To Marshall, you aren't allowed to read this book, but it wouldn't exist without you. Love you, chicken.

yes

&

i love

you

RONI LOREN

Published by Sourcebooks Casablanca, an imprint of Sourcebooks
P.O. Box 4410, Naperville, Illinois 60567-4410
(630) 961-3900
sourcebooks.com

Library of Congress Cataloging-in-Publication Data

Names: Loren, Roni, author.
Title: Yes & I love you / Roni Loren.
Other titles: Yes and I love you
Description: Naperville, Illinois : Sourcebooks Casablanca, 2021. | Series: Say everything; 1 |
Summary: "Everyone knows Miz Poppy, the vibrant reviewer whose commentary brightens the
New Orleans nightlife. But no one knows Hollyn Tate, the real face behind the media star...or the
fear that keeps her isolated. When her boss tells her she needs to add video to her blog or lose her
job, she's forced to rely on an unexpected source to help her face her fears. When aspiring actor
Jasper Deares finds out the shy woman who orders coffee every day is actually Miz Poppy, he
realizes he has a golden opportunity to get the media attention his acting career needs. All he has
to do is help Hollyn come out of her shell...and through their growing connection, finally find her
voice"-- Provided by publisher.
Identifiers: LCCN 2020037366 (print) | LCCN 2020037367 (ebook)
Subjects: GSAFD: Love stories. | LCGFT: Novels.
Classification: LCC PS3612.O764 Y47 2021 (print) | LCC PS3612.O764
    (ebook) | DDC 813/.6--dc23
LC record available at https://lccn.loc.gov/2020037366

Printed and bound in the United States of America.
VP 10 9 8 7 6 5 4 3 2

chapter **one**

Sometimes Hollyn Tate pretended she was in a movie. She had the script. She knew her lines. Her curly blond hair was blown out to perfection and not frizzing like crazy in the New Orleans humidity. Her heart wasn't pounding too hard in her chest. Her facial expressions were totally under her control and appropriate for the situation instead of her Tourette's calling the shots. She was a confident chick in the city on the way to the rest of her life.

Her big career break was just around the corner. Her gaggle of whip-smart, funny friends was texting her about meeting up for drinks and gossip after work. The future love of her life was waiting to bump into her and knock her bag out of her hand—the perfect meet-cute. She was Carrie in *Sex and the City*. She was Meg Ryan in anything. She was Mary Tyler Moore throwing her hat in the air. She was *that* girl. The camera would zoom in on her as other people strolled along the streets around her, their presence only a blur in the background. This was her day. Her world. She was *owning* it.

Hollyn tried to imagine the scene playing on a movie screen as she walked, seeing this better, bolder version of herself navigate the uneven city sidewalks with grace, the brightly painted storefronts the perfect pop of color in the background. If this woman bent down to snag one of the clovers pushing through the cracks in the pavement, it'd have four leaves. Hollyn tried to believe the image, believe that this woman existed. The mental movie got her through the walk to work.

Sometimes.

Today, the fantasy was faltering, her lack of sleep making her extra jumpy. She turned the corner, and the bright-blue, four-story WorkAround building split the sun's morning rays, scattering the light. The converted warehouse took up the entire corner, and the sign advertising *Office Space for the Creative* that hung from the second-floor balcony swayed in the humid breeze coming off the Mississippi River. She took a cleansing breath and worked to unclench her fingers.

Even though she didn't get the overwhelming nausea she had suffered during her first few weeks at WorkAround, her stomach still roller-coastered and her neck muscles balled up like fists. The image of that confident, camera-ready woman slipped away from her like a rogue spirit escaping its temporary host. Another ghost haunting the streets of New Orleans.

She rehearsed her plan for the morning in her head. She'd tried to memorize the people who usually worked on her floor each day so that she knew who to give a quick good morning to (those who responded with a nod and polite smile) and who to avoid (those who wanted to do the dreaded water-cooler chat—even though WorkAround would never have something as gauche as an actual water cooler). But the nature of the coworking space meant the faces were always changing. People renting hot desks on the first floor didn't tend to last long. Those renting actual offices like hers had a little more staying power.

She checked the time on her phone, comforted that it was still early and that most of the people at WorkAround wouldn't be in for at least another hour or so. One of the perks of working for herself was making her own schedule. Most of her coworkers took advantage of that benefit, rolling in around nine or ten and heading straight to the in-house coffee bar where Jackee, a woman with green hair and zero customer service skills, would take your order with a grunt and unceremoniously plunk your coffee or fancy tea in front of you without a word. Hollyn loved Jackee. Coffee and no expectations. Her kind of person.

She dropped her phone into her bag, and her thumb tapped each fingertip on her right hand in a familiar back-and-forth rhythm. *One two three four. Four three two one.* A little twinge of relief went through her at the ritual. She punched in her access code and opened the glass door, which was already covered in dewy condensation, and the blast of frigid air-conditioning hit her along with the sound of fingers on keyboards. She inhaled deeply as she stepped inside, trying to center herself. There was the scent of burnt toast in the air from someone's failed breakfast mixed with one of the "curated" aromas that were pumped into the building to "heighten creativity and productivity"—jasmine today, from what she could tell. Lucinda, the owner of WorkAround, had the aromatherapy on some undecipherable schedule—probably in tune with the moon phases or something.

Hollyn did a quick scan of the main floor. A few of the hot desks were taken—*desk* being a flexible word. Any flat surface with a chair or couch next to it could be rented as a hot desk. The first floor of WorkAround catered mostly to one-person operations—writers, bloggers, online shop owners, app developers. People rented desks so they didn't have to work alone at home—or, worse, from their parents' house—and they could socialize with others from different backgrounds and jobs. Like paying for your favorite spot at Starbucks or the library to guarantee it would be there waiting for you every day.

But unlike a library, there was nowhere to hide in this setup. It was an extrovert extravaganza. The first floor was wide and open with high ceilings, exposed red brick, shiny ductwork, and tall windows lining the back wall. Blue, yellow, and gray couches were set up in groupings to encourage collaboration and socializing. Potted ivies and succulents dotted the tables to make the room feel less industrial. Everything was designed *just so*. This view was the snapshot WorkAround sold to people online. *Look how modern and hip and social this place is! Why work at home when you can be part of something bigger?*

The photo of this floor had originally made Hollyn want to bow out of this experiment completely. She'd been ready to dismiss what her online therapist, Mary Leigh, had suggested could help Hollyn work through some of her social anxiety. At the time, Hollyn had been so freaked out that she'd barely left her house for a month, but maybe becoming a shut-in wasn't all that bad after all. Because an open floor plan full of chatty strangers and nonstop collaboration? *Hell* and *no* and *What kind of monster designed this madness?* But then Hollyn had seen the private offices, had imagined working in a space so bright and modern, and had fallen in love with the idea of getting a little slice of normalcy—an office to go to each day. The price was that she had to get past this part—the good-morning gauntlet.

She hitched her laptop bag higher on her shoulder, doing her finger-counting a few more times, and headed toward the coffee bar with her I'm-busy-don't-bother-me walk—her only defense against getting pulled into anxiety-inducing small talk. She could've stuck earbuds into her ears, but Mary Leigh had insinuated that doing so would be *cheating*. As if Hollyn's mental health was something that had an answer key.

A few people smiled her way or said a generic "morning," and she responded in kind, but she didn't pause. Most of them didn't really want to talk anyway, especially not this early. Eye on the prize, she made it to the coffee bar in the back corner of the main floor as if someone was clocking her speed. She stopped at the counter with a sigh of relief and dug in her bag for her WorkAround card, which got her two free beverages a day. A sharp bang had her attention snapping back upward.

"*Motherfluffer*," a female voice said through what sounded like clenched teeth. More metallic banging ensued, and Hollyn leaned over the counter to see what was going on. A woman with dark-red hair—not Jackee—was crouched in front of a low metal cabinet, her back to Hollyn, yanking at the door with a surprising amount of force, considering her small frame. "Why the hell would they lock this up? Are we really going to steal industrial-sized bags of dark roast? It's not even that good."

Before Hollyn could back away, the woman's head turned, and the scowl she wore brightened into a welcoming smile when she saw her standing there. "Oh! Hey, um..."

The woman didn't know Hollyn's name. Hollyn could see her mentally searching for it. Hollyn knew hers—Andrea, goes by Andi—because she made a point to research everyone who worked on her floor. She was nosy that way.

"Hollyn," she provided after clearing her throat.

Andi snapped her fingers and popped up from her crouch like a jack-in-the-box. "Right, Hollyn. Sorry. Pretty name. We must've never done the name thing." She pointed to her chest. "Andi. I work a few doors down from you."

"Hi." Hollyn shifted and fiddled with her bag, willing her facial muscles to stay smooth and relaxed. She needed coffee, not conversation. Hell, she should have a T-shirt that said that. It applied in so many situations. "Where's Jackee?"

Andi sighed dramatically and tightened her ponytail. "Gone. Apparently, she sold an educational app to a big company and did a whole *Screw you guys, I quit* routine last night. F-bombs were

dropped, aprons were tossed. Somehow no one got this on video."
She rolled her eyes. "The night crew really let us down on that
one. But yeah, she's off to be some kiddie tech mogul, it seems."

Hollyn's eyebrows lifted, and her nose scrunched a few times
against her will, the fight to keep her expression under her full
control failing.

"I know, right?" Andi said, as if Hollyn had answered her.
"I had the exact same reaction. I can't imagine Jackee interacting
with children in any way—unless it was to invite them inside her
gingerbread house in the woods to go all Hansel and Gretel on
them. I was half-convinced she was poisoning the coffee of anyone
who didn't tip well. But yay, good for her, *rah, rah, siss boom bah*
and all," she said, tone droll as she lifted her hands and shook
imaginary pom-poms.

"Bad news for us, though, because I can't get to the supplies,
and Lucinda is locked in her office on a conference call, so I have
no idea where to find the keys." She gave the locked cabinet a
murderous look. "How am I supposed to write a new chapter *and*
record a podcast today with no coffee?" She put her hands out to
her sides with a huff. "I can't work under these conditions!"

Hollyn stared at Andi's whirlwind of rapid-fire words and
expressions. Andi was on her *Avoid* list for just this reason. She'd
learned that podcasters wanted to chat up everybody. So. Much.
Talking. Everyone was a potential guest for them to interview. It
set off all of her run-and-hide instincts. Hollyn didn't know what
to say beyond, "So no coffee?"

Andi gave a grim headshake. "I guess I can go to Chicory
across the street, but it's so expensive, and the owner is this creeper
who's always telling women to 'Smile, it's a beautiful day.'"

Hollyn's nose scrunched again, and she rubbed it, trying to
quell the nervous tic that wanted to take over her muscles.

"Exactly. Does he not realize how aggressive that is? First of all, that's a sign of a sociopath, trying to control my behavior." She lifted a finger like she was making a point in court. "Secondly, dude-bro, I don't need to smile to make you feel more comfortable. I'll smile after I get my damn overpriced coffee and get out of your tourist trap."

A laugh bubbled up in Hollyn's throat, but it got caught and she made a weird choked sound instead. Ugh. *Awkward, aisle one.* Why did this have to be so hard? Why couldn't she just *have a conversation* like a normal person? So much of her wanted to be able to chat with ease with someone like Andi. Why couldn't her body and brain cooperate?

Andi smirked and tapped her temple. "Sorry. Horror writer and true-crime podcaster. Everyone is a serial killer until proven otherwise." She put her forearms on the counter and leaned closer. "But seriously, watch out for coffee-shop guy. Could have bodies in the freezer."

"Ha." Hollyn nodded. "Got it."

"Do you want to walk over together? Safety in numbers?" Andi asked, stepping around from behind the bar. "If he tells us to smile, we can both give him our best resting bitch face."

Hollyn's cheek muscle jumped against her will, her tics surfacing with a vengeance when she had to interact with strangers. She didn't have resting bitch face. She had resting twitch face. But either way, she wasn't going to walk over with Andi. Yes, she was supposed to be here to push past her comfort zone (*I hear you, Mary Leigh!*), but she already felt like she was walking barefoot on thumbtacks today. "Um, sorry. I really need to get to my desk. Maybe next time."

"Wow. You're going to go without coffee?" Andi asked, blue eyes wide. "Brave woman."

"I have a Vitamin Water," Hollyn said, awkwardly patting her bag, which clearly had no room for a bottled drink.

Andi tilted her head, her dark-red ponytail tipping sideways, like she was trying to figure Hollyn out.

Good luck with that, Hollyn wanted to tell her.

"What's your poison?" Andi asked. "I'm going over there anyway, and I can grab you something. I'll get Lucinda to reimburse us for the coffee. We pay rent here and are guaranteed two free drinks. If she doesn't have a barista, we get an IOU." She pinned Hollyn with eye contact, trapping her.

"I, uh…"

"Café au lait, chicory coffee, cappuccino, mocha, latte, cold brew, black tea, green tea, matcha…"

Andi was going to keep listing until Hollyn gave in. "Iced decaf, whole milk, one sugar."

Andi's eyebrows lifted. "Decaf? Actual people order that?"

Hollyn's ears burned. This was why she'd picked up a coffee habit in the first place—because "normal" people drink coffee and not drinking it causes others to comment. But too much caffeine was a big no-no for her, so decaf was her only option. "I had to quit the hard stuff. It messes with my sleep."

"Ah, gotcha. My condolences," Andi said with a smile that made the little ring in her nose glint in the sunlight streaming in through the windows. "I'll bring your imposter coffee to your office."

Hollyn knew it was shitty to let Andi fetch coffee for her. But walking over meant more conversation, and she was already sweating and restless under Andi's observant gaze. So, Hollyn nodded and pulled a five-dollar bill from her purse. "Thank you."

"Not a problem," Andi said in a way that made Hollyn think she really didn't see it as one. Andi plucked the money from her fingertips. "But if I'm not back in half an hour, call the police and tell them to look at coffee-shop guy first."

Hollyn's lips twitched into a brief smile. "Okay. Don't die."

"Yes. Always the number one daily goal." Andi gave a little wave and headed to the main door, greeting people as she passed them, totally comfortable. The envy that welled up in Hollyn became a physical taste on her tongue. What must that be like? To move through life so at ease? To wear your personality on the outside? She shook her head and walked past the coffee bar to the stairs that led to her floor.

Movie-version Hollyn would be friends with a woman like Andi. Movie Hollyn would know what to say and would be able to keep up with the rapid-fire conversation. Movie Hollyn would also go upstairs and create a chance meeting with Rodrigo, the superbuff fitness vlogger who worked down the hall. But there were no cameras, no script, and Real Hollyn just wanted to hide in her office, close her door, and get her work done.

The second floor was mostly quiet when she stepped out of the stairwell. A few people had their office doors ajar, but all the glass-walled conference rooms were either dark or had closed doors, soundproofing them. One of the two podcasting studios was active, the light above the door illuminated, and both video recording spaces were occupied. Through the crack in the door, she could see Emily Vu, a productivity blogger, adjusting the lights inside to shoot a video. Hollyn shuddered. She'd feel like she was in an interrogation room under all those lights.

Hollyn's office was the last at the end of the hall of glass-walled rooms. The space was small but bright, with a big window that gave her a sliver of a view between buildings of the Crescent City Connection bridge. The soft yellow on the one solid wall was soothing, and the mid-century modern desk was so much nicer than anything she'd ever owned that she couldn't help but run her hand over the smooth walnut every time she came in for the day.

When she'd first seen the space, she'd nearly swooned. Anytime she got knots in her stomach about coming to WorkAround, she'd think about this cozy office with its pretty desk, its city view, and its cushy armchair in the corner. It was the office space she'd fantasized about when she'd worked from the beat-up thrift-store table in her mother's house. The only change she would make would be doing away with the two glass walls.

The wall she shared with her neighbor was frosted, but the one facing the hallway was not. If she weren't at the end of the hall, she'd feel like a hamster in a cage. But no one came down to her end unless they wanted to go out through the back staircase to smoke or vape, and she kept her back to the door most of the time anyway. She smiled. Andi would probably tell her to never put her back to a door. Can't see the serial killer coming that way.

Hollyn flipped on her desk lamp and fired up her laptop, wishing she had a hot cup of coffee in her hand. She liked the ritual of sipping it slowly while she went through her email each morning, but the half-empty, lukewarm bottle of water she'd left behind the other day would have to do for now. She got settled at her desk and opened up her inbox.

Something loosened in her body. Outside these doors, she felt like an alien trying to learn the native language. But in here, at her desk, she got to be herself.

Her computer dinged with new mail. There was one nastygram from someone who didn't like her review of their "experimental pop funk" band. She rolled her eyes at the invective. *Get over it, man. The only experimental part was picking a lead singer who was tone deaf and who couldn't stop grabbing his crotch.* Two requests for dates. *No, thank you, overeager strangers.* A forwarded article from her mother about a new supplement she should try. *Delete.* And finally one with a subject line promising a *once-in-a-lifetime* offer. She hovered over the last email, placing silent bets before clicking it. Would it be an offer to refinance her mortgage, a secret bank account in the Bahamas, or a dick pic? She rolled the mental dice and clicked.

And we have a winner!

The screen filled with a high-definition close-up GIF of a dude inserting his penis into the toe of a black high-heeled shoe, the clip looping to give the full thrusting effect. She snorted and then tilted her head, studying the image. Since her entertainment column on the NOLA Vibe site had taken off in popularity, she received these kinds of emails often enough that she'd started to categorize them. Frat boy who drank too much and made bad choices? Lonely soul? Potential stalker?

Miz Poppy, the moniker she used for her reviews of movies and local entertainment, got the gamut in her inbox. Hollyn was amazed by the assumptions people made about a person based on their cartoon avatar. The red lips, long dark hair, and tight black outfit of her cartoon alter ego got more date requests in one week than she'd gotten in her entire life. If she could live life in a cartoon world, she'd be *killing* it. But alas, Miz Poppy only existed in the imagination of her readers. If they knew Miz Poppy was really some chick with unruly blond curls, an even more unruly anxiety disorder, and a penchant for high-top Vans instead of high heels, they'd be vastly disappointed.

Lucky for her, no one but her editor and boss at the NOLA Vibe knew who the real Miz Poppy was, which meant misguided penis guy got to keep his fantasy about Miz Poppy's shoes. What he would *not* get was a reply. She lifted her hand to delete the email, but before she could, a knock sounded at her door.

Her body tensed, and she automatically went into if-I-stay-still, maybe-they-won't-see-me mode. No one ever knocked on her door. There was a *Do Not Disturb* door hanger that she'd bought in the French Quarter hanging off the knob. It had a picture of a voodoo doll full of pins. The message was pretty damn clear. But before she could go into full flight-or-fight mode, she remembered Andi was bringing coffee. She needed to turn around. Be a functioning human for a few more minutes.

The glass door made a soft whooshing sound as it opened. "Um, hello?"

Not Andi. The voice was male and one she didn't recognize. She really needed to turn around now, but she could feel the electricity moving through her, her nerve endings jumping. Her fingers twitched against the arms of her desk chair, tapping the pattern. *One two three four.*

"You ordered a coffee?" the guy said, his tone unsure.

Hollyn wet her lips—*get your shit together, babe*—and forced herself to spin her chair to face the door. A guy she'd never seen before was standing inside her doorway, holding a cup of coffee and watching her. Her breath caught. One, because he was a stranger and *in her office expecting her to speak words.* Two, because, *holy shit. Hot.*

He looked like he could be modeling for a WorkAround ad. Tall and lanky with an untucked, short-sleeved button-down and skinny jeans that said he was trying but not too hard. Square tortoiseshell glasses framing hazel eyes. And dark, shaggy hair that was just a little too long on top to be considered neat.

He gave her a chagrined half smile, and his gaze traveled over her, making her insides ripple with awareness. "Whew. So she *is* alive," he said. "That's a relief."

"Excuse me?" Her throat had narrowed to the circumference of a pencil, and the words came out broken around the edges.

He pushed his glasses up the bridge of his nose, and his smile went full span. "Well, it would suck if on my first day at a new place, I was the one to find the body."

She was supposed to smile back or laugh or something, but as usual, her body didn't cooperate. She didn't do well one-on-one with any stranger, but this guy was launching her system straight to Armageddon level. Attraction was *the worst.* It was like detonating a bomb inside her, setting off all the most embarrassing aspects of her anxiety and Tourette's. Most people got a little nervous when they were attracted to someone, but for her, it was amplified a hundred times over. She was doing everything she could to act chill, white-knuckling her neurons, but she knew it couldn't last. She was bound to tic or say something awkward. Her tension increased—a rubber band being pulled, pulled, pulled. "Did you need something?"

Inwardly, she winced at how rude it sounded.

He flinched and his smile dropped a few watts. She felt a pang at the loss of it. "Uh, yeah, sorry. This woman I met downstairs, Andi, asked if I could bring you this." He lifted the coffee like he was offering a sacrifice to the gods. "I didn't mean to interrupt your—" His gaze flicked over her shoulder to her screen, and his eyes widened behind his glasses. "Work? Private moment with your boyfriend? Shoe-fetish research?"

She closed her eyes, mortified, not even bothering to look behind her. "It's...spam."

"Hey, no judgment. You do you, friend," he said genially. "I was just looking for Lucinda, and Andi said you'd know where to point me."

Hollyn's face was so hot she felt sunburned. She forced herself to meet his gaze, and fought to keep her tics at bay, *hating* the fear, *hating* this thing that took her over when she was around other people. Her fingers tapped on the arm of her chair, and she tried to breathe in the way Mary Leigh had taught her—slowly, deeply. She didn't need to be afraid of Cute Guy. Cute Guy was just here to bring her coffee and get directions and look amazing in a pair of jeans. It wasn't the end of days. No need to panic or stock up on canned goods.

Her body didn't get the memo, though, and she could barely get the words out. "Her office is at the other end of the hall. Last door before the big conference room. Knock first."

But he wasn't looking at her. He was still staring at her computer screen, amusement dancing in his gold-green eyes. "If there's such a thing as athlete's foot, do you think one can…catch that in other places? I mean, maybe he should use a condom."

She glanced at the computer. "Or a sock."

The words had jumped out without her planning it, and his attention flicked to her, that infectious grin returning. "A sock." He laughed. "Obviously. The only proper protection from a shoe." He shook his head. "Why don't I ever get spam that interesting? I just get offers from Russian models wanting to be my wife. They promise to"—he made air quotes with his free hand—"'make me so happy in a special way.' I'm assuming this means they make a kick-ass borscht."

Hollyn pursed her lips at his faux Russian accent and looked down, wanting to laugh but knowing that if she did, it would come out like a parrot squawk with her muscles so tense. "Sounds like a good deal."

"Right? I mean, the beet really is an under-appreciated root vegetable. I'm weighing all the offers carefully," he said with mock seriousness and set the coffee on the corner of her desk, bringing the scent of his shower-fresh soap into her space. He put out his hand. "I'm Jasper, by the way."

She stuck out her hand, knowing there was no way to avoid the handshake, and his warm, confident grip wrapped around hers, sending a zinging awareness straight up her arm and spreading through her chest. His gaze met hers and held, like he was trying to see inside her head, to read her. The connection was too intense, the eye contact impossible for her to hold. Her fingers wanted to count. She quickly released the handshake. "Thanks, for uh, bringing the coffee."

"No problem." He stepped back, giving her an expectant look, and then asked with a teasing tone, "And you are?"

She looked down at her hands, which were clenched tightly, and she realized that she'd let this go too far. If Jasper was new here and got the impression she was someone he could chat and joke around with, she'd have to go through this rush of anxiety every damn day at work. She needed to get better with people, but she couldn't start with someone like Jasper. That would be like deciding to learn guitar and going straight to a Jimi Hendrix song. She needed to learn her chords first. Best to cut the hot new guy off at the pass.

"Busy," she said flatly.

"You—" He paused, as if checking he'd heard her correctly. "Oh, right."

She looked up, finding him frowning, and the room seemed to dim around her.

He squinted like he couldn't quite tell if she was being serious, but then he pushed his shoulders back, straightening. "Yeah, well, sorry to bother you. Good luck with your...shoe-fetish guy."

She nodded again, not trusting herself to speak.

Jasper headed back toward the door, wearing the confused expression of a guy who wasn't used to being shut down. And why *would* anyone shut him down? He was hot. He was funny. One of those people who was probably comfortable in any situation he walked into. He and Andi would get along great.

A pinch of jealousy made her gut tighten.

He stood in the doorway and jabbed his thumb to the left. "I guess I'll go find Lucinda."

He was giving her an opportunity to make things right. To undo her rudeness.

She couldn't look him in the eye, and her urge to tic had hit the breaking point. She quickly turned her chair toward her laptop, putting her back to him. "Thanks."

Her tone was clipped, dismissive.

"Sure. Okay." There was a heavy beat of quiet as if he was

going to say something else, and she braced herself. Some strange part of her wanted him to push back, to not let her off that easy, to not let bitch mode scare him off like it did everyone else, for him *to see* that she didn't really mean it but didn't know how else to get through this kind of thing. But then the door shut quietly behind her because what else could he possibly want to say to someone who wouldn't even tell him her name?

There. It was done.

Jasper would turn into another coworker who would put a label on her—bitchy, awkward, snobby, weird, rude—one of the many adjectives that she'd been pinned with before. Didn't matter which one he picked. This time she'd earned it fair and square, and it would keep him away.

Mission accomplished.

She should feel relief.

She peeked back over her shoulder. The hall was empty, and she slumped in her chair. She didn't know why she felt so disappointed. As if she would've done anything but cower if he had still been standing there. It wasn't like she could morph into another person, go after him, and be all, *"Oh, so sorry, Jasper. It's just been a bad morning. You know how it is. I'm Hollyn. Thanks so much for the coffee. Why don't I show you around the building and introduce you to a few people? After that, we can grab some lunch and you can tell me all about yourself, and then I'll tell you why we should start up a sordid office affair and hook up in the copy room. You like Thai food? Great, let's go."*

She put her head on her desk and banged it softly.

Maybe this whole WorkAround thing had been a terrible idea. Maybe Mary Leigh was wrong and had given her shitty advice. Maybe the whole online therapy business was a sham, and she was being life-coached by some nineteen-year-old operating out of her parents' basement.

Her computer dinged with an email notification, and she took a breath before lifting her head and clicking. The numbers were in for last week's Miz Poppy posts and two new freelance assignments had hit her inbox. *Work.* The sight of it unwound some of the tension and put an end to her pity party of one.

Calm. The hell. Down.

Don't catastrophize. That was what Mary Leigh would say.

Okay, so she'd had a minor freak-out. Fine. She couldn't expect perfection. She couldn't let one embarrassing incident shake her confidence in this plan. She'd worked too hard to get to this point. This didn't have to be a *thing*. *Jasper* didn't have to be a thing.

Look, Mary Leigh, coping mechanisms in action! Mark that in your chart and stamp it with a smiley face.

....

By the time lunchtime rolled around, Hollyn had tucked away the stressful morning into the let's-pretend-this-never-happened file and was in the zone, crafting her next post. She was feeling pretty good, resolved even, until she went downstairs for decaf number two and froze a few feet away from the coffee bar. Jasper was behind the counter, pouring a cup for someone else, a blue apron tied around his waist.

Her stomach sank.

He wasn't just another person renting a hot desk—someone easily avoided. He was the new Jackee. He was the new keeper of the coffee.

Jasper smiled her way and lifted a hand in greeting. So freaking friendly. So damn nerd-hot. "Hola, Ms. Busy."

Smile back! Smile back! Smile back, she silently screamed at herself. *Be a functioning human!*

Instead, a grimace pulled at her face, a yank of muscles she couldn't control. His smile fell, a startled look flashing in his eyes. Then annoyance. A little part of Hollyn died inside. She turned on her heel and walked right back the way she came.

In the stairwell, she leaned against the brick wall and closed her eyes, mortification bleeding through her and making her limbs tingle. *No no no.* She could feel the telltale signs, but it was too late to stop it. All systems had already been engaged.

Hello, panic, my old friend.

She mentally reset the calendar she kept in her journal where she tracked how many panic-free days she'd had in a row with the title *Don't break the chain.* The chain had been broken. Again.

If her mother were here, she would be shaking her head at her with that knowing look on her face. *See, honey, I told you moving to the city was a bad idea. You're not ready for this. You may never be. That's okay. Just come home.*

As Hollyn's heartbeat raced and sweat glazed her skin, all the things she'd pictured in that imaginary movie of herself melted into the ugly reality. There was no four-leaf clover for her. There was no meet-cute. Her awkwardness was not *adorkable* like a movie heroine. She was a goddamned disaster. This monster that clamped its hand around her throat and took control of her muscles was real and it was bigger, meaner, and more determined than ever.

Maybe her mother was right.

She slapped the wall with the palm of her hand and let out a sound of frustration, the noise echoing through the empty stairwell.

No.

She. Would. Not. Run. She loved working in her cozy office. She loved that she was finally earning her own money—even though there wasn't much of it. She loved having the freedom to go out in the city at night instead of having to watch life go by through a TV screen in her small hometown. She was *Miz freaking Poppy*, goddammit. She was *famous*. You know, regionally. Microregionally. Like very micro. On the internet.

She groaned at her lame pep talk, but it at least distracted her from replaying the awkward encounter with Jasper over and over in her head. This didn't have to be a big deal. She would not let her attraction to some cute barista derail her plan. She could deal with this.

He was just a guy. In a world full of them.

So what if this particular one thought she was rude? It's not like she was trying to date him. She wasn't capable of dating *anyone*. In fact, she never had to speak to Jasper again.

She had nothing to worry about.

Everything was cool.

Totally cool.

Ugh. Maybe she needed to find a new office.

chapter **two**

BE COOL. JASPER'S CASEWORKERS HAD ALWAYS TOLD HIM TO think before he acted. They said *impulsive* like it was a dirty word. Like it was some disease he had contracted. *Jasper can't control himself. Jasper can't keep his mouth shut. Jasper is just* too much. He could hear them in his head now, telling him to just let things lie and pour the damn coffee. But when he smiled at the mystery woman from the second floor, and her pretty face twisted into a look full of disgust before she hurried back in the other direction, he wanted to shout out, "Hey, what's your problem?"

What did he ever do to her besides bring her coffee this morning and *not* embarrass her about her porn perusing? Jasper set down the carafe he'd been holding and opened his mouth to call out to her, but she'd slipped into the stairwell before he could get the words out. He frowned and shook his head. "What the hell, man?"

"What's that?" the dark-haired woman in front of him asked, looking up from her phone. *Emily Vu. Vlogger-blogger. Intense vibe.* He'd made his mental notes, determined to learn as many names and personalities as he could.

"Sorry," he said, putting a lid on her coffee and setting it on the counter. "I just... I think I must've done something to annoy the woman who works at the end of the hall upstairs." He cocked his head toward the stairwell. "She was heading this way and then bailed when she saw me working the counter. Maybe she doesn't trust me with her coffee or something."

Emily's brows lifted, and she looked toward the stairwell. "Last office...the woman with the curly blond hair?"

"Yeah, you know her?"

Emily tucked her phone into the pocket of her suit jacket before taking her coffee. "Not really. I mean, I've passed her in the hall, but she keeps to herself. I think she's a writer, maybe. Something that doesn't require the video or podcasting rooms."

"I wish I knew what I did to offend her or whatever." He poured a cup of coffee for himself, replaying their earlier interaction in his head, trying to figure out where things had gone wrong. "Maybe she really loved the person who had this job before me, and now she's mad that she's gone."

Emily choked a little on her coffee and then smirked at him. "I promise that's definitely not it. No one loved Jackee." She grabbed a napkin to dab her lips. "Jackee made sure of it. Maybe she's just having a bad day and you were in the line of fire."

"Maybe," he said, unconvinced.

Maybe he just had that effect on women these days. They saw him and ran in the opposite direction.

Emily's gaze flicked to the clock above the coffee bar. "Well, I have to get back to my desk. My coffee time slot is almost up, and I'm time-mapping this week. I have to stick to it to see if it works." She lifted her drink as if toasting him. "Welcome to the WA, Jasper. Don't let any of the techies talk you into investing in their app. And friends don't ask friends to join their Patreon."

He smirked and touched his paper coffee cup to hers. "Thanks for the tips. That bad, huh?"

"Nah, don't worry. You'll find most people here are pretty friendly, especially when you're giving them coffee. Don't stress about the outliers." She shrugged. "Some people work on their own because they're self-starters. Others only do it because they can't manage to work with anyone else."

"Right. Which one are you?"

"Probably both," she said with a chagrined smile.

"And self-aware, too," he teased.

"I have my moments." Emily checked her smart watch and nodded as if she were marking the period at the end of her sentence, then headed off toward the stairs with a purposeful stride, her heels clicking against the polished concrete floor.

Jasper grabbed a rag to wipe down the counter and tried to shake off the feeling that the mystery woman had given him when she'd looked at him with such disdain, but he couldn't get it off his mind. His sister, Gretchen, teased him that he had this need for everyone to like him—an actor's cross to bear. Or maybe just his foster-kid self-preservation instinct. So maybe that was all this was. He'd wanted to make the woman laugh this morning. She'd had this lost look in her eyes that said she needed a little boost. He'd only been trying to make friends at this new job.

Okay, maybe that wasn't entirely true. He might have been attempting to flirt just a little. Those big green eyes and that mass of blond curls had made him think of the girl on that show Gretchen had watched obsessively when he'd first moved in with the Deares family—*Felicity*. He hadn't joined in watching the show back then or on Gretchen's annual binges since, but he'd always thought the lead actress was hot.

So fine, whatever. Mystery woman was easy to look at. But the flirting Jasper had done had been of the harmless variety. The last thing he needed right now was to get involved with someone he'd see every day. Or anyone at all, really. After what he'd gone through with Kenzie, he didn't feel up for any kind of dating—casual or otherwise. He'd mostly been trying to break the ice with the woman upstairs. He figured if he could find some decent people to chat with, maybe it would make the fact that he was twenty-five and back to pouring coffee a little more bearable. Maybe.

But if Ms. Busy wasn't interested in knowing him, then that was her issue and not his problem. So instead of doing what he really wanted to do—go upstairs and knock on her door again to see what the deal was—he put the *Be back in fifteen minutes* sign on the counter, grabbed his coffee, and found an unoccupied table.

Working the coffee counter and offering in-house improv classes one night a week for WorkAround members would get him free hot-desk time, video room access, and rehearsal space for his group. The pay wasn't great, but the perks made this a better option than anything else he could find right now. Plus, the office setting was the perfect place to gather material both for his improv show and for his newest TV series idea. He pulled out the little Moleskine notebook he kept in his back pocket and jotted down a few notes.

His improv group had a few shows coming up, and though there was no preparing for the actual content of the show, they'd asked him to be the monologist for the next three performances. He liked having as many stories as possible knocking around in his head for those monologues even if he couldn't predict what audience suggestion he'd get. The request from the group had been the first signal that they were beginning to forgive him for bailing on them and chasing Kenzie to LA. When he'd left, his group had just landed a prime spot at the Lagniappe Comedy Theater doing a sketch and improv show, but they'd been dropped off the rotation when he and Kenzie had moved to LA.

He planned to make it up to the group by killing it onstage and getting them back to a better venue than the crappy dive bar they were performing in now. He turned the page and made a few more notes, the sound of the workspace around him fading away as he got lost in thought.

After a few minutes of writing, his phone buzzed in his pocket, and he set his notebook aside. He groaned when he unlocked his screen. A Google alert on Kenzie. Why the hell hadn't he turned these off already? He needed to delete this soul-destroying, low-key stalking bullshit. Instead, he found himself clicking on the box.

Newcomer Kenzie Lord to star in and cowrite a new
Netflix original comedy sketch show, *Aurora Boring*.

Kenzie's smiling headshot accompanied the article, along with a candid of her leaving a restaurant arm in arm with Ames Thoren, one of the hottest comedians on the stand-up circuit at the moment. Jasper's ex-girlfriend and former improv partner looked so happy, so goddamned effervescent, that he had to squint from the glare of all that bliss coming off his phone.

The worst part was he couldn't even hate her for it. The woman was talented as hell. She'd earned her spot.

He hadn't. He'd gotten the audition of a lifetime along with her and had blown it. Then she'd broken up with him because she *really needed to concentrate on her career* and they were *going in different directions*.

Her direction was clearly *up*, so he knew which direction she thought his career was heading.

"*JASPER?*"

The loud male voice startled Jasper from his internet stalking and almost made him knock his coffee onto his lap. His head snapped up and he steadied his coffee cup.

"Holy shit. It *is* you, man," said a refrigerator-sized African American guy, grinning wide. "Jasper fucking Anderson."

Jasper felt like he'd walked into some frat party he wasn't a member of. The dude looked like he could pick Jasper up and force him to do a keg stand. But before Jasper could respond to his old surname or place the vaguely familiar face, the guy put out his hand. Jasper took it on reflex, and the stranger pulled him to a stand and into an enthusiastic man hug, thumping Jasper on the back hard enough to make him cough.

"Uh, hey?" Jasper managed.

The guy leaned back with a knowing grin. "Don't give me some weak-ass *hey*." He put a hand to his chest. "Fitz McLane."

"Fitz..." The name snapped the missing puzzle pieces into place in an instant, and Jasper got an image of a scrawny, hyper kid whose voice was always a little too loud for the uptight teachers at the Wesley Alternative School for Boys. Jasper could almost hear the prim voice of his eighth-grade math teacher. *Turn down your volume, Mr. McLane. Inside voice, Mr. McLane.*

Those comments would be interspersed between her, *Please pay attention, Mr. Anderson. Please stop talking, Mr. Anderson. Is what's outside the window more interesting than my class, Mr. Anderson?*

Yes. Always.

The only reason Fitz hadn't gotten detention over his infractions like Jasper had was because *Mr. McLane* always knew the right answers. But Jasper had always liked the guy. It'd been nice not being the only foster kid at Wesley.

Jasper smiled. "Fitz, wow. You look..." *Like a goddamned linebacker who ate the former Fitz McLane.* "I would've never recognized you."

Fitz stepped back and put his hands out to his sides, beaming proudly. "Finally grew into my voice after I took up weight lifting in college."

"Cool, man. You look great," Jasper said. "What are you doing here?"

Fitz pointed toward the ceiling. "The company I run is temporarily renting part of the fourth floor."

Jasper's eyebrows jumped up. "Your company? Get the fuck out of here."

Fitz McLane owned a company? When Jasper had known him, the guy had barely been able to tie the Wesley uniform tie. Fitz's had always been crooked.

He shrugged, as if owning a company was no big thing. "Yeah, I'm the CEO of GetFIREd. It's an online investment firm. We specialize in working with people working on a FIRE plan."

"A fire plan?" Jasper got the image of money actually burning. That felt like *his* current investment plan. Or as he liked to think of it, *the artist's way.*

"It stands for Financial Independence, Retire Early. Helps people who want to retire in their thirties," he said, glancing past Jasper as if to see if anyone was working the coffee bar.

"Their thirties?" *What the hell?* Jasper was still figuring out how to start his actual career and people his age were already nearing retirement? "Sounds...wow."

Fitz grinned and looked back to him. "Right? It's all about choosing the right assets and cutting expenses. Easy as pie. Get some property in your portfolio, investments that will bring you passive income, live on a shoestring for a while, and *boom*!" He clapped, the sound echoing. "No more working for the man." He pulled a card out of his back pocket and handed it to Jasper. "If you're interested in talking more about it, let me know."

Jasper snorted. "Thanks, man, but the only part I have covered is the shoestring budget."

"Ah, gotcha," Fitz said genially. "What are you up to these days?"

Jasper shrugged. "This and that. You know, all the things our teachers figured I'd grow up to do—petty crime, letting lonely widows use my body for a fee, selling organs on the dark web."

Fitz laughed. "Excellent. Sounds lucrative."

"Yes, all of those would probably make me more money than

what I actually do," Jasper admitted. "I'm an actor in an improv group. We perform a few nights a week here in town."

Fitz snapped his fingers. "That's right. You got roped into the school's theater program."

"Yeah, first by force but then I got hooked." Jasper didn't have great memories from Wesley. He'd been living with an awful family that year and had been determined to cause enough trouble to get moved. But Mrs. Hernandez, the English teacher, had been the one shining light of that year. Instead of giving him detention for acting up in class, she'd forced him to "volunteer" for the play. *Put all that energy to good use, young man.* He'd fallen in love with the high of being onstage, of making people pay attention to him, of making them laugh.

"Wow, so you're still acting. That's great. Living the dream," Fitz said, genuine enthusiasm in his voice. "Your own theater."

"I… Oh, no. I don't own a theater. We just do our shows at a local bar for now." It sounded pathetic even to his own ears. "But we're going to be offering classes soon, too. Lucinda wants us to give a few classes here at WorkAround as a perk for members— you know, improv skills for business or whatever."

"That's cool." Fitz gave him a pondering look, his brown eyes narrowing. "But you really should look into getting your own theater, one that has room for the classes, too. That's where the real money is."

Ha. The money. The real money wasn't anywhere in comedy except at the very top, where there was only enough air for the chosen few to breathe. Right where Kenzie was headed. "I don't think—"

"Plus, property's where it's at right now," he went on. "I got a great deal on a place in the central business district. We're renovating it now, but it's going to save us a ton once we move out of here and into the CBD."

"That's cool," Jasper said noncommittally, already backing

away from the conversation. Business talk was not a pool he wanted to swim in. He'd drown. In fact, he was actively trying to ignore the fact that he was about to start teaching classes with the word *business* in the title.

"I'm telling you, man. There are still steals to be had in the city. Get yourself something that never got a post-Katrina reno, doll it up, and you're in business," Fitz said, making it sound like it was as easy as picking up a sandwich from the corner po-boy shop. "Best to snap the deals up before this city turns into Austin East and all the rents skyrocket."

Jasper shifted. "Thanks, but that's not in the cards right now. I just moved back from LA and am staying with my sister. Can't go and buy buildings."

"Details." Fitz pulled his phone out of the back pocket of his slacks. "I might know a place. One of my clients looked at it and decided on something else, but I still have the info." He scrolled through his phone with a look of concentration. "Damn, I must've archived it, but I'll find the email and send it your way. Here, give me your number."

Jasper took Fitz's offered phone and typed in his number even though there was seriously no need.

His own theater? The idea was so ludicrous he shouldn't even allow his brain to entertain the thought. He was pouring people's coffee and living at Gretchen's for fuck's sake. He'd never owned anything beyond a used car. And even if he had the money, he couldn't run a business. He'd flunked out of college the third semester because...math. It was a no-go idea. *Look away, brain.*

But the possibility snuck into his mind anyway, like a Vegas show girl in a shiny gold bikini—sparkly and sexy and impossible to ignore. *Hey, sugar, let's have some fun. Wouldn't owning your own place show up all those people who told you that you couldn't make it? Wouldn't that be a good way to catch the attention of the big leagues?*

Shut. Up. Brain.

He handed the phone back to Fitz. "I appreciate it, but I'm not really in the property-shopping position right now." He cleared his throat and jabbed a thumb toward the coffee bar. "Living the actor's life in every sense of the word. But I could make you a mean espresso."

Fitz's dark eyebrows shot up. "You're the new coffee guy?"

Jasper smirked. "At your service. Feel free to judge my life choices."

Fitz laughed and clapped him on the shoulder. "No judgment, brother. If that's what you have to do in order to do what you love, then screw anyone who judges you for it. I'm telling my clients that all the time. You want to live off ramen to save up and sail around the world? You want to go off the grid and live on a farm and raise goats or whatever? Go for it. Life's short. Find a way not to starve and do your thing."

Jasper walked back toward the coffee bar, break time over. "Yeah, well, I'm working on the not-starving part first." He put a napkin on the counter. "What can I get ya?"

"Black coffee, two sugars," Fitz said, a wrinkle between his brows.

Jasper turned his back to grab a cup.

"What about investors?" Fitz asked.

Jasper pulled a carafe from the warmer and poured the dark-black coffee, the scent both delicious and depressing. It was his personal smell of failure. "What do you mean?"

"If you don't have the funds to get your own theater, what about getting some investors to go in with you? I mean, it'd be a tough sell to VCs." When Jasper gave him a blank look, Fitz clarified. "Venture capitalists. Because the arts usually aren't their cuppa. The growth is too slow and, in this case, too local. But you could find some angel investors. Locals who care about the arts and the entertainment scene of the city. They'd get some equity in the company and, in return, front you some money to get off the ground, do renovations, that kind of thing."

Jasper shook his head as he dumped sugar into the coffee. "You're nuts." He turned and set the cup on the counter in front of his old schoolmate. "Who's going to want to invest in some ragtag improv group they've never heard of?"

"Are y'all any good?" Fitz asked, pinning Jasper with a challenging look.

"We kick ass," Jasper said without hesitation. The Hail Yes group *was* good. That part he never doubted. He'd missed their effortless chemistry the minute he'd moved to California with Kenzie and had tried to join in with other groups. "But we're in a tiny bar and off the beaten path and just one little show in a big city packed full of entertainment options. People don't come to New Orleans looking for improv. They come for booze, music, and food. Maybe a burlesque or drag brunch in between. This isn't LA, Chicago, or New York."

Fitz leaned onto his beefy forearms. "Fuck that noise. You're seeing old New Orleans, the one we grew up in. Have you looked around lately? The invasion is happening. There's a place on Decatur that literally only sells avocado toasts. Like twenty different kinds. Walk down the street and there are more people with green juice than hurricanes. There's a vinyl record store two doors down. The hipsters and West Coasters have arrived, looking for cheap property and cool shit. Look around." He swept his hand toward the main floor and all the people working at hot desks. "You think these people want to go see burlesque every night or get wasted in one of the tourist traps on Bourbon?"

"Howie, the guy with the bow tie over there, is definitely into burlesque," Jasper said with a serious tone. "I bet he has a habit."

Fitz snorted and sipped his coffee. "You know what I mean. You give them a chill, casual theater with great improv done by people their own age, throw in a few potent drink options, and you've got yourself a real business."

Jasper blew out a breath. "You make it sound easy. But you're forgetting the part where I have no money. And no connections."

"So what?"

"Fitz—"

"Look, how about this? You work on building some buzz around your group—get the tastemakers and Instagrammers and bloggers there—then put together some videos, a good business proposal, and I bet I can help you get investors. You don't have connections, but I do," he said, dropping the statement like it was a nothing sentence when it was, in fact, a big, whopping *something*.

"What? Why would you do that?"

Fitz swigged his coffee again and shrugged. "Why wouldn't I? You were cool to me when everyone else treated me like I had a disease. And foster kids have to look out for each other. We don't get the benefit of family connections." He set down his cup. "Plus, my clients are people our age who are looking to invest in start-ups. Some of them are locals who want to be part of the city's new scene. It could help me, too. I can't make any promises, obviously, but if you can build some buzz and put together a business plan with some numbers, I could pass it along to a few people."

Numbers. Business plans. Those words sent shudders of dread though Jasper. He stared at his friend. "Fitz, you're insane."

"And?"

Jasper groaned, the look on his old friend's face too Labrador-retriever-eager to shut down. "And I'll think about it."

Fitz lifted his arms over his head like he was calling a success-ful field goal. "Awesome. Jasper Anderson is in the house."

Jasper choked on a laugh. "It's Jasper Deares now. And you did not just say I'm 'in the house.' I no longer feel comfortable working with you. I'm sorry this partnership must end before it begins."

Fitz flipped him off. "Go to hell, Jas. You're going to love me by the end of this."

"Aww, Fitz, don't sell yourself short. You don't have to buy my love with favors," he teased. "Straight-up cash is so much easier."

Fitz put his hand in his pocket and then dropped two quarters and a cough drop on the counter. "That should cover what that's worth."

"Ha." Jasper nodded approvingly at the quick comeback. "Be careful. If I see that you're any good, I'll pull your ass up onstage with us."

"Hell no. That improv shit is terrifying." Fitz grabbed the sugar canister and dumped more into his coffee. "But I do want tickets to a show so I can see your group in action. I need to know what I'm helping pitch. If you suck, I'm out."

"I'll text you some dates and leave your name at the door with an open invitation."

Jasper needed to shut up. This wasn't happening. Fitz was selling him some oceanfront property in Arizona. Who would want to invest in him? Pay a few bucks to see him act like an idiot onstage and make people laugh? Sure. That, people would do. Convince businesspeople that the hyper dude who dropped out of college because he couldn't pass a math class was capable of handling their money and running a business? No freaking way.

He wouldn't invest in him. How could he ever expect other people would?

Hell, he couldn't even get the woman upstairs to trust him to make her coffee.

He promised Fitz that he would text him, but when he ended his shift for the day, Jasper vowed to put the ridiculous idea out of his mind.

He was done going down dead-end roads.

chapter **three**

"You do not need a new office. You can't give up on the plan."

Hollyn tucked her phone against her shoulder and shoved a frozen pizza in the oven before responding to her best friend Cal's frustrated words. She bumped the oven door shut with her foot. "It's not giving up on the plan. I'm just not sure if it's the right work space for me anymore. It's a lot of extra money to spend, too. There's a cheaper place in Metairie."

"No *hella good* way," Cal said, one of his regular verbal tics sliding in. "You're being a *panic station* chicken."

Her brows lifted. She was so used to Cal's tics that they were like background noise these days, but that second one caught her attention. "Panic station? That's a new one."

He grunted. "Yeah, it's a Muse song. Great riff. And my brain *panic station* clearly thinks it's a great title. *Hella good.*"

Cal loved music and played lead guitar with a local band in Baton Rouge, where he was finishing up his master's degree in digital media arts and engineering at LSU. Music had always been the thing to give him some relief from his Tourette's, but the side effect was that he often picked up verbal tics from the lyrics. He had to be careful what he listened to. In third grade he'd been stuck with *hokey pokey!* as a tic for months.

"That one's strangely appropriate right now. I think I take the train to Panic Station every day I go into WorkAround." She pulled a bottle of Tabasco sauce and a can of sparkling water out of the fridge. "And I'm not a chicken. I'm just not sure it makes sense for me to put myself through that every day. It's distracting me from my actual work. WorkAround might just be too big of a leap."

"Oh, don't *hella good* give me that bullshit," Cal said dismissively. "You love your *panic station* office. Plus, you and Mary Leigh came up with this plan for a reason. This is the next logical step. You shouldn't be surprised that people are starting to strike up conversations with you. *Hella good.* They're reaching out to you because you've been there a while now, and people like to get to know their coworkers. That's a positive thing. You can't go back to working from home. You'll end up back at square one. Or worse, moving back home."

Square one. She didn't want to think of square one. And she especially didn't want to think of moving back home.

"I promise I'm not going back to how I was. I go out at least three nights a week now for content for the Miz Poppy posts," she said, her fingers tapping in her four count. "I promise I won't become a shut-in."

But the words didn't come out with the amount of force she'd been hoping for. She'd been spurred to seek online therapy with Mary Leigh almost a year ago when she'd realized that she hadn't left her house for a month except for a handful of Miz Poppy assignments. Delivery groceries. Takeout. A month and she'd barely noticed. That had scared the hell out of her.

She couldn't risk that again.

The image of her rental house with aluminum-foil-covered windows, six cats, and ceiling-high stacks of newspapers filled her mind. *Ugh.* She'd watched too many reruns of *Hoarders*. She didn't even subscribe to a newspaper. How would she end up with stacks of them? Plus, she was allergic to cats. But still, the image was imprinted on her nightmares.

"I'm going out tonight, in fact," she added for good measure. "I'm still working the plan."

"That's not the same thing. You go out *hella good* anonymously. You don't talk to anyone. You're a *panic station* ghost, Hollyn."

"Anonymous is the whole point of Miz Poppy," she said, losing her patience with the conversation. Cal's intentions were good, but she was not in the mood to be armchair psychoanalyzed. She had Mary Leigh for that. "No one knows who I am so I get the same experience as anyone walking in off the street. I can do a legitimate review."

"I get that, but it doesn't have to mean you're anonymous in your actual life," he said, words firm but tone gentle. "You said you were going to WorkAround so you could meet *rolling stone* people, get used to being social, maybe make some friends. This is supposed to be getting you ready for job interviews and working in an office full-time somewhere. Hiding in your office and praying no one talks to you—or worse, leaving all together—is not moving the ball forward."

"Cal."

"You know I love you and don't want you to be stressed out, but the only way you're going to get over your phobia of talking to people is to *talk to them*."

"Oh is that all?" she said, her sarcasm going to eleven. "Wow, so super easy, Dr. Cal. Okay, let me just do that. I never thought of actually talking to people. Genius!"

He groaned. "Don't try to bitch me away. That doesn't *hella good* work on me. All I'm saying is that you don't need to hide from people. If you're ticcing out, just tell them, 'Oh, by the way, I have *panic station* Tourette's.' You'll be surprised by how cool people can be. We're not eight years old and on the *hella good* playground anymore. No one's going to call you names. People aren't out to hurt you."

She winced, the horrible memories trying to leak into her brain like a poisonous fog. She shook her head and popped the top of her drink. "If I tell people, then that's all they're going to see. I don't want to be that 'chick with the tics.'"

"Holls, you *are* the chick with the tics. Just like I'm that loud dude who blurts out random words. That doesn't mean it's all we are. You're also *rolling stone* a great writer, a fantastic reviewer, and a good person. I'm clearly a rock god. We all have our crosses to bear."

She laughed. "A rock god?"

"Obviously. All I'm saying is give people a chance to not be assholes." He let out a string of *hella goods* before clearing his throat. "Worst-case scenario, you come across a few jerks. So what? They don't deserve your time. But right now you're *panic station rolling stone* poisoning the whole lawn, killing all the potential flowers just to avoid a few weeds."

Hollyn tipped her head back to stare at the water-stained ceiling, hearing the words but having no faith that she could implement them. Cal understood her situation on so many levels. They'd been friends since they'd met in a therapy group when they were kids. But Cal had never had any shyness. Probably because there was no hiding his version of Tourette's. She'd never had verbal tics beyond some throat-clearing and humming noises. Her twitching muscles could sometimes be hidden with hair covering her face or by turning away or pretending to sneeze. Plus, her mother had plucked her out of school and homeschooled her once the teasing had gotten bad. Cal, on the other hand, had been forced to deal with the schoolyard bullies.

"I hear what you're saying," she said finally and took a sip of her drink. "But it's not that easy. Logically, I know that my coworkers aren't going to burst out laughing or make fun of me. But my body doesn't get that message. If I get pulled into conversation with someone, my words just freeze up and I panic. And then I tic out and become even more self-conscious and it's just a bad cycle." She sighed. "You should've seen me with that guy today. I think my body ran through every horrible face I could make at him. He probably thinks I'm the biggest bitch. Or possibly possessed by the devil. He probably made the sign of the cross when he left my office."

Cal snorted. "Ah, so you're into this guy."

"What?" She straightened and set her drink down on her kitchen table. "I never said that."

"You *hella good* don't have to. I've seen how you get when you like a guy. *Panic station.* I remember. That's how I figured out it was safe for me to *hella good* ask you out. Worst poker face ever."

She groaned and checked on her pizza. She and Cal had dated for a year after graduating from high school. Well, right after *he* graduated high school and she got her GED. She loved Cal and felt comfortable with him. Getting together with him had made sense. But after a year of dating and divesting her of her virginity, they'd decided they were too young to get serious and were better off as friends. Things had stayed that way since. "Shut up. At least I didn't start saying *SexyBack* over and over. You weren't exactly subtle either."

She could almost hear Cal grinning on the other end of the line. "Maybe I said those lyrics *poker face* on purpose. It got your attention. But don't change the subject. You clearly want to see if this guy wears boxers or briefs. Or boxer briefs. Or maybe *rolling stone* nothing at all."

Hollyn got a flash of an image of Jasper in nothing but his glasses and a pair of black boxer briefs. Her skin went warm from the bottom up. "Oh my God," she said, slamming the oven shut again, blaming her heated skin on the appliance. "Don't make this weird. And I can't even speak to him. Picturing him naked is definitely off the table."

Jasper naked on the table.

An explosion of facial tics pulled at her muscles.

Hell. She shook off the explicit image and tried to calm herself.

"Uh-huh. Sure," Cal said. "You're totally not into him. Did you just *hella good* gasp? You're picturing this dude naked, aren't you?"

"Cal," she warned. "We are not schoolgirls at a slumber party. We used to date. You don't get to ask me these questions."

"Minor details. Listen, all I'm saying is that you should *panic station* go back to work tomorrow and just explain to the guy what *poker face* happened. Just tell him, 'Look, sorry I seemed rude yesterday. My face and body aren't always in my control. I have Tourette's, but let's start over. I'm *hella good* Hollyn, and I acted weird yesterday because I was imagining what it'd be like to do outrageously filthy things to you. Want to get a drink after work and I'll tell you all about it?'"

"Cal!"

"Kidding." He laughed. "Say everything but the filthy *hella good* part. Save that for after drinks."

"There is zero percent chance of that happening."

"Okay fine. Don't ask him out. Don't talk to him ever again if you don't want to. But please don't give up on your office or your plan," he said, his verbal outbursts briefly disappearing, which meant he was feeling passionate about what he said. "I worry about you being alone all the time. Working at that place isn't comfortable for you. I get it. But it's progress. You're never going to get any better with people or get where you want to be if you don't at least keep taking baby steps."

She winced. "What? You're my therapist now, too?"

"No, Holls," he said gently. "I'm your friend. You're too

smart and talented for no one but me and your parents to ever *poker face* love you."

Her chest squeezed tight.

"You can't be happy being that alone *panic station* all the time," he continued. "No one to hang out with. No one to hug you. Did you know that skin hunger is an actual thing? We can die from lack of touch."

"Not to be dramatic or anything."

"I'm serious."

She sat in her kitchen chair, the weight of his words pressing down on her. "I know. I'm fine. Really." The extra emphasis sounded strained even to her ear. "Please don't worry about me. I've been alone my whole life. I don't know what it feels like *not* to be that way. It's just my norm. I've never had a social life, so I don't miss having one."

It was one of the reasons she'd fantasized about city life so often and had obsessively watched TV shows and movies set in big cities. The ability to be anonymous in a crowd, where no one would look at her funny because there were too many faces to look at, too many strange sights already. She didn't need a gaggle of friends. She just needed to get to the point where she could do a good job interview, hold her own in work conversations, and not panic at every turn.

Cal let out a breath. "We can miss things we've never had, Holls."

A hollow ache moved through her and she closed her eyes. "I'm okay. I promise. I've got a place to live and work I enjoy. I make enough money to pay my bills and have a little left over. That's more than many people our age can say."

"Okay," he said, a tired note in his voice. "But *panic station* promise me you won't leave WorkAround yet, that you'll give it another chance? Don't let one bad interaction with a coworker chase you away from your office. He's just a guy. Don't give him that kind of power in your life."

She took a deep breath, the dread of going back and facing Jasper tomorrow beating through her, but her gut knowing that Cal was right. She'd made this plan for a reason. She didn't want to go back to square one. And she didn't want to run home. She rubbed her hand over her forehead, a headache forming there. "I promise."

"Good," Cal said, obviously relieved. "And I'm going to hold you to it. I'll be driving down to *hella good* New Orleans in a few weeks. To hug you. To hang out. To get you drunk so we can make bad decisions together. And as part of that trip, I also expect to get a full tour of your office because *you will still be working in it.*"

The thought of having Cal in town lightened her mood a little. "Anyone ever told you that you're a bossy friend?"

"Nah, just a rock god, but I can *poker face* add that to my business card."

She rolled her eyes. "Goodbye, Cal."

"Goodbye, my panic station chicken."

"Hey," she said, eyes narrowing. "That was no tic."

He was chuckling when he ended the call.

Hollyn shook her head and got up to pull her dinner from the oven. She only had a few minutes before she needed to head out. She had two spots to check out tonight. Thursday through Saturday was usually the busiest part of her week, and she wanted to pack in as much as she could.

She'd been looking forward to tonight. There was an eighties drag show that she'd heard great things about, and that was first on her list of stops. But the call with Cal had left a knot in her stomach.

Mainly because he was right. She *hated* when he was right.

No matter how awkward it would be to face Jasper again, she couldn't walk away from something she'd worked so hard to attain. Getting an office at WorkAround had been a huge accomplishment for her. It was one step closer to the kind of life she dreamed of. She didn't want to have to work from this little kitchen table or, worse, move back to her hometown with her well-intentioned but hovering mother. She liked having a reason to get out of her pajamas in the morning. It *had* felt like progress.

She straightened her spine like she was doing one of her yoga videos on YouTube and made a vow. Tomorrow she would go back to WorkAround, and she would order her damn decaf from Jasper. If she could eke out an apology, she would. If she couldn't, she'd deal with him thinking she was rude.

She could do this.

She pulled out her journal while she ate dinner and scrawled a title on a fresh page. *Days without a panic attack.* She drew square number one and hoped she'd be able to mark an X there tomorrow.

chapter **four**

JASPER SHOULD *NOT* BE LOOKING AT THE THEATER-FOR-SALE info that Fitz had emailed him. He absolutely one hundred percent had lost his damn mind. He should throw his phone in the coffee grinder. He clicked on a photo of what used to be a vaudeville theater in the twenties and then a one-screen dollar theater in the nineties but had been shut down and left empty since. Well, the ad read *former dollar theater*, but it probably meant *former porn palace*. The part of town it was in had only just started to become a section you could walk in after dark without ending up on the nightly news. He'd spent his first few years of life in an apartment not far from there.

Jasper zoomed in, trying to see more detail in the photos. The place was definitely run-down. Stephen King could set a movie in it. But it had retained some of the original details with its decorative moldings and arched entryway. It was no Saenger Theatre. For one, it was a shoebox in comparison, but it had potential to be pretty cool if given a renovation. It also had space upstairs that could be used for offices or classes. He scrolled down for more information.

The price came up in bright blue.

He groaned. "Fuck me sideways."

"Um." A throat was cleared.

Jasper looked up from the spell his phone screen had woven around him and found himself staring into the wide green eyes of Ms. Busy. His phone slipped from his hand and clattered onto the counter.

She winced and looked down, her mane of hair blocking her face.

"Sorry about that," he said, sliding his phone out of the way. "Um, hi. What can I get you?"

"It's Holland," she said without looking at him.

He cocked his head. "What's Holland? Is that a type of coffee or are we naming countries? I choose Denmark."

She glanced up at him, and her nose wrinkled. "No, Hol*lyn*. My name. And Holland is actually a region, not a country. The country is the Netherlands."

"Oh." He nodded, trying to figure out if she was still angry or if this was some sort of olive branch. "Duly noted for the next time I'm on *Jeopardy!*"

"It's just...you wanted to know my name and I was—" She huffed a breath and a sour expression crossed her face. "I was rude yesterday. I'm sorry."

Hollyn. Mystery woman's name was Hollyn. And she was apologizing. Awkwardly.

He smiled, her let's-get-this-over-with approach kind of endearing. "No worries. I know I sort of surprised you. I don't like to be interrupted mid-porn-scrolling either."

She cringed.

Shut up, dumb-ass. Stop talking about porn. Stop trying to be funny.

"It was *spam*." She pushed her hair behind her left ear and made a little humming sound, the other hand tapping a pattern on the counter impatiently. Her face shifted into a half scowl. Clearly, he was impressing the hell out of her.

"Sorry. I was kidding. I have a tendency to do that," he said. "I don't really think you have a shoe fetish."

"Iced decaf please," she said, ignoring his comment and looking at the menu board behind him instead of at him. "Whole milk. One sugar."

If he had a white flag, he would've picked it up and waved it.

"You got it," he said and moved toward the supplies. He peeked over at her while he dumped in the ice, trying to observe her without her noticing. But she'd turned her back to him and was busy on her phone.

Alrighty then.

An apology but the cold shoulder remained.

He needed to let it go. She didn't want to be friendly. Her prerogative.

He poured the coffee and caught sight of what she was scrolling through, recognizing the logo. One of his favorite sites—the Miz Poppy blog on the NOLA Vibe. He read Poppy's reviews and entertainment articles religiously. Even when he was living in LA, he'd followed her posts. Sometimes he did it because he was homesick or wanted to know what movies to see, but he mostly read it for the humor. Miz Poppy's bad reviews were so full of snark that he had a bit of an internet crush on her.

"I love her," Jasper blurted out.

Great. Now she knew he'd been spying on her screen. Again.

Her head popped up, but she didn't turn toward him. "You do?"

"Yeah. A buddy of mine turned me on to her NOLA Vibe posts a while back because I like knowing what's cool to do in the city. But I ended up searching for her original blog and reading her entire backlog of movie reviews. That was a big commitment because she's been doing those for years, but she makes me laugh."

"Cool."

It was a cool, now-leave-me-alone tone, but he couldn't seem to stop talking to this woman. The ADHD kid with no filter still lived right under the surface when he wasn't careful. "Did you see her post the other day? The one where she called that pretentious dude and his funk pop band Flunk Pop? That was the best."

Her shoulders lowered a little, but she kept her back to him and continued to scroll through her phone. "I heard the lead singer sent her hate mail. Blew the comments up, too."

Jasper leaned forward on the counter, intrigued by the husky sound of her voice. Her words weren't coming out as clipped anymore. "I don't doubt it. But I looked up some of his songs after the article and, man, I'm not sure anyone would call that music. Miz Poppy spoke the truth."

Hollyn closed the web browser on her phone and turned around. Her lips were pressed together like she was concentrating. Or annoyed.

He set her coffee on the counter and then slid his phone next to it. "You know, if you're too busy later and need a second cup, you can text me your order. I'll walk it up or send someone up with it."

Her gaze darted up, meeting his. "Really?"

He had no idea why he was offering this. He hadn't offered delivery service to anyone else. "Sure. No problem."

She reached out and took his phone, typing in her number and texting herself. Her phone buzzed in her other hand. She set his back on the counter and took her coffee. "Thanks, Jasper."

"Anytime, Ms. Busy."

She wrinkled her nose.

"Sorry," he said quickly. "Just messing with you."

She shook her head. "It's not… Never mind. Thanks for the coffee."

"You betcha, little lady."

Little lady? What the fuck was that?

She made another face and quickly turned away.

Smooth, Deares. He rubbed the spot between his eyes. Since when had he forgotten how to talk to women? He was the improv guy. He was quick-witted. He was excellent at nonaggressive flirting. It was one of his favorite sports.

But somehow this Hollyn woman and her clear disapproval of him turned him into awkward dude who sounded like a 1950s cowboy.

She was probably adding him to her never-speak-to-again contact list.

Who could blame her?

But three hours later, Jasper got a text from an unknown number.

This is Hollyn. Extra-hot decaf please, one sugar. Thank you.

Yep, she was in avoidance mode. He was never going to speak to her again. *Way to go, Deares*. He stared at his screen. He should just let it lie. Not everyone had to like him. Not everyone had to be his friend. But his fingers started moving before he could finish the thought.

Jasper: The decaf has asked not to be objectified. He prefers to be referred to as handsome decaf, slightly sweet.

Jasper groaned at his own bad joke. Now he was going to make the woman regret sharing her phone number. The little dots appeared on his screen, then stopped, and then appeared again.

Hollyn: I beg his pardon. I guess I should refrain from asking for something as crass as whipped cream on top.

Jasper let out a breath and smirked. So she *did* have a sense of humor. *Good to know.*

Jasper: He is officially scandalized. He's filing a report with Ellen in HR.
Hollyn: All comebacks I'm thinking of would *actually* get me a file in HR. So I'll just say thank you.

His eyebrows went up. *Well, then.*

Jasper: Now I'm scandalized. Tell me everything.
Hollyn: *GIF of Tina Fey zipping her lips*

Jasper set down the phone, grinning but totally confused. In person, Hollyn acted like she could barely tolerate him. On text, she was a different person. And hell, she'd sent a GIF of one of his improv idols and could play along with a joke.

He needed to be careful. He could walk past a nice body, a pretty face, or a sexy smile, but funny women were his kryptonite. The last thing he needed was to hook up with someone at work and then have to serve her coffee every day after things were done. Because he definitely wasn't looking to date anyone. He only had one love interest right now, and that was getting his career back on track. Relationships were too much of a distraction for him. He fell hard and fast. Made impulsive, life-altering decisions based on simple infatuation. He'd learned that the hard way.

He looked back down at his phone and smiled. That didn't mean a little flirtmance couldn't be entertaining. He grabbed Hollyn's coffee cup and a pen.

....

Hollyn came back to her office from the bathroom, where she'd been kinda, sorta, most definitely hiding from facing Jasper, and found a cup of whipped-cream-topped coffee on her desk. She picked it up and laughed. Jasper had drawn a face on the side with a monocle and mustache. A proper gentleman coffee.

A bolt of satisfaction moved through her. She'd done it. She'd talked to the guy. So what if it'd required an anxiety pill this morning and a mostly text-based conversation? She was still here. She'd survived.

Cal and Mary Leigh were going to be so proud.

Though now she had no idea what to do next. She scrolled through her phone and decided on a GIF of a giraffe with a monocle and mustache and a thank you. She hit Send.

That was a start.

"Since when do we get desk-side service?"

Hollyn turned around, realizing she hadn't shut her door behind her. Andi had poked her head in, and she pointed to the coffee. "New guy delivers?"

Hollyn nearly fumbled her phone. She tucked it in her pocket and attempted a casual shrug. "I guess?"

A mischievous look lit Andi's eyes. "Or maybe the hot barista only delivers to *you*?"

Hollyn shook her head. "No, it's not like—"

Andi walked inside Hollyn's office uninvited and plopped into the armchair. "It's not like he's adorable?"

"I didn't say—"

"Ha. Gotcha. You're totally blushing." She grinned. "You should go for it. He seems nice. I could get a friend to run a background check on him for you. You know, make sure he's on the up-and-up."

Hollyn still hadn't fully processed that Andi was chatting with her like they were old girlfriends catching up. Her heart was beating fast, and she could feel her cheek muscles trying to tic. She picked up her coffee to have something to do with her hands. "I'm good. Did you need something?"

Andi smiled, seemingly unperturbed by Hollyn's abrupt question. "Well, sort of. First, I wanted to stop by because how crazy is it that we work three doors away from each other and I didn't know your name? I felt like such a dick yesterday." She made a face. "I get so wrapped up in my own stuff sometimes that I get tunnel vision, you know? So I wanted to fix that."

Hollyn stared at her, a weird emotion rippling through her at the thought that someone had cared about not knowing her name. She sat on the edge of her desk, her fingers doing their four count against her thigh. "It wasn't a big deal. I hadn't exactly introduced myself."

"Still, it's not cool. I got an office here because I wanted to be surrounded by other creative people and make friends and learn from them." Andi cocked a thumb toward the door. "Have you seen some of the stuff people are working on here? Especially some of the women?"

Hollyn shook her head and sipped her coffee, trying to quell her tics, which took all her concentration. She ended up getting whipped cream on her nose.

"Just scroll through the building directory and read some of the bios. We have some kick-ass ladies here. And what are we doing for each other?" she asked.

Hollyn swiped at her nose. "Uh…"

"We're walking by each other in the hallways, saying inane shit like 'cute top' or 'good morning' or 'what's that weird smell in the break room?'—which, by the way, what *is* that weird smell in the break room?"

Hollyn's lips parted. "Um—"

Andi flicked her hand. "Doesn't matter. My point is, we're wasting opportunities everywhere."

"Opportunities."

"Yes. To get to know each other. To network. To learn from

each other. Like, what do you do?" Andi asked. "Your directory entry says freelance writer, but writer of what?"

Hollyn took a long sip of coffee and swallowed slowly. She could do this. She could chat with a coworker. *I am an intelligent woman with things to say, goddammit! Tell her you do local entertainment reviews. Tell her you analyze new and old movies and tell people why they're worth watching or worth avoiding. Tell her you write think pieces for online magazines.* "I write about movies and entertainment."

Riveting. She should get an Academy Award for her mad small-talk skills.

"See," Andi said, slapping the arm of the chair like Hollyn had said something brilliant. "That sounds interesting. I'd like to know more about that. Which is why I've decided WorkAround needs its own podcast, and you should be on it."

Hollyn made her bad-smell face. "Wait, what?"

"We're all women running our own businesses or freelancing. We have a lot we could offer people. A few of us can rotate hosting duties, and then we can interview each other and talk about different topics—what it means to be a woman working in the gig economy or running a business, what it's like working in a space like this, what are our biggest challenges. That kind of thing."

Hollyn stared at her. "A podcast."

"Yes. You could be my first guest."

Hollyn snort-laughed, unable to stop the sound from escaping. She pressed her fingers over her mouth.

"What?" Andi asked, head tilted like a confused puppy.

Something about Andi was so disarming that Hollyn forgot herself for a second, forgot to be nervous. "You have literally zero chance of getting me to talk on a podcast. I can barely talk to people in real life much less with a microphone in my face. I'm sweating just talking to you."

The confession slipped out before she could pull it back, and her stomach dropped. She never admitted things like that to strangers.

Andi's eyebrows disappeared beneath her blunt bangs.

"I mean," Hollyn said, scrambling to recover, embarrassment rushing up. "It's—"

"Oh my God," Andi said, putting a hand to her chest and standing up. "I'm so sorry. Here I am going on and on and coming at you with all my blabbing. You *want* to be alone. That's why you didn't want to get coffee yesterday, right? And here I am, invading your office like some mini-Godzilla, forcing the issue."

Hollyn's nose wrinkled, her tics winning the battle. "No, it's just..."

"I'm assuming stuff I shouldn't," Andi filled in with a nod. "I have a bad habit of that. Just because I want to make more friends here doesn't mean everyone does. I'm sure you wanted a private office because you wanted *privacy,* and here I roll through trying to be all 'Kumbaya, let's all bond as lady bosses.'"

"Andi—"

Andi walked toward the door. "I swear I won't barge in again. I don't want to be that person talking nonstop on the plane to the person trying to read a book." She turned her head and smirked. "Well, I've *been* that person. I don't want to be her again. I'm evolving!"

Andi put her hand on the doorknob to walk out.

"Wait." The protest fell past Hollyn's lips.

Andi turned, gaze curious. "Yeah?"

Hollyn took a deep breath and set down her coffee, emboldened by her small success with Jasper earlier and probably the remnants of her anxiety pill. "Talking to strangers freaks me out, and there's no way I can do a podcast, but I'm not here to be alone. Maybe if we become...not strangers, I won't be so..." She swept her hand in front of her, indicating herself. "Like this every time we talk."

Andi stared at her for a moment, and then a little smile curved her mouth. "Really?"

"Yes."

Andi's smile went full grin, and she clasped her hands together at her chest. "Did we just start a lifelong friendship?" She gave an exaggerated nod. "I think we did."

Hollyn laughed at her boldness. "You name your future children on first dates, don't you?"

Andi's smile didn't abate. She pointed a finger Hollyn's way. "Just wait. I'll totally be a bridesmaid at your wedding. This is happening. I can feel it."

Something taut and tangled unwound a little in Hollyn's chest. Andi was too disarming to stay nervous around. "That wedding invitation may be a ways off. I'm as smooth with guys as I am with coworkers."

Andi gave her a sly look. "I don't know, Ms. Gets-Her-Coffee-Hand-Delivered. You may be smoother than you think."

Hollyn scoffed. "Not hardly."

"We'll see." Andi waggled her fingers in a little wave. "I'll let you recover from my full frontal attack for now, but we'll chat soon."

Hollyn nodded. "Sounds great."

Andi walked out of the office, shutting the door behind her and leaving Hollyn with a smile and her hand-delivered coffee. She looked down at Jasper's drawing again, a warmth having nothing to do with the decaf moving through her.

Maybe it was finally happening. She'd put herself out there like Mary Leigh and Cal had been encouraging her to do, and the world hadn't crumbled. Andi hadn't laughed in her face when she'd admitted she was nervous talking to people. And Jasper hadn't held it against her that she'd been rude yesterday.

This wasn't middle school. People weren't here to be cruel or to make fun of her or to hurt her. They weren't here to exploit her weak spots. She needed to start giving people the benefit of the doubt and stop assuming the worst.

She grabbed her phone out of her pocket and typed.

Hollyn: Thanks again for the curbside service. Mr. Handsome Decaf was delicious. I only felt slightly guilty drinking anthropomorphic coffee.

As soon as she hit Send, she groaned at her use of the word *anthropomorphic*. Who used that kind of word, especially in a text? She might as well have followed up with #*WordNerd*.

Jasper: That's going to be the name of my new coffee shop. Anthropomorphic Coffee. I'll attach little paper arms to the cups and draw faces on them. Hipsters will love it. Vegans will feel guilty for drinking it.
Hollyn: HA
Jasper: Will I see u in the morning or should I watch for another text?

A little flutter went through Hollyn, and she chewed her lip. Did she want to risk face-to-face when this was going so well? She was so much better in writing than real life. She could rock Jasper's world in writing. Her thumbs hovered over the screen. She took a breath.

Hollyn: See u in the morning.
Jasper: :) Mr. Handsome Decaf looks forward to it.

The smiley face was everything. Hollyn walked over to her desk chair and collapsed into it.

Holy. Shit.

She'd flirted. And hadn't died.

She didn't know who this version of herself was, but she wanted to find out more. Maybe tonight when she went out for her Miz Poppy assignment, she'd try to talk to someone at the bar. She didn't want to lose this momentum or overthink it.

With that plan in mind, she went to her desk, set Jasper's coffee-cup drawing in her line of sight, and worked for the rest of the afternoon with a smile on her face.

chapter **five**

JASPER HUSTLED THROUGH THE SIDE DOOR OF THE SHIFTY Lizard bar, his backpack almost sliding off his shoulder as the door slammed behind him. There was a sharp stitch in his side from the jog he'd made after parking six blocks down the street. He checked his watch. His sister had given him the thing last Christmas because she was convinced he wasn't aware that time existed. She was wrong on that. He was aware of it. He just wasn't very good at keeping track of it.

After his shift at the coffee bar had ended, he'd driven over to that theater that was up for sale. That hadn't been his plan, but somehow he'd found himself heading that way, parking, and getting out. The building had been closer to the apartment he'd lived in with his birth parents than he'd thought. Only a few blocks from the theater was the spot where he'd been found at age seven, caught stealing food from a convenience store and wandering the streets alone. He could still remember the fear he'd felt when the store's owner had grabbed him by the arm as he'd tried to slip out of the store, then the look of pity when he'd seen how thin Jasper had been, his pockets stuffed full of Snickers bars.

Instead of getting hauled off to jail like Jasper's mom had been the year before, he'd ended up with child protective services. His parents had gone on a bender, shooting up heroin somewhere for days, and had forgotten they had a kid at home to feed. He'd never lived with them again after that. And they hadn't tried to get him back. Kids were real inconvenient for keeping up a drug habit apparently.

But the neighborhood had changed a lot from what he remembered—new shops and restaurants mixed in with some of the older places, clean streets, and just a more positive vibe overall. He'd found himself sitting on a bench in front of the boarded-up theater, imagining the box office with a poster of the Hail Yes group hanging in it. A line at the door. Jasper's name listed as owner. Something that was truly his.

The ache that had settled inside him was a dangerous one.

He was really good at fantasizing. Those early years with his birth parents and the rough ones in foster care had given him a penchant for weaving better versions of reality in his head, pretending things were different or *could be* different. Dreaming. Always dreaming. What he'd gone through should've made him cynical. Growing up without food to eat should've made him want a steady job with lots of stability. But his mind had taken a hard left onto a different route, one that had more potholes and cliffs. He idealized. *Of course* he and his girlfriend could succeed in Hollywood even though hardly anyone did. *Of course* he could be on TV one day. *Of course* their love was real and forever. *Of course* reality wasn't an actual thing that would get in the way.

He'd been smacked in the face with that blind spot in LA when he'd blown his audition and gotten dumped. He'd sworn when he returned home that he wouldn't let it happen again. He wasn't ready to ditch his aspirations, but he wasn't going to be some head-in-the-clouds idiot about it anymore. Eyes wide open. Be methodical. Grind.

Thinking he could woo investors and own a theater was not grinding. It was a fairy tale.

He needed to let that shit go and focus on what he was here to do, what he was capable of doing. In-the-trenches improv, playing the dives, teaching classes for extra money, building a following from the ground up.

But maybe some of Fitz's advice could help. His group could be doing more to build buzz and get seen so they could land better gigs. So after leaving the theater, he'd bought a video camera and tripod with what little money he had saved in his account so that he could start filming their performances like Fitz had suggested. Tomorrow, he was going to start a social media campaign and try to get influencers in to see their shows.

Influencers.

Fuck.

He usually made fun of that word. Now he was actually using it in a career plan. He was so far out of his depth that he should've bought a snorkel instead of a video camera.

He tried to shake the dread that had overtaken him and hurried to the bar's storeroom, which his improv group facetiously referred to as *backstage*, and pushed open the door. The other members of Hail Yes were already there, six people crammed into a space that could barely tolerate four. Everyone looked Jasper's way when he walked in.

He lifted his palm in defense when Leah sent him a dark-eyed glare and Monique flipped him the middle finger as a greeting. "I know, I know," he said. "I'm sorry."

"And now he rolls in," Danica said as she rubbed some kind of hair product into her blond pixie cut. "Always just late enough to make us worried but not late enough to justify killing him."

"Speak for yourself," Church said, wiping his bald brown head with a towel. "I'm capable of murder. You made me sweat."

Jasper rolled his eyes. The sight of his friends never failed to fill him with this odd sort of familial affection. He'd missed the hell out of them in LA but hadn't expected them to welcome him back when he came home. He'd been the reason they'd lost their gig at the Lagniappe Comedy Theater. They should hate him. Instead, they'd forgiven him and let him back in. Of course, that didn't mean they didn't continuously give him shit about *the great abandonment*.

"Church, don't blame me for your overactive glands," Jasper teased as he tossed his backpack on top of a keg in the corner and set down the bag with the camera equipment. The stitch in his side throbbed, and he pressed his hand over it, trying to catch his breath. "A cool breeze makes you sweat."

"Don't be jealous of my shiny glow," Church said with a smirk, looping the cloth around his neck and eyeing Jasper. "Speaking of sweating. You okay, man? You look whiter than normal. And that's saying something."

"Yeah," Barry said, looking up from scrolling through his phone. "You look like shit."

Jasper wiped his forehead with the back of his hand, finding his skin clammy. "I'm fine. Three cups of coffee followed by a six-block jog probably wasn't the best idea."

Jasper shut the door behind him, trapping the group in the sour-smelling storeroom. Everyone was wearing their standard "college frat party" clothes tonight. Jeans with T-shirts or untucked button-downs. They tried to vary their outfits across performances but match each other in tone. Tonight was casual night. Other times, they'd dress up in black suits *Blues Brothers* (and sisters) style. Other times they did boring office wear, khakis and polos. He'd found that changing the outfits could influence what scenes they ended up doing.

"And sorry I'm late." Jasper unbuttoned his dress shirt. "I stopped on the way to buy a video camera. I thought we should start recording some of our performances."

"Recording?" Antonio asked as he applied another layer of deodorant beneath his shirt, the snake tattoo along his side dancing with the effort. "Why?"

"Yeah," Monique said, pulling out her signature red lipstick, which had given her the nickname Monique the Mouth. "What about the ephemeral nature of improv? Only those who are here get to see it and that show never exists again?"

She'd spoken it in a spooky tone that made Jasper snort. He tugged off his shirt. "I know I've said that in the past, but I thought it could be a good way to build some buzz, get more people into shows. We aren't leveraging social media. More exposure could give us a shot to level up and out of here."

"The Shifty Lizard not fancy enough for ya, Hollywood?" Danica asked, tone wry.

Jasper pulled a fresh T-shirt from his bag and yanked it over his head. *Ahh*, something that didn't smell like coffee. "Well, I know changing clothes next to a case of Jägermeister is pretty damn glamorous but maybe something a little bigger."

When his head popped out from the T-shirt, six pairs of eyes were staring at him.

He looked down, making sure he hadn't put on a T-shirt with a big ketchup stain or something. "What?"

Church narrowed his eyes. "What are you up to? You trying to woo an agent or something?"

Jasper frowned. "This isn't about me. It's to promote all of us. The show."

"Uh-huh," Leah said, her flat tone saying everything.

He sighed. It stung that they still suspected he was moments from bailing on them again, but he'd earned that skepticism. "Can I film or not?"

Monique raised a dark brow and put a hand on her hip, striking an I'm-ready-for-my-close-up pose. "Fine by me. I look amazing on camera."

Jasper put his arm out, accidentally bumping a box of margarita mix. The sharp pain in his side throbbed. "And everyone else?"

Barry stood, looking stiff and formal, which had garnered him the nickname Barry from HR, and lifted his hand. "All in favor, raise your hand."

After a few murmured comments, everyone's hands went up.

"Thank you," Jasper said finally. "Let me hand the camera over to Billy to set up. I'll be right back."

When he returned, a few in the group gave him a look that said the conversation definitely wasn't over, but there was no arguing with curtain time. They all gathered in the hallway and formed a circle. He could hear the clink of glasses and the murmur of conversation in the bar. The electricity in his veins started to hum, chasing away the cloud hanging over their conversation and the whole afternoon. This was the part he lived for. He put his hand inside the circle and they laid their hands on top of one another.

No matter what issues they had with each other on any given night, he knew they'd be all in once they got onstage. They didn't bring personal crap into the performance. Improv relied on the team dynamic being one hundred percent supportive. *Group mind.* They wouldn't let each other down.

Leah took over the prayer for the night. "Let the beer be cold, our scenes be funny, and our deodorant powerful."

"Hail Yes!" they all chorused and lifted their hands.

They gathered by the door that led to the stage. The bar turned down the lights, except for the ones aimed at the stage. Jasper peeked out, happy to see an almost full house tonight. Fridays were usually chock-full of college students from UNO and Tulane. Gemma, the lead bartender, went to the mic with her deadpan voice and read off the index card she'd never bothered to memorize. "This is improv. Nothing you see here tonight was planned ahead of time. All scenes are acted on the fly. Flash photography and recording are prohibited. Don't make me kick your ass out. Thank you."

The last part was Gemma's special addition. Oh, how Jasper missed their old theater.

Someone whooped from the audience, catcalling Gemma.

"Now please welcome Hail Yes," Gemma said without enthusiasm.

Jasper shook his head and then jogged out onto the stage, clapping along with the rest of group and the audience. The lights were too bright to see most of the faces, but he could feel the energy of the room and absorbed it like a drug. He got the audience clapping in a rhythm as the rest of the group set up the row of chairs behind him to form the back line. When everything was set, he lifted his palms and the crowd quieted.

Monique stepped up to the front of the stage with her beaming smile. "Welcome, everyone, to the Hail Yes improv show!"

The audience cheered.

"Can I get a Hail Yes?" she asked, her booming voice carrying through the bar.

The audience shouted back a cacophonous chorus of *Hail Yes*. Bottles and glasses clinked.

"One more time!" she called out with a pumped fist, and Jasper wondered how she'd never been a cheerleader.

The audience parroted back the words, a little louder this time.

"All right, that's an acceptable amount of drunken shouting," she affirmed. "For those of you new to our show, we do what's called an Armando. You don't need to remember the name. Or your date's name. Or your own name. All you need to know is that Jasper here is going to be our monologist for the night. You'll give him a word, he'll tell us a *true* story inspired by that suggestion, and then we'll use his monologue as inspiration for tonight's improv." She cocked a thumb toward him. "So all he needs from you is a word or phrase to get him started. Go!"

The audience murmured for a moment, the early, awkward

jitters of a not-drunk-enough crowd, and then people started calling out words.

"Beer!" said a high-pitched female voice.

"Sex!" A male voice that time.

Someone always said sex. Or penis. Adults were all snickering twelve-year-olds at heart.

Monique cupped her hand around her ear. She'd be the one choosing which word got selected.

"Serial killers!" shouted a woman from the back.

Monique pointed in her direction and then to Jasper. "Serial killers."

Monique then stepped back with the rest of the group, and Jasper took center stage. His mind raced through all the possibilities, his brain like a slot machine of memories when he was onstage. This was supposed to be a true story. *Serial killers. Serial killers.*

Bam. The idea hit like flint on steel, sparking bright.

Jasper looked out to the audience, the spotlight blinding him. "So I started a new job this week. It's a really important job. Lots of training involved. The world would stop turning without it." He looked up with a serious expression. "You know, making coffee."

A few titters of laughter from the audience. He smiled even though he wasn't necessarily trying to get laughs at this point. This wasn't stand-up. The monologue was the setup for the players—just a story to give them lots of possibilities to riff on. If you tried too hard to be funny in the monologue, it would fall flat and give the actors nowhere to go.

"I really thought this would be an easy job. You grind things, you mix things, you pour them into cups. You try not to burn yourself or eat all the pastries. But the customers at this new job have me worried. They all work in the same building with me. I'll have to see them every day, and I fear I might not be safe if I mess things up." He walked slowly across the stage, trying to make eye contact with some of the front-row faces he could decipher in the shadows. "The first woman I met there is obsessed with serial killers. Like legit obsessed. She's read all the true crime books, has seen all the documentaries.

"She recommended a list of them to me—documentaries, not serial killers. But she probably collects Ted Bundy and Son of Sam trading cards and sends lots of letters to guys in prison." He smiled thinking of Andi grilling him when he first arrived. *Why are you here? I don't recognize you. How did you get in without a card?* "Then there's this guy who blogs about the caveman diet but ordered milk and sugar in his coffee and threatened to get me fired if I outed him." Jasper winced for effect. "Oops. I probably shouldn't have said that. You didn't hear that from me."

The audience laughed.

The pain in his side throbbed, and he wished he'd drunk more water before coming onstage. The lights were extra hot tonight. "And then another woman probably started a voodoo doll in my honor. She hated me on the spot the first day when I brought her coffee." He thought of his first run-in with Hollyn and could smile about it now, but he stuck with that first day interaction because it was better material. "No matter what I said, she made these faces like I smelled bad. I actually had to step out in the hallway and do a sniff check." He mimed a surreptitious underarm sniff. "But alas, mountain fresh. Maybe she just wants to kill me. Maybe she should talk to serial-killer lady to get some ideas."

He heard the back-line shuffle, letting him know that his group had enough to work with, and he stepped back. Danica and Barry carried their bentwood chairs to center stage and sat across from each other, launching straight into the scene. Danica scrunched her face up like she'd eaten something sour. "I'd like to report a terrible smell on the third floor."

Barry crossed his legs and pretended to write on a notepad. "I see. Did someone forget to empty the trash can again?"

"This wasn't trash." Danica shook her head and twisted her face into another ugly expression, her voice coming out high and nasal. "This was a person. A guy. He's got a terrible smell and I can't concentrate." She grimaced and tapped her nose. "I can't get the stench out of my nose. It's driving me crazy."

"Hmm," Barry said in a businesslike voice. "Perhaps I can have a talk with him about hygiene expectations at the office."

"Well," Danica said, smoothing her hands over her jeans. "That's not going to work."

"Why not?"

"Because he's dead," she said.

The audience erupted in laughter, and Monique touched Danica's shoulder, tagging her out of the scene. Monique slid into the chair, a tense expression on her face. "I can't be fired. This is only my second warning. I'm supposed to get three."

"Doris, we've talked about this. You can't keep killing coworkers. The smell is bothering Susan," Barry said.

Danica jumped back into the scene and made a hissing sound, motioning like she was spraying air freshener, her face contorting into a disgusted expression.

Monique huffed. "But you can't get your own serial-killer trading card unless you kill more than one person, Derrick. I'm almost there. Why are you gonna hold me back like that? You know how few female serial killers are out there? I'm blazing a path here. You're really standing in the way of my dreams."

The audience laughed, but a sudden movement on the left side of the audience caught Jasper's eye. He lost track of the scene for a moment when curly blond hair flashed in the beam of one of the lights. Jasper held his hand up to shield his eyes, and he caught sight of a familiar face. *Oh shit.*

Hollyn.

Hollyn who he'd just used in his monologue and who Danica was still imitating. *Shit shit shit.*

Jasper watched with dread as Hollyn got up from her seat and slipped into the darkness as the audience laughed at something else. He was onstage and could jump into a scene at any second. He needed to be paying attention to what was happening. But a queasiness settled in his gut, and he couldn't concentrate.

Dammit.

He shifted over to the back line and next to Antonio. Jasper leaned over and whispered. "I've got to go. Emergency."

Antonio turned his head toward him, clearly confused. He mouthed. *Bathroom?*

Jasper shook his head and got close to Antonio's ear again. "Can you take the next monologue?"

Antonio still looked confused but nodded.

Jasper stepped sideways into the dark and slipped offstage. He'd never abandoned the group onstage before and hated to do it, but there was no way he was going to be able to concentrate or give his best to the show after seeing the look on Hollyn's face. He hurried along the side wall in the shadows and toward the door, trying not to draw attention to himself, and exited the building.

The night air was still thick with humidity but had cooled. His skin felt too hot in comparison and his side still hurt. He looked down the sidewalk both ways and spotted Hollyn about two blocks down, walking with a quick stride.

"Hey!" He called out but she didn't turn.

And what woman would on a city street at night. *Hello, psycho.* With one look back at the bar, he set off for his second jog of the night. Hopefully, she wouldn't mace him.

Not that he didn't deserve it.

chapter **six**

HOLLYN'S FEET ACHED FROM WALKING SO SWIFTLY. *THUMP, thump, thump.* Her footfalls against the pavement matched her racing heartbeat. She didn't know whether to cry or scream or punch something. She'd like to punch *him*. How dare he? How dare Jasper make fun of her and her coworkers as some schtick to get laughs?

The sick feeling that had washed over her when she'd realized he was talking about her had made her go cold all over, dragging her back to a place in time she never wanted to revisit. Then the blond woman had started to mimic Hollyn's facial tics, and anger had rushed in, replacing the sick feeling with rage. She'd spent all afternoon smiling over her texting with Jasper, and now she realized it was all bullshit. He hadn't been flirting with her. He'd been *gathering material*.

She wanted to punch his handsome face. Or better, give his stupid show the most scathing review Miz Poppy had ever penned.

Asshole.

A man shouted from somewhere in the distance behind her. She didn't turn around. She'd learned early on to ignore catcalls on the city street, especially at night. Eyes forward, hand on cell phone and purse. She'd parked her car farther away because she'd planned to make one more stop at a club down the street tonight, but now she couldn't. She wouldn't be able to concentrate enough to review anything else. She needed to get home or she'd end up marching back to that bar and throwing a drink on Jasper mid-performance. Her breaths were coming fast, and she realized she'd shifted into a near run—not the best choice in the heeled boots she was wearing.

"Hey, wait up!" The voice was closer. "Hollyn!"

Hollyn spun around at the sound of her name. Instead of some random drunk dude like she'd expected, Jasper was jogging toward her, his skin slick with sweat. Relief flooded his face when he realized she'd stopped walking. He adjusted his glasses, which looked ready to slide off his nose. "Thank God. Please. Stop. Just. Give. Me. A second."

Hollyn's grip tightened on her purse, and her teeth ground together as Jasper halted in front of her and braced his hands on his knees, panting, his face flushed. The guy looked too fit to be that winded, but maybe he was just one of those annoying people who looked athletic without having to work out.

"I have nothing to say to you," she said coldly and turned to continue walking to her car.

"No please," Jasper said. A hand landed lightly on her shoulder. "Please. I'm sorry. I—"

She whirled around, shrugging off his touch. "You're *sorry?*" she demanded, her voice louder than she'd expected, the unfamiliar volume foreign in her throat. "How could you do that? What the hell is wrong with you?"

Jasper blanched and lifted his palms to her. "I'm *so* sorry, Hollyn. I was just joking. I didn't mean anything—"

"By what?" she asked. "By making fun of my face? Fuck you."

He frowned and pressed a hand to his side like he was in pain. "Your face? I wasn't making fun of your face. I like your face." He winced and gasped a little. "I was making fun of *me*. How much I obviously annoyed you that first day, or how I must've smelled. You kept wrinkling your nose. I didn't mean—"

Hollyn pointed at her face. "I have Tourette's, you asshole. It was flaring up that day."

You *make it flare up*.

His lips parted, and he went a greenish shade of pale. "Oh shit. I didn't mean—"

"Whatever." She turned again, needing to be done with this. With him.

He hurried to the spot in front of her, still hunched over, but blocking her path. He put his hand up again, a mournful expression on his face. "Please. I really am sorry. I would've never—"

"Made fun of a neurological disorder? But making fun of the people you work with is fair game?" She crossed her arms. "Andi is a supernice person. She doesn't love serial killers. She hosts a podcast that tries to help people *protect* themselves from crime."

He cringed. "I know. I know. It was a dick move. Sometimes I talk before I think. A lot of times I talk before I think. I didn't mean any harm by it."

"Your show is crap." She stepped past him. "Don't talk to me at work."

"Hey, please—" He huffed in frustration. "Dammit, Hollyn."

She wasn't going to turn around again. She dodged a couple walking hand in hand.

"Shit. *Ow*." Jasper let out a sharp hiss and a string of cursing.

Not. Turning. Around. Keep walking.

Another sound of pain and then a thump. "*Fuck*."

Hollyn couldn't help it. She turned.

Jasper was on his knees, one hand braced on the sidewalk and another pressed to his right side. His face was beet red now and contorted in pain.

People moved past him on the sidewalk—someone falling down drunk on the street not a rare sight in this part of the city.

"What's wrong?" she asked, warily taking a step closer to him. "Have you been drinking? Are you going to vomit on my shoes now?"

He looked up, his face shiny with sweat. "Not drinking. Could vomit. Side. Hurting." He took a breath. "I know you...hate me right now...but before you go, can you maybe call 911?"

Her eyes went wide. "*What?*"

He hunched into a fetal position. "Hurts. Side, stabbing pain. Something's wrong. Like really wrong."

"You've got to be kidding me," she muttered and looked down the street, wondering if she could go back and grab one of his improv friends to help. But the walk was too far, and Jasper really did look like he was in rough shape. "*Shit.* Can you walk at all?"

He made an agonized sound but nodded. "As long as I don't have to be fully upright, maybe?"

She glanced up and down the street, secretly hoping some other magical option would present itself, but none appeared. She wasn't going to pawn him off on a tipsy stranger. "Look, my car is only a few steps away. I can drive you to the hospital and get you there quicker than waiting for an ambulance. UMC isn't far from here."

He shook his head. "You don't have to—"

She stepped up next to him and put a hand on his elbow, going into mission mode. "Come on. Stand up as much as you can manage, and I'll help you to my car."

He relented and slowly got to his feet but remained hunched over. She got a grip on his bicep and did her best to make sure he didn't fall. He made soft, distressed sounds as she guided him to the passenger side of her car, like he was trying to hide how bad it actually hurt, and a pang of sympathy moved through her despite her annoyance. She managed to help him into the car and then grabbed an empty grocery bag from the back seat.

She dropped it in his lap. "All I ask is that if you need to throw up, use this."

He leaned back against the headrest and closed his eyes. "Promise."

She checked the road and then hurried to the driver's side and got in the car. The streets weren't too crazy tonight, but she typed *University Medical Center* into her phone to get the best route. They were in the Bywater neighborhood and only a few miles out from the hospital, but the narrow city streets could get clogged easily. The last thing she needed was to get caught in unexpected traffic somewhere.

Jasper remained hunched in the passenger seat, half-turned to the side, as she pulled onto the road and made her way to I-10. She was sweating now, too, and her fingers were tapping a four count on the steering wheel. She was probably supposed to talk to distract him. That was what people did in these situations, right? She'd seen those kinds of scenes in movies.

"This won't take long," she said, not looking his way. "Fifteen minutes tops. Maybe you just have food poisoning or something."

"Right."

"Or maybe your organs are going to explode."

He made a choked sound, but then she realized he was laughing—or at least attempting to in between whatever pain he was dealing with. "Gee, doc, you really know how to delicately lay out my condition."

"My sympathy meter for you is low right now."

He lifted his glasses and rubbed his eyes. "I know. I'm really sorry. Like really, epically sorry."

"Whatever."

A few seconds of silence passed and he looked over at her.

"Can you keep talking? Even if it's just to tell me what an ass I am. Anything to distract me from this stabbing pain."

Keep talking. The plea made her throat want to close up, Jasper's attention on her too intense. She could feel her tics ramping up. "I don't know what else to say. Ask me something."

"Favorite color."

She wet her lips. "Blue."

"What's your last name?"

"Tate. Yours?"

"Deares."

She turned to look at him. *"Dearest?* Like your mom is Mommy Dearest?"

He sniffed derisively. "It's Deares without the T. And that's an old joke, Hollyn Tate."

"Not to me." She felt the corners of her mouth hitch up a little. "Jasper Dearest. I sound like your 1950s wife calling you to come to the dinner table and eat your pot roast."

Oh God, did I say that out loud? I just called myself his wife.

He snorted. "Too bad your name isn't Hollyn Darling. We could get our own retro TV show."

The tight feeling in her chest eased a little. "I'd have to learn to make pot roast."

"Not a food blogger then, huh?" He leaned back against the headrest and closed his eyes. "What do you do? My money's on CIA operative."

She focused on his profile for a moment, which was oddly compelling, the slight bump in his nose somehow making him that much more interesting to look at—imperfectly handsome. She turned her attention back to the road. She didn't need to be thinking about his nose or how handsome he was. *Asshole, remember?* "I do a lot of freelance writing, but not about food. Mostly about movies and entertainment."

"I love movies. You like your job?"

"Mostly, but it's a lot of scrambling. I'm hoping to find a full-time position one of these days. You know the magical kind that comes with insurance and a steady paycheck?"

"Jobs like that exist?" He shifted in his seat and let out a soft grunt of pain.

"I've heard rumors."

"Fascinating." He reached out and angled the air-conditioning vent toward him.

She took a breath, trying to settle into the rhythm of the conversation. "So you do coffee and improv."

"Yeah. And I'm going to teach some classes at WorkAround."

"On how to trash your coworkers?"

Jasper's head turned her way again. "Ouch."

She didn't look over at him. No way was she apologizing. She needed to remember she was mad, that he'd been a jerk. Not get distracted by his hotness or his struggling-actor state.

"Look, Hollyn," he said, his voice quiet. "I'm truly sorry. What you saw tonight...that isn't the spirit of our show." He paused and took a ragged breath, like the speech was a lot of work. "I made a mistake. The serial-killer thing naturally brought my mind to Andi, and I bet if you asked her, she wouldn't have taken what I said seriously. When I talked to her, she made fun of her own obsession. She embraces her weirdness."

"Right," Hollyn said, jaw tightening. "So I should just be cool with being made fun of. I'm the one who's too sensitive. Got it."

"God, no," he said with frustration. "I'm saying I was a dick to use you in the monologue, and I'm sorry. I didn't know about your tics. I just thought you were annoyed with me."

Her grip tightened on the steering wheel as she took the exit for Canal Street, and she inhaled a deep breath. "I've grown out of the worst of them but they flare up when I'm...nervous."

She could feel him watching her, and her fingers tapped more quickly.

"So I made you nervous?" he asked.

"Yes."

He frowned in her periphery. "Why?"

She rubbed her lips together, not liking this line of questioning at all. *Because you were funny and boy beautiful and have the sexiest smirk.* "I'm not great with new people."

He shifted in the seat again. "Good thing I'm not new anymore. You can relax now."

She glanced over. The guy looked like hell. Flushed and sweating. But his eyes had a little spark of invitation in them.

"You're still exceptionally new," she said. "Cellophane-wrapped with the price tag still on."

"Nope. The seal's been broken. We've texted. You helped me limp off a city street. Hey, we've even had our first fight and planned our TV show, Hollyn Darling. I'm no longer new to you." He winced and gripped his side. "We're old friends now."

She stared at him for a moment, part of her wishing it could be true. But who was she kidding? One, how could she trust that any interaction they had wasn't going to turn into material? And two, she'd been fooling herself when she'd thought they'd been flirting. Jasper was a comedian. Funny quips were his business. Charm was his currency. She'd read the whole situation wrong. "We're not friends, Jasper."

He flinched, and this time she knew it had nothing to do with the pain in his side. "Not big on forgiveness, huh?"

She faced the road again. The sign for University Medical Center came into view, and she shook her head, feeling bone-deep tired. "Look, I was rude to you that first day. You were a jerk onstage. We're even. Let's just call a truce and be polite to each other at work."

"But—"

She pulled up to the emergency room entrance. "Go see a doctor, Jasper. Your organs could explode."

One of the hospital staff stepped up to the car, and Hollyn unlocked the doors.

Jasper gave her one last injured look and then sighed. "Thanks for the ride, Hollyn."

"Hope you feel better."

A stocky guy in scrubs helped Jasper out of the car and guided him to an awaiting wheelchair. Jasper looked back once before the guy wheeled him through the open doors. Hollyn sat there for a minute, trying to get her breathing back to normal. She stared at the closed doors, feeling a little guilty for just dumping him at the hospital without going in, but what was she supposed to do? They weren't friends. If it was something serious, they'd call his family or friends to be there with him. She drummed her fingers on the steering wheel. She was not going in after him.

Nope. She was not going to do it. This weird night ended here.

She put her car in gear. She needed to get home, get to bed, and forget this night ever happened. But right as she pulled out, something thumped onto the passenger floorboard. She veered the car closer to the curb so she could stop and clicked on the interior light. Sitting on the floor of the passenger side was a silver rectangle—Jasper's phone.

She closed her eyes. *Come on, Universe, give me a freaking break here.* With a groan, she turned the wheel and headed for the parking garage.

She was never going to escape Jasper Deares.

chapter **seven**

JASPER AWOKE IN A HAZE OF COTTONY THOUGHTS AND confusing dreams that involved chimpanzees replacing his group members at his next improv show. He shifted in bed, and a strange, harsh scent filled his nose. He gripped his sheets, but a pinch of pain in his left hand had him releasing the fabric just as quickly. *What the hell?*

His eyelids felt too heavy to lift, and unfamiliar sounds filled his ears. Maybe he was still dreaming. Monkeys were going to show up at any moment. Or maybe he was drunk? He didn't remember drinking. He tried to lick his lips, but his tongue was dry as sawdust. He turned his head and forced his eyes open. A pale-beige wall came into view along with some kind of machine. Confusion filled him. This wasn't his bedroom. He squinted in the low lights, small details coming into focus. The bed rails. The IV line. The rolling table.

A hospital room. He was in a hospital.

Oh. Flashes of memories came back to him like they'd been part of his dream. Being wheeled into a busy ER. A male nurse talking to him and bringing him to a room for tests. A doctor explaining things to him in quick, firm words. Talks of getting Jasper prepped for surgery. *Appendix. Could burst. Need to get him in now.*

Jasper groaned quietly. He'd had surgery. *Fucking hell.* He glanced down at his left hand where an IV was taped to the top. A wristband with his name circled his other arm. Then a dull pain in his abdomen registered. They'd taken a piece of him out. That was going to hurt a lot more when whatever medication he was on wore off.

He closed his eyes, dread filling him. Maybe he should just go back to sleep, linger in denial for a little while longer.

But a soft sound off to his right had him lifting his eyelids again. He turned his head, every movement feeling like he was encased in Jell-O. He blinked a few times at the sight that greeted him. A woman curled up in a chair and sound asleep, snoring softly. *Hollyn.* The shock of seeing her there cleared some of the fuzz from his mind.

Hollyn had *stayed*? She hadn't even come in with him last night. Or had she? Last he remembered she'd dropped him off at the door, basically telling him to get lost. What was she doing sleeping in his room?

He wanted to ask her, but his voice wouldn't work. All he could do was make hoarse, unintelligible sounds like he was some drunk coming to on Bourbon Street. He gave up trying and just watched her for a few moments. Last night flooded back to him. What he'd done onstage. Her anger. Finding out she had Tourette's.

He winced. *Jesus.* He'd never felt like such a world-class asshole. Those faces she'd made at him had been out of her control. And he'd just assumed it was about him. *Self-centered much?* He could almost hear his sister's voice berating him. And even after what he'd done, Hollyn had still offered to bring him to the hospital. Now she'd stayed in what looked to be the world's most uncomfortable chair.

Who was this woman?

He'd learned some of that answer last night. She was someone who wasn't afraid to yell at him when she was angry but who said new people made her nervous. A woman who had traded flirty texts with him but who could barely look him in the eye. A woman who seemed very guarded.

He frowned, watching the gentle rise and fall of her chest as she slept. He didn't know much about Tourette's, but in sleep, her face was smooth and relaxed. Her features were soft, her lashes long against her cheeks and lips slightly parted. He'd already known she was attractive, but in the unguarded state of slumber, her makeup a little smudged, her curly hair even wilder than normal, he realized she was a knockout.

This was what she'd look like if he woke up next to her in bed.

Annnnd that was not a thought he should be having in a hospital bed about a woman who had basically declared she'd never speak to him again. He closed his eyes. Maybe it was the drugs.

Maybe it was just that need to have everyone like him. Getting Hollyn into bed would prove that she liked him quite a lot. In fact, he would make sure she walked away very satisfied with her new friend Jasper.

Shut. Up. Pervy. Brain.

He had bigger things to deal with right now than inconvenient attraction. Like goddamned recovery from surgery and hospital bills and starting classes and figuring out this whole theater situation. No more thinking about Hollyn. Or how she'd look in his bed. Or how she'd just sighed in her sleep in a way that made him think of what she'd sound like when she—

Nope. Not going there. He turned his head away so he couldn't watch her anymore. He just needed more sleep. He wasn't in his right mind. She'd probably be gone by the time he woke up anyway.

....

Hollyn's joints protested and popped when she woke up in the uncomfortable hospital chair. She groaned and rubbed the back of her neck, trying to work out the crick. A barrel-chested nurse was leaning over Jasper's bed, checking on the IV bag. He smiled Hollyn's way. "Sorry, didn't mean to wake you."

She shifted, putting her feet to the floor. "It's fine. How is he?"

"Has he woken up again?" the nurse asked.

"Not that I know of." She'd sat for a good while after they'd wheeled Jasper in from the recovery room, hoping that he'd wake up so he could tell her who she should call for him. He'd been semi-awake when they'd first wheeled him in but still heavily drugged. He'd called her Felicity for some reason and then had talked to her like she was another nurse. She'd given up and decided to wait until the anesthesia wore off. But she'd apparently fallen asleep at some point along the way.

She checked the clock on the wall—a little past five in the morning.

"Will you be the one taking him home when he's discharged?" the nurse asked.

She blinked. "Um. I'm hoping when he wakes up again that he can tell me who to call. We're just...coworkers."

The nurse gave her a kind smile. "Well, you're a very good friend to stay with him like this. No one likes waking up in the hospital alone."

Hollyn rolled her lips together and nodded, feeling like a jerk because her original intention *had* been to leave him here solo.

"The doc will be making rounds in the next hour or so." The nurse marked something on an electronic tablet he'd brought in. "We can't discharge him until he shows that he can keep liquid down and urinate, so if he wakes up, there's ice water in this pitcher."

Hollyn cringed on Jasper's behalf. She'd known him for only a couple of days and someone was discussing his urination with her. She couldn't imagine he'd appreciate that. "Right."

The nurse plunked the plastic pitcher onto the side table. "I have to check on a few more patients, but why don't you try to talk to him and wake him gently? Then, if he's up to it, get him to eat some ice chips or sip some water. I'll check back in with you in a little while."

Hollyn froze. "Wait, you want me—"

But the nurse had already strode back into the hall, too busy to worry about Hollyn and her awkwardness. She stared at the closing door and then swung her attention back to Jasper. His chest was rising and falling with steady breaths. In the thin hospital gown and in slumber, he looked a lot less intimidating, but her heart was beating fast at the thought of waking him up and explaining the situation to him.

You had surgery.

I'm here because...because you left your phone? Because I couldn't leave you alone? Because I totally ignore personal privacy and have been creepily hanging out in your room like a stalker? Ugh.

And not only was she supposed to wake him up, but she was supposed to talk to him about *peeing*?

Just kill her now and be done with it.

With a groan, she pushed herself to her feet, her fingers doing her four count. She cleared her throat and stepped closer. "Um, Jasper?"

His eyelids didn't move.

She wet her lips. God, she didn't want to do this. She'd rather him not know she'd been there at all. She glanced back to the chair. Her purse was on the floor with Jasper's phone sitting on top of it. She'd tried to get to his contacts last night, but the phone was locked. She needed his code or... She looked back to Jasper and the hand that didn't have an IV sticking out of it.

A jolt of relief went through her. If she could get his thumb on his phone to get the fingerprint signature, she was home free. She hurried over to grab his phone and then went back to the side of the bed. She peeked at his face one more time, making sure he was still sleeping soundly, and then turned her back to him, gingerly grabbing his wrist and lifting his hand. His hand was warm and rough against hers, his long fingers gently curled. She put the phone on the bed and then tried to guide his thumb to the button to get it to read his fingerprint. If she could get to his contact list, she could call someone to come to the hospital for him.

She lowered his hand toward the phone but the angle was wrong, his thumb curling in a little too much. Gently, she shifted her hold and gripped just his thumb, trying to turn it.

"So you really are CIA, or are you just trying to steal my bank-account information?"

Hollyn startled and dropped Jasper's hand. She turned, finding him with a groggy smirk.

"I hate to break it to you, but the bank account would be disappointing," he said, his voice Marlon Brando hoarse. "I've moved all my millions to an offshore account."

Hollyn's heartbeat was a hummingbird trapped in her throat. "You're awake."

"I think so." He tried to sit up a little and hissed, the pain apparently catching him off guard. He collapsed back against the pillows. "Unless this is another dream. Are you going to morph into a chimpanzee?"

Her facial muscles were ticcing. Even if she hadn't felt the familiar tug, she could see him studying her expressions. She looked down at the blanket. "I was trying to unlock your phone to see who I could call for you. They may be able to discharge you soon."

"Yeah?"

She nodded. "Yeah, as soon as you..."

The hospital bed squeaked as he tried to move again. "Do cartwheels? Headstands? Long division? Because I feel totally ready for that."

She cleared her throat again. "No. More like drink something and you know..."

She made some ridiculous motion with her hand.

"Ah," he said with a low chuckle. "I've got to piss in a cup."

"Yeah."

"Fantastic. Performing under pressure," he said. "I guess I better try to drink something so I'm prepared for the big moment. I want a ten out of ten on this event."

Her head lifted, her gaze darting to him.

"What?" he asked.

She stared at him for a moment. "Nothing, it's just...you say things that other people would feel awkward about."

He gave her a disarming smirk. "Improv will do that to a person. It's a no-shame game." He looked away and adjusted his sheets. "Plus, I was a foster kid. Being the new kid in a family six different times kind of inoculates you to awkward."

Her eyes widened. "Wow."

"And really, all awkward means is showing someone else that you're human. I think that secret's already out." He gave her a somber look. "Hollyn, I'm not a robot—much to the disappointment of my former nine-year-old, Transformers-loving self."

She smiled a little, but his focused attention on her was too much. She busied herself, pouring him a glass of ice water, and held it out to him.

He reached out, but before she realized what he was doing, he clasped the hand she'd braced on his bed railing instead of the cup. She jolted at the warm touch but didn't move her hand away. He squeezed her fingers. "So you stayed."

She felt frozen in his gaze, his hand around hers. Cal's suggestion of *skin hunger* floated through her brain. "I—"

"That's, like, amazingly cool of you." He released her hand and accepted the cup from her. He took a small sip and winced a little. "Especially after everything that happened last night."

"It's fine," she mumbled.

"No, it's more than that. I was a jerk and you stayed anyway. So before I lose all toughness points and start whining about how much my stomach hurts and beg you to get a nurse with some serious pain medication in here, I want you to know that I really appreciate you staying. I woke up a little earlier when you were sleeping and...well, I'm just glad I didn't wake up in here alone." His gaze met hers. "You're a good human being, Hollyn Darling. Thank you."

The words and the newly minted nickname hit her harder than they should've, and she had to look away. She took a few steps back and crossed her arms. "It wasn't a problem."

He was quiet for a moment, studying her, and then he gave a quick nod. "I'm going to call my sister and let her know what happened. She'll come up here, fuss at the doctors about something, and then bring me home whenever they're ready to discharge me. Why don't you go home and get some rest? I know it's been a long night. You're officially relieved of Good Samaritan duty."

She rolled her lips together and glanced at the door. "You sure you'll have someone to bring you home?"

He gave her a small smile. "Yeah, I'm covered."

Hollyn wanted to get out of there more than anything, to escape back to the safety of her house, but another small piece of her felt reluctant to leave Jasper. "Do you need anything before I go?"

"Lots and lots of drugs," he said with a serious nod. "Like all of them."

She laughed softly and walked over to grab her things. "Got it. I'll tell the nurse to stop in again. I hope you feel better."

"Thanks, Hollyn."

He was watching her too closely. Every tic felt amplified. She wanted to hide her face, hide her tapping fingers. *Hide. Hide. Hide.*

But she forced the next words out instead. "And"—she took a deep breath—"we'll talk soon. At the coffee bar."

It took him a second to register what she'd said, but then his lips spread into a smile. "Yeah?"

"My face will be doing"—she pointed at her twitching nose—"this. And I will be awkward because I suck at small talk."

He looked pleased as punch. "I am one hundred percent here for awkward small talk."

"And you will never, ever use me in a routine again."

"I swear."

At that, she finally felt herself smile fully. "Cool. See ya, Jasper Dearest."

"Later, Hollyn Darling."

Before she could blush from head to foot, she slipped out of the room, let the nurse know to bring Jasper meds, and headed out. Exhausted but, for the first time in a long time, hopeful.

chapter **eight**

TWO WEEKS AFTER THE SURGERY, JASPER LEANED AGAINST his sister's kitchen counter and stared down at the first hospital bill that had arrived in the mail. *Fucking hell.* Even with some insurance coverage from his parents, he was in the hole for thousands. The little nest egg he'd been trying to build by living rent-free at Gretchen's for a couple of months was going to be obliterated. So much for getting his own place anytime soon or having any money at all to invest in promoting his group.

"You look a helluva lot better," Gretchen said, stepping into the sun-dappled kitchen and grabbing the coffee carafe off the island. She was dressed for her research job at the university in a white blouse and gray pants, her blond hair pulled into a twist. The only hint that she wasn't one hundred percent humorless scientist were the bright-red cherry earrings dangling from her earlobes. "How are you feeling?"

Jasper scrubbed a hand over his jaw. "I was feeling pretty good until I opened the mail. How can surgery cost this much? I was only there a few hours." He flipped the bill her way.

"You're lucky you're still on Mom and Dad's plan. One year older and you'd be in the hole for three times that. Emergency surgery is crazy expensive."

He tossed the bill on the counter in frustration. It was no one's fault that his appendix had decided to quit, and being in debt was better than being dead from exploding organs, but he wanted to tear the damn bill to pieces and burn them. How could he never manage to get ahead? Or not even *ahead*—just simply *caught up* would be nice. "I know it's a lot to ask, but I'm going to need to crash in your guest room for a while longer if I have any shot of paying this down."

Gretchen frowned and set the coffee carafe down. "Jas, you said you'd be able to move out at the end of this month."

"I know, but that was before my appendix decided to go all time bomb on me." He flicked his hand toward the bill. "I can't pay on this and afford rent solo. And my guess is that there are more bills coming."

His sister folded her arms and glanced out the window, squinting like she was concentrating hard. "Well, you're going to have to figure it out."

It took him a minute to process what she'd said. "What?"

She let out a breath and looked back to him, her brown eyes meeting his. "You can't stay, Jas."

"I can't stay," he repeated. "You're being serious?"

She nodded, expression grim but determined. She used to wear the same expression when they were teens and she'd refuse to cover for him with the Deareses when he'd done something to break the rules.

His heart picked up speed, some old, etched-in reaction to being told he can't stay somewhere firing up all his *oh shit* systems. *Sorry, Jasper this placement just isn't working out. Sorry, Jasper, but your parents refused rehabilitation, so you won't be going home.* "Why? I mean, I know it's a pain having me here, but I'm really not going to be here much with two jobs, and don't think I'm taking your place for granted but—"

"I'm moving in with Timothy," she said, cutting him off. "I

already put in my notice here, and the owners have another renter ready to go."

Jasper sagged back against the counter, the news knocking him backward. "Moving in? I didn't even realize you guys were that serious."

"Because you haven't *been here*. We've been dating for over a year. I was already planning this move before you called from California and said you needed to come home. I pushed back the date and asked Timothy to be patient, but I can't delay it anymore." She sighed and held her hands out to her side. "And I shouldn't have to. You're twenty-five and—"

"I should have a steady job and insurance and all that important adult stuff," he said in a mocking, formal voice.

"Don't," she warned, fire coming into her eyes. "Don't act like I'm being a bitch about this. I know you love improv and you're good at it, but you've tried to make a career out of it and it hasn't worked. College didn't work out. Acting hasn't worked out. It's time to make other plans—real plans. *Practical* ones."

He grimaced.

"Practical isn't a dirty word, Jasper. I know you think I'm the boring one with all my ten-year plans and spreadsheets, but look where it's gotten me. Steady job. Steady relationship. Money to pay my bills."

Jasper glowered at her. What did she want from him? A sheet of gold stars? The Good Responsible Person medal? He managed to keep his mouth shut because whatever was going to come out wasn't going to be nice.

"You don't want to look up in your thirties and realize you're still making lattes and don't have a penny in the bank. You're not always going to be able to get by on a wink and a joke," she said, bracing her hands on the island and pinning him with a pointed look. "Do the improv for fun, for a hobby, but start looking for a real job. It's time. You're too old to be crashing at your sister's house and riding on your parents' insurance."

Jasper's jaw was clenched so hard he worried for his teeth.

She crossed her arms in challenge, like she knew he was about to explode and go toe to toe with her. "Mom and Dad would tell you the same thing if they weren't afraid of hurting your feelings."

Her flaming spear landed solid. "Don't," he said in a low voice, a warning. "Don't bring Mom and Dad into this. They have never been anything but one hundred percent supportive of what I wanted to do."

"Supportive because they love you, but that doesn't mean they agree with the path you've chosen. They worry about you *all the time*," she said, a pained note in her voice. "They think they failed you in some way."

His stomach dropped and his surgery scar twinged, the words deflating him like a pin to a balloon. "*What?*"

"Think about it, Jas. Their job was to take you in and prepare you for life but"—she put her arms out to her sides—"you're still living like you're eighteen. You've failed to launch. They think it's something they did."

Her voice was quiet, but the blow was harsher than anything else she'd said. He looked down, gripping the back of his neck. The thought that he had disappointed the Deareses made him sick to his stomach. The best day of his life was the day they told him they wanted to adopt him, not to let him stay until he aged out of foster care, but to make him an official part of their family, give him their name. The very last thing in the world he wanted to do was let them down.

"Fuck." The curse was a whisper, and most of the fight drained out of him.

"Look, I can help," his sister said in a soothing tone as she stepped around the island and moved closer to him. "Timothy said he could get you a data-entry position at his job. It doesn't pay a ton but it has benefits, training, and a chance to move up."

Data entry. Just put a damn noose around his neck and kick the stool out from under him.

Jasper looked up and tried to keep the edge out of his voice. His sister was *trying* to help in her black-and-white, overachiever, practical way. And he couldn't call her out for lies. His life today didn't look much different than his life at eighteen. But data entry? *Hello, hell*. It sounded like a death sentence. Sitting at a desk for the rest of his life? The ADHD kid inside him grabbed a box of matches, wanting to set fire to all the things. "Gretch, I appreciate that, and tell Timothy thanks for the offer, but I don't need him to give me a job."

"He doesn't mind," she said, her voice growing more eager. "Timothy's great, and he could take you under his wing and—"

"I don't need it," he blurted out, the walls of the kitchen feeling like they were closing in around him. "I'm going to buy a theater here and run it."

The words hung in the air between them, and everything went silent save for the hum of the refrigerator and the echo in his brain. *Buy a theater. Buy a theater. Buy a theater.*

Then, after a long moment, Gretchen's lips parted in shock and she barked out a laugh. "Did you just say *buy a theater*?" She shook her head. "Oh, come on, Jas. I'm trying to have a serious conversation with you, and you're making jokes."

He loved his sister, but she was super great at making him feel like he was still a clueless kid. It wasn't lost on him that he'd thought Fitz was joking when he'd originally suggested the plan, but suddenly it seemed like the best idea ever because it was one that didn't involve *learning data entry from Timothy* and chaining himself to a desk for the rest of his life. "I'm not joking. I met up with a guy I knew from school. He owns an investment firm and offered to help connect me to investors. I'm going to put together a business proposal, build some media buzz with the group. There's a hole in the market. New Orleans doesn't have a dedicated improv or sketch theater."

She gave him a look that could only be translated as *Are you fucking kidding me right now?* "There's probably no improv theater here for a good reason. Do you know how hard it is to get a business off the ground? Any kind of business, but especially one that involves taking on property and investors to launch? You don't know anything about starting or running a business."

"A lot of people don't when they start," he said, spine straightening. "You should see all the people at WorkAround who are starting their own thing. They don't all have MBAs from Harvard or Tulane. They're just regular people with ideas that mean something to them."

Gretchen pinched the bridge of her nose. "Jas, you're not thinking this through. Most of those people are starting up one-person operations with very little overhead or risk. A theater is a big-ass deal. Other people's money would be *your* responsibility. You can't even juggle your own finances right now. Who's going to invest in someone with no experience?"

He bristled at that. "No experience? I may not know the ins and outs of running a business, but I know improv. I can perform it, and I can teach it. And I believe in it. I just need to convince investors of that."

"And we're back to the wink-and-a-joke plan." She tipped her head back and looked at the ceiling as if answers were scrawled there. "Even if you could pull it off—and that's a monumental *if*—you need money *now*. You need a place to live *now*."

"I've got the barista job, and now that I'm mostly healed up, I can start giving classes. If those go well, I can charge outsiders to take them. And I still make a little from the shows at night." He grabbed the hospital bill and shoved it in his backpack. "Don't worry. I'll be out of here on time. I'll figure it out."

She stepped closer and put a hand on his arm before he could leave. "Wait." She let out an exasperated breath. "You know it's not that I don't love you or that I don't believe you have talent. And it's not even that I don't want you here. I've enjoyed having you back in town. I hated you living so far away. But I'm saying all this *because* I love you. Someone needs to be straight with you."

"And that's you."

"Yes." She smirked and squeezed his arm. "It's the big sister's job to kick the little brother's ass."

Jasper was still irritated, but being called her little brother always stroked some starved part inside him. He never got tired of hearing that he was part of an actual family—even when it was his sister being a self-righteous nag. "Noted. I love you, too. Even though you just took a big stinking dump on my life plan."

She puckered her lips and made a smooch sound. "Having any kind of plan would be a start, but maybe focus on finding a place to live first."

"Believe me, that's item number one," he said, tone wry. "At least at my next place I can save myself from the sound of Timothy in the throes of passion. The guy sounds like he's being murdered. What the hell are you doing to the dude? Beating him?" He put his palm up. "Never mind. Don't answer that."

Gretchen's eyes went wide, and her hand dropped from his arm. "*You can hear us?*"

He snorted. "People three houses down can hear him. I've never heard *you*, thank God. I don't think I'd recover from *that* trauma. But believe me, I want my own place more than you want me out of this one."

"So what are you going to do? Like, for real?" she asked. "Do you need me to loan you a little—"

"No," he said with a shake of his head. "I'll figure it out."

I always do.

chapter **nine**

GIVE ME MORE MOVIES WITH AWKWARD GROWN-UPS

By Miz Poppy

One of the most popular tropes in teen movies is the awkward girl or boy working through their social ineptitude. We know the routine. The hero or heroine is hopelessly shy or awkward. They don't know how to dress or fix their hair. The girl has never swiped on a coat of lipstick—because apparently, shyness equals not being able to properly apply makeup. Also, glasses, they usually need glasses because myopia and introvertedness must be genetically linked. They also have a tendency to bump into things and knock over chairs. The character is the Before picture in the makeover side-by-side. We've seen it time and again, so why do we watch?

We watch these movies because we can identify with the hero and heroine in some way (because everyone feels weird and out of place as a teen, right?), and we know what's going to happen. There's a comfort in knowing the hero or heroine is going to be saved from the plague of awkwardness. They are going to land the supercool/hot/out-of-their-league love interest (See: *Sixteen Candles, Dirty Dancing, Mean Girls, American Pie, Twilight, Pretty in Pink, To All the Boys I've Loved Before, Dumplin'*, and *The DUFF*) get a gaggle of cool friends (See: *The Perks of Being a Wallflower, Clueless, The Breakfast Club*), and, if they're really lucky, a makeover montage (See: *She's All That, Clueless, Mean Girls*). Or, if you're in a horror movie like *Carrie*, you're going to kill all those bitches in a PMS rage and get the ultimate revenge. Either way, you're going to be relieved of that pesky shyness. And probably get a happy ending. Hooray! High school cures all!

Yeah. Okay. I don't know about you, but speaking as a card-carrying introvert, that's not how it works. If you're shy and awkward as a teen, you're probably going to be shy and awkward as an adult. And there's nothing cute or adorable about it. So where are my awkward adult movies, Hollywood? Where is my heroine who doesn't always have the snappy comeback and who isn't effortlessly chill? Where is the woman who isn't in need of a makeover montage but also doesn't have a pack of friends to hang with because she's too intimidated to strike up a conversation with new people? The most the awkward adults get are side roles for comic relief.

Do we not want to see those movies because identifying with an awkward teen is universal but imagining yourself as an awkward adult is just sad? When does it become not okay to be shy? What happens when people don't grow out of the awkward? I want to see those movies. Am I the only one? Show me what happens after graduation, people!

If you have suggestions I'm missing, email me! In the meantime, here are a few movies with awkward adults...

1. *Never Been Kissed*—This one only half counts because Drew Barrymore's character has to go undercover (with a makeover of course!) and return to high school to get over her awkwardness. See, high school cures all!
2. *40-Year-Old Virgin*—Steve Carell is a master at awkward. We even get the requisite makeover scene—but with hot wax and "Kelly Clarkson!" used as an expletive. Now let's see this kind of movie with a female lead.
3. *Bridget Jones's Diary*—
4. *Must Love Dogs*—

Hollyn's phone rang, jarring her from the concentrated state she was in while writing her post. She'd come into WorkAround extra early this morning, before the coffee bar even opened, to get this post up on her blog so that she could spend the rest of the day writing up her official reviews. The office had been quiet without her neighbor in yet, so the shrill sound of her ringing phone seemed extra loud.

She grabbed for her phone and got a little zap of adrenaline when she saw it was Emmanuel Melancon, the editor-in-chief of the NOLA Vibe. He rarely called. Almost all of her work for the site was done by email, and if anyone called her, it was the entertainment editor. She took a quick sip of water to wet her dry throat and answered. "Good morning, Mr. Melancon."

"Morning, Hollyn," he said, his deep voice an impressive rumble over the phone. "How's life treating you?"

"I, uh, good. Great. Everything's great," she said, her nose scrunching a few times. "And you?"

"I'm fine," he said in a clipped tone, clearly wanting to move on from the small talk. *Praise Jesus.* "Do you have a minute?"

"Of course." Her stomach somersaulted at his serious tone, and her mind scanned through what this could possibly be about. Did he hate her last review? Was he calling because her numbers had dipped? Had he realized she was a total fraud and wasn't at all cool like her online persona?

She was so lost in the possibilities that she almost missed what he said next.

"I wanted to let you know that we're thinking of expanding the Miz Poppy role on the site."

Her spinning thoughts screeched to a halt, and she sat up straighter. *Expand the role?* Her office chair squeaked beneath her like it was excited on her behalf. "Oh?"

It's happening!

Be cool. Be cool.

"Yes. Your posts do really well and sometimes get the top number of hits in a week." He coughed loudly in the phone, making her startle. "You and the restaurant critic seem to volley that top spot back and forth."

"Wow, that's great. It's hard to trump food in this town." She grabbed a pen and a notepad and put her phone on speaker so she could take notes and also not get his booming cough in her ear again. "So what are you thinking?"

She was proud about how calm she sounded. She'd always been better on the phone than in person. She didn't *love* the phone, but no one could see her tics, so it took a layer of self-consciousness off the table. Her initial NOLA Vibe interview had been by phone. She doubted she would've landed the gig otherwise.

"Well," Mr. Melancon went on. "We've been analyzing the

competition, and the only other entertainment posts getting better numbers are over at Buzz of the Bayou. Their entertainment reporter is doing live streaming at some events and is posting flashy videos for his reviews. I forget his name. Blue hair. Loud."

"Billy Blues." Hollyn's pen pressed hard against the paper. She'd crossed paths with the guy a few times when she was out to do a review. She'd heard him asking random women if they were Miz Poppy. Thankfully, he'd never turned his eye on her. But his approach had rubbed her the wrong way just the same. She also thought his posts were big on personality but thin on quality content.

"Yeah, that's him," Mr. Melancon said. "I find the kid annoying, but his technique is working. Video content is what the readers are wanting. Their site is getting the younger demographics. I want those eyeballs on *our* site."

Hollyn was taking notes, but when she wrote down *video content*, she stilled. "Right. I'm good with a camera. I could take some great shots of the venue. Maybe film a few live clips of performances. I mean, obviously, we wouldn't want me on camera. That would ruin the whole mystique of Miz Poppy."

Mr. Melancon was quiet for a moment, but she could hear something tapping on his end, maybe his pen. "Actually, Hollyn, I don't think the mystique is what drives the posts. Your writing and attitude do. Readers like your humor and how straightforward you are. I think we could get a lot of momentum if we build up to a reveal and then unveil the real person behind the posts. Then that frees you up to be on video."

Hollyn went hot all over and then bone cold, a rush of *no, no* and *hell no* going through her. "Mr. Melancon, I'm a writer. I don't know the first thing about editing videos."

He grunted. "We have an intern who can edit the videos and put the graphics in. It will be the same type of content. You'll just have to speak it instead of type it."

Her hand was trembling, and she flattened it against the notepad to stop the shaking. "I don't know if—"

"I'm aware that this will take a lot more time and work on your part and that you do a lot of freelance work," he said, oblivious to her silent panic. "So if you agree to this, it would be a promotion. A salary instead of per-article pay. Full-time benefits. I don't have the office space here in the building, but we could chip in a little for that office you rent since I know they have video rooms."

Hollyn closed her eyes. The carrot he was dangling was what she'd been working for since moving to the city. An actual writing job with full-time pay—writing about things she loved. But this wasn't writing. It was writing *with video*. It was Miz Poppy coming out of the shadows and being on camera. The thought made her want to hurl herself into traffic.

Mr. Melancon hadn't noticed her tics during her follow-up interview. She'd taken an anxiety pill and had worked to exhaustion to suppress them as much as possible for the hour. But if he knew he was hiring someone like her to be on camera, he'd never be making the offer.

"Mr. Melancon, I really appreciate the offer. That sounds amazing, but I do think the anonymity is important and—"

"Hollyn," he said, voice underlined with impatience. "I don't mean to be blunt, but this is the direction we need to go in. If you're not willing to do the videos, I'll be forced to recruit a new Miz Poppy. One who can take on this extra work and do videos. We can't be left behind and lose readers to Buzz of the Bayou."

Her hands went to the arms of her chair, gripping hard. "A new Miz Poppy? But that's *my* pen name."

"In your contract, it states that we have the right to keep the name if you leave," he said matter-of-factly. "It's part of the site's brand now."

Hollyn tilted back in her chair like he'd shoved her. "Oh."

Oh.

"Hollyn," he said, his gruff voice softening, "I'm not trying to get rid of you. I'm trying to promote you to a bigger job. I believe you can do this. But I need you to be willing to learn some new things and move with the market."

Her fingers were tapping in her four count on the arm of her chair, her thunderous heartbeat hurting her chest. "I understand."

"So what do you say?" he asked.

Hollyn's skin was damp, and she wanted to cry. She didn't want to lose this opportunity, but how the hell was she going to do this? Video? She froze up talking to people face-to-face. How was she supposed to talk to thousands through a video camera? And she could already imagine the Internet comments. *That's Miz Poppy? What's wrong with her face? God, what a disappointment.*

But she couldn't afford to lose this job right now. Without it, she was going to be headed straight back to her hometown to move back in with her mother.

No way.

"Can I have some time to work on my skills?" she said, scrambling to come up with a way out of this. "There are a number of video bloggers here at WorkAround. I'd like to partner with them and learn some tricks of the trade first. If we're going to do a Miz Poppy reveal, I want it to be polished. Otherwise, I'm going to look like an amateur next to Billy Blues, and that won't get us anywhere."

Mr. Melancon made a humming sound like he was pondering and then cleared his throat. "That's probably a wise plan of action. Let's put our best foot forward with the launch video. Take the next six weeks and work on your video presentation skills. I want upbeat and fun, but don't lose that signature snark. Miz Poppy is your wry best friend telling you about what's worth seeing and spending your money on. Keep that brand. Don't try to match that blue kid's over-the-top enthusiasm. I don't want a goddamned cartoon character."

Thank God for small mercies.

"Right. Got it." She swallowed hard. "And thanks for the opportunity, Mr. Melancon."

"You've earned the chance," he said firmly. "The new position will be effective once the reveal goes live. I'll email you with the specifics. I look forward to seeing what you come up with."

The phone call ended before she could say goodbye.

She watched her phone screen go dark and then put her elbows on her desk, her face in her hands. *Reveal herself on camera. Be on video. Be a freaking vlogger.*

He may as well have asked her to build a spaceship and land it on Mars.

She sat there in a panicked, wallowing spiral, not planning to move for a while, but her phone dinged and had her lifting her head a few seconds later.

She glanced over at the screen.

Jasper: Handsome decafs are back in stock. U want?

The sight of Jasper's name on her screen made her belly flutter, but the breath she'd been holding released—some odd combination of relief that he was back and anxiety...*for the exact same reason. Ugh.* Brains were weird.

Her brain was weird.

She picked up the phone, pondering how to respond.

Lucinda had used a rotation of temps to cover the coffee bar over the last two weeks when Jasper had been out recovering from surgery. The coffee had been nearly undrinkable. Hollyn had texted Jasper once, two days after surgery, and he'd responded with enough typos to make her suspect he'd been blitzed on pain meds. But she'd at least confirmed that he was okay. She hadn't had the guts to text him again, though. The longer he was away, the more it felt like he was a stranger again, like their whole interaction had been some kind of waking dream. She'd mostly convinced herself that the night in the hospital had just been a glitch in the universe, and now everything would be set back to normal.

But right now, she could use a coffee and a pastry and maybe a glimpse of that friendly face of his. So instead of following her first instinct—to text her order and hide—she typed a quick response.

Hollyn: Welcome back! Heading down. I'm starving and need to get out of this office.
Jasper: Your pastry and awkward small talk await.

She smiled, a warm, tingly feeling moving through her and chasing away some of the panic over her new job assignment. Jasper remembered their conversation. That was something. She rolled her chair backward, ignoring the notes she'd taken on the traumatic phone call, and headed down. She had bigger things to worry about than being awkward with the cute barista right now. Suddenly, talking to Jasper seemed like child's play compared to what she was facing at work.

chapter **ten**

HOLLYN WAS FEELING RELATIVELY CONFIDENT ABOUT SEEING
Jasper until she got to the bottom floor and stepped out of the stairwell. She had a brief moment of alarm when she saw Jasper leaning
on the counter and laughing at something Andi said. The last time
Hollyn had made this walk, she'd embarrassed herself. And had he
been this hot when he left? Her memory must've fogged the level
of hotness, some built-in mental protection from the intense attraction. Maybe she wasn't ready for this. Jasper and Andi looked so at
ease and comfortable. Maybe she shouldn't interrupt.

But then Jasper turned and caught sight of her. His face lit with
an open-mouthed smile, and Andi waved her over like she'd been
waiting for her to arrive. Hollyn took a deep breath, smoothed the
front of her black capris, and headed over.

"Look who's back!" Andi announced and swept her arm out
like she was presenting Jasper as the prize on a game show.

Hollyn could feel her nose twitching, but she smiled to counter-
act it. "I heard." She turned to Jasper, bracing herself for the full
impact of her small-talk nerves. "How are you feeling?"

Jasper put a hand over a spot on his lower abdomen, making
his gray T-shirt pull tighter against his abs. "Strong like bull. Bull
without appendix."

Hollyn smirked. "Well, you look gor—" A ripple of horror went through her. "Grrreat!"

Andi's eyebrows lifted at Hollyn's Tony the Tiger impression, and she bit her bottom lip, no doubt catching Hollyn's slip. Yes, she'd almost said *gorgeous*. To Jasper's face. Fantastic.

Jasper, blessedly, didn't seem to notice. Or he was actively ignoring her gaff. "Thanks." He reached back to grab a cup of coffee and a cinnamon roll and then placed them in front of Hollyn. "And the pastry's on me because without you, I'd basically be dead."

"Dead?" Andi asked.

"True story," Jasper said with a nod.

Hollyn cocked a brow. "So your life is worth three whole bucks?"

"No. It's worth a sweet, delicious mouthful of heaven," he said with mock offense. "Obviously."

Sweet, *delicious*, and *mouthful* all ended up sounding completely filthy in Hollyn's head, and her face heated, her cheek tic doing a dance.

She *noticed* Jasper *noticing* her tic and only got more mortified.

Andi gave Hollyn a knowing look. "Welp! I have a chapter to write. You kids have fun! Good luck with your house hunt, Jasper."

"Andi—" Hollyn said, but her new friend was already making tracks to the stairwell. She looked back to Jasper. "I'm sorry. I didn't mean to interrupt."

"You didn't," Jasper said, swiping a bit of icing off the edge of her plate and licking it off his finger.

Hollyn slid onto one of the stools in front of the bar and broke off a piece of cinnamon roll. If she had something to do, this awkward small talk would be easier. "What'd she mean by house hunt?"

Jasper stretched his arm down the counter, making his T-shirt ride up a little at his hip—not that she noticed and took a mental picture. *Whatever. Shut up, brain.* He grabbed a little handwritten sign—card stock he'd folded into a table tent—and turned it her way.

Hollyn read it aloud. "'Need a roommate? I make coffee, am a clean freak, and don't steal food.'" She looked up. "You're looking for a new place?"

She popped the bite of cinnamon roll into her mouth, and tried not to make a sex noise. It really *was* sweet and delicious.

"Yeah, I moved back from California not that long ago and have been staying with my sister. But she's *in lurve* and moving in with her boyfriend, so she needs me out. I was planning to get my own place but"—he patted his side—"medical bills aren't cheap. So a roommate is needed."

Her face scrunched. "That sucks."

He gave her a bemused look.

"What?" She touched her mouth. "Do I have icing?"

He shook his head. "No, it's nothing."

She narrowed her eyes. "Liar. What is it?"

He shrugged. "It's just, we're having small talk and it's not awkward. I feel cheated. I was promised awkwardness."

She pointed at her face. "I'm ticcing like crazy."

"That's not awkward. You're just wrinkling your nose a lot. Like a bunny. It's kind of cute."

She groaned. "You're full of shit, Jasper Deares. There's nothing cute about it. Don't try to make me feel better."

"I'm not." He gathered up a few left-behind coffee cups from the side counter. "I mean, on some level, I can relate. I've always been a fidgeter. I still don't sit for long without bouncing my knee or clicking a pen or whatever. When people ask me to stop doing it, I find it really tough. So I'm not pretending I can fully understand what you're dealing with, but I get what it means to not be able to control certain things." He tossed the cups in the recycle bin and washed his hands. "So now that I know you're not making faces at me because you're pissed, it's not as noticeable as you think."

His words made something sharp and defensive inside her smooth out a little. She took a sip of her coffee. "It's not always this bad. Some days are better than others. Different things aggravate the condition. Caffeine, stress, lack of sleep." *Guys I'd like to see naked.* "That kind of thing."

"So what's going on today? Late night?" He nodded at her cup. "I swear that's decaf."

"It's not the coffee." His eye contact was too much. She looked down and traced her finger around the rim of the cup. "It's just been a rough morning."

"Oh." She could almost hear his frown. "What's up?"

She tore another piece off the cinnamon roll, letting the gooey icing drip off her fingers. "It seems I'm about to lose my job. Yay."

She shoved the bite in her mouth and chewed viciously, like the pastry has caused her current woe.

"Damn," he said, tone full of sympathy. "I'm sorry. Been there." He paused for a second. "But wait, I thought you were freelance. You can't get fired from that, right?"

She looked up and sucked icing off her thumb. "It's my main gig. The one that pays most of the bills."

His gaze flicked to her mouth and then back to her eyes. "Why do they want to let you go?"

She pushed her plate toward him. "This thing is huge. Want some?"

He broke off a piece of cinnamon roll and popped it in his mouth.

She pulled the plate close again. "They don't want to let me go. They want to promote me. But they're asking me to do something I can't."

"What's that?" he asked, the words muffled.

She met his curious gaze. "Do my posts on video. Become a *vlogger.*" She waggled her sticky fingers. "Reveal who's behind the anonymous persona I write under on the website."

His eyebrows went up. "And you don't want to do that?"

She let out a huff. "Jasper, have you met me? I can barely talk to people, much less a camera. And the video will catch every damn tic in full HD color. This"—she swept her hand in front of her face, almost knocking her coffee over with her elbow—"is not who people want to see as Miz Poppy."

The words escaped before she could stop them. Her fingers pressed over her mouth. *Shit.*

Jasper blinked. Then his lips parted. "Hold up. Did you just say…"

She shook her head and lowered her hand to grab a napkin. "No, I did not. You didn't hear that. Ignore me."

But Jasper's eyes had grown big. "Holy shit," he said, keeping his voice low and leaning forward. "*You're* Miz Poppy. Like leather-clad, black-haired cartoon vixen Miz Poppy?"

She dabbed her mouth with the napkin. "I said you didn't hear that."

"*Hollyn.*"

"What? You don't see the resemblance?" she asked dryly.

"I… Wow."

"You seriously cannot tell anyone," she warned, her free hand doing her four count against the counter. "Like no one. They're planning this big reveal thing. Not that I'm going to be able to do it."

Jasper let out a sound of wonder and shook his head, delight on his face. "You're messing with me right now. I told you I loved her."

She sniffed. "Yeah. That wasn't uncomfortable at all."

He laughed and grabbed a towel to clean the icing off his hand. "And—oh, *oh.*" A flicker of horror went over his face, and he dropped the towel like it'd burned him. "You were at my show that night to *review it?*"

She nodded. "Give the boy a prize."

"*Son of a bitch.* We were going to get a Miz Poppy review?" His tone sounded heartbroken. "That would've been... Dammit. I screwed it all up."

"Your appendix saved you." She lifted a brow. "You should be glad you caught up with me that night. I almost annihilated you guys."

"But you didn't. You didn't review us at all." He grinned like he'd just received the main item on his Christmas list.

"I'm not heartless. I couldn't take down a guy who had to pee in a cup. Plus, I only saw a few minutes of the show. That wouldn't have been a fair review."

"Hollyn, this is—I know you're having a freak-out and I'm sorry about that, but this is the best news I've heard all day." He gave her this adorable look of wonder. "Do you know what this means?"

"I'm about to lose my job?"

"No. You can't lose your job. If you could get my group a good Miz Poppy review, that would be everything." He put his hands in a praying motion and leaned closer, eyes pleading. "I need you to give us another chance. I swear we're good. I swear I'm not usually an asshole. That night was an anomaly."

She made an exasperated sound. "You're not *hearing* me, Jasper. I'm going to have to quit. And they're going to have to hire someone else to be Miz Poppy. I can't do what they're asking me to do."

He frowned and dropped his hands to his sides. "Of course you can."

She scoffed. "Says the improv guy who isn't afraid of anything."

"Well, I don't know about not being afraid of *anything*. I'm not a sociopath. And have you ever seen a black widow spider? Those things are fucking scary," he said gravely. "But not being afraid to be onstage in front of people? That's just something you can learn. I wasn't always that way."

"Maybe not, but I bet you were never *this* way." She pointed to herself. "I can't imagine you shy."

He tilted his head. "Okay, I'll give you that. But that doesn't mean—" His eyes brightened. "Hey, I could teach you."

"Teach me? Jasper—"

"No, I'm serious," he said, a crackle of electric energy in his voice. "I'm going to be giving improv classes here. They'll be free to members. You could join up. Learn with your coworkers. It will help you to loosen up and move through the fear. You can practice in front of people here. You'll learn to think quicker on your feet and won't be so afraid of making a mistake."

She stared at him like he was speaking another language. "Me? In an improv class with my coworkers? You're out of your goddamned mind. I'd rather go to the dentist and get all my teeth pulled without pain meds or enter a cage with a hungry lion. That's like worst-nightmare stuff for me. Black widow spiders everywhere."

His enthusiastic expression dimmed, and he reached out and put his hand over hers. "Come on. It won't be that bad. This could help us both. I need my group to get noticed. I want to buy a theater, but I need investors. You don't want to lose this job, and you shouldn't. You're freaking amazing at it. We could help each other. Win-win."

His hand was warm and heavy over hers, and she appreciated his earnestness, but the thought of getting up in front of a group of WorkAround people and trying to do improv was ludicrous. No way. Not ever. "I'm sorry. I can't. People…freak me out. Performing in front of people might actually kill me dead. I'm serious. I'm in therapy for this."

He considered her, brows knitted, and then he tipped his head toward her. "What about just me then?"

She tried to read his expression. "What do you mean?"

"Private lessons. Free ones. Just one-on-one," he said, talking slower, like he was choosing his words carefully. "I can teach you some of the tricks of improv. We can get you practicing on video. But no one else has to see you or the videos yet besides me. Safe space."

She stared at him. "Safe space. Embarrassing myself in front of you?"

That didn't sound safe at all. That sounded horrible. Super extra horrible.

"Of course. You don't have to worry about looking ridiculous in front of me. My job is to look ridiculous." He lifted his hand from hers and braced it on the counter, leaning closer, his gaze fervent. "Do you know how much power there is in learning not to give a fuck if you look stupid?"

She wet her lips, his nearness making her all kinds of nervous. He smelled like dark roast and cinnamon. "I can't..."

"It's like a drug, Hollyn," he said softly. "It's taking control back from everyone else and saying, 'This is who I am and I don't give a damn what you think.' When you get to that place, you hold all the chips in the poker game. They can't beat you. The fear fades."

She closed her eyes, the picture he was painting pure fantasy but tempting nonetheless. "I don't think I'm capable."

"What's the alternative?" he asked, voice quiet. "Giving up? Quitting your job? Isn't it worth at least trying?"

She gripped her coffee cup with both hands, looking down at her bloodless fingers, nerves pulsing through her. "I don't know."

"Hey," he said, his tone cajoling her to look up. "I promise you're safe with me. I'm not going to make fun of you. I'm not going to tell you you're doing it wrong. If it doesn't work, I'm not going to blame you." He smiled. "And I swear, this isn't some ploy to get alone time with *the* Miz Poppy."

Her lips parted in surprise.

"I mean, I *did* tell you I loved her."

Her. Like Miz Poppy was a different person.

"I wouldn't think that. I know what you meant." He meant *not* Hollyn. He loved the image of Miz Poppy like everyone else, not the reality.

"Classes will be a pressure-free zone. Just one friend teaching another." He shrugged. "And if, in return, you can give my show an honest review, I'd be forever indebted."

The look he was giving her was so openly earnest that she couldn't look away. Take one-on-one classes with a guy she was hopelessly attracted to and embarrass herself trying to do improv in front of him? This sounded like the worst plan in the history of the universe.

But he was right. She didn't want to lose her job. What could it hurt to try?

If nothing else, she'd just had a full conversation with him. Jasper had somehow, without her knowing it, moved from the stranger zone to a person she could talk to without a panic attack. That was a precious thing in her world.

She *wanted* friends at work. With Andi and now Jasper, she would have two people she could talk to.

She inhaled deeply and tried to quiet the screaming banshee in her head. "Okay. I'll...give it a try. But I reserve the right to back out at any time. And I'm not promising you a great review. An honest review will be *honest*."

Jasper's face lit up, and he lifted a fist in victory. "Fantastic. You made the right call, Hollyn Darling. This is going to be so much fun."

"This is going to be absolute torture," she replied, deadpan.

He laughed and then nodded at her plate. "Hush that negativity and eat your cinnamon roll. We've got plans to make, my friend."

My friend.

That sounded...kind of amazing.

She vowed then and there that this was what Jasper would be. She could ogle him because...*hello*, she was human and had hormones and hadn't been touched by hands other than her own in a really, *really* long time, but she needed to stop thinking about him as someone she was attracted to. That only amped up her nerves and made her tics worse, anyway. She needed to take that layer out of play. He wasn't interested in her like that, and she could use a friend more than she needed an unrequited crush. She had been through enough of those already.

As if on cue, Rodrigo, the former marine turned fitness vlogger sidled up to the coffee bar. Hollyn had admired him from afar since her first day there and had kept a steady crush simmering on her mental back burner. Where Jasper was *artsy hot*, Rodrigo went straight for the *obvious hot* category. Good-looking in that way that wouldn't go unnoticed by anyone with a pulse. Dark hair and eyes. Light-brown skin. Body built for combat.. He smiled her way and gave her a nod of greeting. "Hey."

"Hey." She gave a quick smile and then concentrated on the cinnamon roll like it held the answers to the universe.

She caught Jasper giving her a curious look in her periphery, but then he shifted his attention to Rodrigo. "What can I get you, man?"

Rodrigo made his order, and Jasper struck up an easy conversation with the guy, making him laugh like they were old friends. God, if he could teach her five percent of that, she'd be good to go.

Maybe he could.

It was a *big* maybe.

Jasper finished up with Rodrigo and waited until the guy left before moving back down the counter to Hollyn. He cocked his head in the direction Rodrigo had walked. "What's that guy do for a living? Get paid for selfies?"

She snorted. "Pretty much."

Jasper chuckled. "Don't blame him. If I looked like that, I'd cash in, too."

She wanted to tell Jasper that she'd buy his selfie any day. But she kept her mouth shut. Friends didn't tell other friends that.

"So is that what happens for you with anyone you don't know?" he asked.

"What?"

"You go into avoidance mode." He jabbed a thumb to where he'd been talking with Rodrigo. "I was going to pull you into the conversation, but it was like you'd put up a force field around yourself. You wouldn't even look up. You became one with the furniture."

She groaned, shoved her plate to the side, and put her head down on the counter. "I'm hopeless."

"Oh, don't be so dramatic." Jasper palmed the back of her head and gave it a playful pat. "By the end of classes with me, *you'll* be the one making gym boy nervous. Just wait."

She didn't believe Jasper for a second. She lifted her head. "Maybe this is a waste of time."

"A couple of weeks ago, you couldn't talk to me. Now look at you. We're sharing food." He grabbed another chunk of cinnamon roll and then touched her nose with it, leaving icing there. "It won't be a waste of time. I promise."

She gave him a small smile and wiped the icing from the tip of her nose. "You're full of big promises, Jasper Deares."

"I've got no place to live and no theater. But promises, I've got." He shrugged. "And I'm not bullshitting you. Improv saved me. I believe in the process. You just need to be open to it and give it a chance to work. The first rule of improv is to always say yes." He met her gaze. "So, Hollyn, what do you say?"

She wet her lips, tasting sugar there, and forced herself to hold his gaze even though she could feel her facial tics cycling through their dance. "I guess I say yes."

"Welcome to my world, Hollyn. We're going to have a grand ol' time." He slipped the bite of cinnamon roll in his mouth and smiled a smile that made her insides melt.

Goddamn. She was doomed. *Artsy hot* was so much sexier than *obvious hot*.

chapter **eleven**

"FITZ, ARE YOU SURE ABOUT THIS?" JASPER ASKED AS HE spun around slowly, taking in the killer top-floor apartment in all its converted-warehouse, exposed-brick-walls, high-ceilinged glory. "You could get some serious rent off someone to stay here. Or film a reality show. I can't pay you what this is worth."

Fitz crossed the main living area, his footfalls heavy on the refinished parquet wood floors, and dropped his laptop bag on the kitchen island. He smiled before going to the commercial-style fridge, pulling two beers from it, and popping the tops off. "I didn't ask you to, and I'm sure." He walked over to Jasper and handed him a bottle of Abita. "I've got the extra space, and I don't actually need rent money. I do have a proposition for you, though."

Jasper tipped back the beer and sipped, marveling at the words *I don't need rent money*. "What's that?"

Fitz propped a hip on the back of his leather couch and pointed the neck of his beer toward Jasper. "You can stay here for the next few months rent-free—"

"Fitz, no, I don't need charity."

His friend lifted a hand. "Hear me out. It's not charity. You don't have to pay me rent. Just cover half the utilities, and when we get this theater thing worked out, you give me a ten percent stake in it."

Jasper lifted his brows. "You want to invest in my hypothetical theater?"

"It's not going to be hypothetical if you stop doubting my brilliance and actually pursue it," he said pointedly. "Did you look at the listing I sent you?"

He nodded. "I passed by. The price tag is steep."

"It's a steal. The neighborhood's on the upswing. Many of the buildings are being converted into lofts. A younger crowd is moving in. I think with the right vibe and design, and a group like yours, an improv venue could be golden. I mean, don't get me wrong, I like investing in people who are passionate about what they do." He shrugged his wide shoulders. "But I'm also an opportunistic bastard, and I think there's money to be made here."

Jasper laughed.

"Seriously, though, this could really turn into something," he said between sips of beer. "I want in on the ground floor. Let's do this shit."

The genuine eagerness in Fitz's tone sent a pang through Jasper. How could this guy he knew in middle school so easily believe in him? Fitz hadn't even seen him perform yet. But Jasper wasn't stupid either. Free rent for a sweet apartment? *Hell* and *yes* and *where do I sign?* No rent for a few months could do wonders for paying off his hospital bills. Plus, he liked Fitz, and the guy was going to be key in getting a shot at the theater project if Jasper was really going to attempt this. If Fitz could actually make this happen, ten percent seemed like a small price to pay.

"I don't know what to say," Jasper said, floored by Fitz's generosity.

Fitz stood and put out his hand. "Say yes, asshole."

Jasper chuckled. "Well, that *is* the first rule of improv."

Fitz gave him an expectant look. "So?"

Jasper let out a breath and grabbed Fitz's hand. "You realize I have no idea what the hell I'm doing, right?"

Fitz gripped his hand. "You think I had a clue when I started my business? You learn as you go. Plus, you have me. What's life without a little risk?"

Jasper smirked. His whole life seemed like a bad bet lately, all risk and no reward, but he shook Fitz's hand. Risk or not, he couldn't shake the idea of the theater. It had burrowed into his brain and wasn't leaving without some blood spilled. "Then I guess I say, yes, asshole. Let's do it."

"That's what I'm talking about. Confidence." Fitz pulled him in for a half hug/half hard thump on the back.

Jasper stepped back and took a long pull from his beer, his mind spinning and his gaze scanning the luxury apartment. "I can't believe I'm going to be living in a fucking penthouse and trying to start a business. Life is weird."

"Yeah, this place doesn't suck." Fitz grinned as he settled onto the couch and hooked his ankle over his knee, looking every bit the confident businessman. "I got it mainly because it reminded me of that apartment in that old Tom Hanks movie *Big*."

"Huh." Jasper looked around at the open space, remembering the movie. "Yeah, I can see the resemblance. No trampoline though."

"That could be arranged," Fitz said, no jest in his tone. "I loved that movie when I was a kid. The thought that I could just instantly be grown up and make my own decisions, not have to deal with another foster home or caseworker. That sounded like living the dream."

Jasper met his gaze, seeing the kid Fitz used to be for a brief second in his mind's eye. Scrawny. Scattered. No one would've suspected that hard-to-corral, too-loud boy could've landed in this spot. "I'm glad you finally got here, man."

"Me too. But don't get too sentimental." Fitz ran a hand over his close-cropped black hair and stretched his arm out over the back of the couch. "Let's be real. I also got this place to impress women."

Jasper snorted and took a seat in the armchair across from him. "Of course. Does it work?"

"What do you think?" Fitz's smile turned sly. "Feel free to test out its magical powers for yourself. Our rooms are on opposite sides of the apartment. You'll have all the privacy you could want if you bring someone home."

Jasper stretched his neck from side to side, tension building at the thought of getting involved with anyone again. "Thanks, but I don't see that happening. I've got too much on my plate right now to worry about dating or any kind of social life outside of work. Plus, this"—he flicked his hand toward the wall of windows— "would be false advertising. You don't want a show a woman a caviar lifestyle and then break it to her that you're a coffee-pouring starving artist."

He'd learned that with Kenzie. He could almost pinpoint the moment when her view of him shifted from seeing him as a passionate, ambitious performer to someone who was weighing her down. The only difference between hot, up-and-coming star and guy who can't pay his bills was a break in show business. But the gap was a big one. They'd fallen on different sides of the chasm.

Fitz snorted. "True, but you won't be that for much longer. Give it a little time, sprinkle in a little of my networking magic, and you'll be owner of the hippest new theater in town before you know it. All the ladies will want a ticket to your show."

Jasper rolled his eyes. "I'm glad you're so optimistic."

Fitz shrugged. "After what we went through as kids, I learned you have to be your own cheering squad. The world doesn't want to believe that you can be special—that the kid with no family support and all kinds of issues can actually make shit happen. But look where I've landed. Screw all that negative noise. If you don't believe you can do it, how the hell will you convince other people you can? Investors are going to want to see confidence." He leaned forward, brow cocked. "So why not you, Jasper? Why the fuck can't you have your own theater?"

Jasper stared at him. "I don't know. It's just—"

"Are you a shitty actor?" he asked, tone full of challenge.

Jasper's teeth clenched. "No."

"Does your group suck?"

"Of course not."

Fitz leaned back as if pleased with himself. "Then there you go. Why not you? Why not now?"

Jasper let out a breath, the condensation rolling down the side of his beer bottle as he gripped it hard. Fitz was right. Why *not* him? It's not like someone was going to give him official permission or a stamp of approval. Hell, even his family, who were more supportive than most artists could hope for, were losing faith in him. If he wanted this kind of opportunity, he was going to have to take it, fight for it, believe he was the best damn person to make it happen. Buy the story he was selling. He was going to have to treat this whole venture like he did improv. Onstage, in a scene, you couldn't waffle. You had to fully commit. Create the *base reality*.

In this base reality, Jasper needed to be a guy who could start a business and make it successful. He needed to trust himself and his team to be good enough to pull off this show. He met Fitz's gaze. "That theater is going to be mine."

Fitz smiled a brilliant, toothy smile. "Fuck yeah, it will."

....

Hollyn sat in the back of the newly minted improv classroom at WorkAround with Jasper's promise that he would *definitely*, *absolutely not, under any circumstances* call on her to participate. She'd threatened death and dismemberment if he broke that promise. But even with that assertion, she was having trouble relaxing.

She shifted in her chair and pulled a notebook and pen from her bag because taking notes would give her something to do. Plus, if anyone asked why she wasn't joining in, she had a prepared answer. She would tell them she was writing an article about the class offerings at WorkAround. She needed to focus on that and therefore couldn't volunteer.

Andi was next to her, cross-legged in the chair, and chewing on the edge of her blue-polished thumbnail, looking almost as nervous as Hollyn felt.

"You okay?" Hollyn asked.

Andi turned to her. "Yes. No. I kind of feel like I'm in line for a roller coaster. Like sort of excited but also kind of vomity."

Hollyn gave her a sympathetic smile. "I'm familiar with that feeling."

It was how she felt every time she was around Jasper.

"Maybe I should've gone out and had a margarita or something first," Andi said, her gaze flicking to the people still wandering into the class. "I mean, I have to improvise on the podcast, but I can edit my mistakes out, you know? And when I'm writing, obviously I can delete the crappy stuff. Plus, the pressure to be funny kind of makes it hard to be funny."

"I don't think anyone has to be funny. Jasper told me this is going to be a no-mistakes, judgment-free kind of thing," Hollyn said, looking for the man in question. "I'm sure it will be fun, you know, for people like you."

Andi scrunched her nose like she'd smelled something bad and turned her attention back to Hollyn. "People like me? Clarify."

Hollyn looked down, doodling googly eyes on her notebook page, and shrugged. "You know, outgoing, confident, unafraid."

"Ha." Andi sniffed derisively. "Unafraid? Girl, we need to get to know each other better. You know what running a true-crime podcast and writing horror stories does to a person?"

Hollyn looked over.

"It shows you how freaking terrifying the world can be and turns you into a huge chicken," she said. "I'm surprised I haven't sprouted feathers yet."

Hollyn frowned. "I guess I hadn't thought of that."

"The stories I come across..." Andi shook her head ruefully. "Well, it'd be ludicrous to be unafraid, especially as a woman." She reached in her purse, which was by her feet, and pulled out a pack of gum. "But outgoing, yeah, I'll give you that one. Gum?"

Hollyn took the offered stick, feeling a new camaraderie with Andi. Maybe her new friend wasn't as fearless as she appeared to be. Maybe everyone was carrying something heavy in their personal-life backpack. "I'll make you a deal," she told Andi. "I'll keep an eye out for murderers for you. You watch out for strangers wanting to have small talk with me."

Andi grinned and popped the stick of Big Red in her mouth. "Deal."

Movement near the door caught Hollyn's eye, and she spun that way, catching sight of Jasper just as he walked in with a pretty African American woman with short curly hair and the brightest red lipstick Hollyn had ever seen. They were chatting quietly, serious expressions on both their faces. Jasper had changed out of his apron and button-up shirt into a T-shirt that said *Maybe Tomorrow, Satan*. His hair was a little mussed like he'd been running his fingers through it, and he just looked slightly undone in the best way possible. Something deep inside Hollyn gave a kick of appreciation.

He had a stack of papers in his hand and a backpack over his shoulder, and was chattering away. But when he turned his head and saw Hollyn and Andi, he gave a little wave with his paper-filled hand and a pleased smile. Jasper's companion followed his line of sight and gave the two of them a quick once-over.

Hollyn waved back, trying to suppress her tics.

"Your boyfriend's here," Andi whispered as she raised her hand in greeting and beamed a smile their way.

Hollyn could feel her tics fighting to the surface. She turned back to Andi and poked her playfully. "Hush. We're just friends. Not even. *Acquaintances.*"

Andi chewed her gum, still smiling, looking zero percent remorseful. "Uh-huh. You literally perked up like a puppy seeing a treat when he walked in."

Hollyn groaned and shoved her own stick of gum in her mouth, the hot cinnamon flavor matching the heat in her face. "We are not in eighth grade. No whispering about crushes in the back of the classroom."

Not that Hollyn had ever had the opportunity to do that, but she'd seen it in movies.

"Can we pass notes instead?" Andi asked, elbowing Hollyn gently in the side and then stealing her pen and writing Jasper + Hollyn = ❤ in big looping letters on Hollyn's notebook page.

Hollyn laughed, almost choking on the gum, and snatched her pen back. "You're going to get me in trouble with the teacher."

Her face lit. "Ooh, that could be fun."

"Don't even," Hollyn warned as she scratched out the doodle, though she couldn't stop her smile. "You get in trouble with an improv teacher, they make you perform."

Andi sobered, looking a little worried again. "Good point. I'll behave."

Jasper set his stuff down at the front of the room, said something to his companion, and then headed up the center aisle of chairs to where Hollyn and Andi were sitting.

"Uh-oh, maybe we're already in trouble," Andi whispered. "Act innocent."

Hollyn's hand gripped the bottom of her chair, trying to will her fingers not to count.

"Hey," Jasper said, stopping next to their row and greeting them both.

"Hey, Teach," Andi said.

"Ugh. That sounds weird." He leaned a little closer, bringing the smell of his laundry detergent and a whiff of dark roast coffee into Hollyn's orbit. "Don't tell anyone, but I've never taught before. Everyone in here is a guinea pig tonight."

"Except me," Hollyn said firmly.

His lips quirked. "Of course. I wouldn't break my promise. There is an invisible force field around you," he said, drawing a square in the air in front of Hollyn. He looked to Andi. "What about you? You game, Podcaster?"

Andi blew a bubble with her gum and tipped her head to the side. "How painful is this going to be? Like on a scale of brain freeze to getting a tooth pulled with no anesthesia?"

"Nowhere on that scale I hope," he said with a laugh. "This is supposed to be fun."

"Uh-huh," Andi said, unconvinced. "I'll play along. Just don't pick me first."

"Got it," he said and then reached out and put his hand on Hollyn's shoulder, catching her gaze. "We still on after the class is done?"

Acute awareness rushed through Hollyn—not just at the thought of what was to come but at his nearness, his warm hand on her. Her body almost didn't know how to react to the friendly intimacy. An ache went through her chest, but she swallowed past the bubble of emotion and forced a smile. "That's the plan."

"Great." He gave her shoulder a squeeze. "I'll see you after class then. Wish me luck."

"Break a leg," she said, her throat dry and voice cracking a little.

Jasper checked the clock on the wall and then headed back to the front of the room. Hollyn sagged back in her chair, her bones like water.

Andi leaned in. "You didn't tell me you guys were going out after. Good for you, girl."

"Not going out," she said, trying to get her heartbeat and her tics in check. "He's giving me a few private lessons to help me with a new video project I need to do for work. He knows I'm too anxious to participate in a group setting."

"Private lessons, huh? That's cool of him," Andi said, looking back toward the front and then frowning. "Maybe I should run that background check on him. If you're going to be alone with him, better to know he's got a clear record."

The comment snapped Hollyn out of her own thoughts and she laughed. "You just said it was cool of him. Why would you background check him?"

Andi gave her a *girl, please* look. "The best serial killers know how to be charming. And that boy is full of charm. He oozes with it."

Hollyn eyed her friend with amusement and shook her head. "You're a mess."

Andi patted Hollyn's knee. "Told ya. Don't go around thinking everyone else has it together. We're all just falling apart in different ways."

"That's depressing."

Andi shrugged. "Meh. Or comforting."

Hollyn put her hand over Andi's and gave it a little squeeze. "Thanks."

She gave her a puzzled look. "For what?"

"For making the first friendship move," Hollyn said. "I needed that."

"Anytime." Andi leaned her shoulder into Hollyn's. "And when you pick out those bridesmaids dresses for you and Jasper's wedding, remember that I look great in blue."

Hollyn groaned. "You're relentless."

"Part of my charm."

The lights flickered, and everyone's attention was drawn to the front. Jasper was near the light switch, a smile on his face but a hint of tension in his stance. "Ready to get started?"

Hollyn wasn't ready to start improv, but for the first time in a long time she felt like maybe, finally, she had started *something*.

Quite possibly, her life.

chapter **twelve**

JASPER'S STOMACH WAS QUEASY AS HELL AS HE STOOD IN front of the room with Monique and tried to center himself for the first class. He'd taken a ton of improv classes as a student but had never taught one, and standing up there, all those entrepreneurial eyes on him, made him feel like a giant fraud. Sure, he could probably make these people laugh, but that's not what he was there for. He was there to try to help them with their businesses. The guy who was bumming off a friend for an apartment and who served coffee for a living was offering business advice. Why should they listen to him? Easy answer: they shouldn't.

Monique moved closer and gave him an evaluating look. "You look pale again. Another organ gonna give out on you?"

"I'm fine. Just...this feels weird." He gripped the stack of index cards where he'd listed improv games and notes and resisted the urge to fan himself with them like a southern lady on a hot day.

Monique's red lips curved. "What? Being nervous? Yeah, I know what you mean. I feel like I'm the one taking my first class again." She lifted her fist toward him. "But we got this, Jas. It's just another audience. Another performance. You know, with a slide presentation and talking points and shit."

Jasper let out a breath and rolled his shoulders before bumping his fist to hers. "Right. I think prepping for this has made it worse."

"Has it?" She plucked his stack of notecards from his hand. "Problem solved."

"Hey," he said, reaching for the stack, but she held it out of his reach.

"Nope." She tucked the cards into her back pocket. "Don't start overthinking things now. You're magic without a net, and I'm magic no matter what. We don't need the cards. We just need our quick brains and stunning good looks."

She batted her eyelashes at him and he laughed. "You're right. Let's do this."

Jasper stepped over to the light switch and flicked it a few times to get everyone's attention. "Ready to get started?"

Once the group had quieted down and everyone had taken their seats, Monique cleared her throat. "Welcome, ladies and bros, to our inaugural Hail Yes Improv for Business class!" She paused and when no one in the group responded, she put her hands on her hips. "Rule to remember: When I say exciting things in my cheerleader voice, you're supposed to clap. Clap now, people. The quietest gets called on first."

Cheers and claps erupted.

She smiled her bright smile. "Good job. Now I know you're all chickens."

A few nervous laughs drifted from the group. The first row of chairs was empty, which meant everyone was definitely dreading being called on.

Jasper joined Monique, facing the class, and mentally shook off his nerves. The group would never relax if he looked like he had a stick up his ass. His job was not just to teach them but to show them there was nothing to fear. "Before we get started, give yourself gold stars for showing up. I know the thought of doing improv is scary to most people. That's completely normal. So it's okay if you feel a little—or a lot—freaked out about this. The world tells us to 'always be prepared' and to 'never let them see you sweat,' and basically that it's not okay to reveal to anyone that you don't have it one hundred percent together at all times."

There were a few nods of agreement in the audience. His gaze inadvertently flicked to the back row where Hollyn was sitting. Even though she wouldn't be participating, something about having her there made him feel more energized about this whole venture. He wanted her to feel confident going into their one-on-one lesson tonight, so he needed to project his own confidence. He also maybe wanted to impress her a little. He knew from her Miz Poppy articles that she wasn't easily impressed. At shows, he sometimes picked the most grim-faced person in the audience as his target. If he could get that person to laugh, the show was a success. Tonight, Hollyn was going to be his audience of one.

"But there's nothing to fear here in this classroom," Monique added. "This is a judgment-free zone."

"Exactly," he said. "There are no mistakes. That's one of the most important rules of improv. In fact, what can feel like a mistake often leads to the best scenes or the biggest laughs—which, in your businesses, could mean the best ideas or opportunities. Think about how many things were invented by happy accident or by improvising—Post-It Notes, PlayDoh, microwaves, potato chips."

"Right," Monique said, jumping in. "Improv isn't about making jokes. It's about being open to discovery and possibility. This isn't stand-up comedy. You don't need to have one-liners in your pocket. This is a team sport. It's about saying yes to others, thinking on your feet, supporting your team members, and removing road blocks to creativity."

"All things that can translate into your business and to your team," Jasper said, hitting his stride. Monique had been right about the index cards. Notes weren't his style. He knew this stuff.

He could do this. He loved this shit. "So we'll start with going over a few more rules of improv. Then, we're going to find some willing victims to do a few short-form games up here."

"And by willing victims, he means I'm going to pick the quietest." Monique cupped her hand around her ear.

The group cheered and Jasper laughed. They were off and running.

Forty-five minutes later, Jasper was buzzing with adrenaline as Monique wrapped up her section on the importance of agreement in improv. He and Monique had focused mainly on the "Yes, and" principle for this class—how to never block your partners' ideas. Go with the ideas and then add to them. They linked the concept to brainstorming in a business and how it can help not to shut down any ideas during that initial stage.

They'd played a few simple games with a couple of brave volunteers, but now it was time to get the whole group involved. No more hiding. He raised a hand. "All right, everyone, class is about to wrap up, but before you go, we're going to play a quick game that involves everyone. Please turn all of your chairs so that they form a circle."

There were a few panicked looks.

"I promise this won't hurt at all," he added.

After a few murmurs, people got up and started dragging chairs across the floor to get them in order. Jasper watched Rodrigo, the fitness vlogger, head over to Hollyn and Andi to help move their chairs for them. Jasper frowned as Hollyn shook her head and lifted her notebook up to Rodrigo. Rodrigo ignored her protest and waved his hand to encourage her to join in. She glanced toward the front of the room, sending Jasper an SOS look. He was already striding over.

Jasper reached them before Hollyn's chair could be moved. He put a hand on her elbow. "Hey, can I see you for a sec?"

She nodded quickly and smiled briefly at Rodrigo and Andi. "Excuse us." Hollyn went with him, and he guided her off to the side. He could feel a little tremor go through her, like her anxiety was flooding in. When they got a good enough distance from the group, she said in a low, urgent voice, "It's going to stand out if I don't join in, but I'm not down with this."

"I know. I'd already thought of that," he said, releasing her elbow. "I have a plan."

"Run out the back like I'm on fire?" She gave him a hopeful look.

He smiled. "Yes, that's option one. You can bail now if you want and just meet me back here after everyone leaves *or* I can give you a behind-the-scenes role in the game."

Her throat flexed and her facial tics pulled at her muscles. He had the urge to reach out and smooth the tension from her cheek, to soothe her in some way, but kept his hands at his side.

"How behind the scenes?" she asked.

He dipped his head and caught her gaze. "Ever played duck, duck, goose?"

She frowned. "Sure."

"Well, you'd be the goose in this game. You just have to touch people's shoulders to let them know it's their turn to talk. You don't have to talk or participate in any other way."

She rolled her lips together and glanced toward the circle the group was forming. Her chest rose and fell with a breath, and he could almost see her brain working, but finally, she nodded. "I guess I can do that. I kind of want to see the game. This has been..." She met his eyes. "You're really great at this, you know?"

Something warm and potent spread through his chest at the simple compliment. He could tell she wasn't the type who would say it if she didn't mean it. "Thanks."

"So I won't have to talk?" she clarified.

"I swear. I've got you." He put out his palm in offer.

She eyed him for a moment, and he worried that she would go with plan A, but then she took his hand. His fingers closed around hers, pleasure suffusing through him at her trust, and he led her back to the group.

Monique was critiquing the group's circle-making skills when they rejoined the class. "There are no mistakes in improv, but this is a poor-ass excuse for a circle, people. Aren't some of you computer geniuses? Do you remember kindergarten? Show me a circle. Three-hundred and sixty degrees. No corners. Make me proud."

A few people laughed and others were smiling. Monique had the group in the palm of her hand, so they dutifully complied. She glanced over at Jasper while the circle was being adjusted, and cocked a brow at his and Hollyn's clasped hands. He quickly released the hold.

Monique strode over. She put out her hand to Hollyn. "Monique, or Monique the Mouth as my group so lovingly calls me."

Hollyn's cheek tic was going a little wild, but she managed a friendly smile and shook Monique's hand. "Hollyn. I'm apparently going to be your very silent goose."

Monique's red lips curved. "Ah, easiest job in the place. You must've paid Jasper off to get that gig."

"Something like that," Jasper said, saving Hollyn from more of his friend's not-so-subtle prodding. "Everyone ready?"

Monique turned, put her hands on her hips, and sighed audibly at the group. "This is an oval, people, not a circle, but I can only do so much. Let's get started."

Jasper left Hollyn's side so that the attention wouldn't be on her and moved closer to Monique. He lifted his hand to get everyone to quiet down and then started. "Okay. The way this game works is we're going to write a Dear John–style breakup letter together. When your shoulder is touched, you add a line to the letter, building on whatever was said before. This will help you practice that rule of agreement and the 'Yes, and' principle.

"Don't deny what the previous people have said, only add to it. This is also a good exercise for learning to listen carefully to the group." Jasper cocked his head toward Hollyn. "Hollyn will be walking the perimeter of the circle and can touch whoever's shoulder she wants, so you won't know when your turn is coming. When she touches you, it's your turn. No passing. Try to answer without thinking. And don't plan your answer ahead because then you'll miss the listening component."

"Everyone understand?" Monique asked.

Jasper glanced at Hollyn, and she nodded and moved closer to the circle.

Monique went on. "Great. Then I'll start. 'Dear Jasper...'" Jasper sent Monique a narrow-eyed look at making him the recipient of the breakup letter, and she gave him an innocent shrug. "What? This will make it more interesting. Poor Jasper, y'all. His girl is dumping him."

Jasper snorted. Well, the best improv setups often started with a true story. His ex, Kenzie, never would've bothered with a letter, though. She'd wanted to live through the dramatic moment and soak up all that emotion. Fodder for future acting gigs. He'd probably see their breakup scene in one of her *Aurora Boring* episodes one day.

"Dear Jasper..." Monique repeated, and Jasper dragged his attention back to the game.

Hollyn touched Andi's shoulder. "I'm so sorry to be typing all this in a letter instead of an email, but I'm really into analog right now, and I wanted to try out my new typewriter."

Someone laughed. Hollyn continued walking around the circle. She touched a redheaded guy. Toby? Jasper couldn't remember his name.

"But I need to tell you that this isn't working out. The way you eat peanut butter straight from the jar..."

Hollyn touched a guy wearing a backward baseball cap.

"While we're having sex is really getting to me," the guy said. "And *on* me."

A few people laughed and Jasper smirked. These games always led back to sex jokes.

Hollyn tapped Rodrigo. "I'm tired of being sticky, so I'm leaving for good. I've taken half of the furniture and the dog."

Back to Andi. "I took the front half of the dog because you deserve the messy end."

Jasper laughed, and Monique pointed at Andi. "Good listening."

Hollyn moved to the next guy. "I know the furniture wasn't mine, but the couch really matches my new apartment better."

Hollyn tapped Emily, the productivity blogger. "And this is actually your typewriter. Well, it used to be. But I've seen your writing. I've done you and the world at large a real favor."

Much of the group was into it now.

Another tap. "I know this will be hard to hear, so that's why I thought I'd share it in a letter. I've met someone else. He has a huge..."

Hollyn tapped Toby. "Allergy to peanuts so there's no food allowed in bed."

Tap to backward-hat guy. "And he's got a really massive—"

Hollyn quickly touched Emily again, an amused expression on her face. "Instagram following. I'm including the link so you can obsess about how cute we are together."

Hollyn continued to move around the circle, the story getting more complicated, and only one person freezing up during their turn. When Hollyn returned to Andi for the third time, Andi wrapped it up. "I wish you hell, sweetheart. Oops, darn typewriter, no spell-check. I wish you *well*."

Monique laughed at that.

Hollyn touched Rodrigo. "Yours no more, Fifi."

"Oh, Jas," Monique said sympathetically. "Fifi broke your poor heart."

Jasper snorted and lifted a hand to cue Hollyn to stop. "I'm truly shattered." He stepped closer to the circle. "Give yourselves a hand. Great job!"

Jasper applauded along with the rest of the group and then spent the next few minutes answering questions as the class broke apart and everyone started putting chairs back in their places.

He lost track of Hollyn in the process, but as the room emptied out, he caught sight of her standing near one of the windows, presumably watching the sunset or the city below. Or maybe just hiding from the after-class small talk.

Monique walked over to him, her skin glowing with a little sheen and her eyes bright. "That was fun. Far less boring than I imagined."

Jasper grinned. "Yeah, it was. They loosened up toward the end. Plus, I knew you'd enjoy being in charge."

"Always." She lifted a business card between them. "And I got a date out of the deal."

"Oh yeah? Already crossing the student-teacher lines?"

She waved a dismissive hand. "We're all grown-ups here."

"Which guy?"

"Toby," she said. "Turns out he really did break up with someone because she thought peanut butter was a sexy thing to bring to bed. I figured I needed to hear the rest of that story."

"Ha. So are you going out with him for material or because you like him?"

She shrugged. "Too early to tell." She nodded toward Hollyn. "How about you? What's up with you and the goose? I thought you were taking a break from the dating game."

"Oh, it's not a date. She's—" He started to say she was Miz Poppy and was going to give their group a review, but he'd promised Hollyn he wouldn't blow her cover with anyone. "She's going to take some one-on-one lessons with me. She's intimidated by the class setting and needs some specific help for a work project she has to do."

Monique's eyebrows arched. "Private lessons? How much is she paying you for that?"

"I, uh..."

She pursed her lips. "You're not charging her."

"We've come to a mutual agreement," he said carefully. "It's not about money."

"So a date," she said flatly.

When he protested, she raised a palm, cutting him off. "Look, you're a grown-ass man and can do what *and who* you want, but promise me you won't get distracted by a woman again. We're starting to build momentum with the shows, and now you're looking at that theater, which could change all of our lives if it works out. Don't veer off course. You know how you get when you get involved with someone."

His jaw flexed. "And how is that?"

"Blind," she said, not pulling any punches. "You chased Kenzie to LA without thinking about what it would do to anyone else, to the show, to you."

Great. They were back to the Great Abandonment talk. "Monique—"

"All I'm saying is that we need you one hundred percent focused right now. If you need to get laid, go hook up with someone for a night. Don't date someone at your job."

He made a face. "Please stop giving me sex advice. And it's not a date, all right? I'm not interested in her like that. I'm just helping her out with some issues she's dealing with. Totally sexless endeavor."

Monique's gaze flickered with something, and Jasper felt the hairs on the back of his neck rise with awareness. *Hell.* He gave Monique a look that said *She's right behind me, isn't she?*

Monique smiled a smile that said, *Yep.*

Wonderful.

He turned and found Hollyn cringing, her nose tic in full effect and her gaze trained somewhere near the floor. "Sorry, didn't meant to interrupt."

He had no idea how much she'd heard so he tried to play it off. "Not interrupting. You ready to get started?"

Her gaze jumped to his. "I guess."

Monique clapped her hands together. "Alrighty, I'm headed out. Hollyn, it was nice to meet you. Jas, I'll see you at the next show. Good luck with the private lessons."

"Thanks," he said, not missing the warning look Monique gave him. The look that said, *You've fucked up things before. Don't do it again.*

But really, Monique had nothing to worry about. It didn't matter that Hollyn was attractive or that he loved her articles or that they were going to be alone tonight. He hadn't been lying when he'd told Fitz that he wouldn't be bringing women home. He didn't have time to worry about dating right now, and he especially didn't need to try something with the woman behind Miz Poppy. Because he had one guarantee in life—he sucked at relationships. If he went down that road, he'd mess it up with Hollyn and he'd end up with either no Miz Poppy review or worse, a bad, vengeful one.

The opportunity for a hookup wasn't hard to come by. The opportunity for a career break was much more precious. Which made Hollyn a straight-up diamond.

"So," he said, turning fully to Hollyn, "you ready to play?"

chapter **thirteen**

DID SHE WANT TO PLAY? HOLLYN GLANCED AT THE DOOR like a spooked horse ready to bolt in response to Jasper's question. Beyond the all-encompassing fear of trying this improv stuff, she was mortified that she'd walked up on him telling his friend how completely uninterested he was in Hollyn and how she had "issues." *A sexless endeavor.* God, how had she ever suspected that he'd been flirting with her? *Of course* he didn't see her that way.

He was just a nice guy offering to help out *that awkward chick with Tourette's. Ugh.* She cleared her throat. "Look, I'm not sure this is the best idea. Maybe—"

"No way," Jasper said, stepping between her and the path to the door and catching her gaze. "Please don't back out now. If you heard—"

"I didn't hear anything," she said quickly.

His mouth hitched up at one corner. "You're a terrible liar."

She pressed her lips together. *Fucking tics.*

"I'm sorry you heard any of that. Monique was just being Monique—a great friend but blunt," he said with a shrug. "I'm coming off a shitty breakup, and she wants me to make 'good choices.'" He made air quotes at that. "She was worried our private lessons were a cover for me starting up some kind of on-the-rebound work affair."

Hollyn blinked at his frankness. "Oh."

"Which obviously they're not," he said. "So, she has nothing to worry about. *You* have nothing to worry about. I'm here to help you with your job stuff. You're going to help me by getting my group an honest Miz Poppy review. We know what's what. I just couldn't tell Monique the whole truth because I don't want to blow your Miz Poppy cover."

Hollyn worked not to cringe at the word *obviously*. "Right."

"So," he said. "Ready to get started now?"

"I'm still kind of freaked out over the idea of this," she admitted, trying to refocus on why they were there.

"That's just the initial panic trying to scare you away. Try to shake it off." He put his arms out to his sides and shook his hands. "It's only nervous energy."

She huffed. "I can't just shake that kind of thing off. I'm literally composed of rogue nervous energy."

"Sure you can. Come on and try it. Hands out. Shake it off. Don't make me sing the Taylor Swift song." He continued to shake his arms and hands like he was trying to get a bee out of his shirt or something.

She pursed her lips in frustration but put her hands out and gave them a half-hearted shake.

He gave her sad attempt a look that said he was wildly unimpressed, and then he took her by the hands and shook her arms with his, training his face into an ultra-serious expression until she smiled. "There you go. You said you wanted to give this a try. Don't quit before you even give yourself a chance."

"Jasper—"

He let go of her hands and gripped her gently by her shoulders, his hazel eyes earnest. "Look, it's just me, okay? Everyone has left.

This is a completely safe space to act like a fool. No mistakes to worry about. If you freeze up or panic or whatever, it's no big deal. I'll help you breathe through it. And if your mind goes blank at any time during a scene, just do the funky chicken."

Her eyebrows shot up. "The what?"

Jasper tucked his hands beneath his armpits to make wings and started flapping his arms and bouncing on his toes, his head moving like a chicken's.

She put her hand over her mouth to stanch the laugh that bubbled out. He stopped dancing and gave her that sexy half smile of his, sending a ripple of heat through her. Leave it to her to be turned on by the guy's funky chicken dance. Good God, she was hard up. She needed to go home, binge-watch *Pride and Prejudice*, Colin Firth version, and knock the dust off her vibrator. She couldn't be trusted out in the world like this.

"See. It's always funny," he said, misinterpreting her flush of attraction as amusement. "So, when your brain wants to freeze up, just do the funky chicken. It will help snap your mind out of the panic. No one can take themselves too seriously when acting like a yard bird."

"The chicken seems apropos for this situation," she said, trying to reel in her errant thoughts. "My inner chicken is flapping her wings hard right now, trying to fly right out of here."

He hooked his thumbs in the pockets of his jeans and gave her a contemplative look. "What's your biggest fear about all this? Just off the top of your head."

She was already sweating, and they hadn't even started. She prayed her extra-strength deodorant was improv-proof. "That this is going to be super embarrassing. That I'm not going to be able to do what the other people did tonight. That I'm going to look stupid or pathetic."

"Okay. So let's say all of those happen," he said. "What then?"

"I—" Her words left her as she searched for an answer. "I don't know."

"I have a secret to tell you." He cupped his hands around his mouth and leaned forward like he was about to whisper. "Looking stupid is kind of the point. And embarrassing yourself can be really freeing."

She gave him a droll look. "That is a bullshit statement. No one likes to be embarrassed."

"I didn't say we have to *like* it. I said it can be freeing. Think about how it feels to hang out with your friends or family who you can be completely yourself around. People you don't have to worry about embarrassing yourself in front of. Do you have anyone like that you can think of?"

She shifted her weight from foot to foot, her body still wanting to run out of there. "My friend Cal. We've known each other since we were kids, and...he has Tourette's, too."

Jasper nodded. "Okay, good. Think of how you feel when you're hanging out with Cal, how relaxed that feeling is."

She took a breath, trying to channel that Cal-comfort sensation and nodded. "All right."

"Now, imagine," he said, spreading his hands out and indicating the room around them, "that you could feel that comfortable in front of a roomful of strangers."

Her stomach dipped. "That's impossible."

"I promise it's not," he said, lowering his arms to his sides. "Of course the audience isn't our best friend who we're going to share our deepest thoughts or feelings with. The people who come to my shows don't get to know me on a personal level, but they *are* fellow humans who have all experienced embarrassing situations or awkwardness or looking like a fool at some point in their lives. If I mess up, they laugh along with me. They *want* me to mess up. Think about how much everyone likes the outtakes at the end of movies."

She crossed her arms. "That seems kind of mean for the audience to root for mistakes."

"But it's not. It takes the pressure off the performers. Sure, the audience wants a good improv show. But I know if I fumble something, I'm giving them some of what they want, too," he said. "And knowing that lifts a lot of the stress. I get rewarded for looking like an idiot."

She gave him a skeptical look.

He leaned forward conspiratorially. "If you embarrass yourself tonight, I'll reward you, too. Very handsomely."

Her heartbeat quickened at his nearness and the words. "With what?"

He lifted a finger indicating that she should give him a second and then headed to the front where he'd left his bag. He dug inside and then turned to her. He lifted both his hands, each holding a bag of candy. "Pick your poison—Skittles or M&M's?"

She laughed. "You're baiting me with candy? What am I? A toddler?"

He waggled his eyebrows and jiggled the bags of candy. "You know you want it."

She wanted something all right. The hot actor. She groaned. "Okay, I do love a Skittle. But no grape ones."

He tossed the M&M's back into his bag and grinned as he walked her way. "Okay, Eddie Van Halen, all purple Skittles will be removed."

She sighed. "You're pretty good at the hard sell, Jasper Deares."

"Have I convinced you not to run out on me?"

She glanced at the door once more and then nodded. "For now."

"I'll take it. Come on. I'll strike while I've still got you under my magical Skittle spell." He put his hand out and she reluctantly took it. She didn't know if he realized how physical he was. To her, it felt like an intimacy—one she didn't mind—but she had to remind herself that Jasper was in comedy. Improv, from what she'd seen on television, was inherently physical. He probably didn't even notice how much he touched her. He led her over to the line of chairs and dragged two out. He released her hand and turned the chairs back-to-back. "Here. Have a seat, Hollyn Darling."

She sat but kept her eyes on him. "What are we doing?"

He stepped around her and sat in the other chair, putting his back to her. "We're going to tell each other embarrassing stories or things about ourselves. It's easier if you don't have to look at the person."

She turned her head to look back at him. "Oh, hell no. This sounds like a terrible idea. Can't we just do another *Dear Jasper* letter?"

He turned, which brought his face close enough for her to see his dark, thick eyelashes behind his glasses. She lost her train of thought for a moment and could feel her tics giving him a show. His expression softened. "Trust me. This will help us get to know each other, and the more we know of each other, the more comfortable you'll feel. You're not the kind of person who's going to be able to let go with a stranger. At least not yet. You need to know some of my secrets and vice versa. Build a circle of trust so that your stranger alarm system doesn't go off when we start playing the games."

She stared at him for a moment and then closed her eyes, unable to counter his argument. "Fine."

"Great. I'll go first," he said.

They turned back-to-back again, and she stared at the windows on the other side of the room, wishing she could climb right out of this situation.

He cleared his throat. "I once was out of clean laundry, so I went to a performance commando. I didn't think it'd be a big deal, but when me and another guy in our group got into this mock fight scene, my pants ripped and I ended up mooning the audience."

Hollyn bit her lip, imagining the scene. "Oh no."

"It gets worse," he warned. "I thought the audience was laughing so hard because I was doing such a good job. I didn't notice the draftiness until I was well into the next scene. The theater manager ended up giving me a lecture about their nudity clause afterward, and I had to pay a fine. My group now refers to this as the Jasper Ass Tariff."

She looked down at her lap and grinned. "Your group didn't signal you that something had happened?"

"And break the scene and lose the laughs?" he asked. "Not a chance. Those bastards would've let it go on for ten scenes."

"No mistakes in improv, right?"

"Exactly," he said. "Your turn."

She took a breath and picked at a loose thread in her jeans. "I don't know what to say."

"What about something when you were little? We all do embarrassing things as kids."

She thought for a moment, her fingers naturally going into their four count. "Um, okay. When I was seven, I was cast as an angel in the church Christmas play. They told us that we couldn't leave the stage no matter what. I guess they'd had problems with kids wandering back to their parents. I had to go to the bathroom but wanted to follow the rules. So, the whole performance I was basically twisting and squirming. Then when baby Jesus was brought out, instead of singing my part, I peed. In a white dress."

Jasper chuckled. "That sounds like a failure on the adults' parts, not yours. Was that the end of your days onstage?"

"No, that was before the tics. I bounced back from that one." She looked to the ceiling, squinting at the memory, trying to remember how it felt *not* to be afraid of people watching her. "The next year they made me a camel, though."

"Ha." His hand touched hers, making her startle, but then he tucked a piece of candy into her palm.

She relaxed her shoulders and popped the red Skittle into her mouth. "Your turn. How about something embarrassing about *you* instead of a story?"

Something to make you less sexy and adorable would be nice, please and thank you.

"All right, let's see." She could feel him shifting in his seat. "Oh, I've got one. I have a deep, secret love for boy-band music. Like an unironic love."

Her thoughts skidded to a halt at that. "Hold up. Really?"

"Yep."

She wanted to turn around to see his expression and determine if he was screwing with her, but she forced herself to stay facing forward. "Like a particular boy band?"

"Nah. I'm equal opportunity—old ones, new ones," he said, tone casual as ever. "I met this girl in one of the group homes I lived in early on who told me that you can't stay sad or angry listening to boy bands. She'd filched all these different CDs from the group home's ancient collection, and we used to listen to them together. One Direction. NSYNC. Backstreet Boys. New Kids on the Block. I got kind of attached. The harmonies just do it for me. So soothing." He shifted in his chair, making it squeak. "She was right, too. You really can't stay in a bad mood listening to boy-band songs."

Hollyn's heart gave a little kick, imagining Jasper without a family, living in some group home, but her lips curved thinking of him belting out boy-band tunes. "That's kind of an amazing one."

"Thanks. I'll eat a Skittle," he said with a smile in his voice. "Now you. Tell me an embarrassing unironic love, Hollyn. Death metal? Reality TV? Gossip about British royals?"

"Hmm, let's see." She stared at the windows and pondered. "Not reality TV, but I do have an obsession with movies and television shows set in high school. Angsty ones. Funny ones. Cheesy ones. Over-the-top dramatic ones. It kind of doesn't matter the type as long as they're teens in high school."

"Yeah?" He sounded delighted.

"Yep. My mom pulled me out of public school to homeschool me when I was in sixth grade, so high school still seems like this mythic, fictional place I needed to learn about in order to not be a complete alien. I studied those movies and TV shows like a detective."

"Wow, so all you know about high school you learned in movies?"

"'Fraid so."

He was quiet for a moment as if digesting that. "So do you think that all high school dances have synchronized dance numbers?"

"They don't?" she asked with mock shock. "At least tell me everyone is involved in an angsty love triangle where one guy is the girl's long-pining best friend."

He laughed. "Sorry to disappoint. Most school dances involved a lot of standing around and...not dancing. And no love triangles that I know of."

"Dream crusher."

He passed her a Skittle. "So why'd your mom pull you out of school?"

She winced at the question, though she appreciated that he didn't automatically assume it was because of her Tourette's. "That is its own horrible, truly embarrassing story."

He was silent for a beat. "Want to share or is that one too much?"

She worried the green Skittle between her fingertips. The story *was* too much. But maybe if she laid bare her worst childhood story, it'd be like ripping the Band-Aid off. Nothing else she shared going forward could be more humiliating. She wet her lips. "It's not a funny one."

"That's okay."

She looked down at her hands, holding the candy like a totem. "That year, sixth grade, I had a crush on this older boy—Maddox. My first real crush that wasn't someone on TV or whatever. I had no intention of pursuing it. I mean, I was already on the outs of the social circles by then, so I didn't think it could turn into anything. It was the write-his-name-in-your-notebook kind of crush—a fun secret," she said. "But somehow he found out."

"Maybe one of the girls I'd confided in told him or maybe he sensed it. I don't know. But one day, he sent me a note to meet him under the big oak tree at recess for a kiss. I was a romantic kid—already into movies with happy endings—and it didn't cross my mind to question it. It just seemed exciting." The green of the Skittle was staining her fingertips, her hands starting to sweat. "But when I showed up, he'd brought a group of his friends and the pet mouse from science class. He called me 'rodent' and told me he had found my prince."

Jasper made a disgusted sound in the back of his throat. "What an asshole."

She swallowed hard. "Yeah, his friends grabbed me to hold me in place and he forced me to kiss the mouse." Her stomach tightened, nausea trying to well up. "My mom pulled me out of school for good the next day." *Right after I announced I wanted to die.* She tucked the candy in her mouth, chewing harshly, and wiped her hands on her dark jeans. "So now you know my most embarrassing moment. You can feel better about your boy bands."

She could feel the air shift as Jasper turned toward her, but she wasn't ready to face him yet. Her facial muscles were ticcing, and her fingers were counting.

"That sucks, Hollyn. I'm sorry you had to go through that," he said quietly. "Kids can be absolute dicks."

"They can," she agreed. "I also should've known better. My tics were terrible by then. Way worse than they are now. The notion that Mr. Popularity said he liked me should've tipped me off as a red flag."

"Fuck that noise," he said, grabbing her chair and turning her toward him. "You were a kid. Not one bit of that was your fault."

She couldn't look at him, so she focused on the hand he had braced on his knee. He was flexing it as if he was angry. "I thought this was supposed to be improv, not a therapy session. I know it wasn't my fault. But it was a lesson in seeing the reality and not painting some delusional fantasy picture on top of that."

"Thinking a boy could want to kiss you is not delusional."

She glanced up at that.

He smiled and then reached out and took her hand, flipping it palm up. He poured the entire bag of Skittles into her hand and then started picking out the purple ones.

She frowned. "What are these for?"

"Because if you can survive that kind of sadistic bullying, you can survive anything onstage or in front of a camera," he said, expression serious. "And it took guts to share that with me. You win all the candy."

"Please don't give me pity candy," she said, her voice tight.

"Hollyn, this isn't pity candy." He leaned in, almost nose to nose with her, a spark of mischief in his eyes. "I'm a former foster kid with junkie birth parents who literally forgot to feed me when I was little. And I pour coffee for a living. Compared to a talented writer with a few tics and some social hang-ups, you've got nothing on me. I could out-pity-party you on any given day, *amateur*."

The words shocked her into a laugh. "That's messed up, Jasper."

He shrugged and leaned back with an unapologetic look. "I'm kind of messed up."

He put the handful of purple Skittles in his mouth and stood. Only when he walked back to his bag did she register that he hadn't been making a joke. She'd caught the barely there shift in his demeanor, the closing off. He'd said more than he'd meant to.

He peeked back over his shoulder, easy expression back in place. "Ready to play a game that has nothing to do with painful childhood memories?"

"Well, with a sales pitch like that…" she said, standing up and setting her candies in the chair.

She wanted to ask him more questions, to see what was underneath that thick layer of charm, but she tucked away the urge. They weren't on a date. *I'm not interested in her like that.* She wasn't going to make this into something more than it was. She'd learned that lesson with Maddox. This was just a lesson. Games.

Nothing more.

chapter **fourteen**

JASPER HAD NO IDEA HOW THE SILLY EXERCISE HE'D STARTED had taken such a personal turn. He didn't talk to people about his birth parents. He didn't share why he'd gotten removed from his home. But somehow, his dark-closet shit had spilled out and into Hollyn's lap without him realizing it. Hearing what that kid had done to her had made him want to break things. Smart, quiet Hollyn getting held down and a fucking rat shoved in her face? His fists clenched at the image. He wanted to go back in time, find that kid, and punch him in his sadistic little face.

He also realized, to his horror, that he'd wanted to kiss Hollyn. He'd almost done it when he'd seen that wounded-little-girl look in her eyes. He'd wanted to erase that ugly memory right out of her mind, show her that *of course* she was worth kissing, pull her to him and kiss her until they both forgot their pasts. *Thank God* he'd resisted that urge. There'd be no better way to mess up this whole thing than making out with Miz Poppy.

So, in a panic, he'd tried to out-traumatize her with his childhood as a distraction instead. *Way to go, Deares. Way to make it weird.*

"So what's the game?" Hollyn asked, tucking her hands in the back pockets of her jeans and making her blue T-shirt stretch tight across her breasts, which he was totally not checking out. Nope.

He held up a stack of cards he'd grabbed from his bag. "Each of these has a suggestion of a topic or scene we can act out. We'll take turns, each giving lines in the scene, until we run out of things to say or hit an obvious end."

She glanced down at the cards, and her posture curled inward, her apprehension obvious. "I don't know if I'm ready for that. The thought of being on the spot stresses me out. I mean, I know that's kind of the point of improv but I just... I don't know."

He frowned. He was losing her. He could feel her mentally backing away from the experiment already. And in his gut, he knew if he let her walk out without trying a game today, she was never coming back to a lesson. He needed her to get past the initial panic, to jump into the ice-cold pool so that her body could adjust to the water.

"Okay. I have a potential backup plan." He went back to his bag. "This is not an official part of the curriculum, but if you want to use the old-school method of shaking stage fright, there's always this." He turned around and held up a bottle of bourbon he'd taken from Fitz's stash, which his new roommate had graciously given him full access to.

Hollyn's lips parted. "You brought *booze?*"

"And red Solo cups because I'm fancy," he said. "Look, I don't endorse alcoholism as an answer to stage fright, but many of the people I've done improv with, even the experienced ones, knock back a beer or a shot before going onstage just to loosen up. Too much booze and you're sloppy, but just a little bit of something can take the edge off, especially when you're new and feeling self-conscious."

She eyed the bottle. "I don't know."

"No pressure. Just wanted to offer it as an option."

She let out a heavy sigh. "Maybe just this first time."

"Yeah?" he asked, wanting to make doubly sure.

She nodded. "I really don't want to give up on tonight, but the thought of acting out scenes one-on-one has me seriously jittery. Plus, that's ridiculously good bourbon."

He smiled. "My roommate has good taste. Okay, I'll do a shot with you. I'm off duty as an official teacher, right? I don't think Lucinda would approve of drinking with the students."

"Officially off the clock."

He grabbed the red cups, set them on the table, and poured a shot into each. He handed one to her. He lifted his drink to tap hers. "Cheers."

They both knocked back the shots, the bourbon smooth and instantly warming. He glanced over at Hollyn, who winced a little when she swallowed, and then she shook her head, looking sheepish. "I can't believe I'm doing shots in the name of work."

"You're very dedicated."

She laughed and licked her lips. "So dedicated."

"You good?" he asked.

She shifted her weight from foot to foot like she was trying to gauge her body's reaction to the alcohol. She held out her cup. "Maybe one more. A small one."

A pang of sympathy went through him. He wished he could lift the heavy weight of anxiety from her, see what was beneath. But he also didn't want to get her hammered. That would ruin the point of the lesson. He tipped about an ounce into her cup and did the same in his own cup. They both swallowed down their shots.

Afterward, he put away the bourbon, gave her a few minutes to let the liquor take effect, and then grabbed the cards again. "How are you feeling?"

She shook out her arms at her sides like he'd shown her earlier. Her cheeks were stained with a bright flush of pink. "I'm warm and tingly all over. But it's not a panic attack, so there's that."

"Progress!" He held up the stack of cards. "Ever watch *Whose Line Is It Anyway?*"

"A few times."

"This is kind of like their game Scenes from a Hat," he explained. "Remember, there's no pressure to be funny or say the exact right thing. It's just riffing on a topic and having fun with it. You want to give it a go?"

Her throat bobbed, and she rubbed her hands together like she was trying to psych herself up. "Okay, let's try."

He fanned the cards out and held them out toward her. "Pick one."

She reached out and plucked one from the stack. Her eyes skimmed over the typed words. *"Things you can say about your house but not your mate."*

He lifted a finger. "First, approval to be R-rated—yay or nay? I want you to be totally comfortable."

"R-rated is fine," she said with a casual wave of her hand, the booze obviously taking effect. Her posture was already looser, her facial tics less frequent. "Have you read my columns? Being shy doesn't mean I have delicate sensibilities."

He smirked. "I have. Miz Poppy is definitely not a pearl-clutcher."

"Not hardly."

"Cool. Fewer restrictions make it easier to come up with stuff." He set the cards down on the table at the front and then faced her. "Okay. 'Things you can say about your house but not your mate.'" He sniffed and made a disgusted expression. *"Mine has this weird smell."*

She huffed a quiet laugh. She looked around like she was examining a house. *"Uh, mine's really old but has good bones."*

"Mine's falling apart."

She sighed. *"Mine really has depreciated in value over the years."*

Jasper crossed his arms and mimed looking something up and down. *"I think I need a new one."*

She frowned and pointedly looked down at his crotch, her nose wrinkling. *"Mine's not big enough."*

He grinned. A dick joke. Nice.

He loved that she wasn't holding back and that he was getting a glimpse of her Miz Poppy side. He leaned closer as if he was telling a secret and waggled his eyebrows. *"I like to rent mine out on weekends."*

"Oh really." She put her hand to her hip and tilted her head, getting into character. *"I like to share mine with the neighbors, but only if they don't leave a mess behind."*

He chuckled, a flicker of pride going through him. *"There's not a lot going on upstairs. But I really like what's happening downstairs."*

She cocked a brow in challenge. *"I like to enter mine through the back door."*

Jasper choked, and then he burst into a laugh. He shook his head and put his hand out for a high five. "You win that one. Where are my pearls to clutch?"

She grinned, ducking her head, and then tapped his palm with his. "I didn't realize it was a competition."

"It's not. But you got me to break the scene and laugh. So you win." He eyed her. "I think you may be hustling me with this anxiety thing. You're quick on your feet, Hollyn Darling."

"Blame the bourbon."

"Yeah? How are you feeling?"

She pinched her fingers together. "A little tipsy and warm all over but...better. Once I got into the rhythm of the back-and-forth, I was able to forget that I was on the spot. I just wanted to outdo you."

He lifted a brow. "A competitive streak, huh? That can work to your advantage." He grabbed the stack of cards. "Let's do another one then. This time, try to get fully into character and treat it more like a scene. Don't be afraid to be physical and move around a little. You'll have more fun, and movement will help your mind not lock up."

She nodded, expression serious like she was taking mental notes. "Got it." She pulled another card. Her mouth hitched up at one corner. *"Things terrible actors would say to each other in bed."*

He rolled his eyes. "Monique must've planted that one. We can do something else."

She gave him an arch look. "What? Too close to home, Jasper?"

He took in her expression, enjoying the little streak of cockiness the liquor had revealed. Someone was forgetting that she was supposed to be nervous. "Oh, I'm fine. No shame, remember? If you're game, I'm game."

She tossed the card onto the table. A wrinkle appeared between her brows. "I'm not sure how we're supposed to act this one out though."

"We can just speak it or we can play it like we were actually onstage. Your choice."

She eyed the space between them. "How would it be onstage?"

He cocked his head to the side. "Come on. I'll show you."

She followed him over to the nearest wall and then he sat down, leaning his back against it. He patted the spot next to him. "Join me in bed."

Her cheeks got a little darker than the flush she was already sporting, and her nose tic appeared, which made him smile, but she joined him on the floor. He looked over at her. "Say stop at any time if this gets weird."

She gave him a surely-you-can't-be-serious look. "We did shots and are sitting in a pretend bed. This is already weird. But I hear you."

"All right, let's give it a try." He squinted, tipped his head toward the ceiling, and jostled her slightly to the left. *"Move over. You're in my light."*

"I'm..." She looked confused for a second, then realized he was already playing the game. "Oh. Right." She gave him an annoyed look. *"Cut! That was terrible. Is that what you call a sex scene?"*

He paused, wondering how far he should take this but then dismissed the thought. This was improv. No overthinking. He needed to act like he would with a member of his group. He moved toward her and straddled her calves. The bourbon was making his limbs feel warm and liquid, but he was careful not to put his weight on her. He frowned down at her and put his hands on his hips, swiveling a little from side to side. *"Can we do that again? I missed my mark."*

He waited a beat, half expecting her to shove him away for taking it to that level. Instead, she surprised him by grabbing a hank of her hair. *"Really, Steve? In my hair?"* She twirled her finger in the air. *"Makeup!"*

He almost choked, her comeback dirtier than what he'd lobbed at her. He bit down on his smile and waved a hand in front of her. *"I don't believe you in this scene. Show me you're enjoying this. I need more enthusiasm."*

"Oh, oh, oh," she said deadpan.

"That's all you've got? This is your big audition to be my girl, Lorraine." He bent forward and braced his hands on the wall next to her. *"Don't you know I'm kind of a big deal? I've been in three car-dealership commercials."*

She put the back of her hand to her forehead Scarlett O'Hara style and closed her eyes. *"Oh yes, Steve! Sell me a car!"*

He was having way too much fun now and losing himself in the scene. *"With more feeling! I don't believe you."*

Hollyn's eyes were tightly closed, and she panted as she tossed her head back and forth, *"Yes, Steve! Yes! Yes! Yes!"*

He slapped the wall behind her. *"That's it. Say my name."*

"Oh God, Steve!" she gasped.

Jasper lost his train of thought for a second, seeing Hollyn's face tipped back and hearing the breathless sounds escaping her short-circuited him for a second. "Uh…"

She opened her eyes, brows lifted in surprise at his stumble.

"I got my start in porn," he blurted out.

She blinked. "Was that another line or a confession?"

That broke him out of his distracted state. He cleared his throat, realizing their faces were only inches away and that he might possibly be getting turned on. *Not good.* "A line." He licked his lips and tried to regain his focus. "You're doing great. Your turn."

Her eyes met his, searching, a little dazed. He could feel her breath hitting his neck. "I, uh…"

"Don't think," he whispered. "Just follow the first impulse."

She stared at him for a millisecond longer, and then she grabbed the front of his T-shirt, pulled him closer, and kissed him.

Jasper froze, momentarily shocked by the contact, by the hot press of her lips against his, but then his own *don't think* instincts kicked into gear. He let out a low sound in the back of his throat, and his lips parted, opening to the kiss and the woman offering it. His hand went to the back of her neck, and Hollyn whimpered, her grip on his shirt tightening. Their tongues touched, and the alcohol-induced warmth in his body heated into something entirely different. Fire raced through him, and he tipped her head back, deepening the kiss and savoring the sexy groan she made and the sweet bourbon taste of her.

Heat flooded lower, the front of his jeans tightening. His fingers tangled in her hair. He wanted to lay her down on this floor, straddle her properly, hear those *Oh God* sounds she'd made earlier for real. But a thought hung on.

The sweet bourbon taste of her.

The sweet *bourbon* taste of her.

Shit. Jasper pulled back, his heart beating fast and his blood pumping hard. Hollyn's eyes blinked open, a dazed look of shock there. *Shit. Shit. Shit.* He was kissing a woman he'd just fed shots to. A woman he was supposed to be teaching, not trying to get naked.

He scooted back. "I...uh..."

A look of panic flashed over Hollyn's face and then her cheeks went apple red. "I..." She cleared her throat and looked down, pretending to button up her shirt. *"I have one question. Did I get the part?"*

Jasper stared at her for a moment and then it registered. She'd given him another line. She was going back to the game. Or maybe that had all been part of the game, and he'd taken it too far? He'd kissed lots of improv partners onstage, but what he'd just done had been decidedly *not* a stage kiss.

He let out a tense breath and ran a hand through his hair. He tried to find a casual smile to plaster on his face, and he just hoped to God the half-hard state of his cock wasn't obvious in this position. "Wow, you, uh, really committed to that one. Good job!"

She rubbed her lips together and looked away. Her nose scrunched a few times in succession, and her fingers were moving in some kind of pattern against her thumb, like she was counting. He frowned. He was starting to learn the signs of her freaking out.

"I'm sorry," she said. "That was... I don't know what the hell that was."

"Bourbon, probably," he said, trying to keep his tone light. "You were in the moment. And don't apologize. I think we both got a little caught up in the scene. It happens."

Her gaze darted to his, a skeptical look on her face. "It does?"

"Sure," he said with a tight shrug. "I've kissed every one of my improv group onstage at some point, girls and guys." Not with tongue and he certainly didn't get hard kissing any of them, but he wasn't going to mention that part. "You do what will make the scene the best for the audience. It's all in good fun."

She rubbed the spot between her eyes. "Maybe drinking was a bad idea."

"Right." He cleared his throat and sat next to her, leaning against the wall. "But for what it's worth, you were great." He winced. "With the scene, I mean. Not the kissing."

She stiffened.

"Though that was fine, too," he said quickly. *Fine? What the fuck, Deares?* He was blabbering. *Hello, hole, let me dig you a little deeper.* "You know what I mean."

He didn't know what he meant, but maybe she had a better shot at deciphering it.

"I need to get going," she said, tone abrupt.

He looked over at her. "Oh. Already?"

"I… Yeah." She got to her feet, her movements a little jerky. "Thanks for the lesson."

He scrambled to stand. "Hollyn—"

She gave him a tight smile. "I'll see you tomorrow."

He frowned. "Are you okay to drive? I mean…the bourbon."

She was already walking over to grab her purse and bag off a chair. "I'm not drunk. And I walked to work today anyway."

"I can walk you home."

She hooked her bag over her shoulder. "No, I'm fine. It's fine. It's a short walk."

Shit. He'd screwed this all up. She was in full retreat. "Wait. Are we going to do another lesson?"

She looked away.

Dammit. "Hollyn, I'm sorry. This was my fault. I shouldn't have brought liquor into it, and I should've taken the suggestive ones out of the stack. Please don't let my screwup scare you away from the lessons."

She scoffed and finally looked at him. "Your screwup? Jasper, I *kissed* you. Literally less than an hour after you made it very clear that you have no interest in that *chick with issues*, I mauled you."

The words were like cold water in the face. "What? I never said—"

She groaned and tipped her head back. "Congratulations to me. I have the uncanny ability to turn an already awkward situation into a mortifying one. It's like some reverse superpower." She shook her head. "I can't do this."

"Sure you can. You—"

"No." She looked over at him, voice tired. "I can't do this *with you.*"

He frowned. "What does that mean?"

"It means—" She shook her head. "Never mind. I've got to go."

She turned to walk out, but he jogged over to her, grabbing her elbow before she could take another step. "Hold up. Don't leave yet. Tell me. What does that mean?"

Her eyes were shiny, her frustration all over her face. "It means I'm pathetic. It means I haven't learned my lesson from underneath that oak tree. I'm still that girl who wants the popular boy to kiss her. Only this time, I forced the issue even knowing outright that he's not interested."

Jasper's lips parted, the confession knocking him backward. She *wanted* him to kiss her? "Hollyn, I..."

"Please let go," she whispered. "Please don't make this more humiliating than it already is."

He released her elbow, and she spun and took a step toward the door.

"I kissed you back," he blurted out.

She paused, her back still to him. "What?"

"What I said about the stage-kiss thing was a lie. You don't use tongue in a stage kiss." He wet his lips. "I kissed you back. I wanted to."

"Jasper, you don't have to pretend—"

"I'm not. Jesus. I'm not *that* good of an actor."

She turned around, a confused wrinkle between her brows, her cheek twitching.

He let out a sigh and raked a hand through his hair. "Look, Hollyn, no bullshit, all right? I like you. As a person. As a writer. I think we could be good friends."

She winced.

"I'm not finished," he said, tone grim. "I like you as a person, but I also had exceptionally not-safe-for-work thoughts about you when you feigned that orgasm, and it only got worse when you kissed me. If you had looked down before I climbed off of you, you would've seen exactly how it affected me."

Her eyebrows shot up.

"But it's an epically bad idea for us to get involved that way," he said, forcing the words out when all he really wanted to do was haul her up against the nearest wall and kiss her until they were both dizzy. "I wasn't lying. I'm fresh from a breakup. My life is basically in shambles at the moment. And the last thing I need to do is drag someone into that with me. I'm not in a place to date anyone. I need to put everything I have into getting this theater thing to work. If I let anything physical happen between us, I'd just be using you, and I don't want to do that. You deserve so much more than that."

Hollyn was staring at him. Her neck was flushed, and her throat worked as she swallowed. "I see. So you'd just be using me for sex because you're attracted to me but wouldn't actually be interested in dating me?"

He grimaced. "Damn, it sounds even worse when you say it back to me."

"No, I appreciate your honesty," she said, voice strangely calm. She gave him a long look and then adjusted her bag on her shoulder. "Let's do another lesson tomorrow night."

The offer threw him a little. "Great. Yeah. Okay. We can... Oh, wait, no, we can't. I don't have the room reserved tomorrow."

"Oh." She frowned.

"We could use Fitz's place," he said without thinking.

"Fitz's place." She cocked a brow. "Isn't that *your* place?"

He cringed. God, he was making a mess of this. Tell a woman you want her but really just for the sex, not an actual relationship, and then invite her over to your place. *And the creepy douchebag award goes to...* "I mean, yes, technically, it's where I'm living. But I didn't mean it like how it sounded. Fitz has a huge apartment. There's open space in the living room that would work. I'm sure Fitz will be there, too. I can order pizza."

Hollyn gave him a considering look, her nose twitching a little.

Jasper couldn't get a read on her. He was happy she hadn't slapped him. He was even happier that she didn't want to quit their arrangement. But something had shifted in her. Maybe having it all out in the open and clearing the air took some of the awkwardness away. They were attracted to each other. Acting on it was a bad idea. Okay, done. *Moving right along, nothing to see here.*

She shifted on her feet. "Uh, sure. I guess that could work."

He let out a breath. "Okay, great. It's a—*Not* a date."

"Right." She smiled. "Glad we got this cleared up."

"Me too?" he said, hearing the lack of certainty in his own voice. He wasn't sure what they'd cleared up. Things felt messier than ever.

She lifted a hand. "See you tomorrow."

And with that, she turned on her heel and strode out, leaving him to wonder how the hell their lesson had ended like this.

chapter **fifteen**

"WHAT IS *THAT* SMILE FOR?" ANDI ASKED AS SHE SLIPPED into a small booth and sat across from Hollyn the next morning. Andi's maroon hair was covered with a flowered head scarf, making her look like some glamorous 1950s starlet about to take a drive in a convertible.

"Love the scarf," Hollyn said.

Andi patted her hair. "Thanks. It's a bad-hair-day lifesaver. So...the smile?"

Hollyn had arrived early at WorkAround and had already gotten her cup of coffee from a very busy Jasper. Then she'd taken a spot by the window to enjoy drinking it while she waited for Andi. The two of them had taken to meeting up in the mornings before heading to their offices. Hollyn still avoided talking to most people she passed in the morning and always grabbed the booth that was tucked away in a corner, but she marked it as progress nonetheless. She wasn't racing to her office first thing. Mary Leigh had told her during their last therapy chat that baby steps counted as steps. Baby steps still meant she was moving forward.

Hollyn set her cup on the table. "Was I smiling?"

"Yes. You were. Like you had a big, juicy secret that no one else is in on." Andi set her bag down. "Which means you need to spill whatever it is because I spent my night researching a horrible murder case—like gave-me-nightmares horrible—and I could use some sunshine. Tell me something good."

Hollyn frowned at her friend. "You sure you're okay? You want to talk about it?"

Andi looked up, her normally bright-blue eyes a little bloodshot. "I'll be fine. I just don't know how anyone can ever feel safe in this world. There's an open serial case in Mississippi right now where women are disappearing and showing up dead and dismembered. The police thought they had the killer in jail, but another woman was murdered and found near the Louisiana line while he was in custody. The victims were all members of a dating app, so they're looking to see if the killer is linked to that. I just... Dating shouldn't be a life-or-death gamble. Being alone forever doesn't sound great, but it sounds way better than dead on the side of the road. I'd make a cute spinster, right?"

"Andi—"

"I know I'm being dramatic, but it just freaked me out. It's one of those things you can't unknow. It makes dating feel like a literal minefield instead of a figurative one." She took a long sip of her coffee and then waved her hand. "But enough about my internal screaming. Tell me why you're smiling. Did your lesson go well last night?"

Hollyn leaned back in the seat, her hands wrapped around her coffee cup. "It went...interestingly."

Andi perked up. "Yeah? Tell me, tell me, tell me."

Hollyn glanced toward the coffee bar. Jasper was on the opposite side of the building, bustling behind the counter with a decent-size line of people to manage. She looked back to Andi, a hum of pleasure going through her that she had a girlfriend to share this with now. "Well, we may have drank a little and a scene may have gotten a little out of hand and I may have kissed him."

Andi gasped and then bounced in her seat. "Holls! You minx. I'm so proud."

Hollyn snorted. "I nearly died of embarrassment afterward. I'm not sure what came over me."

"Badass bravery, that's what," Andi said pointedly. "So, what did he do?"

Knocked me off my goddamned feet. Hollyn took a demure sip of her coffee, enjoying the bit of suspense. "Kissed me back."

"Ha! I knew it." Andi slapped her hand on the table. "No way was that dude hand-delivering coffee just to be helpful. He's got a thing for you. Did he finally ask you out?"

Hollyn gave her a rueful smile. "No, he basically said he wanted to sleep with me, but isn't in a place to date anyone right now so isn't going to use me like that."

Andi's lips formed an O. "Wow. He actually said that to you, like *out loud*?"

"Yep. He seems to have a thing for blatant honesty. I think he says everything that comes into his mind."

"Damn. I mean, yay, honesty. But maybe keep some things to yourself." She wrinkled her nose. "Way to make it awkward, dude."

Hollyn's fingers tapped along her cup. "I don't know. It was actually kind of amazing."

Andi tipped her head to the side. "Seriously?"

"I mean…" She frowned, trying to put together her thoughts on what she'd been feeling since Jasper had blurted everything out. "Everything felt so tense last night. I live my life walking on eggshells, but this felt even worse. Because beyond having to deal with my normal social anxiety, I was dealing with this crush I was trying to hide, too. It was like walking on eggshells while juggling and doing long division. That's why I drank the booze even when I knew it probably wasn't a good idea. I could barely breathe around him."

Andi sipped her coffee, listening intently. "Crushes are *the worst*."

"Right? But once he just put it out there—that he was feeling it, too, that he was having the same kinds of thoughts about me, it just…" Hollyn shrugged. "Took the air out of the too-full balloon."

Andi nodded and set her cup down. "I get that. Like naming Voldemort."

Hollyn blinked. "Huh?"

"Harry Potter," Andi said, giving her a look that said she was disappointed Hollyn hadn't immediately caught the reference. "There's that line about the fear of saying the name making the fear of the thing worse. You two Voldemorted the sexual tension between you. You took the power out of it. Like, *hey, we both have pants feelings for each other. Let's stop pretending we don't and deal with it so we can stop being so freaked out about it.*"

Hollyn smirked. "Oh, the pants feelings are still pretty powerful. At least on my side."

Andi laughed. "You know what I mean."

"Yeah, I think you're right, because it was like all of a sudden, I wasn't so nervous to be around him anymore. The playing field was leveled."

"Leveled?" Andi gave her a knowing grin. "I don't know. You sure you're not feeling a nice dose of feminine power right now? He wants you and is *having to resist* all that sexy, smart energy you're putting out. You're holding the cards."

Hollyn scoffed and lifted her hands, showing her palms. "I'm holding no cards. Did you miss the part about him not wanting to date anyone right now? The poker game has already ended. There will be no more kissing." She resisted glancing over at Jasper again. "But I'm glad it happened. I feel like I can actually get some use out of these lessons now without being locked up with all that anxiety. I obsess about what people are thinking of me. That's part of what makes it so hard to talk. But now I know what Jasper thinks, and I can trust that if I ask, he'll tell me. That's a game-changer."

Andi's eyes narrowed. "Come on. You're not feeling just a *little* powerful?"

Hollyn laughed and gave into the urge, looking over at Jasper again. "Okay, maybe a little."

Andi beamed. "Good. Make that boy *pine*, girl." She made air quotes with her fingers. "'Would only be using you for sex.'" She made a derisive sound. "What a dude thing to say. He didn't even consider that *you* may only want to use *him* for that, too. Like men have cornered the market on that."

"I—" But Hollyn's voice cut off when Andi's words registered.

"Hmm?" Andi asked, looking at Hollyn over the rim of her coffee cup.

Hollyn gave Jasper a long look, watching as he leaned onto the counter, bicep flexing, hair falling across his forehead. Warmth tracked over her, settling low. "Nothing."

"So when's your next lesson?"

Hollyn dragged her attention back to her friend. "Tonight."

"Nice. What are y'all working on?"

"I'm not sure." An idea flitted through Hollyn's head. A dangerous one. "But I may have some suggestions."

....

"We having a party or are you just really hungry?" Fitz asked, eyeing Jasper as he stepped into the kitchen.

"I have a friend coming over tonight from WorkAround," Jasper said, dropping three large pizza boxes onto the kitchen island. "But I got enough for you, if you want any."

"Thanks. Who's coming?"

The scent of the pizza made Jasper's stomach rumble. "You might know her. Hollyn, the woman with the curly blond hair who works on the second floor?"

Fitz pulled a bottle of water out of the fridge and turned toward Jasper. "I don't know her personally, but I've seen her around. Hot date? Need me to be scarce?"

Jasper rubbed the back of his neck. "Not a date. I'm giving her some private improv lessons."

Fitz gave him a sly smile. "Private lessons, huh?"

"Don't give me that look. It's not like that." Though, it sort of was last night. "But we're going to be using the living room and she's...shy. Hence the private lessons. So..."

Fitz took a long gulp of water and then gave him a salesman smile. "Don't overwhelm her with my sparkling personality and good looks?"

Jasper pointed at him. "Bingo. Part of the reason she's doing these lessons is because being in front of people makes her nervous, so I don't want her to feel like she has an audience tonight. She's not ready for that."

Fitz lifted the lid on one of the pizza boxes and grabbed a slice. "No worries. I'll say hi and get out of your way."

Jasper braced his hands on the counter, frowning. "Thanks, man. I feel shitty asking. This isn't my place and—"

"Jas, shut up," Fitz said and took a bite of pizza. "Stop acting like I'm giving you charity. You're paying your way here with the piece of your future business. Take the living room. It's yours to use." He lifted a brow. "Just don't screw on the couch. I don't need to walk in and be traumatized by your bare ass on my new furniture."

Jasper flipped him off. "I already told you. Not that kind of private lesson."

Fitz tilted his head, his expression mocking. "Pity. You seem tense."

The doorbell rang, and Jasper left Fitz chuckling in the kitchen. He strode toward the front door, his shoes squeaking against the shiny hardwood floor, and opened the door to Hollyn. Even though he'd known it would be her on the other side, seeing her almost felt like a surprise. For a second, he just looked at her, taking in the casual version of her as if the door had framed her portrait.

Her hair was pulled up into a messy bun, and she had traded the black jeans and T-shirt she'd worn to work for a pair of white shorts and a sleeveless pink top. Her flesh-toned bra strap was visible, and her lips were shiny with that barely there gloss she always wore. *Strawberry-flavored gloss.* He ignored the sneaky whisper of desire that went through him at the memory of tasting her, at the sounds she'd made when they kissed. He also forced himself not to let his eyes travel down her bared legs. He cleared his throat. "Hey."

"Hey." She smiled tentatively, her cheek twitching, and held out a white box. "I brought petit fours from McKenzie's."

"Payment in tiny cakes," Jasper said, taking the box and wondering if Hollyn had brought a gift to avoid the should-we-hug-or-not-hug question. "I approve. Come on in."

Hollyn stepped inside, shutting the door behind her, and followed him through the foyer, but she halted when they reached the living room. "Holy shit."

"I know. It's ludicrous," he said, turning to her. "Blame Fitz. I told you we'd have room for lessons here."

"Blame me for what?" Fitz asked, stepping out from the kitchen, barefoot and holding a fresh slice of pizza.

Hollyn visibly tensed and her nose twitched. Without thinking, Jasper put his arm around her in a side hug, wanting to calm her. "Fitz, this is Hollyn Tate. She's a writer who works on the second floor. Hollyn, this is Fitz McLane, benevolent ruler of the fourth floor."

Fitz smiled his we're-all-friends-here smile and put his hand out to her. "Pleasure to meet you, Hollyn."

"Same," she said, her body stiff against Jasper's side but her voice pleasant and friendly. "Thanks for letting us commandeer the living room for the night. Your place is gorgeous."

Jasper lowered his arm to his side, knowing he'd already made it weird.

"Thanks. And not a problem. I have a binge watch of *Red Valley* planned," Fitz said. "The TV in my room is better."

"Ooh," Hollyn said, some pep coming into her voice. "That's a great show. Have you seen it before?"

"Nope."

"Oh, wow. I'm jealous you get to see it for the first time. The fifth episode is some of the best television I've seen this year. The plot surprised me in the best way, and the acting is killer," she said, her tics calming for the moment. "Just plan to be up late because they'll get you with the shameless cliff-hanger endings."

Jasper's eyebrows lifted at Hollyn's enthusiasm.

Fitz rubbed a hand over the back of his close-cropped hair, giving Hollyn a more intent look. "Man, now I'm even more jazzed to watch it."

"Hollyn reviews movies and TV shows as part of her job," Jasper said proudly.

"Yeah?" Fitz asked, looking genuinely interested—maybe a little *too* interested. "I'm a TV junkie. You should let me treat you to coffee one day at work, and we can nerd out."

Hollyn's fingers tapped against the side of her leg, but she smiled. "Sounds nerdy."

Jasper noticed she'd dodged the invitation. Despite Fitz's good intentions, he'd put Hollyn on the spot. "Well, we better get to work," Jasper said, giving his flirty friend a cease-and-desist look. "Enjoy your binge watch, Fitz."

Fitz huffed a quiet laugh at Jasper's not-so-subtle dismissal. "Will do, brother. You kids have fun."

Fitz headed down the hallway that led to his bedroom, and Hollyn's shoulders lowered a fraction. Jasper led her to the kitchen and set the pastry box on the island next to the pizzas. He sent her an apologetic look. "Sorry about that. I told him you were shy with new people, but Fitz probably saw that as a challenge. He won't bug you about having that coffee."

She lifted a shoulder and leaned back against the counter. "It's okay. He's nice. I have to learn how to talk to people at some point."

"You actually did great," Jasper said, handing her a paper plate and then opening a pizza box to offer it to her. "You lit up when you started talking about TV."

She took a slice of veggie lover's and put it on her plate. "It's my comfort zone."

"Yeah, but that bodes well for your videos. You'll be talking about things you're into." He grabbed a slice for himself and took a quick bite before speaking again. "If you can talk about it on camera like you talked to Fitz, you're halfway there." He pointed his pizza at her. "Hell, maybe you *should* have that coffee with him. You can practice your shop talk."

"Maybe," she said, unsure.

"Just don't let him use that as a sneaky way to ask you out. He's a charming fucker. You'll be agreeing to have his firstborn child before you know what's happened."

She swallowed her food and smirked. "So now you get to determine who can and can't ask me out?"

He frowned, his pizza slice halfway to his mouth. "I didn't mean... Wait, do you *want* him to ask you out?"

Jasper didn't like the burn that caused in his stomach. Why *wouldn't* she want that? Fitz was a good-looking, friendly guy. He was damn successful. He'd treat her well.

Jasper hated the idea immediately. He wanted to murder that idea, bury it deep in the ground, and salt the earth.

"That's not the point," she said. "And it doesn't matter anyway. I'm not ready for that kind of thing yet."

Jasper set his plate down, his appetite waning. "What kind of thing?"

"Going out with someone. I would probably have a panic attack before the appetizers hit the table," she said grimly. "I don't date."

She folded her pizza New York style and took too big of a bite, like she wanted her mouth to be too stuffed to continue this conversation.

But Jasper couldn't let that one go. "Wait. You don't date?"

She shook her head, her nose twitching.

"Like *at all*?"

She set her plate aside, finished chewing, and gave him an exasperated look. "Like ever. Do you have something to drink?"

"Uh, yeah. Bottled water, sparkling water, and beer."

"Sparkling."

Jasper went to the fridge and grabbed a random flavor of LaCroix, still hung up on what she'd said. He handed it to her. "You're serious."

She took the drink from him, her lips pursed. "Did you miss the part where I freeze up talking to people? Going on a date usually involves speaking to someone you're attracted to. Remember how I was when we met that first day? *That's* my body's reaction to attraction. Tics and then flight."

"Attraction." Her words made him perk up. "So that first day…"

She gave him an are-you-really-going-to-make-me-say-it look. "Yes, Jasper. I thought you were hot, and I completely panicked."

His lips parted. Closed again. "Wow." Then another thought hit him. "Wait. So…have you never, like, spent time…with anyone?"

She leaned back against the counter and took a long sip of the water before giving him a droll look. "Way subtle, Jasper. I know what you're asking. No, I'm not a virgin. I dated my best friend for about a year in college. But that's it."

It wasn't lost on him that her tics had decreased despite the personal topic of conversation. This was Hollyn. He'd somehow gotten into her safe zone, and he was seeing the real her, the one beneath the stranger anxiety. And what he saw there was fascinating and beautiful but also...lonely. Isolated. She hadn't been with anyone since she was in college? "So that kiss..."

She looked away. "It'd been a while."

"I couldn't tell."

She glanced up with a gimme-a-break glare. "Liar."

"I'm being serious." He laced his hands behind his head and let out a breath, absorbing all the information. "I had no clue. Honestly. That's...tough."

"It sucks," she said flatly and set her drink on the counter. "I had an idea, though. About how these lessons could help."

He lowered his arms to his side. "With the dating stuff?"

"Yeah."

"Well, I mean, if the improv makes you more comfortable thinking on your feet, I'm sure that will translate to—"

"No," she said, cutting him off. "My idea is that, well, it's about what you said last night."

His brow wrinkled. "What I said..."

She met his gaze, something defiant there. Her nose twitched. "I might want to use you, too."

He stared at her for a second, his mental GPS not tracking. "What's that now?"

She licked her lips and pushed a lock of hair that had escaped her bun behind her ear. Her gaze shifted to some spot off to the left of his shoes like she was losing confidence. "Last night, you said we shouldn't get involved because you didn't want to date anyone right now and that you'd just be using me for, you know, the physical stuff." She tapped a pattern on her thigh with her fingers. "You assumed I'm looking to date. That's not the case. I'm not prepared for that either. But I'm never going to be if I don't... work through some things."

Jasper's ears started to ring like he'd been to a loud concert. He wasn't hearing what he thought he was hearing. "Some things."

She pinched her temples. "God, this is hard to say and like super embarrassing, but I'm giving this blatant honesty thing of yours a shot." She took a deep breath. "I've been in therapy for this anxiety stuff for a while, but it can only do so much." She closed her eyes. "I literally ache, Jasper. To be touched. To have that skin-to-skin contact with someone I'm into. I'm alone *all the time*. A vibrator can take care of some things but can't fix what's wrong."

Fuck. The visual. His whole body lit on fire. "Hollyn—"

She looked up, cheeks scarlet, but her gaze resolute. Brave. "So if you weren't bullshitting me—if you're actually into me that way, but would just want the physical stuff, to use me for that— well...I'm kind of in a place where I *want* to be used. Where I want to use you in the same way."

He'd fallen asleep. That was the only explanation. He was on the couch, having some sort of erotic dream where Hollyn was begging him to touch her, telling him that she had an ache she wanted him to satisfy.

She closed her eyes and winced. "For the love of God, please say something before I suffer death by mortification right here in your kitchen."

Not a dream. He swallowed past his parched throat and ignored his thundering heart. "Don't do that. And please don't be embarrassed. I'm just...processing that a beautiful woman asked to use me for sex. I'm determining if I've suffered a head trauma. Maybe I should try to count backward by sevens from one hundred. One hundred...ninety-three..."

She put her hands over her face and laugh-groaned. "*Jasper.*"

He stepped forward and took her wrists, gently bringing her hands away from her face. "Come on, it's okay. Don't hide. Look at me."

Reluctantly, she opened one eye like she was afraid of what she'd find.

"You're serious about this?" he asked softly.

She finally met his gaze, her facial tics doing a little dance. "I know it's...unexpected. But once the idea got in my head, it started sounding more and more like an...elegant solution."

"An elegant solution." He hid his smile. This woman could be damn adorable.

"Yes." She shrugged a shoulder, the movement tight and self-conscious. "You're going through some stuff and are on the rebound, and you don't want the strings that come along with relationships. But I'm guessing sex is still something you would like to have on occasion?"

"I'm twenty-five and male. So, pretty solid assumption."

"And I want that, too, but I'm not ready to tackle the dating scene," she said, not pulling her wrists from his gentle grip. "There are so many paths to navigate with that. Even Andi, who's literally the most socially comfortable person I've ever met, is struggling with dating. I'll drown. I just want to...practice with a guy I'm comfortable with who, you know, happens to be really hot."

His eyebrows lifted. "You think I'm *really* hot? Not just standard hot?"

She groaned and tilted her head back. "You are the worst. No fishing for extra compliments, Deares."

"Hey, if you're not going to tell me how great I am in bed, this deal is off," he said in a haughty tone. "I expect effusive praise before, during, and after, preferably at high volume so the neighbors can hear."

She shoved him in his shoulder, his fingers still around her wrist. "You're teasing me. You think I'm ridiculous."

"No, I think you're ridiculously sexy. And brave. And I think the universe might possibly be paying me back for the early years." He released her wrists and stepped back to give her a little space. "But I want to make sure I understand what you're proposing here. You're talking a friends-with-benefits kind of situation?"

Her forehead scrunched. "Sort of. But maybe a little more… instructive? Like role-playing. Or a dress rehearsal for the real show."

After his mind took a brief jaunt to a very dirty place at the word *role-playing*, her meaning sank in. "Like improv for dating?"

She cringed. He couldn't tell if it was a tic or a reaction. "That sounds so weird." She shook her head and pushed away from the counter. "Maybe I *am* ridiculous. Let's just forget we had this talk, mmkay? I've hit my pathetic-meter limit for the day. Can we just get to the improv games and pizza?"

This was a bad idea. Not a ridiculous one—a perilous one. He was not prepared for this. Monique had already warned him not to get involved with Hollyn. He had yet to meet a relationship he couldn't destroy or that wouldn't destroy him. He didn't want to hurt her.

He should let her run.

Run, Hollyn, run.

He grabbed her hand.

chapter **sixteen**

HOLLYN WAS READY TO BOLT AND LEAVE A HOLLYN-SHAPED hole in the door. This had seemed like a good idea at the time, but now that she'd said everything out loud and had seen the shocked look on Jasper's face, she realized how bent she sounded. Mary Leigh was going to have a field day with this one in their next session. *So what'd you do this week? Oh, just shamelessly threw myself at a guy and asked to use him for sex.*

She tried to stride past Jasper, but he grabbed her hand as she passed, halting her. "Hey." He tugged her back closer, his hazel eyes intent. "Don't run. I was clarifying, not criticizing."

"You don't have to—"

He leaned down and touched his lips to hers, effectively shutting her up with the soft press of his mouth. Her body went still and hot, and she forgot to close her eyes.

He pulled back and smiled a half smile. "I'm in."

She released a sharp breath, her heart hammering, her body just catching up to the kiss. "*You are?*"

"Yeah." He pulled her against him, linking his arms around her waist and giving her a very serious, un-Jasper-like look. "I'm not going to pretend I'm an expert at dating rituals. And I blow at relationships. Awards could be given for how bad I am at them.

But if you mean you want to practice feeling comfortable around someone, flirting, kissing, touching..." His gaze tracked over her face. "Sex, if that's where it leads."

If that's where it leads... Her blood was pumping, her nipples sensitive against his chest, and her skin warm in all the right places. Her body was already leading that particular parade straight to the bedroom.

"Then, yes, I'm game. Very happily game," he said. "I just... don't want to risk hurting you. This won't—can't—turn into anything more than a friendship."

She nodded, truly listening. Her mother had once told her that people tell you who they are if you listen closely. Jasper was telling her he was a leaver. She had to be okay with that. "I know. I'm not here for that. This isn't some bait and switch."

He gave her a rueful look. "I'm saying that as much for myself to hear. I have my own confession."

Her brows lifted. "Oh?"

"Yep. Truth be told, I've never done the casual hookup thing."

She scoffed. "Don't bullshit me."

He held her eye contact, no jest there. "No bullshit. Blatant honesty night, right?"

She nodded.

"I've gone on dates with people that didn't turn serious, but when I start sleeping with someone, I see it as a relationship." His fingers absently traced a circle on her lower back, sending tingles along her spine. "I mean, I tried once. I had a one-night stand when I was in college. She snuck out after I fell asleep—pretty standard operating procedure in college. But the way I felt when I woke up..." His fingers stopped moving. "Well, it felt like shit. I knew I didn't want to do that to anyone else. And I didn't want to experience feeling left like that again."

Feeling left. The words made her think of what he'd said about his birth parents and his foster homes. Suddenly, it made sense. Sure, Jasper was charming and a performer and could probably have a regular rotation of one-night stands, but constantly saying goodbye would take its toll. Feeling abandoned would feel too familiar. He'd had a lot of goodbyes. A lot of people had turned him away. She pressed her hands against his chest. "I get that. And if this feels like that, then please—"

"It doesn't," he said. "This feels like…two friends helping each other out. Like"—he gave her a playful look—"an elegant solution."

She considered him. "Two friends helping each other out. How am I helping you? Wait—I can't exchange sex for a good Miz Poppy review."

He grimaced. "Whoa. I swear that wasn't in my head at all. You don't have to give us a review. I'll figure something else out to get us some publicity."

She frowned. "Then what's in this for you?"

"Is that supposed to be a serious question?" When she shrugged, he let out a sound of disbelief and touched his forehead to hers. "Fuck, Hollyn. You really need to take a hard look at yourself. You're hot as hell. And smart. And funny. Plus, you have an exceptionally nice ass. Like top-notch."

She laughed, her head dipping.

"But besides all that," he continued. "I'm getting over a breakup. Having someone to hang out with who I can also kiss and touch without any worry of drama or the weight of heavy history—that's a pretty fantastic deal."

They were so close, she could feel his breath tickling her cheek, his heart beating against her chest—quick and strong. "Yeah?"

"Of course."

She licked her lips. "I can still give you a review, you know. I'll just have to put a footnote disclosing that I'm friends with one of the members."

He brushed a thumb over her cheek. "I don't want you to feel like you owe me that."

"It's something I want to do. I was going to review you from the start. And I'll still be honest."

"You're amazing." He put a finger beneath her chin and tipped her face toward him. Her breath stalled as he stared down at her. "I'm going to kiss you again. Possibly with tongue this time. You've been warned."

She wet her lips, her heartbeat jumping into her throat. "To seal the deal?"

"No, because I want to kiss you like I did last night and not have to pretend it's because of a scene." Then he leaned down and closed the last of the space between them.

The feel of his mouth on hers was nothing like the chaste kiss from a minute ago. This one had intent, purpose, promise of more things to come. Desire wound through her bloodstream like a drug, making her limbs go heavy. She let out a soft whimper against Jasper's mouth, the tension in her body unwinding. He slowly backed her up against the counter and slid a hand to the nape of her neck as he deepened the kiss. His tongue parted her lips, and her hands tracked further up his chest, his taut muscles flexing beneath the fabric. Her fingers curled. His T-shirt was soft and warm in her hands as she gripped it, holding him in place, only half-believing that this was actually happening.

His tongue stroked against hers, and he made his own sound of pleasure as he clasped her neck with gentle pressure and aligned his body with hers. When she shifted, she felt the hard length of him against her hip and gasped. A rush of sensation went through her. Any lingering doubt she'd been harboring about his attraction to her burned up in the electric space between them. He *wanted* her. No. He wanted *her*.

Enough that he'd been willing to sacrifice a review that could bring his group a lot of attention.

Riding a surge of bravery, she let her hands track down and slip beneath the hem of his T-shirt. The smooth heat of his bare skin branded her fingertips, the muscles in his abdomen flexing against her touch. She had the sudden, intense desire to lick along the path her fingers traced, to know the taste of his skin. She resisted. Barely.

There'd be time for that. There'd be time for *everything*. The thought sent a wash of pleasure and hot anticipation through her, her body going slick and needy at the possibilities.

Jasper broke away from the kiss but only to move to a spot along her jaw. "You ache to be touched?" he asked, voice roughened. He pressed his mouth softly along her jawline and then to the sensitive spot behind her ear. "Like here?"

"Yes," she answered in a whisper, her head tilting back, her belly fluttering.

He kissed down her neck, along her collarbone. "And here?"

"So many places," she said, her nails scraping gently over his stomach.

His hand traced up her side slowly beneath the hem of her shirt, giving her time to stop him. When she didn't, he continued higher and cupped her breast, the thin lace of her bra doing nothing to shield her from the heat of his touch. His thumb circled over her nipple just as he pressed his lips against her throat. She groaned from deep inside her gut.

Her body was on fire. Throbbing. Aching. Ready.

"Jesus," she said, breathless. The stroke of his thumb over her nipple, the heat of his palm cupping her breast, the hard length of him pressed against her were like an avalanche to her system, every nerve ending activating, her skin hypersensitive. It'd been so long. So. Long. *Years*. Since a guy had touched her like this. The sensations overwhelmed her, shooting straight downward and lighting up every deprived part of her. *Please. Please. Please.* Every cell of her being was begging for relief. Her inner muscles clenched involuntarily. Her breath quickened in a very specific way.

Holy hell.

That couldn't be what it felt like, right? That was impossible. But she felt on the verge of something, overwhelmed by the sensations. "Jasper. Please."

She had no idea what she was asking of him. Just that she needed *something*.

Jasper shifted his position and pinched her nipple, rolling it between his fingers, and his erection pressed against the apex of her thighs, right where she needed the pressure. Hard. Thick. Hot. The cotton of her shorts and panties did nothing to blunt the reaction. Something inside her detonated, and she let out a sharp cry as her body spasmed in places he hadn't touched yet. She gripped the waistband of his jeans, holding on as the sensation rumbled through her and her knees went weak. *Holy shit. Holy shit. Holy shit.*

She held on, swallowing down the louder sounds that tried to escape, and Jasper lifted his head, surprise on his face. "Hollyn?"

She turned her face away, embarrassed, as she tried to discreetly pant her way through the last vestiges of the orgasm and not rut her hips against him like some animal in heat. "I... It's hot in here."

He blinked. "Did you just..."

Her hands slipped from his waistband. "I think I need some air."

He released her and took a step back, but she still couldn't look at him—especially at the impressive outline in his jeans. Her body gave another jolt. *God.* Was she so deprived of touch that a guy copping a feel could send her over the edge?

She looked down, trying to come up with something to say.

"You came," Jasper said, almost in wonder.

"Jasper," she warned, her gaze firmly on a spot on the floor.

He reached out and took her hand. "Hey." He wiggled her arm playfully. "Look at me."

She flexed her jaw and turned her head. Her facial tics were going wild. She probably looked like a rabbit having a seizure. "Can we not... Can we just...move on?"

He smiled a melt-her-panties-off smile. "No, we cannot." He traced a finger over her twitching cheek. "That was the sexiest fucking thing I've ever seen. You came from me touching you over your clothes. I think we both get sex merit badges for that or something. That's like a survive-the-apocalypse skill. We could get off while running from the zombies without ever having to take our clothes off. Go, us."

She snort-laughed. "You're seriously bent."

His smile went even wider. "I can't wait to see what happens when you actually get to see me naked."

She groaned and then shoved him. "Narcissist."

"Hey, I just made a woman come from a kiss. This is life news. I'm apparently a sexual dynamo. A gift to women, really. Who knew?"

"Hey." She poked his shoulder. "Only *I* get the badge. You didn't actually come. Slacker."

"Oh, is that the requirement?" He crowded her against the edge of the counter again and braced an arm on each side of her, caging her in, a wicked grin on his face. "Don't worry. I will later." He gave her an up-and-down once-over. "All I'll need to do is think about the look you just had on your face, and I'll be good to go."

Her smile fell, and she licked her lips at the image of Jasper touching himself while thinking of her. Her arms were trapped between their bodies. She boldly brushed her knuckles against the length of his erection. "I might be able to help with things."

Jasper let out a soft groan and gave her a heated look, no more humor there. "I want to say yes to that more than I can possibly describe, but I don't want to fuck this up by rushing. I don't want you to wake up tomorrow and regret that we moved too fast. We have time. Plus, you want to learn about dating, right?"

She swallowed hard. "Yes."

"Well, lesson one: Don't date a guy who requires a tit-for-tat even orgasm exchange. This isn't a bank transaction, and an orgasm isn't a favor. Find a guy who thinks making a woman come is its own reward." He kissed the tip of her nose. "That was crazy hot. You don't owe me a thing."

The words only made her want to touch him more. "I wasn't offering out of obligation. But"—she sighed heavily—"maybe you're right. I don't want this to be a close-my-eyes-and-jump-off-a-cliff thing. If I rush it, my panic might kick in and send me into hiding."

He dipped down to brush his lips over hers. "Slow and deliberate then," he said, voice low. "I can definitely get on board with being slow and very, very deliberate with you."

A hot shiver worked its way through her. The thought of Jasper slowly and deliberately kissing down her body had her heartbeat quickening again. She put her hands to his chest and gently pushed. "We better get to work or I can't be held responsible for what happens next."

He stepped back with a smile. "I know. I'm sorry I'm so irresistible. It's a burden."

She grabbed a napkin from the counter, balled it up, and launched it at him. "Literally, the worst."

He caught the paper missile in the air and his smile softened.

She shifted to walk past him.

"Hey," he said, halting her.

She met his gaze. "Yeah?"

"Thank you."

She tilted her head. "For what?"

"The trust." He hooked his thumbs in his pockets like he was resisting reaching out for her again. "All joking aside, I know this was a big, fucking brave thing you did—asking to do this. So thank you for thinking I'm worthy of your trust. It's rare that anyone throws that kind of thing my way."

She frowned.

"I know it's hard to believe." He gave a self-deprecating smirk. "But people seem to think of me as flighty and self-involved. Only half-true, obviously."

He had a teasing tone but the words sent a pang through her. "Jasper..."

"But I want you to know," he said, gaze serious, "you can be whoever you really are with me. No judgments, no fake bullshit, no games. Just like in the improv scenes, I want you to know you're safe. If you're scared, tell me. If something isn't working, tell me. If I'm doing something wrong, tell me. I've got you."

The words were exactly what she didn't know she needed to hear. Something unlocked inside her, letting her take a deep breath. They were going to try this unconventional experiment, and it would be okay. Jasper wasn't going to make fun of her or talk shit about her to his bros. He wasn't going to pretend to be interested, only to show up with a rodent beneath a tree.

"Thank you." She stepped closer to him and kissed him on the cheek. "Your dirty talk is on point, Jasper Deares."

He laughed and gave her an illicit look. "Oh, you have no idea, Hollyn Darling."

They grabbed the boxes of pizza and moved to the living room. For the rest of the night, they worked on improv scenes, and Hollyn forgot to be nervous. She forgot to apologize for her awkwardness. She forgot to be self-conscious about her tics. For those few hours, she forgot about everything except the fact that, at least for a little while, she could have fun and be fully herself with a guy she liked.

Normal.

Free.

chapter **seventeen**

JASPER FIDDLED WITH THE TRIPOD IN THE VIDEO ROOM that was meant to hold smartphones, but he couldn't get the thing to clamp the right way. The tripod tipped over, bringing his phone with it. "Oh come on, you piece of sh—"

A light knock from behind him had him cutting off his invective and turning his head. Emily had poked her head in the doorway, her black ponytail swinging sideways. "Need some help?"

Jasper frowned as he rescued his phone from the floor. "That obvious?"

Emily pinched her thumb and forefinger together. "Just a little." She stepped inside, her heels going quiet on the carpet. "What are you trying to do? An improv video?"

"Sort of." Jasper righted the tripod as Emily stopped next to him, hands on her hips, the crisp scent of her perfume filling the room. "Hollyn and I are working on a little project."

"You and Hollyn." She gave him a skeptical look. "Doing a project together?"

He felt his hackles rise. "Yeah. Why?"

"Nothing. Just the first time I saw you two in the same room, she hauled ass in the other direction. Here, let me." Emily put her hand out for his phone, demanding more than asking. He gave it

YES & I LOVE YOU | 183

to her, and she went about securing it in the tripod with a practiced ease that said she could do it in her sleep. "I thought she didn't like you. Or, you know, anyone."

Jasper tried to pay attention to what Emily was doing so he could do it for himself next time. "It was a misread. She's just quiet. She's actually pretty cool once you get to know her."

"Huh." Emily angled the phone just so and then tapped her fingers against her lips, pondering the area to be filmed. "Go stand over there for a sec. Be my model."

Jasper walked over and stood in front of the white wall.

"Do you have any particular background in mind?" she asked, adjusting the phone again. "They have a green screen you can use. You can superimpose any background onto it."

"Nah. This is just practice so we don't need any effects."

"Okay, just good lighting then." Emily went to the wall and flipped a few switches. A bright ring light glowed to life. Jasper squinted in the white light as she walked back to the tripod and looked at his phone screen. "Smile pretty."

Jasper obliged, amused by Emily's no-nonsense instructions, and he pretended to flip his hair and bat his eyelashes. "I'm ready for my close-up."

"Very nice. You look good on-screen. That light makes your eyes stand out," she said with a tone a doctor would use to declare he'd passed his physical. She adjusted something on his phone screen and frowned. "You know, I have a real camera. You can borrow it if you want—as long as I can set it up, because if you break it, then I'd have to murder you."

Jasper laughed. "Thanks but I won't risk death. I actually bought a DSLR recently, but today's supposed to be a quick test run. For what we're doing, the phone is fine."

He wasn't even sure he and Hollyn were going to hit the record button today. Hollyn had done well a few nights ago when they'd run scenes at Fitz's, but he suspected the post-orgasm relaxation effect had something to do with that. When he'd told her he wanted to try some camera stuff today, she'd sounded less than enthused. He smiled. Maybe he'd just have to get creative to help her loosen up again...

"Is it just going to be you two in here today?" Emily asked.

The question startled Jasper out of his dirty thoughts. "Huh?"

"Is it just going to be you and Hollyn in here?" she asked again as she futzed with the lights, her eyes narrowing each time she adjusted something.

"Uh, yeah," he said, sensing there was a question within the question. Maybe she'd sensed his R-rated thoughts about what he and Hollyn *could* do in here with a locked door. "Why?"

She glanced over at him and shrugged. "No reason. I just see you chatting with Fitz McLane all the time. I didn't know if he was part of this project."

"Oh, no, not part of this," Jasper said, watching her as she plugged a wire on the tripod into something that made the camera view come up on a computer monitor. "But we're old friends, and I'm staying at his place."

"Wait." Her attention jumped his way, her ponytail whipping around. "You're his roommate?"

Jasper's eyebrows lifted at her breathless tone. *Oh.* He hid a smile. "Yeah, why?"

She bit her lip and then straightened as if remembering her normally perfect posture. "No reason. I was just...curious."

He folded his arms. "Curious."

"I mean," she said, pushing a stray hair away from her face, clearly flustered. "I was only wondering because I'd like to interview him for my vlog. You know, he's gotten so much accomplished so young, and I know he's probably got a ton of productivity hacks to share."

Jasper looked down, hiding his laugh as he stepped away from the lights. The idea of Fitz having some detailed productivity system was amusing, but more entertaining was Emily's paper-thin story. Ms. Put Together was blushing to her roots. "Well, I can get you an introduction if you want. I don't know his schedule, but I bet he can make some time for you."

She lifted up on her toes like an excited kid. "Really?"

"Of course." He went to the camera and checked the view. *Perfect.* He turned back to Emily to thank her for her help, but she surprised him by throwing her arms around him in a hug.

"Thank you so much," she said, giving him a squeeze.

A little startled by the normally formal Emily being so effusive, he awkwardly patted her on the back. "No problem."

"Oh, um, hey," a familiar voice said. "I–I can come back."

Jasper looked over to the doorway, his arm still loosely around Emily, and found Hollyn staring at them, a frown on her face, her cheek twitching.

"No, you're right on time," Jasper said.

Emily released him immediately and gave him a chagrined smile. "Sorry. I'll… I'm going to go. Just let me know. Do you need my number?"

Hollyn looked off to the side, her hands clasping her elbows tight. "Really, I can—"

Oh, hell no. That resignation in her voice wouldn't do. Jasper stepped around Emily to get to Hollyn. He reached up, cupped her chin to turn her face toward him, and planted a quick kiss on her lips. "Hey, gorgeous. Just give me a sec."

She blinked up at him in shock, and he turned back to Emily, whose eyebrows had disappeared beneath her bangs. "Just bring me a business card the next time you get coffee. I'll pass it along."

Emily gave a little nod, her curious gaze darting between him and Hollyn. "Great."

Jasper smiled. "Thanks again for your help."

"Anytime." Emily moved toward the door, offering Hollyn a conspiratorial smile. "Good luck with the project. I'll put the *Occupied* sign on the door."

Hollyn's nose wrinkled and she grimaced, her tics making her look annoyed. "Thanks."

Emily slipped out of the room, letting the door shut behind her. Hollyn's cheeks were pink when she turned back to him. "I didn't mean to interrupt."

"You didn't," he said, reaching past her to lock the door. "Emily was helping me set up the camera."

"Sure," she said, sounding skeptical. "That's...nice of her."

"She is nice—in this sort of blunt, take-charge kind of way," he said. "Though I don't know if it was totally altruistic this time. I think she's got a thing for Fitz. Wanted me to set up an intro."

Hollyn's attention flicked upward, finally letting him see her eyes. "Oh. Fitz."

"Yeah." His lips curved, a wash of pleasure going through him at Hollyn's obvious relief. "What? You thought she was hitting on me?"

Her cheek twitched. "I—"

"Emily's nice, but I can assure you that Ms. To-Do List would want nothing to do with someone like me—unless she was going through a rebellious phase." He shrugged. "Fitz the CEO is much more her type."

Hollyn tilted her head. "You disappointed by that?"

Her line of questioning surprised him. Did she really think he was interested in Emily? He'd wanted nothing else but to kiss *Hollyn* when she'd walked in the room wearing a navy-blue wrap dress that looked like it'd come off with one tug on the knotted belt holding it together. "Nah, we can't all be successful CEOs. There have to be some guys around to provide women with the opportunity to make bad decisions and have morning-after regrets. Or to have improv dating lessons with."

She shook her head and then rubbed the spot between her brows. "I'm sorry. This is a weird situation. I didn't mean to act like the jealous girlfriend or whatever. You can like who you want to like. Obviously."

"Good. Because I like you. But it is cute that you got jealous." He put his hand to his chest. "I feel so special."

She gave him a petulant look. "Don't be a dick, Deares."

He laughed and pulled her against him, relishing the soft feel of her. He loved that he could do that now—touch her, be in her space. Improv dating was like eating candy without the calories. They could have fun without all the serious shit. "I'm this close"—he pressed his thumb and forefinger together—"to getting the beautiful and talented Miz Poppy into my bed. Why would I waste my time flirting with other women?"

Her brow arched. "You do realize that you wouldn't be getting Miz Poppy into bed, right? No confident cartoon vixen is going to appear. This is what you get. Just me."

He frowned at the implication. "I'm very aware of who I want in my bed. I don't follow your posts because of your image. I follow it because of your thoughts, your attitude. That's all you, Hollyn Tate."

She blinked up at him.

"And I hate to break it to you"—he rubbed his thumb along the small of her back—"but you're way hotter than that cartoon image."

She released a breath. "Oh."

"So," he said, trying to read her expression. "We good? Or would you like me to do a formal presentation on why I'd like to lick all of your body parts?"

She laughed, the sound muffled by the acoustic paneling in the room, and a blush stained her cheeks. "Well, maybe we could skip the presentation and just have a demonstration later."

The answer made his blood heat. He wanted to pick her up and take her back to his place right this very second to start that demonstration. He brushed his lips over hers and let his hand drift over the curve of her ass, making his groin tighten. But he let his hand drop before he took it further. Neither of them would get what they wanted if they started skipping the lessons. The physical stuff had to be secondary. Their jobs had to come first—or they'd both end up sex-sated but flat broke. "Noted. But we better get to work first. I only reserved the space for an hour."

She sighed. "Do we have to do the camera thing? Can't we just run scenes again?"

"Nope," he said, releasing her. "You're ready for the next level. But I promise whatever we record won't leave this room. I just want to get you used to the idea of being on camera. Of feeling its eye on you."

Her fingers tapped a pattern against her thigh. "I can't imagine ever getting used to that."

"The key is to know where it is but then to forget it's there." He reached out, took her elbow, and then hit a button on his phone with his other hand. "Just walk over here with me."

He led her to the lighted space in front of the camera. She gave him a panicked look. "Jasper, this feels—"

"Don't think about the camera right now," he said, turning to face her, the lights making her skin look luminescent and her eyes sparkle with starbursts. "Just keep looking at me."

"Jas—"

"We're going to play the ABC game," he said, his voice low and calm, his gaze locked on her. He needed that camera to fade into the back of her mind.

"I think I covered that in preschool."

"Not like this," he said with a smile. "We start with A, and then each line has to start with the next letter of the alphabet. Okay?"

She rolled her lips together and nodded but then glanced at the camera.

He gently touched her cheek and guided her attention back on him. "Eyes on me. ABCs, easy peasy. I'll start," he said. "All I wanted to do today was show you how the video room worked."

Her throat flexed as she swallowed, but she kept her focus on him. "But then I walked in on you with another woman."

Her voice was shaky and unsure, but he gave her an encouraging nod.

"Can't you see she means nothing to me?" he asked, using his dramatic soap-opera voice, trying to get her to see this was just a silly game, nothing to stress about.

She narrowed her eyes, slipping into character. "Don't tell me lies."

He took her hands in his. "Each time I see you, all I can think of is the way you looked when I made you come in my kitchen."

She glanced at the camera, but he lifted his hand to her cheek and drew her attention back to him again. She wet her lips. "For once, can we not talk about how great you think you are in bed?"

"Great?" he asked. "How would you know how great I am if you won't let me take you to bed?"

"If you would stop flirting with every woman who moved, maybe I'd give you a chance to show me," she countered, back in soap-opera form.

He pulled her closer. "Just give me a chance to prove how much I want you."

Her gaze held his, and she looked at a loss for a second.

He smiled. K really was a tough letter. He'd once randomly yelled out Kangaroo! in this game onstage.

"*Kiss* me," she said finally.

Well, then. That had worked out nicely. He leaned down, cupping her face and kissed her gently. He'd planned to make it brief, but when he nibbled her bottom lip and her lips parted, welcoming him, he couldn't resist. He deepened the kiss, sweeping his tongue against hers, and tasted the sweet, minty flavor of her mouth. She made a needy sound in the back of her throat, and the surge of desire that zipped through him was made of pure fire. His heartbeat picked up speed and blood rushed downward.

This woman pressed his buttons in so many ways. Sexy and smart, but more than that, he could feel her hunger vibrating in every move. He both hated and loved that she was so starved for this kind of touch. Hated that she'd been neglected but loving that he was the one she'd chosen to give her what she craved. Everything felt so intense and fresh. A kiss wasn't just a kiss with her. It was a full-out experience. She put everything she had into it, like she was drinking up the electricity between them. How long had it been since a kiss had made *him* feel that excited?

He pulled back, a little breathless, and smiled down at her. What the hell letter where they on again? *J*? *P*? No... "Luscious."

Her pupils were pinpricks in the bright lights and her eyes a mesmerizing green. She licked her already slick lips. "Maybe we should go back to my place?"

"Now?" he asked, watching her mouth, wanting it again. Against his lips. On his skin. Other fun and fabulous places.

"Or maybe we should just stay right here." She slid her arms around his neck, her breasts brushing up against his chest and making him grow hard behind his zipper.

"*Please* don't ever doubt how much I want you," he said, trying to remember the thread of the scene.

She met his gaze. "*Quit* talking."

"*Right*." He leaned in and kissed her again. This time he let his hands drift down her back and over the curve of her ass. He pulled her against him, letting her feel what the kissing was doing to him, and she whimpered into his mouth—one of the hottest sounds he'd ever heard. She rubbed her breasts against his chest, and without thinking he lifted her off her feet, wrapping her legs around his hips.

The flowy skirt of her dress slid up her legs, exposing hot, smooth thighs. He wanted to kiss his way up one and down the other. The scent of her arousal filled his head, and he lost his mind a little. He groaned, scene forgotten, and walked her over to the side wall, pressing her into the soft acoustic tiles and bracing her there as he let his hand track up her thigh. She made a soft, breathy sound and her hips bucked. Fuck, she was so sweet and pliant, so goddamned starved for pleasure. He wanted to make up for all the guys who'd dismissed her or walked on by because she was a little different, because she was shy, because she had some unruly muscles. Fucking idiots. This woman was a goddamned gift.

His hand slipped higher, his thumb tracing the edge of her panties. She shuddered in his one-arm hold, and he moved his thumb closer to her center. The thin fabric was damp and hot.

"Christ." He broke away from kissing her, and his cock flexed against his zipper, painfully hard.

"That doesn't. Start. With an *S*," she said between breaths.

"*Sorry. So soft. So sweet. So sexy.* Enough *S*'s for you, *sunshine*?"

She laughed this low, throaty laugh. "*Totally.*"

He feared if he stopped the game, she'd stop everything, start thinking. *U, U, U*... He set her down on her feet. "*Underwear* needs to come off."

Her eyes popped open, and she looked down at him as he crouched in front of her. "I...uh...*V. Very* risky."

He smiled. That wasn't a no. He got to his knees, slid his

hands up her thighs, and found the waistband of her panties. Without giving either of them too much time to think about it, he yanked them down and off.

"Want you," he said, slowly tugging on the tie of her dress. The knot came loose and the dress opened to him. Her fingers dug into the soft wall, but she didn't move to cover herself. Instead, she watched him and his hands. He took in every inch of the delicious view. Hollyn pressed up against the wall, cheeks flushed, lace-clad breasts exposed, smooth belly moving with quick breaths, and then...the sexy triangle of trimmed curls fully bared to him—*well*, that *w*as just a goddamned *w*onder. W, *w.w.* "Wow."

She was trembling and breathing hard, but her eyes were begging for what she needed. "X-rated," she said hoarsely. "This is X-rated."

"Yep." He dragged his knuckles over her center, pink and flushed and so fucking gorgeous. "Screw Z," he said, moving closer. "I'm ready to circle back to O."

chapter **eighteen**

HOLLYN HAD NO IDEA WHO HAD TAKEN OVER HER GOOD sense and replaced it with wild abandon, but there was no way she was moving from this spot, not with Jasper kneeling at her feet and looking at her like he was going to make every sordid fantasy she'd had about him come true. Never had she bared herself so brazenly for anyone. Bright lights. Pinned against a wall. Nowhere to hide. This couldn't actually be happening. They were supposed to be playing an improv game. They were at work. There was a—

Jasper's hot, wet tongue dragged over her center, and all her logic and reason obliterated into mist. Her head tipped back as her body quivered in response, and her hands went to his shoulders and gripped hard. No way were her knees going to hold up for this. Jasper groaned against her flesh like she was the most delicious morsel, and his lips found her clit, tasting her in the most intimate way possible. Lightning flashed through her bloodstream, making her gasp.

"So fucking sweet," Jasper murmured as he kissed and tasted her, his tongue and lips weaving magic that made every feminine part of her sing. He put his hand behind her knee and draped her leg over his shoulder, opening her fully to him, exposing her in a way that made her feel both self-conscious and exceptionally alive all at once. Her hand went to the back of his head, gripping his hair, and unconsciously guiding him where she needed him most.

Jasper didn't seem to mind being directed. If anything, the guttural sound he made said, *Yes, show me what you want. Yes, I'm the one who can give it to you.*

Hollyn's belly fluttered, her breath coming short and fast as he laved at her most sensitive bits with hungry strokes and slid a finger inside her. Her body clenched around his finger, the heat of him both foreign and welcome. She rocked her hips in an involuntary rhythm.

"Fuck yes," Jasper said, his breath painting her skin. "Come for me, gorgeous. Show me what you need."

She pressed the back of his head closer, and she could feel him smile against her before he used that wicked tongue on her again. He slipped another finger inside her, touching just where she needed, and the combination of that and his mouth was too much. The blinding lights of the small room split into colors behind her eyelids, and she cried out, her orgasm rolling through her like a thunderstorm, powerful and unstoppable.

Jasper rode out her jerky movements, continuing to pleasure her until the knee holding her up wobbled. He gently guided her other leg back to the floor, eased back, and stood, supporting her with an arm around her waist. He pushed a damp lock of hair away from her face and dipped down to kiss her.

He paused a breath from her lips, as if asking permission, and she closed the distance. Their mouths met in a hungry collision. The taste of herself on his lips made her shiver with an aftershock, and she let her hand slide down. The feel of his thick erection against her palm made her inner muscles clench again. She felt insatiable, greedy, like one orgasm wasn't enough. Like the years of deprivation deserved payback.

She rubbed him through his jeans, and he grunted against her lips. She broke away from this kiss. "Want you," she said, too blissed out to form complete sentences.

He looked down at her, his head haloed by the bright lights and his eyes dark, a ravenous look in them. "Hollyn, you don't—"

She pressed her fingers over his mouth. "Shut up, Deares. Do you have a condom?"

His Adam's apple bobbed and he nodded. "In my wallet."

She lowered her hand. "Do you want this to happen?"

"So much."

Feeling bold, she reached around him and grabbed his wallet from his back pocket. She fished out the condom and pressed it into his hand. "I don't need chivalry right now. I need you."

Something dark and determined flashed over his face. Selfish, even. He was going to take what he needed now, and she was so here for it. "Turn around, Hollyn. Hands on the wall."

Her heartbeat picked up speed, and her body pulsed with fresh need. She turned around and did as he said, her fingertips digging into the soft foam panels. Jasper stepped closer, the heat of his body radiating against her. His fingers slipped the dress from her shoulders and then he let it puddle on the floor.

"I want to see all of you," he said.

She didn't stop him as he unhooked her bra, leaving her in nothing but her sandals. A few feet away, the people of WorkAround were going about their business, passing this door with the *Occupied* sign, drinking their coffee. The knowledge both terrified her and thrilled her.

Jasper blew out a breath and traced a hand over her breast, her belly, her hip, his breath tickling her shoulder. "You're a fucking sight, Hollyn. I thought about you just like this after you left the other night. My imagination had no shot of conjuring how good the reality is."

She shifted under his perusal, her skin glazed with a fine sheen of sweat. "You thought about me?"

He pressed his clothed body against her bare backside. "I told you I would. I went into my room, locked the door, and imagined you like this—naked, wet, aching to come again. Then I wrapped my hand around my cock and came harder than I had in longer than I can remember."

Her forehead tapped the wall. "Shit, Jasper."

He kissed the curve of her neck. "Too much?"

She laughed under her breath. "No. But I'm nearly a born-again virgin. If we don't do this soon, my brain may melt from the images alone."

His hand slid back to her belly, spreading over her abdomen and tilting her hips back. Then she heard the blessed sound of him unzipping his pants and opening the condom wrapper. When he reached around her, gently teasing her clit with his fingers, and the smooth head of his cock pressed against her opening, she shivered with anticipation and braced herself. It'd been so long, and she didn't know what to expect, but her body was so slick and ready for him that when he eased forward, all she felt was the sweet, blissful pressure of being filled completely. She sucked in a breath at the sensation and drank up the gritty moan Jasper let out as he seated himself deep.

His nose buried in her shoulder as he held himself still, their bodies joined. "Now *I'm* feeling like the born-again virgin. Fuck, you feel amazing. Are you okay?"

She wet her lips, trying to find her voice. "Five out of five stars."

"Good." He stroked between her legs gently with his fingers as he canted his hips back and pumped into her again. "I'd like to take my time but…"

Need welled in her anew, her body urgent again. "Slow is overrated."

He chuckled under his breath. "Next time."

Next time. That was when it hit her fully. They'd get to do this again. This was a thing they could do now, that they'd decided to do together. The thought was enough to make Hollyn giddy. And that was the last thought she had because Jasper begin to move quickly then, pumping into her with long, deep strokes, his fingertips circling her clit in rhythm and sending a sunburst of sensations through her.

She dug her fingers into the wall, trying to hold off the oncoming freight train of her orgasm, but her body was too keyed up, the feel of him too sweet, the images of Jasper touching himself still too fresh in her mind's eye. Everything inside her went tight and hot at the same time, her body vibrating like a plucked string. "Jasper."

"God, baby. So good." He pumped harder, his breath harsh against her neck and the scent of him driving her higher. Then, she fell apart. Her eyes squeezed shut, and a sharp cry escaped her throat, the soundproof room absorbing their secret.

Jasper's groan joined in, and he seated himself deep, the searing heat of his release spilling into her as he tipped over his own edge. The jagged, primitive sounds he made, mixed in with a few gasped *fuck*s, were going to be forever imprinted on her brain. She wasn't a virgin, but she'd never heard a man so openly undone, so raw, so goddamned sexy. She wished she could see his face. His body.

Next time.

Jasper held on to her as they coasted back to earth. The lights and sounds of the room came back to her in a gradual awareness, like waking up slowly from a dream. She breathed deeply, trying to settle herself, trying to find some semblance of self-control again. Jasper slipped out of her and kissed her between her shoulder blades. "Just give me a second, and I'll get your things for you."

She turned around, catching Jasper as he slid off the condom, tied it, and then quickly tucked himself back into his pants. She bit her lip at the glimpse of him. They'd fooled around twice, and she had yet to see him naked. He lifted his head and caught her watching. His mouth quirked at one corner, his hair mussed and falling in his face. "Probably shouldn't throw this away in the company trash bin."

"Probably not." She reached for her dress and covered herself, feeling way too naked all of a sudden. "There's a box of tissues in the back corner."

He found the box and wrapped up the evidence before tossing it in a stray Target bag someone had left in the room. Then he snatched her panties from the floor and her bra off a piece of equipment and handed them to her.

"Thanks." She didn't know what to do with the dress, her movements awkward and jerky, her limbs not fully back online yet.

"Here, let me." Jasper set down the bag, took her dress from her, draping it over his shoulder and then let her tug her panties back on. He slipped the bra straps over her shoulders and then stepped behind her, gathering her hair to one side, and hooking the bra. He kissed her shoulder before slipping her dress on for her.

The move was so unbearably intimate that, for some reason, it made her want to cry. She took a deep breath and gathered herself before turning around.

"Thanks," she said, her brain still whirling and her body still pulsing with aftershocks. "I can't believe we just did that."

He smiled, his face a little flushed. "Me neither. Apparently, our improv games are dangerous with or without alcohol."

"We just had sex at work," she said, still not believing it. "Improv must be an aphrodisiac."

He lifted a brow. "Funny, this never happens with my group. Though, Church has looked pretty sexy at times."

She laughed, thankful to see that he was still the same Jasper she'd gotten to know. Sex didn't have to make this awkward. It didn't have to make it heavy or serious. "I'm not sure how to do non-awkward after-sex talk."

"Oh, no one knows how to do that," he said, running a hand through his hair to get it back in some kind of order. "You don't get into a rhythm with that until you're with someone for a while. Embrace the awkward."

Her cheek muscle jumped. "I'm a pro at awkward. Still don't know what to say."

"How about this? That"—he nodded toward the wall—"was a helluva lot of fun. I think we should continue to do that."

"Agreed," she said with a resolute nod.

"Excellent. See, look at us not being awkward. I... Oh fuck." Jasper's eyes went wide.

"What?"

He tipped his head back and closed his eyes with a fuck-my-life expression.

"What is it?" she asked again.

"Well," he said, looking at her. "Dating lesson number two: Never let a dude tape you having sex because you will end up on the internet."

Her lips parted and her attention swung to his phone. "Oh my God. It was *recording*?"

"I thought we were going to do an improv scene and then take a look at it," he said, going over to his phone. "I didn't think we'd... Obviously, I'll delete it."

"How much did it catch?" She stepped over to stare at the camera with him. He hit Stop and then dragged his finger to rewind to the beginning to see what the camera had captured. She leaned over to see.

"We should probably just delete it without watching," he said resolutely.

"Probably," she agreed.

But neither of them hit the delete button. The video ran. It started with the two of them talking about the improv scene. They were facing each other, fully under the lights. Hollyn watched with curiosity at first and then with avid interest. As the scene went on and off the rails, she watched their expressions changing. Her and Jasper's gazes heating, their faces more serious. It was kind of hot. Like she was watching two other people. But that wasn't what stood out to her. "I'm not ticcing."

Jasper glanced at her. "What?"

She nodded at the video. "After the initial few seconds, my tics stopped. It means I was totally focused. The tics tend to get quiet when I'm concentrating on something else—or I guess in this case, *someone* else."

Jasper looked back to the screen, a small smile touching his lips. "You're right. You look super into me."

She smacked his arm and he laughed.

The scene got to *K*, and they started to kiss. Both she and Jasper went quiet at the sight, each watching their past selves intently. Jasper had been so tender with her, his touch sweet and gentle. Her chest tightened with something unfamiliar, something out of bounds, and she tapped that ridiculous feeling down right quick. None of that. Feelings couldn't get involved.

"We're kind of hot," she said, trying to distract herself from her errant thoughts.

Jasper nodded. "Right? We're nailing this kiss."

Their counterparts shifted on the screen, heading to the side wall. The camera had only caught a sliver of the action, but the sound was fully captured. Hollyn's skin got hot all over again. "We should, uh, delete all of this right now."

Jasper nodded resolutely. "Definitely."

They kept watching.

A loud banging on the door startled them, and Jasper almost knocked the tripod over.

Panic zipped through Hollyn. "Uh, one second," she called

out, but she knew whoever was on the other side wouldn't hear her from the soundproof room. She quickly ran her hands over her hair and made sure her dress was all back in place. "I'll get it."

Jasper stopped the video and went to the wall of equipment, putting his back to the door and pretending to be busy with something.

Hollyn took a breath and unlocked the door. When she opened it, she found Andi standing on the other side with a worried look. "Hey, oh, it's you. Everything okay?"

Hollyn blinked. "Uh, yeah. Why?"

Andi frowned. "You're fifteen minutes past the time slot, and I had to knock really hard. Plus, since when do you do videos?"

"I don't. I mean, not yet. We were practicing. I'm sorry about being late. We were just finishing up. I guess we lost track of time." Hollyn ran a hand over her hair.

"We?" Andi's eyes narrowed, and she peered past Hollyn to where Jasper was. Her eyebrows went up. "Oh. Ha. Um, never mind." She smiled at Hollyn. "I didn't realize it was a…group project. Carry on. I can book a different time slot."

"Andi, no, it's fine, we were—"

But Andi was already striding away, wiggling her fingers in a backward goodbye. "Ta!"

Hollyn shut the door and leaned back against it, cringing. "She totally knows."

Jasper turned around and grinned. "Doubtful. Either way, she seemed delighted to leave us to it. Good friend, that one."

She put her hand over her face. "I had sex. At work. On video no less. Who am I? What is my life?"

"Did you enjoy it?" he asked, voice closer.

"Obviously. But not the point."

"Definitely the point." Fingers circled her wrist, and Jasper tugged her hand away from her face. He kissed her knuckles.

"Don't stress about it. Andi's not going to tell on us. No one is going to find out. The video will be deleted. And who you are is a woman who might possibly get off on a little risk. Nothing wrong with that." He pulled her against him. "In fact, it's quite a winning quality."

She huffed. "I'm literally the opposite of a risk taker. Sheltered homeschool kid remember?"

He gave her a look. "I call bullshit on that, Hollyn Darling."

She frowned.

"I know we're new to each other, but here's what I do know. You're a woman from a small town who grew up in a protective shell and broke out of it as soon as she could. Despite being on her own, despite having anxiety and a neurological disorder to contend with, she came to the city and made a name for herself. A woman who literally goes undercover like a superhero to do what she loves. A woman who, no matter how terrified she is, is pushing herself to do what it takes to get over her fears and get the job she wants. A woman who straight-up, no bullshit asked a guy to help her get more comfortable dating. You, Hollyn Darling," he said, touching his forehead to hers, "are a motherfucking, risk-taking badass."

She laughed at the final declaration, but a pool of warmth spread through her chest, making her limbs tingle and her eyes get watery. "Jasper."

He lifted his head, giving her a gentle look. "I had a counselor once tell me that we need to be careful with the stories we tell ourselves because our brains believe them. Maybe it's time you start telling yourself a different story. You're not that little girl under the tree, unable to stand up to the bully. Not anymore."

She swallowed hard. "You and my therapist been having drinks behind my back?"

He laughed. "All I'm saying is that this Hollyn would kick that kid in the balls."

"Hell yes I would."

He smirked. "And this Hollyn would totally sneak away into the video room and get off with her practice boyfriend."

Her brows lifted. "Is that what we're calling it?"

He stepped back and shrugged. "I don't know what to call it, but people here are going to figure out something's going on between us. I mean, I kissed you in front of Emily. Andi apparently knows something's up."

"The Andi thing may be my fault."

"Ah, so you talked about me?" he asked, looking enormously pleased.

She rolled her eyes. "Narcissist."

"All I'm saying is that we probably should get on the same page about how we're going to interact here. We don't owe anyone any explanation, but if you're planning on keeping this a secret, I need to know. I'll also need to ask Emily to keep what she saw to herself."

Hollyn rolled her lips together, pondering. On one hand, not having to hide it would be easier, but on the other hand, she needed to be careful. This wasn't a real dating relationship. She'd seen those rom-coms. People got hurt when they pretended to be together and one got attached. She didn't want to be the unlucky one who caught feelings and had her heart broken. Could she handle this? Was she really the tough person Jasper saw her as? Not the desperate girl just looking for a guy to like her?

Ugh. She really, really hoped she wasn't the latter anymore.

"So we would just tell people we're seeing each other if they ask?"

He nodded. "Works for me."

She tipped up her chin, trying to write her new story. "Okay, I'm cool with that. But you better not fall in love with me. You know how those fake relationship movies can turn out."

A flicker of something unreadable flashed across his face but then that winning smile returned. "Now who's the narcissist?"

She tilted her head. "I've got to keep up with you, right?"

He reached out and took her hand. "You're keeping up just fine, darling. And this isn't a fake relationship. It's just a unique friendship. One with lots of orgasms."

"*Those* definitely weren't fake." She gave him a pointed look. "Now, go delete the video evidence because I've seen that movie, too. And I don't wanna be in that kind. That kind ends with jail or murder."

He laughed. "Done."

A few minutes later, they headed out, back among coworkers and the noise of the office, the real world a harsh contrast to the quiet video room. Rodrigo was coming down the hall toward them. Hollyn stiffened and shifted a little further from Jasper, hoping she didn't have *I just had sex with this guy in the video room* written all over her face, but before she could process what was happening, Jasper reached out and grabbed her hand, keeping her close.

She watched as Rodrigo's eyes went from Hollyn's face to her and Jasper's clasped hands. His eyebrows arched as he stopped in front of them. "Hey, guys."

"Hey, man," Jasper said genially. "Ready for your afternoon green juice?"

"Yeah, I was just headed that way," he said, glancing at Hollyn and then back to Jasper.

"Just wrapped up my lunch break. I'll walk down with you," Jasper said. He lifted his and Hollyn's joined hands and kissed her knuckles. "I'll see you tonight."

Hollyn's belly flipped over, some weird combination of emotion going through her, the publicness of all this both exciting and a little terrifying. "Yeah. Sounds good."

Jasper gave her a little wink and then turned to walk downstairs with Rodrigo.

She stood for too long in the hallway, watching Jasper go and trying to ignore the fluttery feeling inside her chest.

No, girl. Not yours. Not really.

Maybe she *had* been telling herself a lie about not being a risk-taker because, suddenly, this arrangement with Jasper felt like the biggest risk of her life.

chapter **nineteen**

JASPER FROWNED DOWN AT HIS LAPTOP, THE WORDS OF HIS half-finished business plan blurring together into a bunch of meaningless letters. Maybe he shouldn't have had that third coffee. He rubbed the bridge of his nose and tried to come up with the names of similar businesses.

Fitz had gone over the basics of a business plan with Jasper two nights ago and had sent him a shit ton of links to examples, but trying to keep his mind focused was like trying to herd cats hyped up on catnip. Numbers and graphs and analyses. How was he supposed to sound like he knew what he was talking about? He was in over his head with this. He wasn't some MBA grad. He was just an actor who liked to make people laugh. Maybe his sister had been right. This was just another doomed-to-fail, harebrained scheme. Another useless whim he'd chased.

Fuck.

"Wow, you look intense," a familiar voice said. "Everything okay?"

Jasper looked up from his spot at the hot desk, finding Hollyn wearing black skinny jeans, a sleeveless green blouse that gave him a hint of her lacy bra beneath, and a tentative smile. She'd wrangled her curly hair into a big, messy bun atop her head and stabbed through it with a pencil. Adorably sexy as usual. He let out a sigh, the sight of her a welcome respite from the work at hand. "I'm fine." He flicked his hand toward his laptop. "Just coming to the realization that I'm dumb as shit and doomed to fail in business."

Her smile dropped into an instant frown. "Stories we tell ourselves, Jasper."

Great, she was throwing his own words back at him. *Perfect.* He raked a hand through his hair, irritated all over again. "True stories in this case."

She grabbed a chair from an unoccupied table and sat down facing him, her tics quiet, which he was beginning to recognize as her singular focus mode. She gave him the look an interrogator would give a criminal. "You're not dumb and doomed to fail."

He leaned back in his chair and crossed his arms, feeling petulant. "How would you know? I've had official people in education tell me this."

"I know because I'm not attracted to dumb," she said matter-of-factly. "And whoever told you that needs to be fired from their job and not allowed to work with children." Her nose scrunched a few times in succession. "Plus, what you do onstage, how quickly your mind works and the clever stuff you come up with? That takes brains. So don't give me your sob story, Deares. I'm not buying it. What's the actual issue?"

He dropped his attitude. Hollyn wasn't the enemy. This goddamned piece-of-shit plan was. "Business plans suck."

"Ah." She leaned over and peeked at his computer. "Competing analysis. What's that?"

"Area businesses that are similar to what I'm proposing and how my theater would stack up," he droned, repeating what he had learned from Fitz and the Google gods.

"Oh." She smiled, perking up. "I can help with that. I review a lot of places that would be competing with you. I've worked that area. I could put together a list."

He sat up from his slouch. "Yeah?"

"Of course." She shrugged as if it were no big deal. "Off the top of my head, I can think of at least three in the immediate area of the theater. You'll be unique enough to stand out. There's no comedy club out that way. But there are a few bars where local bands play. A movie theater that plays retro movies. There's also a karaoke and craft beer place. The last one will probably cross over with the kind of crowd you're hoping to attract."

Something tight in Jasper's neck unlocked. He leaned forward, took her face in his hands, and kissed her soundly. "You are a goddess among women."

She rolled her eyes. "I didn't say I was writing your plan up for you."

He mock pouted, even though that hadn't been what he was asking her to do.

"Not gonna work," she declared with a smirk. "I did enough homework for cute boys in my early days. I'm not going down that thankless road again. You give them their assignment and then they forget your name."

He frowned. "Boys can be shitheads."

"Yep. That's been my general conclusion. I'm trying to amend my study, though, with fresh research." She lifted her brows. "Up for the challenge?"

"Absolutely. I'm aiming to wreck the curve," he said, meaning it. He couldn't give Hollyn what she really deserved, but he sure as hell wasn't going to use her and forget her. "And I don't need you to write it, but I would much appreciate the list if it's not too hard to throw together."

"Not a problem." She pushed a stray hair behind her ear,

and her gaze shifted away. "In fact, it makes me feel better about asking a favor of you."

"A favor?" He crossed his fingers for her to see. "Please let it be sexual favors, please let it be sexual favors..."

She laughed under her breath, dipping her head and a little pink staining her cheeks. "Sadly no. But it does involve our arrangement."

He tilted his head, catching the shift in her tone. "Okay."

She crossed her legs and grabbed the edge of her seat like she was trying not to fidget. "My best friend, Cal, is driving into town tonight from Baton Rouge, and he'll be staying with me for a few days."

Her best friend Cal. That sparked something in the back of Jasper's mind. He reached for the thread of thought, but he couldn't grab ahold of it. "All right. Do you need me to lie low?"

"Kind of the opposite actually," she said, meeting his gaze. "He's convinced I'm hiding away here in the city and spiraling into being a hermit. I need him to see that I'm doing okay. And it would help a lot if he could see that I'm dating someone. I usually tell him everything, but if I tell him about our arrangement, he's going to worry even more that I'm going off the deep end. So..."

Jasper smiled. "I need to be the boyfriend."

She let out a breath. "I know that's a big ask, but can you act like we're the real thing with Cal?"

He pressed his hand to his chest in mock horror. "Hollyn Darling, I'm a serious thespian. Of course I can act like I'm totally hot for you. I mean, it will be a real hardship to behave like I want you. I'm totally not thinking about you naked right this very second."

She smacked his arm and laughed. "I'm being serious. Like I'm asking you to spend time with me outside of lessons and, you know, the bedroom for this."

He reached out and dragged her chair closer to him. Since that day in the video room, they'd barely passed a day during the last two weeks without a lesson and a little after-hours fun at his place. The fact that she even had to ask him for this said he wasn't doing a good enough job showing her how much he was enjoying spending time with her. "I'm being serious, too." He kissed the tip of her twitching nose. "Happy to do it. And by *do it...*"

"*Jasper.*"

He grinned, loving that he could rile her up so easily. "I'm kidding. I've got your back. We'll show your friend how unhermit-like you are. Totally well-adjusted Hollyn with her totally under-employed slacker boyfriend."

She pursed her lips. "Who is going to start his own kick-ass theater."

"Yeah, yeah, yeah," he said dismissively, but her confidence in him sent warmth through his chest.

"Thank you." She put her hand on his knee and leaned over to kiss his cheek. "You're a good guy, Jasper."

He flipped his collar up *Grease*-style as she backed away. "You're totally killing my bad-boy image here."

She tilted her head, a quizzical look on her face. "Wait, you had a bad-boy image?"

"Hey," he said in mock offense and reached for her.

She laughed and stood before he could grab her. "I'll email you that list of businesses. And if I bring Cal to your show tonight, will you come out for drinks with us afterward?"

"Of course." He fixed his collar and smoothed it down.

"Great." She bit her lip. "By the way, just FYI, Cal has Tourette's, too, but he has more verbal tics. So he'll say some stuff that doesn't make sense in the conversation. Usually snippets of song lyrics."

Jasper nodded. "Got it. Thanks for the heads-up."

"Also..."

"What?" he asked when she hesitated.

Her nose and cheek tics cycled through their dance. Something was bothering her, but all she said was "Never mind. See you later."

Then, she lifted her hand in a quick goodbye and strode off toward the stairs that led back to her office. Only when she was out of sight did his brain finally come back online and retrieve the snippet of conversation he'd been reaching for earlier.

"No, I'm not a virgin. I dated my best friend in college."

Her best friend.

Hell. That had to be the guy who was coming into town. Hollyn didn't have a long list of friends. She definitely wouldn't have a long list of *best* friends.

That was what she'd almost told him just now but chickened out on. He was going out for drinks with her ex. The only other guy she'd slept with. *Fantastic.*

He wasn't particularly bothered by meeting someone's ex-boyfriend. If Hollyn and Cal wanted to be together still, they would be. But he had no idea if she had an ulterior motive. She should've briefed him. Was she trying to make the guy jealous? Prove something? Was Jasper supposed to be cool and friendly? Overly affectionate and protective?

He didn't like not knowing Hollyn's motivation or his role.

Well, this should fun. Not awkward at all.

He turned back to his business plan. Suddenly, the numbers seemed like they might end up being the easiest thing on his agenda today.

FIVE FAKE-DATING MOVIES TO BINGE THIS WEEKEND

By Miz Poppy

When I was figuring out what movies I wanted on my docket last weekend, I realized I was in the mood for a fake-dating marathon. You know the trope. For some reason—sometimes financial, sometimes revenge-related, sometimes for a wedding date—two people who (often) don't like each other decide that the best solution to their current predicament is to fake date. There are rules to be followed, à la *Fight Club*: don't tell anyone what's really happening, keep your stories straight, decide on the appropriate level of public affection, decide whether you're actually going to sleep together, and most importantly, *do not* fall in love. So simple in theory. So hard in practice.

Another version of this setup is when only one partner knows it's fake and is being paid or encouraged to trick the other person into a relationship. The person in the dark has real feelings. Though those movies can work (fine, fine, who can resist Heath Ledger in *10 Things I Hate About You*?), I'm not including them here in this list because that version of this plot has a sharper, crueler edge. In my perfect world, fake dating should be all about the consent on both sides. No one wants to fall in love and realize they've been duped.

So, want to fake it this weekend? Here are my top picks:

1. *Pretty Woman*
2. *The Wedding Date*
3. *To All the Boys I've Loved Before*
4. *Can't Buy Me Love*

A knock sounded on Hollyn's door, startling her from her blog post. She grinned and snapped her laptop shut, rushing to the front door to open it.

"Someone order a houseguest?" Cal asked, filling up her doorstep and smiling wide.

"Cal!" Hollyn breathed in the familiar cedar-soap scent of her old friend as Cal stepped through her doorway, dropped his bag with a *thunk* onto her floor, and enveloped her in one of his big, all-encompassing bear hugs. "Oh my god," she said into his shoulder, her voice muffled by his shirt. "It's so good to see you."

Cal picked her up off her feet and kissed the crown of her head, his broad body making her feel like a little kid again. He set her down and gave her an affectionate smile. "Back at you, my *panic station* chicken."

She groaned and shut the door behind him. "I refuse to accept that as a new nickname."

He sniffed. "Too late. Burned into the brain."

"Don't make me kick you out this early in your visit," she said, giving him a stern look.

"Don't do that. I'll be good. I feel like it's been *rolling stone rolling stone* forever." He gave her an up-and-down look, his shoulder lifting in a shrugging tic he'd had since she'd known him. She'd changed into a white sundress and gold sandals right before he'd arrived, forgoing her usual blend-in-to-the-background Miz Poppy wear since she was off duty tonight. He let out a low whistle. "Looking sharp, Tate. *Rolling stone*. Taking me out on the *hella good* town tonight? Am I underdressed?"

She took in Cal's black T-shirt from The Glorious Sons concert he'd told her he'd gone to a few weeks ago and his dark jeans. His wavy brown hair was shoulder length now and tucked behind his ears. He'd also grown out his scruff to the just-woke-up-and-rolled-out-of-bed look. Cal had always been cute, but in the last two years, he'd moved into the hot-guy-in-a-band zone. "You look rock-star chic. Are women throwing their panties at you onstage yet?"

His lips curved, dimples appearing and his shoulder ticcing again, giving him this image of nonchalance. "It's not 1987 on the Sunset Strip so no, *hella good*, but I do all right. And are you saying I look pretty, Tate?"

He mimed fluffing his hair, and she snorted. "You look great. Honestly. And not underdressed. We're not going anywhere fancy. I was thinking shrimp po-boys for dinner and an improv show for our evening entertainment. You game?"

"Improv?" he asked. "I thought we were going to *panic station* check out some local bands."

That had been the original plan, but she hadn't yet told him about Jasper. She hoped just introducing them after the show would be the easiest route, so she could avoid Cal giving her the third degree beforehand. Jasper could win him over with that easy charm of his. "Maybe tomorrow. Tonight is a local improv group. I think you'll like the show."

He shrugged for real this time. "Cool. I'm *hella good* game. I'm just glad we get to *panic station* hang out." He leaned over and gave her a side hug. "It's good to see your face."

"Same." She leaned her head against his shoulder, her nervous tension releasing a little. Why was she so wound up? This was just Cal. Her favorite person. So she'd be telling him a little fib. It didn't have to be a big deal. This wasn't like one of the fake-dating movies she'd binged last weekend. She and Jasper *were* basically seeing each other. No, they weren't going out on dates. No, they weren't trying to build a future. But they were sleeping together and hanging out, so it wasn't *that* big of a lie. She just wanted Cal to see that she was doing okay, put his mind at ease. She hated that he worried about her so much. She didn't want to be *that* friend—the one who was a burden, the one who had to be taken care of all the time.

All she needed to do tonight was have a good time with him

and Jasper and show her oldest friend that she was doing just fine. That should be easy. Because right now, for the first time in a long while, she was feeling pretty damn good.

"Come on." She cocked her head toward the living room. "Grab your bag, and I'll get the sofa bed set up so we don't have to worry about that when we get back. Then we can head out."

He followed her. "I get turndown service? I'm impressed. Does it come with mints on the pillows? I have *rolling stone* high standards, you know. I'm in the band. Girls consider throwing their panties at me."

She didn't look back. Just flipped him the bird as she walked.

He grabbed her finger and kissed the tip. "Love you."

She shook her head. "Love you, too. Still not getting mints on your pillow, though."

"You can't blame a guy for *hella good* trying."

She shook her head and smiled to herself. Yep, Cal and Jasper were going to get along just fine.

Cal helped her unfold the creaky sofa bed, and they covered it with fresh sheets and a blanket. He tossed a few pillows on it and she frowned, staring down at the bed. "Are your feet going to hang off of this?"

He shrugged. "Dunno. I'll be fine either way."

"If this is too small, you can sleep in my bed."

"Oh, you want to cuddle?" he teased. "You must've really missed me."

She rolled her eyes. "I meant we could switch beds."

He gave her a look. "I'm not kicking you out of your bed, Tate. This is *hella good* fine. I'll go diagonal if need be."

She sighed. "Okay. I just want you to be comfortable. You're my first official overnight guest here."

He glanced up as he fluffed a pillow, something unreadable in his expression. "Yeah?"

She winced inwardly. *Oops.* Tonight she was going to introduce him to her "boyfriend." How exactly was she going to explain that Jasper had never slept over? Ugh, lying sucked. She would be a total fail in the fake-dating movies. "You ready to go? The improv show starts at eight. I don't want to have to rush dinner. Inhaling a po-boy too fast does not a good night make."

Cal stepped around the foot of the sofa bed and put his hand out. "I'm ready. Show me your new *hella good* town."

Hollyn took Cal's hand, inhaled a deep breath, and they headed out. *Here we go.*

chapter **twenty**

As soon as Jasper jogged onto the stage for that night's show, he caught sight of Hollyn in the second row, her mane of curly hair catching the light and glinting gold. An odd rush of jitters rolled through him. *Miz Poppy is here.* That fact was intimidating. Yes, he and Hollyn had been hanging out for a few weeks now and had seen each other naked on multiple occasions, but this was different than performing for a woman he was seeing. In this world, she wasn't only Hollyn. She was Miz Poppy—a woman with an evaluating eye and impeccable taste in entertainment. She'd never seen their full show, and last time she'd been here, he'd blown it completely. Tonight, he wanted to impress the hell out of her.

Hollyn's head was turned to the side, and Jasper was ready to give her a little wink of acknowledgment whenever she looked his way, but then he noticed the big dude sitting next to her and how that guy had draped his arm on the back of Hollyn's chair. Jasper's flutter of nerves morphed into something decidedly different. That had to be Cal. Hollyn wouldn't look so relaxed with a stranger being that casual with her.

Jasper surreptitiously checked out the best friend she used to sleep with while Barry did the intro onstage. Cal had longish hair, that scruffy-on-purpose look, and was built like a fucking wall.

Plus, the guy played guitar in a band. He probably didn't even have to flirt with women. He could just smile and strum a power chord and they'd jump in bed with him.

Cal leaned close to Hollyn's ear and whispered something that made her laugh and lean into him.

Ugh. Jasper's fists clenched.

He tried to ignore the territorial impulse that welled in him. He didn't have the right to be jealous. Hollyn wasn't really his girlfriend. This guy had been her friend since childhood. The one she'd had her first time with. Jasper was the new guy in this scenario, the easily expendable one. Cal would still be around when Jasper and Hollyn ended their lessons. Cal was the fixture. Jasper was the whim.

That thought dug right under Jasper's skin, but Monique was starting the monologue, and he needed to pay attention. The last thing he wanted to do was mess up the performance. He needed to nail this shit. He wanted Hollyn rolling with laughter in her chair—breathless with it. Because after the show, she was going to introduce him to Cal as her boyfriend, and he wanted her to be proud of the man she had on her arm.

And if her goal was to make the boy jealous, Jasper was suddenly very down with that plan. He put on his game face. *You may play guitar, rocker boy, but I can make her laugh. And I can make her forget herself enough to have a screaming orgasm up against a wall at work.*

He recognized the pathetic act of setting up a nonexistent pissing contest, but that didn't mean he wasn't going to use that ire as fuel to kill this performance tonight. The monologue wrapped up, and Jasper jumped in.

Showtime.

The applause was loud and raucous as Hail Yes wrapped up the show. Jasper was riding high on adrenaline and the energy of the crowd. They'd *killed*. Not just him but the whole team. Some nights he felt like it was a good show, sometimes a not-so-great one, and other times, there was a special kind of buzz that told him they'd climbed higher that particular night, had achieved true *group mind*, had brought the audience along with them on that magic carpet ride where everyone forgot there was a world going on outside the doors.

The group was all high fives and back thumps as they gathered backstage and changed out of the *Men in Black*–style suits they'd chosen tonight and back into their street clothes. The hum of adrenaline had Jasper's blood pumping, his mood giddy. His hands were trembling with it. He shook out his arms, trying to work out the tremors. "Great job, y'all. That was… We kicked ass."

"Hail Yes we did!" Antonio shouted, pulling on a fresh T-shirt.

Danica groaned at the old joke and tossed her necktie at him.

Antonio ducked the projectile and ignored her. "Did you get this one on film, Jas?"

"Yep," Jasper said, running a towel over his damp face. "I'll get the video up on the new YouTube channel tomorrow." He looped the towel around his neck and unbuttoned his shirt. "Tonight was gold. Danica, that bit with the appliance-store commercial? I almost broke character and lost it. So fucking funny. You could expand that and make a sketch."

"Thanks." Danica beamed and scrubbed her hand through her damp pixie cut. "You were on fire, too. The male stripper scene at the political convention? Hilarious. Even though I know you were just looking for an excuse to take off your shirt and flash some nipple at the audience."

Jasper snorted. "What scene can't be improved by a little nip exposure?"

"Trying to impress your new lady friend?" Church asked, sitting down on a wooden storage box and pulling off his shoes, which filled the room with the distinct funk of Church's feet and made Danica groan.

Jasper smirked as he tossed the black pants in his bag and then tugged on his jeans. He'd had to admit to the group today that he was seeing Hollyn because he didn't want one of them to slip up in front of Cal. Monique had given him a look that could've peeled the paint off his car, and had pulled him aside to inform him that if he bailed on the group for another woman, she would literally never speak to him again. He'd assured her that this was a no-risk situation, and for good measure, he'd gotten on his knee, knight-style, and had sworn his fealty to Monique and the group.

"I'm not *not* trying to impress her," Jasper said.

Monique rolled her eyes. "Lord Jesus, pray for us sinners. Jasper has another crush."

Barry laughed. "Aw, don't bust his balls. Jas, you should have your lady friend come to every show. Nothing makes a guy be on top of his game more than when he's trying to impress a woman."

Monique shook her head. "I should've known when you said you absolutely weren't interested in that girl that it meant *I'm literally going to do everything to get her to sleep with me.*"

Jasper zipped up his jeans and then lifted a hand, swearing-on-a-Bible style. "I swear this wasn't some master plan. We're just... enjoying each other's company. It is not a big deal. This isn't like last time. This isn't a Kenzie situation."

"It better not be." Monique put two fingers in front of her eyes and then pointed to him, reminding him of their earlier conversation. "Eye on the ball, Jas. The buzz is building. And we're all ready to put money into this theater project of yours. Don't get distracted by another pretty face."

"Not happening. I swear." He reapplied deodorant and then

pulled on a clean black shirt. When he'd confided in his group about his dream of their own theater, he'd been overwhelmed by their response. None of them had a lot of money to throw around, but each one of them had pledged to put in what they could if he could find a couple of investors to help get the building. The fact that they trusted him in that way again, that they wanted to be in long-term business together, meant everything to him. "The theater is my number one priority. I've been working on the business plan today."

"Can we see it?" Danica asked.

"Absolutely," he said. "I'll email copies when I've got the draft done. But right now, I gotta go."

"Wait. No celebratory beers at Jabberwocky's?" Antonio asked.

"Sorry," Jasper said, grabbing his bag. "Can't tonight. Hollyn's got a friend in town, and we're all going out for drinks."

"And so it begins," Monique said with a smirk. "Ditching us already."

"Come on," Jasper said, dropping the light tone. "I know I deserve that, but I can work on the business *and* see someone at the same time. I promise nothing is more important to me right now than this group and getting that theater. Hollyn knows that. We're keeping things casual."

"You suck at casual, Jas," Leah said. "You're all formal attire when it comes to women. Like full tux with tails."

Jasper groaned. "No, I *used* to suck at casual. I'm evolving. I've learned my lesson. But right now I have to go and meet the ex-boyfriend and not act like that's weird. I need to be on my A game."

Antonio chuckled. "Oh shit. A meet-the-ex night. Godspeed, my friend. We'll have a drink in your honor."

"Thanks." Jasper waved, hooked his backpack over his

shoulder, and headed out of the storage room, shoving any worries his friends had stirred up out of his mind. He only needed to be focused on one thing tonight. *Not looking like an ass in front of Hollyn or her ex.*

He took a deep breath and walked out to the main part of the bar.

Hollyn was sitting at the long, wood-topped bar with Cal, sipping an Abita beer and looking like sin on a stool in a white sundress. Her legs were crossed, but the dress had ridden up a little to expose a smooth expanse of thigh. Jasper wanted to stroll over, step between her legs, and slide his hands right up those thighs.

But the big dude next to her reminded him there would be none of that tonight.

Jasper wrangled in his libido and strode their way. Hollyn noticed him almost instantly. Her gaze flicked down Jasper's body almost quick enough to miss, but he warmed at the fact that she hadn't been able to resist giving him a once-over either. She sent him a tentative smile before standing up. Cal had his back to Jasper, but turned when Hollyn stood.

Cal got to his feet along with her and gave Jasper a curious look as he made his way to them. When he reached them, he was childishly pleased that he had at least an inch of height on Cal. God, he was being a douche. "Hey."

"Hi." Hollyn's facial tics cycled in a flurry of movement, her nerves evident, but then she turned to Cal and smiled. "Cal, this is Jasper. We work together at WorkAround."

"Oh, really?" Cal said, putting his hand out, a genial smile on his face. "Great show, man. *Hella good.* Really funny."

Jasper heard a record scratch at Hollyn's introduction. *We work together.* What the fuck was that about? *We also sleep together*, he wanted to add but kept his mouth shut. He accepted Cal's handshake and glanced at Hollyn with a ball's-in-your-court look. He knew how to improvise, but he needed to know what role she was expecting him to play.

She bit her lip and looked back and forth between the two of them. Her nose scrunched, and she cleared her throat. "Jasper's also... We're seeing each other."

Cal's grip instantly tightened and his sharp, brown-eyed gaze collided with Jasper's. "*Panic station*. What?"

Jasper was confused for a second, but then he remembered what Hollyn had said about Cal's verbal tics. Jasper cleared his throat. "I'm the boyfriend."

Cal's shoulder lifted in a little jerky motion, and he gave Hollyn a quick questioning look, but then pasted on a smile. He released Jasper's hand. "Oh. That's cool. Wait. Are you the coffee guy?"

"*Cal,*" Hollyn complained.

Jasper's brows lifted. Hollyn had talked about him to Cal? "Ah, well, I do pour coffee at WorkAround, so I guess yes, I could be the coffee guy."

Hollyn looked sheepish. "I may have mentioned to Cal how I freaked out on you that first day. I didn't know your name then. Hence, coffee guy."

Cal gave him a second, more critical look. "Yeah, she hasn't mentioned you since. *Rolling stone. Rolling stone.* At all."

A dig. Nice. Well, this was going to be a fun night. Jasper smiled. "Well, you know how things are when it's new. You want to keep it just between the two of you for a while." He gave Hollyn his best we've-got-a-secret look that made her blush. "But I'm glad I finally get to meet her best buddy."

Cal's lip curled, a knowing look in his eye. The guy hadn't missed the subtle message the word *buddy* implied. "Well, *panic panic station.*" He grimaced. "If she didn't mention it, I have Tourette's. I can't control these *rolling stone* extra words."

Cal's verbal tics were almost in the cadence of a sneeze, sharp and sudden. Also, the more he talked, the more Jasper's ear kind of skipped over them, editing them out, because they sounded different from the rest of his words. "She mentioned it. No worries."

Hollyn gave Cal an affectionate look and bumped her shoulder into his. "Onstage, it all goes away, though. He's freaking amazing with his band. I'm hoping it's going to be the same effect for me on video."

Cal looked down at her with an adoring smile. "You're going to *hella good* nail it, Tate."

Jasper couldn't stay irritated with the guy for long. Clearly, he cared for Hollyn and wanted what was best for her. If Cal was feeling protective of his friend, then Jasper would just have to win him over, show him that he wasn't going to hurt Hollyn. "We're working on it. We did a little camera work already, and she was very smooth."

Hollyn's gaze darted to Jasper's, startled, and her cheeks went full red. Jasper bit his lip. He hadn't meant any double entendre with the word *smooth*, but now that she had read that into it, he couldn't help the little jolt of heat that went through him. Hollyn had been smooth—and hot and slick and tight.

She cleared her throat, breaking him from his racy thoughts. "I think it's time to get out of here. Y'all ready?"

Jasper surreptitiously adjusted the fly of his jeans and stepped next to Hollyn, offering his arm. "Lead the way, gorgeous."

Hollyn slipped her arm into his, a little shiver going through him at the feel of her, and they headed out.

Cal followed behind and said something under his breath that Jasper didn't catch.

....

The Gee-N-Oh club was buzzing with conversation and music, the air thick with the scent of perfume, sweat, and alcohol as Hollyn scooted into a curved booth, ending up sandwiched between Cal and Jasper. A blanket of awareness and awkwardness wrapped around her as they got situated. The walk over to the club had been fine, but there was some weird vibe going on between Jasper and Cal, and she had no idea what that was about. Penises, she suspected. They were usually to blame. Why had she thought this was a good idea?

A dark-haired guy with no shirt and tight red pants with suspenders sidled up to the table before they'd even settled in. He leaned in, his glittery eye shadow catching the light. "What can I get you beautiful people?"

"The house IPA," Jasper said.

Cal looked over the photo menu on the table. "The high-octane daiquiri."

The waiter turned his eyes on her. "And you, sweetie?"

She leaned over to see the menu. Was there one that cured awkwardness? She picked the biggest and the prettiest. "Um, that one."

"A Cat 5 hurricane for the lady," the waiter said and then glided off, dodging the crowd like they weren't even there.

"A hurricane," Jasper said with a sly grin. "You're going for it tonight, huh?"

"I've always wanted to try one," she said, only half lying.

"I guess she thinks *rolling stone* we're going to be boring company," Cal said with a smirk. "She wants to *hella good* get smashed."

"Says the dude who ordered a drink with the words 'high octane' in its name," she said, arching a brow at Cal.

"I can handle my liquor," he said. "You, on the other hand—"

She quickly pressed her fingers over his mouth. "No embarrassing teen stories for Jasper. You will not do that to me."

Jasper leaned forward on his forearms. "Well, now I have to know."

She lowered her hand and looked at Jasper, shaking her head. "No way."

"Let's just say," Cal said, "someone *hella good* found out that for some people, liquor can *panic station* quiet tics and decided to test the theory when she was fifteen with *hella hella* shots from my dad's whiskey stash. This experiment may have ended up with someone swimming in her underwear in my neighbor's pool and then throwing up on their poor dog when he tried to alert them about the trespassing teenagers. Poor Boris was traumatized for life."

Hollyn put her hands over her face and sank back against the booth. "You're dead to me, Cal. He's totally lying, Jasper. Don't believe a word he says."

Jasper laughed and squeezed her knee. "Did you get arrested for animal cruelty?"

She dropped her hands and gave him a deadly look.

Jasper bit his lip, clearly enjoying teasing her.

"The neighbors. *Hella rolling stone.* Didn't call the cops. But we had to *hella* give the dog a bath in the middle of the night."

"And Mr. Redmond saw me in my bra and underwear. So, there was no looking him in the eye ever again," she added.

"But she wasn't ticcing," Cal announced, clearly pleased with himself. "Experiment successful."

Jasper smiled. "Does it really help with the tics?"

Cal shrugged. "Depends on the *rolling stone* person. *Rolling stone.* It helps with mine. For someone else, it could make them worse. Just like there are happy drunks and mean drunks. Different body chemistry."

"It helps mine, too," Hollyn added. "But that's a treacherous dance. You don't want to lean on that as a fix because then you don't just have a tic problem, you've picked up an alcohol one."

Just as she said it, the waiter came back with their drinks.

Hollyn's eyes widened as he plunked down a tall,

filled-to-the-brim glass in front of her. The orangey-pink cocktail looked harmless in its curvy glass with a wedge of orange and a cherry decorating its brim, but she'd lived here long enough to know the famous hurricane packed a punch. The Cat 5 designation probably meant it'd be even worse than a normal one.

Jasper accepted his beer from the waiter with a thank-you and then eyed Hollyn's drink. "Looks like you're planning for a swimming-in-your-underwear night. Should I warn the neighborhood dogs? Or maybe just get my camera ready?"

She flipped him the middle finger and sipped her cocktail, which was some tasty combination of rums and fruit juices. *Mmm.* That went down real easy. She hadn't ordered it to quiet her tics. She just needed something to take the edge off. She hadn't realized how awkward it'd be going out with her BFF/ex-boyfriend and her fake boyfriend. The two guys had nearly had a dick-measuring contest when they'd met. She hadn't expected that at all, and didn't have a clue on how to negotiate the odd tension.

"I'm not trying to get smashed," she said. "I just never got a chance to try one of these because usually when I go out, I'm on the job and alone. Tonight, I know if I get a little tipsy, I only have to worry about being embarrassing in front of you two. I don't have to worry about getting hauled into an alley and raped or murdered because I've let my guard down."

"Jesus, Hollyn," Cal said, looking horrified. "Is the city that dangerous? Maybe you shouldn't be going—"

"It's not the city," she said, cutting Cal off before he could get all mother hen on her. "It's called being a woman in the world. I can't go out and get tipsy alone. There are demented assholes everywhere. So this...is a treat. I have two people I can trust watching my back."

"The world sucks," Jasper said, jaw clenching. He put his arm around her shoulders and squeezed. "Whenever you don't feel safe somewhere, you call me, and I'll go with you."

She leaned into him, appreciating the offer. "Thank you. I don't need a babysitter, though. Except tonight. Tonight, I might need a babysitter."

She took a long sip and both the guys laughed.

"We've got you covered, Tate," Cal said and took a sip of his own drink. "So Jasper, *rolling rolling*, you do the coffee thing by day and the *hella good* show by night?"

Jasper released Hollyn and draped his arm over the back of the curved booth. "Yeah. I also teach some classes at WorkAround. But I'm drawing up a business plan to try to get investors for a theater. I want the group to have their own place instead of using the bar."

Cal nodded and his shoulder shrugged twice. "That's cool. And sounds like a lot of work."

"It's overwhelming," Jasper said, slowly turning his beer bottle on the table. "But I think if we get word-of-mouth going and some wider publicity, we could get investors interested."

Cal's eyebrows quirked, and he took another deep gulp of his drink. "Publicity. Like Hollyn's column?"

Hollyn frowned. She could see where Cal's mind was going. "Yes. I actually planned to review the show before I even knew who Jasper was. I ran into him after one of his shows, and that's sort of how this whole thing started."

"She rescued me from certain death," Jasper said, obviously trying to shift the mood back to the lighthearted conversation from earlier. "My appendix almost exploded outside the bar. Hollyn brought me to the ER."

"Isn't it a conflict of interest? Reviewing the show of a guy you're dating?" Cal asked, ignoring the appendix story and focusing on her. "Your whole brand is that your reviews aren't sponsored. They're one hundred percent honest."

Jasper stiffened next to her. "I'm not asking her to not be honest."

"But you're asking her to do you a favor?" Cal said, his tics quiet as his focus zeroed in on Jasper. "And it's one that could get her in trouble if someone found out she was dating you."

"I—" Jasper began.

"Cal, stop," Hollyn said, getting annoyed at the line of questioning. "You're making a thing out of something that isn't a thing. I will disclose the relationship at the end of the review. And if I didn't like his show, I wouldn't give it a good review. Just like I wouldn't go and see your band and give it a good review if I thought you guys sucked. No matter how much I love you."

Jasper glanced her way, and she cringed at her use of the word *love*. Cal smirked. "You would not pan my band, Tate. You don't have it in you."

She stared at him for a moment as she drank more of her hurricane and sighed. "Fine. I do love you enough to not do a review at all if I hated it. But I *do* like your band. And I *do* think Jasper's show is great. You saw it yourself. They're awesome." She shrugged. "So it's not a conflict of interest. I just happen to have a talented friend and a talented boyfriend. No big deal. No one's going to be doing some deep investigation into it."

"You don't have to review my show," Jasper said, his attention still on Cal.

"What?" she asked, frowning Jasper's way. "But—"

He leaned in and kissed her lightly. "Your friend here thinks I'm using you to forward my career. That's not what this is."

Hollyn huffed and looked to Cal. "Is that what you're saying?"

Cal sipped his drink and shrugged—not a tic—looking like the petulant kid she'd first met. "Just seems convenient timing. And he *is* an actor."

Irritation flooded her, and her hand landed on the table with a soft smack. "Cal Summers, if you just implied that I'm not worth dating unless someone's getting a favor out of it, you're about to get a very sticky drink poured in your lap."

Cal's expression fell, a frown touching his lips. "Shit. *Panic station*. You know that's not what I meant. You're... Any guy would be lucky to be with you. I just—"

"You just what?" she asked.

He sighed, a defeated look crossing his face. "Nothing. I'm just being a dick. I'm sorry." He looked to Jasper. "I'm sorry to you, too. I was just surprised by all this. *Kill the lights. Rolling stone*. I'm naturally suspicious."

Jasper relaxed next to her and set down his beer, his attention on Cal. "Seriously. We're cool, man. I get it. Hollyn told me what happened when she was a kid. I'm glad she has someone who watches her back." He tipped his head in Cal's direction. "You have my blessing to kick my ass if I'm here for any other reason than the fact that she's smart and beautiful and I like being with her."

Hollyn's chest squeezed at the words, and she looked over at Jasper, trying to determine if he was telling the truth. This wasn't a real relationship. This was an agreement. But somehow he seemed sincere. And really, despite their unconventional situation, would he really have agreed to come out with her best friend/ex-boyfriend if he didn't at least enjoy her company a little bit?

Hope pushed through the tender space in her heart, but she tamped it down, refusing to let it root. She'd promised. No getting *The Feels*. Jasper would end this. That was the only promise he'd given her. She decided to forgo the straw and gulped her drink.

Cal reached across the table and put his hand out to Jasper. "Deal."

Jasper shook on it.

The techno song playing in the background switched to a new one, and Hollyn could take the awkward no more. "I love this song. Let's dance."

Jasper glanced her way, surprise on his face. "Yeah?"

"You game, Deares?" she asked.

"Always." Jasper grabbed her hand. "Let's go."

"Have fun," Cal said before taking another swig of his daiquiri.

She tossed a balled-up cocktail napkin at him. "No. You're coming, too. It's a dance song, not a prom song. Everybody up and on the dance floor."

Cal gave her a wary look, but she didn't know what his deal was. The boy loved to dance. And she never got to dance at any of the fun places she went. With rum running through her veins, her best friend in town, and her whatever-Jasper-was by her side, she'd finally get the chance to let loose a little. She really, really needed that.

"I think someone's hurricane is *hella good* kicking in," Cal said wryly. "You don't dance in public."

"You wanted me to work my way out of my shell. Observe. Stepping out of the shell for a little while." She slid out of the booth with Jasper and then put her hand out to Cal. "Come on. The night is young. You're only in town for a few days. Let's actually act like people in our twenties and have fun."

Jasper laughed. "Totally the rum. But I'm here for it."

Cal shook his head in amusement but put his hand in hers and let her yank him to his feet. The thought that she was going to dance in public with the two of them seemed a little out there, but the buzz from the alcohol had given her some courage. Why shouldn't she be able to have a good time tonight? For the first time in the longest time, she felt safe to just be herself. She wouldn't have to hide her tics. She didn't have to impress anyone. Neither guy was going to take advantage of her—well, Jasper might, but only with her full and enthusiastic endorsement.

So, as she led the two guys onto the dance floor, and pulled them into the pulsing crowd, she let go of normal Hollyn. Normal Hollyn would be worried who was looking. But tonight, tonight she didn't care.

The three of them made a pocket of space on the dance floor and started to move to the music, the beat pulsing through the soles of her shoes and into her bloodstream. They danced near each other, three little islands unto themselves, but after one song, the guys seemed to loosen up and call a temporary truce.

Each took turns dancing with her, spinning her, passing her back and forth. Jasper holding her closer. Cal keeping it friendly. Her blood was fizzy with alcohol and adrenaline and affection for these two guys. Finding anyone she could be herself around was a challenge—finding two was a miracle.

They took brief breaks to drink a little more but were back on the dance floor before they could register that their feet were hurting or that it was getting late. One of her favorite songs came on, and she tipped her head back to sing along. She felt light, filled with helium. Drunk on more than the potent alcohol.

"You look ready for a swim," Cal yelled next to her ear. "Hope you wore your good underwear."

She shoved him in the shoulder and laughed. "No stripping tonight. I promise."

His eyelids lowered a fraction, and he gave her a smile she didn't recognize. *Ha.* She wasn't the only tipsy one. "Is it bad that I'm disappointed?"

His words didn't quite register with her. "What?"

But before he answered, she was spun away from Cal and ended up in Jasper's arms. His dark hair was damp against his forehead, his eyes bright behind his glasses, and his T-shirt was clinging to every muscle in his chest. Something deep in her belly coiled tight. She had the urge to literally sink her teeth into him.

He squeezed her hips and rocked against her. "You look beautiful right now."

"I'm a sweaty mess," she said on a laugh. "And possibly super drunk."

He pressed his lips against her ear. "You're fucking sexy is what you are. It's taking everything I have to keep my hands off you. I wish I could take you home right this second and get you out of this dress. But I don't think your company would appreciate that."

"God, you're hot," she blurted out, her head spinning.

He grinned that confident grin of his. "Back at you, sunshine. You're a fun drunk."

She wet her lips, a hunger for exactly what Jasper was suggesting stirring in her. "Maybe I can offer Cal some earplugs."

Jasper glanced over her shoulder to where Cal had to be a few steps behind her. "He would absolutely hate that. Knowing I was in bed with you."

She stumbled and then looped her arms around his neck to keep steady. "He's a big boy."

Jasper's gaze went serious and he leaned close. "It's not that. Don't you see it?"

The words were running into each other in her head. She saw him. She saw blurring lights. "See what?"

"How he's looking at you."

She frowned, the words not making sense, and looked in his eyes, but Jasper's face went a little hazy and her knees wobbled. "I—"

"Whoa there," Jasper said, wrapping an arm around her waist.

"Jasper, I..." But she couldn't find what she wanted to say. The room flipped over in her vision and she closed her eyes. Her stomach pitched.

She heard Jasper call her name.

Then her mind went black.

chapter **twenty-one**

JASPER TUCKED HOLLYN INTO BED, MAKING SURE SHE WAS lying on her side and had a full glass of water nearby, and then he kissed her forehead. "Get some rest, wild child."

"I'm never drinking again," she mumbled. "Hurricanes are Satan's work."

"You'll start feeling better now that you got rid of most of it," he said. "But I'll check on you before I leave, all right?"

She muttered something but was already pulling the covers over her head with a groan.

Jasper stood and turned off the lamp before leaving the room. He took a deep breath before making his way down the hallway and into the living room. Cal had kicked off his shoes and was sitting on top of the blanket on the sofa bed, ankles and arms crossed. Probably still a little drunk himself because his shoulder tic was quiet.

Jasper cocked his head toward the hallway. "She's almost asleep. She spent some quality time hugging the toilet, but that was probably for the best. And no dogs were harmed this time."

"I could've taken care of her and put her to bed," Cal said, tone flat.

"I'm sure you could've." Jasper sat in an armchair across from the sofa. "I'm sure you'd happily curl up next to her and make sure she was all good for the night."

Cal's jaw flexed, but he didn't deny it.

Jasper ran a hand over the back of his head. How did he end up in this spot? Maybe he should've drunk more tonight. He was way too sober for this kind of conversation. But he also wasn't going to sit here and hold his tongue. That was a skill he didn't possess. "So does she know?"

Cal's expression remained stoic. "Know what?"

Great. Dude was going to make this extra difficult. Jasper let out a tired sigh. "That you love her."

Cal snorted. "She already knows that. I tell her all the time."

"You know that's not what I mean," Jasper said, leaning forward and bracing his forearms on his thighs. "Let me rephrase. That you're *in* love with her, that you *want* her."

Cal looked away, his posture tight, his fingers flexing against his biceps. "Is this the part where the new guy challenges me to a fight or some shit? Because I could fucking take you, man."

"Right. That's what I feel like doing after a night out—brawling with a drunk guy for no good reason. How about we *use our words*?" he said using a kindergarten-teacher voice.

Cal gave him a look that said he'd probably feel better just taking a swing. But Jasper wasn't here to fight. He didn't have a problem with Cal per se, and he'd been in enough fights as a kid to know it didn't get anyone anywhere except a date with a swollen fist and an ice pack.

"Okay," Jasper said. "How about this? I know you and Hollyn dated in college. I know it was serious enough that you were her first and only before I came along."

Cal's expression flickered with surprise. *Oops.* Well, if Cal hadn't yet figured out that he and Hollyn were sleeping together, he knew now.

"But," Jasper continued, "she said you both decided that you were better off as friends. She made it sound mutual."

"It wasn't," he said, tone clipped.

"Oh." Well, that made sense. This guy was still nursing a broken heart. "So—"

"I broke up with her," Cal said, cutting him off.

Jasper blinked. "Wait, what?"

Cal let out a frustrated breath and shifted on the bed, making the metal frame squeak. "I broke up with her, all right? Not because I didn't love her. But at the time, I thought it was for the best."

Jasper clasped his hands between his knees. "Why?"

Cal reached over to the side table and grabbed a bottle of wine Jasper hadn't noticed earlier and took a deep swig. He gave Jasper a look like he was deciding between throwing something at him or ignoring him completely. But when he put the bottle down, he sighed like he was exhausted, and some of the fight went out of his expression. "Because we were kids. Because it's hard to tell what's what when you have so little experience. I didn't want to be her boyfriend by default. I didn't want us to end up married at twenty-one and wondering if we'd missed out on something."

Jasper grimaced at the thought of Cal and Hollyn married.

"So I told her we were better as friends, and I've encouraged her to get out there and date. As much as it sucked to think about, I wanted her to be with other guys. I've dated other women. I wanted us both to experience some life outside of the bubble we grew up in. But I always hoped that..."

The truth landed on Jasper. "That afterward, she would come back and pick you anyway."

Cal gave him a look that confirmed Jasper's conclusion as he gulped a little more wine.

A little flare of possessiveness went through Jasper, but he tamped the feeling down. "Have you told her any of this? Is that why you're here?"

"No, I've been willing to wait. I promised myself when she finally started dating that I would keep my mouth shut and see it as progress, but tonight..." Cal plunked the wine bottle on the side table and shook his head. "It's killing me to stand by and watch some smooth-talking actor sweep her up just to use her for his own agenda."

Jasper's jaw flexed, his sympathy for the guy morphing into irritation. "I'm not using her."

"Right," he said dismissively. "You're looking to find a woman to settle down with. You totally seem like the type."

Jasper's hands, which had been loosely clasped between his knees, clenched. "First, don't pretend you know anything about me, because you don't. And second, this relationship is new, man. No, I haven't bought her a ring and named our future children, but I'm not leading her on to get a damn review. I like her. We enjoy being with each other."

"You like her?" Cal huffed. "You enjoy her company?"

Jasper didn't know what the guy was expecting him to say.

When Jasper didn't respond, Cal's lip curled. "You have no clue, do you? You have no idea how she looks at you when you're not paying attention."

Jasper's stomach flipped. "What?"

"God." Cal ran a hand over his face, his expression weary. "You don't realize what you've stepped into. You don't know what Hollyn's been through. How isolated she's been all her life. How hard everything has been for her." His throat worked as he swallowed. "Kids were cruel to her. People avoid her because they don't understand. Every interaction with a stranger has been anxiety-ridden for her. And her mother didn't help by locking her in a virtual prison to try to protect her. There were times I worried she'd just...decide to not go on at all."

Cal looked down like he was trying to gather himself, and Jasper's throat tightened at the thought of Hollyn being that depressed.

"And finally, she's making some progress, putting herself out there." He looked back to Jasper. "I'm so glad for that. Seeing her working outside the house, making friends, meeting new people. She's been fighting hard to create a life she wants. But as tough as she is in some ways, she's so fucking vulnerable to someone like you."

Jasper's defenses went up swift and tall. How many times had someone referred to him that way? *Someone like you.* The stupid one. The foster kid. The problem child. The fuckup. "Someone like me?"

Cal gave him a smug look. "The good-looking guy who knows how to say all the right things. You're the prom king asking the wallflower to dance just to feel like he did something nice."

Jasper's temper surfaced, his voice rising. "I'm not dating her out of fucking pity."

But the words sounded hollow in his ears. He and Hollyn *were* just pretending to have a relationship. He wasn't actually her boyfriend. He was helping her. Exchanging favors. *Being nice.* Did that mean there was some truth to Cal's accusation? Even though Jasper was attracted to Hollyn, was he doing all this just to feel like a good guy after fucking up so royally? Was he trying to prove something to himself?

"Even if this isn't about pity or getting publicity, even if it's just about getting her in bed and having a little fun," Cal said, "she's not hardened to that kind of thing yet. She hasn't been through the meat grinder of the dating scene. Her defenses are weak at best. She looks at you like…"

"Like what?" Jasper asked.

Cal's frown lines deepened, his eye contact steady. "Like you're the guy."

That took the wind right out of Jasper. No way. Cal had it all wrong. Hollyn was just a better actress than she gave herself credit for. She was selling the lie hook, line, and sinker. He shook his head. "Cal—"

"Hollyn deserves someone who's going to love her and stick around," he continued. "Someone who puts her first. I could be that guy. You—are not that guy."

That pressed all of Jasper's fuck-off buttons. "You don't know me."

"I know enough," Cal said. "You don't do what you do unless you're fame-hungry. I bet your career is everything to you."

"Says the dude in a band. And a career and a relationship aren't mutually exclusive last I checked."

"Right," he said, tone dismissive. "If a big break gets tossed your way, you gonna turn it down to stay with Hollyn?"

"If your band gets a record deal and is asked to tour the world, you gonna turn it down to stay with Hollyn?" he lobbed back at Cal.

"Yes," he said without hesitation. "I would."

"Then you're dumb," Jasper said, derision in his voice. "Nothing like starting a long-term relationship with a big, heaping pile of resentment that you gave up a life dream to be with someone. I wouldn't expect her to do that for me either."

It was why Jasper hadn't fought harder to work things out with Kenzie. She had chosen her career over him. He hadn't liked how she went about it, but he hadn't blamed her for putting her ambitions first. She would've resented the hell out of him if he'd held her back in any way.

"Love is more important than any career goal," Cal said after taking another swig of wine. "See. I know your type better than you think."

Jasper's teeth pressed together. "Look. You're not her dad. I don't have to declare my intentions to you. Like I said, this is new."

"Right. Which means if you don't have any thoughts of it turning into something lasting, then you should do her a favor and let her down now," he said, a plea in his voice. "She's already getting in too deep. I know her. I can tell. She's let you in."

Something twisted tight in Jasper's chest at that.

"Don't get her all knotted up with feelings for you and then dump her. I *will* fucking punch you if you do that, whether you want to fight or not," he warned. "If you care about her at all, do the right thing."

Jasper was so done with this conversation. He was arguing over a fake freaking relationship. Why was he letting Cal push his buttons? He got to his feet. "Right, let her go so that she can go running to you?"

He shrugged. "I love her. She loves me. I could make her happy."

Jasper stared down at him, something new burning in his gut. "I know I haven't known Hollyn for all the years you have. We don't have that kind of history. But I know that she isn't some shrinking violet who would appreciate her friend manhandling her love life and 'protecting' her from the big, bad world. If you haven't noticed, Hollyn is a badass. Quiet and shy but strong as hell," he said, thinking of the woman who boldly asked him for exactly what she wanted, the woman taking her fears head on to make her career happen.

"So maybe you're not with her right now because she's not looking for a shield from the world. She's looking for someone to be on the front lines with her, someone who believes that she can handle herself just fine. Plus, she deserves someone who will fight to be with her, who will lay his ass on the line to get the privilege. Not someone who sits around for years in some passive self-righteous state waiting for her to come to her senses."

Cal grabbed the wine bottle again, his knuckles white against it. "Fuck you. You have no clue what our relationship is like."

"And you have no idea what ours is like," Jasper said. "Maybe we're goddamned soul mates and you're trying to derail the start of our epic love story. Maybe she'll be the love of my life."

The words were out before he could evaluate them, but they reverberated in his brain like a thunderclap. *Maybe, maybe, maybe...*

They should've sent a panic through him.

Didn't.

"Yeah right." Cal snorted, his lip curling. "Go home, Jasper."

Jasper had planned to leave after a quick check on Hollyn. But suddenly, he felt his heels digging in. He glanced down the hallway and then gave Cal a humorless smile. "I'll see you in the morning. I'm gonna keep an eye on Hollyn tonight."

Cal's brows dipped, a line appearing in his forehead.

Jasper slipped off his shoes, gave Cal one last look, and then headed back down the hallway. If Hollyn didn't want him there, fine. But no way was he letting Cal kick him out. He'd just told the guy that Hollyn deserved someone who would fight for her. Jasper didn't know exactly what this thing he had with Hollyn was, but he knew she was having fun with him. He knew she'd been the one to ask him for this type of relationship. This was on her terms. And he wasn't going to bail on their agreement just because her childhood best friend was pining for her and thought he knew what was best for her. If Cal wanted her, he was going to have to step up and prove he was worth her time. Until then, Jasper was going to show her why she hadn't chosen wrong when she'd invited him into her life and into her bed.

He quietly made his way into Hollyn's bedroom and shut the door behind him. The sheets rustled.

"Hello?" Hollyn's sleep-soft voice crossed the space between them.

"It's just me again," he said in a low voice. He squinted in the darkness, trying to make out her form. "How ya feeling?"

"Room stopped spinning," she said. "But I'm having a little trouble falling asleep. I thought you'd already left."

His eyes started to adjust, and he could see she'd propped herself up on her elbow. "I planned to, but…"

"But?"

He shifted his weight from foot to foot. What the fuck had he been thinking coming back in here? His ego had gotten in the way of his good sense. He may as well have taken out a ruler and had a dick measuring contest will Cal. *You may be her lifelong best friend, but I get to see her naked.* God, he was ridiculous. "I, well, I will but I wanted to check on—"

"You can stay," she said, her voice a night flower blooming in the darkness.

His bumbling explanations cut off. "What?"

The moonlight from the window gave her damp curls a silver glow as she reached out and patted the bed. "I'm not going to be much company, but it's late and I know you've got to be tired, too. I'd rather you stay than drive off into a ditch somewhere, falling asleep at the wheel."

He let out a breath. "I can take the floor."

Before he realized what was happening, something soft and solid hit him. A pillow.

"Hey!" He lifted his hands in defense a second too late. The pillow fell to the floor.

"Don't be ridiculous," she said. "You've literally been inside my body. We can share a bed for a night. Don't make it weird."

He laughed. "Fine. But I'm about to strip down to my boxers, so if you could refrain from saying the words 'inside my body' again, that would be great because otherwise, *my body* will not understand that it is not an invitation for him to show up for the party."

She made a husky sound that could've been a laugh. "Just remind him that I vomited up a hurricane an hour ago."

Jasper smirked. "Annnnd, that'll do it." He glanced at her bathroom door. "Speaking of which, do you mind if I take a quick rinse in your shower?"

"Little Jasper still needs some attention?" she teased.

"First, he is offended by the term *little*. Second, no I am not going to jerk off in your shower. I have *some* manners. Third, you don't want me to get in your bed post-performance and post-dancing. The pheromones would be so irresistible, your hormones would just explode. I can't risk it."

She made a derisive sound. "Yes, I bet I'd orgasm at the mere scent of you."

He walked closer to the bed, his dark mood lightening. "It happens." He bent down and kissed her temple. "I'll be back in five minutes. Go to sleep."

She grabbed his hand and gave it a squeeze. The simple gesture did more to him than it should.

When he returned after a quick shower, Hollyn was quiet and on her side, eyes closed. The thin, white T-shirt she was wearing was doing nothing to conceal the lush curves of her breasts. He swallowed hard and looked away—okay, he looked twice more and then finally pulled his gaze away for good. He wasn't a saint. He walked around the bed, carefully peeled the covers back and climbed in. The mattress groaned a little and she stirred. "Shh," he said. "Just me."

"Mmkay," she mumbled and shifted against him, making him the big spoon.

His breath gusted out of him at the sleep-warm feel of her against his skin. Somehow between the time he'd left her in the room earlier and now, she'd ditched the pajama pants and was just in her T-shirt and panties. He could feel the heat of her backside nestling against him, the thin cotton of his boxers doing nothing to blunt the effect. His cock stirred. *Shit.*

"Hollyn," he said in a whispered choke. "Sorry, I..."

But she just snuggled closer, his hardening erection pressing against her ass, and fell asleep. His head sank into the pillow, the sweet torture of her body somehow both the best and worst thing ever. She wasn't going to move, though. And he wasn't going to make a move on her right now. So, after accepting his state, he surrendered and put his arm around her, pulling her fully against his chest and inhaling the scent of her. She sighed in her sleep like she was having the best dream, and he smiled.

He was glad he'd won this round of the fight. He couldn't think of any place he'd rather be tonight.

chapter **twenty-two**

HOLLYN WOKE AT DAWN, HER HEAD ACHING A LITTLE AND her mouth bone dry. She blinked in the semidarkness and froze at the soft, steady sound behind her. It took half a second for her brain to register what the unfamiliar noise was. Breathing. Jasper had slept over.

Being careful not to jostle the bed too much, she rolled over, finding him on his back, covers shoved down to his waist, his bare chest moving with deep, sleep-heavy breaths. Maybe it was creepy to watch someone sleep, but she didn't care at the moment. A gorgeous, half-naked man in her bed was a gift that deserved some study. She let herself take a long look, enjoying the luxury that she hadn't yet been afforded with Jasper—time. Their naked antics thus far had been frantic and intense, no opportunity for savoring.

She drank him in slowly without the worry of him catching her staring. His dark hair had fallen across his forehead and was sticking up in other spots, making him look almost boyish save for the stubble covering his jaw. His lips were parted slightly, the bottom one looking full and bitable. Her gaze drifted lower, over his chest, his flat stomach, along the dark trail of hair at his navel that disappeared beneath the band of his boxers. Her body stirred with awareness. She wanted to keep going with her perusal, to slide those boxers off and take in the whole luscious view. She resisted—barely. But Lord, he was fun to ogle.

And he'd stayed.

She didn't know what that meant. Fake dating didn't involve sleeping over. Anytime they'd hooked up over the last couple of weeks had been at his place after an improv lesson, and she'd always gone home afterward. She'd been content with that arrangement, used to having her own space, but last night she hadn't wanted him to go. And she'd sensed he hadn't wanted to leave either. So despite knowing it was probably a bad idea, she'd invited him into her bed. They'd cuddled.

Cal was going to give her the third degree when he got her alone later. She'd been trying to sell this relationship with Jasper to him, but maybe she'd gone a little overboard.

She sat up, wincing at the dull throb in her head, and reached for the water Jasper had left on her side table. She gulped down the whole thing. Her hangover was mild. Getting rid of the contents of her stomach as soon as they'd gotten home last night—not her most shining moment of the evening—had probably helped, but she needed to brush her teeth more than she needed to take her next breath.

Careful not to wake Jasper, she slipped out of bed and went into the bathroom to take care of all the necessities. She made sure her mouth was minty fresh, washed her face, and drank another glass of water. There was nothing to be done about her wild hair, but by the time she made it back to bed, she felt somewhat human again.

The springs in her mattress protested as she snuggled back under the covers. The memory of last night came back to her in pieces. Jasper standing there in the dark. The scent of his freshly showered body slipping into bed a while later. Somehow her fruity shower gel had smelled completely different on him—enticing in a way she never would've anticipated berry-burst body wash could be. Then there was Jasper spooning her, the thick heat of his erection growing hard against her backside. So much of her had wanted to rub herself against him, to take things to that place. But she hadn't trusted her stomach. She already had a barfed-on-a-dog story in her past, no way was she adding a barfing-on-a-hot-guy tale to that list. A girl could only handle so much humiliation. So despite the physical ache feeling him against her had caused, she'd resisted. And he hadn't tried to persuade her or push the issue. He'd been a gentleman.

No, he'd been Jasper. A guy she was quickly learning could be trusted to respect her boundaries.

However, this morning, she was feeling better, and seeing him lying there next to her, the desire flourished anew, and she was much less concerned with drawing lines in the sand.

She hadn't slept in the same bed with a guy since Cal, and even then it hadn't been an overnight thing. When they'd dated, they hadn't had their own places. Cal had been in a boys-only dorm. She had been at her mother's. This was new. A gorgeous man tangled up in her sheets. She wanted to indulge.

She propped herself up on her elbow next to him and decided to be bold. She let her fingertips trace over his chest, mapping the hard planes there, feeling the little patch of crisp hairs between his pecs, and then circling his nipples and watching them stiffen from her touch. The sheets twitched at his waist, the male part of him coming online before his brain did, and she smirked with satisfaction.

Jasper might not be awake yet, but some parts of him were taking notice. She liked the surge of sexual confidence that came with that knowledge. Yes, she had her issues, but she could be sexy, too. She could entice and tempt. She let her fingers track lower, mapping his abdomen and then traveling the little treasure trail down to his waistband. Jasper's breathing changed as the sheets became tented.

"Hollyn," he said in a sleep-clogged voice.

"Good morning." She didn't look at his face, but instead let her nails scrape gently along the sensitive skin below his navel. A flicker of nerves tried to surface because she didn't *really* know how to seduce a guy, but she shoved down the anxiety. There wasn't like…a seduction *protocol*. She just needed to follow her own desire. She could do this. She could be the aggressor. "I'm touching you. Do you want me to stop?"

His belly dipped with a sharp breath at her touch. "Right, because it's awful to wake up to a beautiful woman getting me hard. Worst nightmare ever. This torture must stop."

She bit her lip and dared a glance at his face. His half-lidded gaze was firmly on her, the hazel in his eyes more green in the early-morning light.

He propped an arm behind his head and smiled that dangerous half smile of his. "Good morning to you, Hollyn Darling. Feeling better?"

She dipped her head, suddenly shy under his gaze. "Much."

He glanced down at his now obvious erection. "Me too, apparently."

Her face warmed, and her nose scrunched a few times. "Sorry I woke you."

"You better not apologize for that. Best alarm clock ever." He reached out and pushed her hair away from her face. "But if you have some secret fantasy to mess around with a sleeping guy, I'm here for it. I can close my eyes and pretend."

She huffed a quiet laugh. "You're safe. No *While You Were Sleeping* fantasies."

He settled into the pillow. "Good, because it's hot to watch you touch me."

Her heartbeat was sinking lower, the *thump, thump, thump* finding its way to the spot between her thighs. "Yeah?"

"Of course." He gave her an evaluating look, his forehead crinkling. "You look like you're thinking too hard for this early in the morning. What's going on in that head of yours?"

She rolled her lips together, trying to work up the courage, to not be embarrassed by what she wanted. "Would it be weird if I asked to, like, explore you?"

His lips parted slightly, and his gaze swept over her, lingering in certain places. No doubt her nipples were hard points beneath her T-shirt, announcing how secretly turned on she was by all this. "Explore?"

Anxiety tried to join the party. She could feel her tics pulling at her face, but she did her best to ignore them. "I know it's going to make me sound like a freak, but I've never really had the chance to just…" *Grimace. Scrunch. Blink, blink.* "Take my time and explore a guy. I want to find out what makes you feel good."

"Ah," Jasper said with a knowing voice. "I see what's happening here."

She frowned and touched her twitching cheek. "What?"

"I'm clearly still asleep and am having an erotic dream. Because there's no way a sexy, panty-clad Hollyn just asked me to lie back so she can find out how to make me feel good."

His joke was just what she needed to release the tension that had gathered in her body and turn her uncontrollable grimace into a very purposeful smile. "So that's a yes?"

He reached out and cupped her breast through her T-shirt, dragging his thumb across the tip and sending a spike of arousal straight down. "That's a huge yes. I literally could think of no better way to spend a morning—except maybe being afforded the same right to play Magellan with you."

She shifted, her panties damp and her body growing more sensitive. "That could probably be arranged. So you don't think I'm weird?"

"First, you say weird like it's a bad thing. I make my living on weird. But no. This is the best kind of learning I could think of. Let's have a lesson in this every day." He sent her an unrepentant grin. "How to Make Jasper Hot and Bothered 101 followed immediately by How to Make Hollyn Come 201. And 301. And if we mix in some breakfast and hydrate, perhaps 401."

She rolled her eyes, but a giddy lightness filled her.

"Seriously, though," he said, his eyes meeting hers and his finger winding a tendril of her hair. "I know we're doing this partly because you want to get comfortable with some things, so don't get so stressed out to ask me stuff." He smoothed a finger down her twitching cheek. "Ask for what you want. Always. Not just with me. If, in the future, a guy ever thinks you're weird or throws shade at you for doing that, then you drop his ass on the hot pavement. Sex can be fun. It can be hot. It can be kinky or serious. It can be a lot of things. But what it should always be is a safe zone to explore what each person likes. If everyone is consenting and it's legal, there really are no limits beyond that." He brushed his fingertip over her lips. "Just be you. Because *you* are pretty damn spectacular, Hollyn Darling. Any guy you invite into your bed should thank the benevolent universe that he has the privilege of being there and should answer any question you have and let you explore all you want."

Something peaceful settled deep in Hollyn's bones at his words. This was Jasper without the facade, without the layer of jokes and sarcasm. She was getting peeks of that guy more and more. Underneath that quick wit of his, he was a genuinely caring person who wanted to make others feel accepted and safe. Not once had he made her feel different or judged or odd. Not for her questions, not for asking for an unconventional relationship, not for her anxiety, and not for her uncooperative muscles. He'd never made her feel like he was hanging out with her despite her issues. With him, she sometimes forgot she even *had* the tics. Because he didn't stare. He didn't make her feel self-conscious. He embraced exactly who she was.

No, not just embraced but seemed to genuinely enjoy being with her—both as a friend and a lover.

He treated her like she was...Hollyn. Not the chick with the tics. Not the woman with the panic attacks. Not the homeschooled freak from the small town. With him, she was label-less.

He saw *her*.

The realization was like a plunge in an icy lake—bracing and clear and bright.

"Hey, you okay?" Jasper asked.

Her expression must've changed, but she couldn't find her words, so she just nodded. *I'm fine. I'm fine. I'm fine.* But she was definitely *not* fine. Her body had gone cold and then hot all over, and her chest had tightened as if her ribs had been cinched up with string. It was like a panic attack only...not. It was her inner voice screaming at her. *Oh shit. Oh no. Don't do this. You promised.* But it was too damn late.

She had caught the plague she'd been determined to inoculate herself from.

She'd caught *feelings*. Motherfucking, knock-her-on-her-ass feelings. For a guy who had told her there was no chance for more.

She was so damn pathetic. She was supposed to be tougher than this by now. *Don't fall for the popular guy. Don't fall for someone who isn't a possibility. Don't be that girl waiting under the tree for the kiss again.* She was smarter than this. She blinked quickly, her eyes burning, and looked away.

"Hollyn?" Jasper asked, concern in his voice.

She took a deep inhale and tried to refocus her thoughts. She *would not* do this right now. She could freak out about this later—alone, when Jasper wasn't here. This morning wasn't about feelings. He'd slept over because it was late, and they were hooking up. This was sex. This was supposed to be about sex.

That was what it had to be about. *Needed* to be about. Jasper wasn't here to love her. He wasn't going to be her boyfriend. She wasn't going to introduce him to her mother. She needed to focus on what was real. What was good.

This didn't have to be a tragedy. There was a gorgeous half-naked man offering himself to her. Someone who was great in bed and attracted to her. She needed to focus on that. On how delicious Jasper looked. On how skilled he was at touching her. Not on the feelings he stirred up.

"Tell me a fetish or fantasy you wouldn't tell just anyone," she blurted out, trying to reroute the conversation and her whirlwind thoughts.

Jasper sank back against the pillow and chuckled. "How long have you got?"

"Ha. Just one for now," she said, folding down the covers and revealing his still-tented boxers. She zeroed in on the physical sensations that sight set off. That was the only kind of feelings she needed to be focused on right now. Her body's response to him. All she wanted to think about was the way Jasper's body was going to feel beneath her hands, the way it would feel to have him inside her again. The images that conjured chased the panic into a dark corner and got her back on track. She traced a line along his length through the cotton, fascinated by the way his cock flexed and jumped at her barely there touch.

His abdomen dipped like he was trying to find a breath. "Just one. Okay."

"An embarrassing one," she clarified, circling the head of his cock with her fingertip, a damp spot appearing on his shorts.

"So clearly torture is one of yours," he joked. "Okay, embarrassing, some fetish or fantasy I wouldn't tell anyone else. Let's see..." He made a disgusted sound in the back of his throat.

That got her attention. "What? Whatever one just crossed your mind, tell me."

He groaned. "God, this one is pretty gross. *I* would judge me for this one."

Her eyebrows lifted and she glanced at his face. "Now, I'm really intrigued."

He cringed and closed his eyes. "So I *may* have this fantasy of a woman getting my name tattooed some place on her body that only I would see. Something that marked her as mine."

Hollyn's lips parted.

He cracked an eyelid open, peeking at her. "It's so obnoxiously egotistical and misogynistic, I know. But there it is. The thought makes me hard. That's definitely something I wouldn't tell anyone else. You can now proceed to blackmail me."

She stared at him, processing that. *Marking her as mine.* That sent a shiver of heat through her. "Isn't that like a kink thing? Like putting a collar or brand on someone or whatever?"

She hadn't done kink, but she'd certainly read about it.

He wet his lips. "Maybe? But that really isn't my scene. It's more. I don't know. I can't really explain it. But like, the thought of making love to a woman and seeing my name on her shoulder or something like that. Something permanent." His cock jumped against her hand, the fantasy clearly sending his blood pumping. "It just does it for me."

The words settled over Hollyn, turning over in her head, as she decided how she felt about that. Maybe Jasper's ego really was off the charts. But then, something clicked into place. Why he might like that idea. She'd bet everything she had that the fantasy wasn't about ownership for him. It was the *permanence*. A tattoo wasn't going anywhere. A ring could be tossed. A foster kid could be moved. Jasper hadn't ever had anything that was one hundred percent his. He probably had never been able to even write his name on a toy until he was adopted. Everything was always temporary or shared. Transient.

She looked at him, saw vulnerability flash through his eyes.

"You think I'm a complete egomaniac," he said with a laugh. "Or a sociopath. I promise I'm not here to serial-kill you."

She smiled, an idea sparking. She moved her hand away from him for a moment and twisted toward her nightstand. She pulled open the drawer and rifled around inside. When she found what she was looking for, she grabbed it and turned back to him.

"What are you doing?" he asked, trying to see what she'd gotten.

She lifted up a black Sharpie to show him and then handed him the marker. "It's not a tattoo, but it's going to take a few days to come off."

His brows dipped. "What?"

She sat up. "I'm going to explore you. And *you*, you're going to sign your name anywhere you want on me."

His eyes widened, his gaze turning almost black. "Hollyn."

She pulled her T-shirt over her head, loving the way he watched her every move, and straddled him. "You can even touch it up or replace it whenever we're together. Your name will be on me. Marking me as just for you, at least for a little while."

He closed his eyes and his body shuddered beneath her thighs. "You're going to fucking kill me."

The pleasure that rushed through her at his response warmed her through and through. She could make this man shudder and twitch beneath her. She couldn't make him fall in love with her, but she could unravel him in bed. That was something. "You game, Jasper Deares?"

He opened his eyes, his gaze colliding with hers. Her nipples hardened at the intense stare, the feel of his warm, bare abdomen beneath her spread legs. "You have no idea."

He clamped the marker between his teeth and then grabbed

her by the waist and rolled her onto her back. She gasped at the sudden movement, her body hitting the mattress with a bounce.

He stared down at her, his gaze hungry, his lips in a half smile. "You better not be bluffing."

She inhaled deeply, feeling a rush of confidence, and cupped her breasts, offering them to him. "Not bluffing. Mark me."

Jasper's teeth pressed into his bottom lip, making him look feral, but he shook his head at her offering. He leaned down and flicked his tongue over her nipples before sucking each briefly into his mouth and making her whimper with the erotic circling of his tongue. But just when her body started to rev, he released her flesh with a soft pop. "Not there," he said, his breath hot against her sensitive breasts. He shifted down and kissed along her belly, making her toes curl with the tendrils of sensation snaking out from the contact. "Not here either."

She arched beneath him, her body going restless and overly hot. She needed him to touch her, to taste her, to do *something* to relieve the growing ache between her thighs.

He reached the waistband of her panties and tugged at them with his teeth. The little snap of elastic against her skin made her tip her head back, her clit now throbbing for his touch.

He kissed down the front of her panties, pressing his tongue against the already damp fabric, making her moan.

"Not here," he whispered.

Then he slid down further and licked a trail up her inner thigh. Her fingers grabbed at him and curled into his hair. All worries and concerns she had earlier evaporated in her mind, all her attention zeroing in on Jasper's touch.

"Yep," he said with satisfaction. "This is the spot."

He kissed her where her leg met hip and then he pulled the cap off the marker with his teeth. The pungent scent of the marker filled the air, and she pushed herself up onto her elbows, needing to watch. Jasper spread her legs, hungrily taking in the view, and then with careful precision he wrote on her upper inner thigh with his slanting script.

The tip of the marker shouldn't have felt so erotic, but the skin there was tender and hypersensitive. Those nerve endings seemed to have a direct line to her core because she felt a rush of hot, slick need between her legs. Jasper dragged the tip over her, making goose bumps chase up her leg, and finished his name with a flourish. When he was done, he gazed at his handiwork and then looked up at her like she was the most delectable meal he'd ever laid eyes on.

She swallowed past the dryness in her throat. "How does it look?"

He shook his head as if he couldn't speak yet and then he crawled up her body. "It looks perfect. *You* look perfect. *Feel* perfect." He braced himself above her, his hardened cock rocking against the front of her panties and making lightning spark through her. "Do you know what it's going to do to me at work the next couple of days, knowing you're walking around with my name on your fucking thigh?"

"Tell me," she whispered, her hips rocking against him without her conscious control.

He bent his head close to her ear. "I'm going to get hard every time I see you. I'm going to think about dragging you into the nearest office, shoving up your skirt, and sliding deep inside you until you're soaking wet and screaming for me. And if I can't have you, I'm going to go home and put my slick fist around my cock and come, imagining you with your legs spread and my name there on your skin."

Holy. Shit. She'd never thought she'd be one for dirty talk or even if Jasper would be the type to use it, but holy hell, she was so here for it. Her inner muscles clenched like he was already making good on the promises. "God, Jasper."

He reached for the marker and set it between her breasts. "No one else gets to see me naked either."

Her heart was beating hard against her ribs. "Yeah?"

"Promise."

She let her hand trail down and close around the marker. "Can I?"

His gaze flared with fire. "You want to?"

She was surprised by the answer that immediately popped into her head. "Yeah, I kinda do."

He smiled a satisfied smile. "I'm all yours, Hollyn Darling."

If only that were true. But she dismissed the unhelpful thought. He rolled off of her and she stared down at him. "Lose the boxers."

"Yes ma'am," he said, a pleased note in his voice. He reached down and tugged off his boxers, revealing the impressively thick erection he'd been corralling. The smooth, flushed head was shiny with arousal. Hollyn's tongue pressed to the back of her teeth. *Have mercy.* Maybe she wasn't as dumb as she'd thought. In fact, maybe she was fucking brilliant. Yes, she had developed *the feels* and was going to have to deal with that. But right now, she was looking like a genius. She had made this happen. She hadn't settled for some awkward one-night stand to break her dry spell. She hadn't chickened out and decided to live the life of a nun. She had taken a risk and asked for what she wanted. She had gotten this gorgeous, funny, smart guy in her bed, where they had no awkwardness, no pressure. Just fun and sex and heat. *Gold star, Hollyn.*

Following her instincts, she lowered her head and dragged her tongue across the head of Jasper's cock, tasting his heat. Jasper groaned and grabbed the base of his erection like he was afraid he'd go off right there. She smiled and got to her knees. She settled in between his spread legs and then pulled the cap off the marker. He'd signed her inner thigh. She had her own place she wanted to mark. She trailed her fingers through the thin dark line of hair beneath his navel, no barrier stopping her now and watched as his cock twitched for her. She leaned over, took him into her mouth, and then signed her name right along his treasure trail, right where it would disappear into his boxers, as she sucked him.

Jasper groaned and fisted the sheets, obviously fighting to stay still. She finished signing, capped the marker, and then threw it onto the floor. She slid her mouth off his cock and stared down at her autograph, tracing the edges with her fingertip.

Jasper reached down and caught her hand. "You like it, don't you?"

Her lips curved and she met his eyes. "You're not the only freak I guess."

"Cofreaks," he agreed. "Excellent match."

"We are." The words made her chest flutter. *No ma'am, none of that.* She shook off the feelings that were trying to fight their way in and then slid her hands down her thighs. "Time to explore."

....

Jasper was going to die. But at least he'd die a happy man. Hollyn lowered her head and kissed a line up his inner thigh, making his muscles jump and his body beg. Any other woman would just get down to business and go straight for the blow job—the sure-to-please thing. But not Hollyn. Hollyn wanted to take her time. To find the nuances of what made him feel like he was going to explode. Somehow, her careful attention was more erotic than her putting her mouth on him—not that he would've turned down more of that. Her mouth had felt like heat-soaked heaven. But her genuine curiosity and desire were the sexiest lingerie she could've worn. He suspected she'd be game for just about anything. An experimenter.

And man, was he ready to be her research subject.

She kissed her way up his thigh, keeping his legs spread,

and then she nuzzled his balls, the brush of her nose against him sending white-hot pleasure through his veins. Her breath was warm against him, erotic, anticipatory, and then the flat of her tongue laved over him.

Christ. He was going to come like a teenager at this rate. Kill the whole mood with his inability to control himself. This woman was *Hot. As. Fuck.* And she had no freaking idea. For some reason, she thought he was doing a favor for her. He needed to fix that misguided notion immediately.

"Does that feel good?" she asked, a tentative note in her voice. "Is that okay?"

Is that okay? He briefly entertained an erotic student/professor fantasy with her in a short little plaid skirt and nearly melted his brain. "I'm sorry. My eyes have rolled into the back of my head. I'll have to get back to you on that."

He could feel her smile against him, her lips tickling the base of his cock. He was definitely going to ruin this and come in her hair. She'd never forgive him for that. He tried to conjugate verbs in his head to stave off his orgasm.

But Hollyn was unrelenting. Her fingers moved over him, touching him everywhere, squeezing his cock, palming his balls, even dipping low with her fingertips and tracing along the most private of places. His bones were going to liquefy. His brain already had. But he'd let this woman touch him anywhere.

She let me write my name on her. His stupid, bizarre fantasy hadn't fazed her. More than that, she'd embraced it and had given him the version she could. Right now, his mark was scrawled on her thigh, damp with her sweat and arousal. God, he was never going to get any work done at WorkAround again. That image was going to be burned into his brain every time she was near him even after the ink washed off.

"Whatever we do, we have to be quiet," she said, wrapping her fingers around his erection and applying just enough pressure to drive him nuts. "Cal will wake up soon. I don't want him to hear."

Jasper's jaw tightened. Part of him wanted to cry out in exaggerated ecstasy—no, he wanted *Hollyn* to cry out—so that Cal could hear loud and clear that Jasper was the one in her bed, that he was the one making her feel good. But he swallowed back the caveman instincts. "I'll do my best, gorgeous, but the sounds I make might not always be in my control."

"Bite a pillow," she said, stroking him now. "That's what I do when…"

"Fuck. Me," he said on a groan. The visual was too much. "Finish your sentence."

She paused for a moment but then said, "When I use my vibrator."

All his breath whooshed out of him. He wanted to see that. Wanted to see Hollyn spread out on this bed, touching herself, making herself come. Later. Another day. Right now, he didn't have the patience for that. If he wasn't inside her soon, he was actually going to die.

"Hollyn, I need you. Please," he said, unable to hold back anymore. "You have condoms?"

"Just bought some." She crawled across him and reached back into the bedside table. She dropped a packet onto his chest.

He grabbed the condom and put it on the bed within reach. "Good. But first, lose the panties and come here."

She quickly divested herself of her underwear, tossing them off the side of the bed. "Where?"

He grabbed her hands and guided her up his body.

When she was straddling his chest, she got a brief look of alarm. "Jasper, what are—"

He tugged her higher. "I need to taste you first, baby. Straddle me and hold on to the headboard."

"You want me to...?"

He answered her by showing her, guiding her upward until she was spread out above him, in perfect position for his mouth. His signature flexed on her thigh in his periphery and his cock jerked in response. *Mine.* He dragged his tongue along her sweet, plump flesh, relishing the taste of her, and she let out a sound that came from somewhere deep in her belly.

"Oh God," she said. "I'm never going to stay quiet."

He reached out and grabbed her discarded T-shirt. "Use this."

She took it from him, balled it up, and bit. So sexy. So game for anything.

He grabbed her hips and tasted her again, the tart, sexy flavor of her making his blood rush. It was a crime that she'd been left alone all this time, no one here to give her the pleasure she deserved. He wanted to make it up to her, to make her feel everything. He curled his tongue around her clit and then sucked the nub between his lips.

She gasped and rocked against his mouth, begging him with her body. *Fuck yes.* He could do this all morning. He loved how hungry she was in bed, how unashamed to take the pleasure. He knew without a doubt, she'd never been in this position with a guy before. She'd clearly been reluctant when he'd led her there, but now, now she was losing herself to it. His fingers dug into the flesh of her ass and he feasted on her, using his nose, lips, and tongue to give her every ounce of pleasure he was capable of offering. She was in a rhythm now, lost to it, her sounds muffled by the T-shirt, and he couldn't get enough.

Hollyn. Hollyn. Hollyn.

His tongue dipped into her and she jerked against him, her muscles stiffening in his hold. He held her firm when she tried to wiggle away, and the feel of her coming apart against his mouth was a revelation. Hollyn didn't come like the quiet woman she was day to day—she came like a freight train, like all those words and thoughts she kept bottled up exploded into a brilliant burst of sensation and ecstasy all at once.

The T-shirt dropped from her mouth, and he softened his attentions as she came down from the high, kissing and licking with softer strokes. She sagged against the headboard, panting, and he gently rolled her off of him and onto her back. She blinked up at him, dazed, her hair a golden riot of curls around her head. "That was... You should charge for that."

He laughed. "I'll consider it as a backup profession if this comedy thing doesn't work out."

She smiled a drunk-on-lust smile and looped her arms around his neck. "Nah, you don't need a backup. It's going to work out. If I haven't told you yet, you're fucking amazing, Jasper."

"I think you mean amazing at fucking," he teased.

She shook her head, the humor falling from her face. "No, I know what I mean. I saw the show last night. You're talented as hell. You'll get your dream."

He leaned down to kiss her, the words meaning more to him than they should. Had anyone ever told him that? Believed in him without adding fine print? It was usually... *You're talented but it's a tough business. It's good to dream but you should have a backup plan.* Never just *You'll get your dream. You can do it. I believe in you.*

But when he looked down into her eyes, he believed her. She really did think he was capable, that it would happen.

"You're pretty damn incredible yourself," he said softly.

She smiled a smile that seeped right into his skin, warming him from the inside out. He didn't trust himself to speak again, so he reached out and found the condom. He tossed the wrapper aside and rolled it on. Then, without any games or jokes or antics, he slid his hand behind her knee, opened her body to him, and made love to her. Slow and deep and never dropping the eye contact.

As he rocked into her, relishing the feel of not having to rush, he watched her watching him back. When they'd first met, all she'd wanted to do was hide from him. Turn her face away. Run. Now she was here with him, as naked and vulnerable as a person could be, and she wasn't running. She was boldly staring back, one hundred percent feeling this moment with him. Confident and sexy. It filled him up with a satisfaction that had nothing to do with how good his body was feeling.

Hollyn cupped the back of his neck, pulling him down to kiss her. He closed his eyes and felt his hold on the situation slipping. All this time, he'd been holding on to the edge of the pool, always with a hand safely on the cement. He wasn't going to sink into the deep end again. He wasn't going to choke on the water.

But when Hollyn whispered his name against his lips and he buried deep inside her, coming along with her, he felt his grip slip.

He was going to drown.

And if he didn't stop it, he was going to take her down with him.

chapter **twenty-three**

HOLLYN PADDED INTO HER KITCHEN IN THICK, FUZZY socks and yoga pants, humming a little tune. Jasper had headed home to shower and change clothes since he had a late-morning shift at the coffee bar today. After he'd left, she'd felt inspired and had typed up a few posts. She'd even started drafting a review of the Hail Yes group. She wanted to do that one on video and surprise Jasper. But until then, she'd get to spend some one-on-one time with Cal because Jasper had a packed schedule for the next two days and she'd taken the time off to spend with her BFF.

She opened the fridge and pulled out the orange juice, debating whether she should offer to make breakfast or take Cal to a jazz brunch. When she set the juice down and reached for a glass from the cabinet, the floorboards squeaked behind her.

"Morning." Cal's deep voice rumbled through the quiet kitchen.

"Morning." She turned with a smile and then winced at the ashen face of her best friend. "Oh shit. I thought you said you could handle your alcohol. You look like roadkill."

Cal grunted and scrubbed his hands over his face. "I can usually handle it fine. But I may have *panic station* finished off that half bottle of wine you had in the fridge after you went to bed. I may be *hella good* hating myself right now."

"You finished the wine?" Her eyebrows lifted. "Okay, George Thorogood. You drink alone?"

"I wasn't exactly *kill the lights* alone." He reached past her to grab a glass from her cabinet and then filled it with tap water. "I needed to *hella good* drink so I wouldn't tic all over the place with your new friend. You know how it is with strangers."

"You and Jasper hung out?" she asked, turning her back to him to pour her juice and trying to sound nonchalant. She hoped Cal had slept hard and hadn't heard anything this morning. Talk about awkward.

"We talked for a while before he went to bed. Your bed." Cal sniffed. "I didn't realize y'all were at the *panic station* sleeping-over stage already. Seems fast."

She turned at that, frowning. "Seems fast? Okay, Mr. Judgy."

He took a long sip of water. "I'm just saying, how long have you been seeing this guy? Half a second?"

"Not that it's your business but over a month. Would you like a side of bacon with that slut-shaming?"

He grunted. "I'm not *hella good* shaming you. I'm just—"

But she was too irritated at the implication to let him finish. "You're just telling me a month is too fast. So the only women you sleep with are long-term girlfriends?"

"No, I'm saying that *kill the lights* I don't have anyone *sleeping over*," he said in frustration. "That's different than sex."

She rolled her eyes. "So you just send them on their way when you're done? Because that's better."

Cal took another gulp of water and eyed her, his mouth in a grim line, his shoulder shrugging. "I'm not trying to be a *kill the lights* dick. And I'm not judging you for hooking up. It's just... I'm worried about you, okay? Sleeping next to someone can make something feel more serious than it actually *hella good* is. It makes it feel...like something real."

Something real. An ache went through her.

"I know it's not that serious, all right?" she said with a petulant tone. Her stomach twisted in a knot, though, Cal's point feeling all too close to that rush of emotion she'd been hit with this morning. "It's not like Jasper is leading me on or something. We're just having fun and seeing where things go."

Cal stared at her over the rim of his glass, his gaze bordering on pitying. "I don't want you to get hurt."

"Cal," she groaned. "Where is this coming from? You were the one who wanted me to put myself out there. Here I am, putting myself out there."

"Emphasis on the *'putting out'* part. Multiple times."

She gasped and grabbed a kitchen towel from the edge of the sink and tossed it at him. "Cal Summers, you shut your face."

He smirked, though the humor didn't make it to his eyes, and caught the towel. "Your walls are *rolling stone* thin, Tate."

Her face burned and she knew she had to be red up to her hairline. "A best friend would pretend he'd heard nothing."

He set his glass down and stepped closer. He snapped the towel toward her, catching her lightly on the thigh. "A best friend would not subject her former boyfriend to hearing her *hella good* screw another dude. *Oh, Jasper. God. Yes. Right there.*"

"I hate you," she said with a huff.

"I love you, too." He pulled her into a one-armed hug and kissed the top of her head. "But take my *kill the lights* advice. Scratch the itch with the actor and move on. He's a flighty one. Told me if he caught a break, he'd *hella good* bail on this town in a hot minute."

Hollyn stiffened and pulled back. "What? No. He's trying to buy a theater here."

Cal shrugged and released her, tossing the towel onto the counter. "Just reporting what your new boyfriend told me. *Rolling stone.* I get the feeling that the theater is the plan for now until something better comes along. You think if some talent scout sees him in a show or online and offers him something bigger, he wouldn't leave?"

She frowned.

"So," Cal said, "after I take a shitload of meds for this hangover, *kill the lights*, what do you want to do today? I've been looking forward to having you all to myself since I arrived."

Hollyn let out a breath and shook her head. "Whatever you want. I'm all yours."

Cal pointed at her. "That's what I like to hear, my panic station chicken." He grabbed her hand and kissed her knuckles. "Because you need to show me the ropes of good ol' NOLA. It's going to be my new home."

She blinked, the words not quite registering. "What?"

He beamed at her. "I wanted to make sure it was a done deal before I told you. But yesterday morning, I met with a company I've been talking to for a while and did a final interview. They offered me the job. I start as soon as I finish up this last semester."

"Oh my God." Her chest expanded with an influx of joy. "You're moving here? Like for real?"

He grabbed her hands and squeezed. "Yeah. For real."

Her mind was whirling with too many thoughts. "What about the band?"

"They're heading down with me. The gigs are better here." He gave her a brow lift. "So what do you think?"

She shook her head, her excitement almost too much to contain. Her best friend was going to be here in town with her. She wouldn't be alone anymore. She threw her arms around him for a hug. "I think this is the best news ever."

He enveloped her in a hug and pressed his nose to her hair. "I'm so happy you're *hella good* happy."

"Of course I'm happy," she said, cheek pressed against his chest, his heart beating hard. "My favorite person in the world is going to be living in the same city. This is amazing news."

Cal loosened his hold on her a little and leaned back to look down at her, his gaze searching hers. "You're my favorite person, too. *Kill the lights.* You know that, right?"

She smiled, a little confused by his earnest tone. "Of course."

He reached up and tucked her hair behind her ear. "Hollyn…"

When he didn't say anything else, her brow wrinkled and she searched his expression, trying to read him. But then she felt the air between them shift, a crackle there. "Cal…"

"Fuck it," he whispered.

"What?"

But he was already leaning in. Her brain couldn't process what it meant until it was too late and his lips touched hers. Her entire body froze in his hold. Cal was *kissing* her. No, *Cal* was kissing her. Somehow it felt both familiar and completely foreign at the same time.

She put her hands to his chest and pushed gently, breaking the connection almost immediately. She took a big step back, her heart racing, and looked up at Cal in shock.

His shoulder shrugged roughly, and his throat worked as he swallowed, but he didn't look away.

Hollyn stared at him. When he didn't say anything, she blurted out, "What the hell was that?"

Cal's jaw clenched, like he was trying hard not to tic. He took a deep breath. "I don't know. I guess that was…the truth."

Her lips were numb, like her body didn't know how to react to this insanity either. "The truth? Cal, *you kissed me.*"

"I know. *Panic station.*" He cleared his throat. "I've been wanting to do that for a really long time."

Hollyn leaned back against the counter, not trusting her knees not to give out on her. Cal, her best friend and ex-boyfriend, had been wanting to kiss her for a long time? What planet was this? "What is this? I don't understand. You've wanted to *kiss me*? You've been the one telling me to date."

"I know." He sighed and shifted to the spot next to her, leaning against the counter and gripping the edge of it. "I thought that was for the best. To not have your whole dating history be just me. Plus, I didn't want to risk messing up our friendship when you were going through so much change already. I was going to wait until I moved down here to bring up the possibility. But..."

She glanced over at him, frowning at his downtrodden tone. "But what?"

He turned his head a little, barely meeting her gaze. "I didn't realize how much it would hurt to see you with someone else." His Adam's apple bobbed, and his shoulder went through a quick succession of hard shrugs. He turned to her, his eyes somber. "Watching Jasper dance with you, touch you? Hearing what I heard this morning? *Kill the lights.* I wanted to bust in there and yank you away from him, Tate. I wanted to make you look at me. See me. Have your hands on *me.*"

Her lungs flattened out and she gripped her elbows, trying to keep it together. Cal wanted her? To touch her? Be in her bed?

Shit. She had no idea what to do with that revelation. She and Cal had dated forever ago. Yes, she'd loved him and thought he was the one back then. She'd wanted him to be her forever person. But they'd been so young. And *he'd* broken up with *her*, had convinced her they were better off as friends. They'd been best friends for years now with no hint of anything more. "I don't understand," she said, shaking her head, the room spinning a little. "Where is this coming from?"

Cal turned fully to her and took her hands in his, his blue eyes big and serious. "I'm sorry. It's my fault this is blindsiding you. I wanted to give you space and time and opportunity to experience things on your own, without any pressure of feelings from me."

"Feelings?" She felt like all she could do was stare and repeat what he was saying with a question mark.

He squeezed her hands, his expression beseeching. "I love you, Hollyn. Not just as a friend. I don't think I ever stopped feeling that way after we dated. *Panic station.* But we needed time apart. I wanted to make sure what I was feeling wasn't just kid stuff. *Kill the lights.* And I didn't want to be your default choice."

Her tics flared, her cheek twitching hard. "My default? Cal—"

"After what happened when we were kids, you stopped taking risks. You got scared and went for the sure things, the safe choices. And I don't blame you. You've been through hell. But I didn't want to be one of your safe choices. I wanted *kill the lights* to be the right choice. The guy who lit you up inside for more reasons than that I also had Tourette's and wouldn't hurt your feelings. I needed you to go out and experience some life, date other guys, be on your own. I wanted to know for sure that if you came back to me, it was because you wanted *me*, not because I was in your comfort zone."

Cal's fingers were firm around hers. Thank God, because he was knocking her worldview sideways and she wasn't entirely sure she wasn't going to tip right over. Cal, her best friend, the big-hearted, beautiful guitarist loved her. As more than a friend. And had apparently felt this way for a long time.

All those late-night phone calls drifted back to her, all those times he'd been there for her, all those times he'd made her feel glad to be who she was. He'd been in her corner for so long she didn't remember what life was like before he'd come into it. Now he was saying he wanted to be that and more to her.

Getting back together with Cal was a secret wish she'd held on to for a long time after they'd broken up. Back then, she'd always hoped that their shift into friendship was a temporary one. They were perfect for each other in so many ways. They understood what it was like to have a disorder, to be looked at oddly, to be different. She'd always thought he was easy on the eyes. They'd been good together in bed—well, as good as the young and inexperienced could be.

But…

Thoughts of the man whose name was currently scrawled on her thigh filled her head, scrambling her brain and her complicated feelings. She closed her eyes. "Cal, I don't know what to say. This is a lot."

"I know. I'm sorry. I didn't plan to *panic station* blurt it all out like this. I was in it for the long haul. I was going to move down here and be as patient as you needed me to be. But seeing you with Jasper…" He made a frustrated sound. "I just can't stand by and let some other guy use you like that. I need you to know you have other options."

Her eyelids popped open, and a snap of irritation moved through her. She slipped her hands free of his. "He's not using me."

"He doesn't love you," Cal said gently.

She tipped her head back. "Of course he doesn't. That doesn't mean he's using me. It just means it's a new relationship. I'm not delusional."

Cal put his hands on her face and gently guided her to look at him. "You forget. I *know you*, Tate. *Hella good.* Whether you think there's something there on his end or not, I saw how you looked at him last night. There are feelings developing on your end."

"Cal—"

"Crushes get you crushed," he said, concern all over his face. "Please don't do that to yourself. Even if you don't feel the same way about me that I do about you, don't let it be this guy. This guy is a bad investment."

She shook her head, and Cal lowered his hands. "You don't even know him."

His jaw flexed. "I know that I told him how I feel about you and he didn't stay here this morning."

That made her stomach clench. "He had to work."

"If I was really into a woman and the guy sleeping on her couch told me he loved her, you can damn well guarantee that I wouldn't leave her without telling her exactly how I feel about her," he said. "Instead, he left you with me."

Hollyn looked down, a tight feeling growing in her throat. Cal wasn't telling her anything she didn't know, but somehow, it felt like grief. Was she doing that thing again? Pinning unrequited feelings on the popular boy she had no real shot with. What did she think would end up happening with Jasper? That he was just going to rethink his whole life plan and jump into a long-term relationship with her?

The flicker of hope that tried to spark at that thought proved that somewhere inside her she'd been keeping vigil with that little candle. *Fuck.*

Cal stepped closer and cupped her chin, tilting it toward him, his blue eyes full of so much—connection, attraction, love. "I can make you happy, Tate," he said, voice full of tenderness. "If you can take off the friendship blinders and really look at what we have, I think you'll see that. We already love each other. We already have each other's backs. We make each other laugh. We have trust. Just think how amazing it will be if we add the other things—the relationship things." He swallowed hard, like this was taking everything out of him. "You don't have to be alone anymore. You don't have to wonder where a guy stands. You'll always know where I stand. Right next to you. Loving you."

Her ribs cinched tight at his words and the fact that he hadn't ticced once. His focus was one hundred percent on her. And the story he was painting was a tempting one, one she had imagined before, one she would've jumped on without hesitation even a few months ago. But her brain was a tangle of thoughts and emotions she couldn't unravel. She couldn't process her feelings about her lifelong best friend after having had the best sex of her life a few hours ago. "Cal..."

"I'm not asking for an answer now," he said. "*Panic station.* I know my timing sucks. But I needed to let you know how I feel. When I move down here, I want to be with you. *Kill the lights.* That's where I'm at. Whatever you do between now and then is up to you. I won't even ask about Jasper. All I'm asking is that you consider the possibility of an us."

An us. Cal loved her. He wanted her. She could have something with him. No confusion. No guessing. No rules about fake relationships. Just a man who loved her and wouldn't let her down. A relationship. Maybe more. A marriage. A long life spent together instead of alone.

She wanted that dream so badly sometimes her bones ached. But did she want that dream with Cal? "This is a lot. I need time to...process all of this. You've flipped my world on its head, Cal."

He stepped a little closer but didn't touch her. "Of course. Look, do what you need to do. Even if that means working this Jasper thing out of your system. I've loved you for a long time, Tate. If I need to wait a little longer, that's okay. I want to be with you, but only if you want to be with me back."

She blinked, her eyes wet. "I do love you, Cal. You know that. I just need some time."

He made a wry sound under his breath and muttered, "Fuck."

"What?"

"I just realized something. I'm having a Duckie moment." He looked up at her with a smirk. "You made me watch that movie so many times, it's burned into my brain. The best friend's in love with the girl, and the girl is dating Mr. Popularity. I really hope this movie ends better than that one did for the best friend."

She choke-laughed, tears clogging her throat. Cal knew how much she had a love-hate relationship with that movie. She'd done blog posts on why the ending of *Pretty in Pink* was bullshit. "Are you going to start lip-synching 'Try a Little Tenderness'? Because I am so here for that."

He laughed a weary laugh and pulled her into a hug, sitting his chin atop her head. The embrace felt so familiar, so warm and comfortable. She could have this all the time if she wanted it. And more. She could have all of it with Cal. "I'll do whatever it takes to show you that you mean everything to me. Including giving you space. I can head back home today."

She stepped back, frowning. "Oh, no, you don't—"

He shook his head. "It's fine. I'm hungover anyway. *A little tenderness*. Dammit."

She cringed. "Shit. Sorry."

He sighed. "Not your fault. *Tenderness*. But this has been a lot for me, too. I'm going to find some hair of the dog and wander like a tourist for a little while and then head back to Baton Rouge. *A little tenderness*." He made a sound of irritation and balled his fist. "God, this fucking disorder."

She reached out and squeezed his arm in empathy.

He took a cleansing breath, obviously trying to calm the tic. "The last thing I want is to make you feel cornered. *Tenderness*. Get some breathing room. I'll be here—apparently endlessly quoting Otis Redding—when you want to talk."

The tightness in her chest softened. How could she not love this guy? This was Cal. The boy who never let his disorder slow him down. The guy who stood up for her when no other kid would. They could be so good together. She loved the guy down to her very soul. A few months ago, she wouldn't have even paused in her response. But her experiences with Jasper were clouding things. Which was stupid because she hadn't been lying to

Cal—she knew what she had with Jasper was temporary. They weren't even technically dating. It was a friendship at best, a farce at worst. Still, she couldn't just take the leap.

Cal deserved someone who would walk into a relationship with him with no doubts, with full enthusiasm. She wasn't there in this moment.

She needed space. She needed to think. This morning had been...mind-warping.

"Thank you," she said.

He smiled, a hint of resignation there. "Sure."

"We'll talk soon."

He nodded and put his hands on her shoulders, expression serious. "Just please. Really think through things from all angles. This is going to sound like a *try a little tenderness* shitty thing to say, and it's the last time I'm going to say anything about Jasper, but I know what it's like to be hot for someone. Sexual chemistry is a legit thing. I've had those kinds of instant physical connections, too. *Tenderness*. And you and Jasper probably have that. But believe me, it burns bright and fizzles fast. Time will show that. There needs to be more than that *a little tenderness* to sustain a relationship. We've got chemistry, but we've also got history and friendship and a lot more layered into that. We've weathered things together. Solid bricks under our feet, not sand."

She wet her lips. "Okay."

He let out a breath and leaned forward to kiss her twitching cheek. Then, without another word, he left the kitchen, leaving her with a pit in her stomach and no idea what to do.

chapter **twenty-four**

JASPER SAT ACROSS FROM FITZ'S DESK, TAKING IN THE VIEW the corner office at WorkAround afforded and trying not to bounce his knee as he waited for his friend. He needed to be focused for this meeting, but he'd been distracted as hell the last two days, knowing Hollyn was hanging out with Cal. He'd wanted to give her time with her friend and not act like a possessive asshole, but Jasper couldn't shake the talk he'd had with Cal that night at Hollyn's.

Cal wanted Hollyn. Not for a hookup, not to date casually, but in the you're-my-one-and-only-forever way. Cal was willing to sacrifice it all for Hollyn, and he had history with her to back it up. Even though Jasper had been the one to spend that night in her bed, he'd been hit with how out of his league he was in the contest when he'd left the next morning. What did he have to offer Hollyn besides some improv advice and a good time in bed? His near-empty bank account? His borrowed apartment?

So for the last two days, Jasper had been running every scenario in his head and driving himself crazy. Had Cal confessed his love to her? Had she fallen into his arms? Were they currently strolling hand in hand through the French Quarter, sharing beignets and licking sugar off each other's lips? *Ugh.*

He'd wanted to ask Hollyn so badly, but all they'd done since the morning he left was exchange a few texts. He'd been crazy busy with work, and she'd told him she'd see him when Cal left town. Plus, he didn't want to be *that* guy, text stalking her. He was trying to give her space, trying to give *himself* space because of all the things he'd been feeling for her that last morning, but it wasn't working. His brain was running around like a dog chasing its tail.

So when Fitz had texted Jasper that he wanted to chat about the business plan whenever Jasper got his break, he'd welcomed the new thing to worry about. But now that he was waiting in Fitz's office, his mental dog was off and running again, chasing in a different direction. What if his business plan totally sucked and no one was interested and Fitz was giving up on him and kicking him out? That was where his mind went. Because if you're going to panic spiral, why not go for it with gusto.

The door whooshed open behind him, and Fitz strolled in, all crisp suit and expensive cologne. He smiled at Jasper as he settled into his chair. "Hey." He emptied two sugar packets into the coffee Jasper had brought him. "Sorry. My last meeting ran long. Thanks for the coffee."

"No problem."

Fitz took a gulp of his coffee and then quirked a brow at him. "So, I've got news."

Jasper rubbed his damp palms on his jeans. "Okay. What kind of news?"

Fitz gave him his CEO look—direct, confident, a little smug. "I've been talking to some people and sharing your business plan." He leaned back in his chair and steepled his fingers in front of him. "I've gotten a lot of noes."

Jasper's heart sank, his worst fears confirmed. "Fuck."

"However." Fitz smiled a smile like a guy with a secret. "I also got some yeses."

"Wait, what?" Jasper sat forward in the chair, gripping the arms. "Seriously?"

Fitz laughed and leaned in, putting his elbows on the desk and looking more like the kid Jasper used to know. "Yes, asshole. I can't believe you doubted me. You should've seen the hangdog face you just gave me. Where's the confidence, man?"

Jasper groaned. "You're a sadistic shithead."

He made a smooching sound, then sipped his coffee, enjoying Jasper's torture way too much. "Yes, but an effective shithead. I've got three potential investors on the hook and interested in what you're trying to do with the theater. They loved your business plan and pitch. And the performance videos really won them over."

Jasper couldn't quite process the words—particularly *loved* and *business plan*. "Holy shit."

"Don't look so surprised. Own that shit. You've got a good idea, and your group is talented. Other people want in," Fitz said, reaching for a legal pad full of notes. "Now, one's a tech guy who loves comedy and is looking to diversify his portfolio. Another is a woman who made her money flipping properties. She likes that the neighborhood is on the upswing. If she can get in early and the theater goes well, I see her buying up more property around there and revitalizing it as an entertainment district. The last one is a bored rich kid playing with inheritance money, but he's smart and has a killer social-media presence so can send influencers your way."

Jasper linked his hands behind his neck and let out a breath, taking all of the information in. "Wow."

"Now," Fitz said, flipping through the pages. "They need to see one of your live shows since they've only seen videos thus far, but I need you to pick a date that you think you can get a full crowd. I don't want these investors showing up to a half-empty bar. Your show needs to look like hip shit, like they've found a pearl in the oyster. Investors like to feel like they're getting in on a secret right before the world knows about it."

Jasper leaned back in the chair, his mind spinning. "Fitz, I'm thrilled to have them see a show, but I can't predict how the crowd is going to be. It varies from night to night. I mean, weekends are better, but I can't guarantee a packed house. If I could do that, I wouldn't be looking for investors in the first place."

Fitz looked unmoved. "Figure it out. Promote. Offer a discount. Plan a special event or special guest that will draw more people in. Get your show's name in front of people and fast. Plant friends in the audience if that's what it takes. You need a full room and a loud, engaged crowd. You have a week. I don't want to leave these investors twisting on the line long. They're like magpies and will get distracted by the next shiny thing."

Jasper's heart had picked up speed. He didn't want to lose the opportunity, but that schedule gave him no time to plan. If he could get a packed house every night, he would. But their location sucked. They had only just started doing shows again, so word of mouth had stayed very local and in the neighborhood. He needed… Wait. "I'll take care of it."

Fitz's eyebrows arched. "Yeah?"

"I can get us a review from Miz Poppy on the NOLA Vibe site. She can talk us up and mention that next weekend, there will be a discounted show."

"How are you going to do that?" he asked, frowning. "I read that blog. Miz Poppy isn't pay to play. She reviews what she wants. That's her thing. You can't guarantee she'll give you coverage."

"I can guarantee it," he said, his stomach flipping over that he was going to have to ask Hollyn not just to review him but to make sure it was an ultra-positive one. "I…know her."

Fitz stared at him for a moment. "Seriously? Why haven't you used that connection before then?"

"It's...relatively new," Jasper said carefully.

"Wait." Fitz leaned onto his forearms and lowered his voice. "Does she work here?"

He shook his head.

Fitz's gaze scanned Jasper's face, searching, then he broke into a big grin. "She does. Holy shit. Holy *shit*."

"What?"

"You only have one new person in your life besides me. It's your girl," Fitz declared. "Hollyn. You're hooking up with the woman who can get you press, you sly bastard."

Jasper froze. "I—"

Fitz waved a hand. "Don't freak out, Jas. I've got you. I won't tell anyone. But damn, you really are an ambitious fucker."

Jasper's jaw clenched. "It's not like that."

Fitz gave him a patient look. "You're telling me that you just happened to start giving lessons to and hooking up with Hollyn, and then you just happened to find out that she could hold the key to helping your local show break out?"

Frustration was building in Jasper, making his mouth go sour. "That's not what this is."

Fitz snorted. "You told me when you moved in that you weren't looking to hook up with anyone. Plus, your last girlfriend was a loud-mouthed comedy actress. Hollyn's cool and seems nice enough, but she hardly talks. She's a project. No guy looking to steer clear of the dating game wants a project."

Jasper stood, fully pissed now. "She's not a fucking project. She's a person. Who's actually fantastic when you get to know her."

Fitz lifted his palms. "Don't get all puffed up about it, Jas. All I'm saying is that if she wasn't Miz Poppy, would you be hanging out with her?"

Jasper opened his mouth but then shut it again. *Technically*, he wouldn't have been. That connection was what had brought them together. And technically, they *were* doing an exchange of sorts. But damn if he was going to let it sound like he was using her. They were helping each other out. Benefits on both sides. He was giving her lessons. She could get him a review. They were both enjoying spending time together. Neither had gone in with any expectations beyond that.

Except he was about to ask her for a good review. He was about to lay an expectation at her feet.

Damn.

"Don't talk shit about her again," Jasper said, quiet warning in his voice. "We started talking because she needed the lessons for her job. The site wants her to do a Miz Poppy reveal and then start doing video reviews. The dating stuff happened naturally."

Mostly true.

"Wait, she's going to do *a reveal*?" Fitz's expression lit like he'd gotten what he wanted on Christmas morning.

"Yeah, that's the plan. In a week or two. I'm helping her get ready for it."

"Jas, that needs to happen at your show," Fitz said, voice brimming with excitement. "Let her be a guest star. She can get the whole thing on video to submit to the NOLA Vibe or even live stream it. You can promote the show as having Miz Poppy as a special guest. That will get people out there. People want to know who she is. It's genius."

Jasper shook his head. "No way. I'm not asking her to do that."

"Why not? It could help you both. She gets her reveal done and has you there to help her through it. She and her website get publicity. You and your group get publicity. Your potential investors get to see the whole thing. Wins all around."

Jasper couldn't let the idea creep into his mind. The amount of buzz that could generate would be killer. But asking Hollyn to get onstage was asking too much of her. She'd made a ton of progress with their lessons and the videos they'd been practicing with, but it was still just her and him. Being in front of a bar full of people, revealing herself as Miz Poppy. It would be a lot. "I don't know if she's ready for that kind of thing. She was going to do her reveal on video, but not live in front of others. The option for multiple takes and editing are important to her."

Fitz gave him a look, clearly undeterred. "Ask her. Tell her you'll be there with her every step of the way. I'd bet she's capable of it. She just needs a little encouragement to take the plunge. It could be her graduation from your lessons."

Jasper let out a sigh. Hollyn *was* capable in theory. She was great when she forgot the camera was there and had a good time. Her tics were still there, but he had a feeling people would get used to that as part of her if she gave them the chance. She even had a bit of a knack for improv. In so many ways, she'd be the perfect special guest. But the last thing he wanted to do was push her too hard too fast.

"Or maybe that's part of it?" Fitz pinned him with a look. "Maybe you don't want the lessons to be over. You sure you're not holding her back just to keep her needing you, Jas?"

Jasper reared back like he'd been hit in the face. "Are you kidding me right now? What the fuck, man?"

Fitz lifted his palms in a don't-kill-the-messenger motion. "I'm not trying to be an asshole, but I've been there. It's nice when someone needs you for something, when being around them makes you feel like the big man. Especially when you feel completely out of your depth in the rest of your life." He ran a hand over the back of his head, a grim expression crossing his face. "I was in a relationship for two years with that setup. She was in a bad marriage and needed someone to make her feel good and worthy. I didn't know what the hell to do with my life, and she made me feel like I was her savior. But in the end, we were just each other's crutch. I know it feels good to be helping Hollyn, to be the guy she can lean on. But is it really about her or is about you trying to repair all the holes your ex and LA poked in your ego?"

Jasper wanted to punch something, possibly his friend, but the words were seeping into him like acid in open wounds. Was that what this was? Was he feeling all these things for Hollyn just because she made him feel better about himself? Made him feel like he wasn't a fuckup?

"Shit," he said under his breath.

"If you really want to help her," Fitz said, voice gently prodding, "get her to do this. Then you'll both be able to walk away with something good out of it."

Jasper's anger deflated and a bone-deep weariness replaced it. He rubbed the spot between his eyes. "I'll talk to her."

"Excellent," Fitz said, a smile coming into his voice. "I have a good feeling about all this, Jas. You make this happen, and you'll get your theater. I'd put my money on it. Just think, in a few months, you could be debuting at your own place. No more pouring coffee. No data entry for your future brother-in-law. Just you and your group headlining and doing what you love."

The image was too much to wrap his head around. Was he really that close to that reality? No more drifting around from shitty job to shitty job, hoping for a big break. No more depending on auditions. A real career. His own business. "You really think it could happen?"

Fitz gave him a serious look. "I *know* it can. But you can't half ass it. That's why I'm twisting your arm to put everything you have into this showcase. You're only going to get one shot with these investors. *Hamilton* this motherfucker, Jas. Don't throw away your shot."

Jasper's eyebrows went up. "Did you just throw a Broadway reference at me?"

Fitz leaned back in his chair, pleased with himself. "I contain multitudes."

Jasper laughed. "No doubt."

"So, we good?" his friend asked, a rare tentative note in his voice.

Jasper scrubbed a hand over his face. "Yeah, man. We're good. I'm ridiculously appreciative of everything you've done. I can't believe you made this happen."

Fitz nodded. "I helped, but you're the one who's going to make it happen. You and your Miz Poppy."

Jasper let out a breath. "Right."

"Don't look so stressed. If this girl cares about you, she's going to want to help you out, Jas."

That was the problem. He knew Hollyn would want to help. But if *he* truly cared about Hollyn, if those feelings from the other morning had been real, he wouldn't ask her to do this. He wouldn't push her to do something she probably wasn't ready for. The fact that he was going to anyway proved what Fitz had accused him of—his feelings for Hollyn weren't real. This was another one of his performances—one so good, he'd convinced himself. But in the end, he'd only been propping up his wounded ego. Using her. A fucking rebound.

As Jasper headed out of Fitz's office, he felt nauseous. A few nights ago, he'd told Cal he wasn't using Hollyn. And he'd promised Hollyn he wasn't one of those guys asking her to do his homework for him. But he was about to drop a big damn assignment in her lap. Pushing her onstage wasn't going to benefit her.

It was all about him.

His dream. His plans. His ambition.

But he couldn't walk away from the opportunity. He didn't have it in him. He was going to ask Hollyn to do this.

And then he was never going to touch her again. Because she deserved so much better.

That sent a hard pang of reality through him. *Hell.* She deserved Cal. A guy who would sacrifice his dream to be with her.

Jasper wouldn't—couldn't—sacrifice his dream for anyone. It was all he'd ever really had to hold on to. Without it, he didn't know who he was.

He was going to have to let her go.

chapter **twenty-five**

WHY LOVE TRIANGLE STORIES ARE SECRETLY TRAGEDIES

By Miz Poppy

We've been talking a lot about rom-coms lately and romantic tropes, in general. So, I would be remiss if I left out the love-triangle trope. This is a favorite of the rom-com genre and the teen TV series. But as I've gone through my favorite love-triangle stories, I've realized something. Love-triangle stories are only romances for two. When you switch point of view to the person who doesn't win the love, you're telling a tragedy. What if *Pretty in Pink* was told from Duckie's POV? That would be a sad-ass movie.

The reason why we see these as happy romances is because we, as viewers, are guided to identify with the two who end up together. But how many of us in our real lives have been the unchosen one? I'd like to see the movie of the person who doesn't get picked. Show me their happy ending. Show me why the best thing that ever happened to them was to not get chosen by that person they wanted. I want to see all happy endings, dammit! :)

In the meantime, here are some of my favorite love-triangle movies and TV shows to fill up your watchlist:

1. *Love Actually*
2. *Bridget Jones's Diary*
3. *My Best Friend's Wedding*
4. *Sleepless in Seattle*
5. *Dawson's Creek*
6. *Buffy the Vampire Slayer*
7. *How I Met Your Mother*
8. *Lost*
9. *Vampire Diaries*
10. *True Blood* (so many vampire love triangles on the list!)

Those are some of mine. What's your favorite? Which unchosen love-triangle character would you love to see get their own movie or show?

Hollyn had been hiding. And lying. And basically being a big ol' coward. She hated that she'd lied to Jasper, telling him that Cal was still in town. She hated that she hadn't picked up the phone to talk to him, but she wasn't in a state of mind to explain what had happened or to jump right back in bed with Jasper and pretend like nothing had changed. Cal's revelation had thrown her like a wrestler tossing her out of the ring of her life. Her head was still spinning.

She'd spent the last two days mostly in her pajamas, watching movies in an endless queue and eating too much junk food. That was what the movies told you to do when you'd suffered a major relationship shake-up. But none of it had helped. Her brain was still as scattered as when Cal had walked out, and her heart had taken a vow of silence on what she was feeling about the two men in her life. Anytime she tried to peek into that particular closet of her psyche, the threat of a panic attack rushed up like a tsunami and she slammed the door shut. This was a maze she wasn't going to be able to navigate solo.

By the second night, she gave up on trying to white-knuckle her way through things alone and pulled out her phone. She opened the familiar app and hit the button, requesting an emergency chat with her therapist. Mary Leigh indicated that she was available to chat in ten minutes. Hollyn watched until the indicator on her app for Mary Leigh changed from unavailable to available and took a deep, bracing breath.

Mary Leigh: Hi Hollyn, what's going on?

Just seeing the words made Hollyn feel a little better. She used to feel ashamed that she even needed therapy, but having a neutral party to discuss things with, one who had her best interests as their job, was the ultimate life hack. She refused to feel bad about doing something that helped her be a better version of herself.

Hollyn: My best friend just revealed he's in love with me, is moving here, and wants to have a relationship. HELP
Mary Leigh: Wow. That's a big revelation. How do you feel about what he said?
Hollyn: If I knew that, would I be emergency texting you?

Mary Leigh didn't respond for a beat.

Hollyn: Sorry. I'm freaking out a little. I didn't mean that to sound as bitchy as it did.

Mary Leigh: Feeling freaked out is a valid reaction. A love declaration is a big deal, especially from someone you consider a friend. You've always talked fondly of Cal. Outside of this new information that he's revealed, how do you feel about him?

Hollyn pulled a throw pillow into her lap and picked at the piping. How did she feel about Cal?

Hollyn: He's the best person I know. In a completely not hyperbolic sense.

Mary Leigh: So you like him as person and a friend for sure. Are you attracted to him?

Hollyn pictured Cal in her mind, trying to be objective, trying to tease apart facts from feelings.

Hollyn: We used to date. A long time ago. We had good chemistry back then. And he's attractive. And plays guitar. I'm not NOT attracted to him. I just haven't thought about him in that way for a long time. I had to shut that part off when we broke up or we could've never been friends.

Mary Leigh: Right. That's understandable. So is that a switch you want to turn back on? Can it be turned back on?

Could she let herself be attracted to Cal again? Could she imagine kissing him? Putting her hands on him? Having his hands on her? She answered with honesty.

Hollyn: The switch isn't broken.

Mary Leigh: Okay, so it can be turned back on. But do you want to do that?

Hollyn groaned and pressed her face into the pillow before answering.

Hollyn: I don't know! It all feels so complicated.

Mary Leigh: It's all right not to know. Remember to breathe.

Hollyn frowned. How did this woman in her phone always know when she was holding her breath? She inhaled a deep, lung-filling breath.

Mary Leigh: How about this? What could you gain in your life by flipping that switch and giving things a chance with Cal?

Hollyn sighed and lay back on her couch. Maybe if she assumed the proper therapy position, something would become clear. She stared at her screen and then typed.

Hollyn: A lot. A guy I already love who cares about me and who has always looked out for me would be my boyfriend, maybe eventually more. I wouldn't be alone anymore. I'm already comfortable with Cal, and he has Tourette's too, so there's zero awkwardness about my disorder. I feel completely accepted.

Mary Leigh: Sounds like a lot of great things.

Hollyn: Yeah.

Mary Leigh: So what would you lose if you start a relationship with Cal?

Hollyn closed her eyes, trying to pinpoint the things that were giving her pause.

Hollyn: I could mess up the best, longest, and most important friendship I've ever had.
Mary Leigh: A legitimate concern. But you two have survived a breakup before, right?
Hollyn: Yes.
Mary Leigh: So what else would you lose or give up to be with him?

The answer was there in her head. The stupid, stupid answer. She tapped her head back against the couch cushion.

Hollyn: Possibility.
Mary Leigh: Of what?
Hollyn: Someone else.
Mary Leigh: A part of starting any committed relationship.

Hollyn cringed. If only it were that simple. That she was just a commitment-phobe.

Hollyn: No, a specific someone else.
Mary Leigh: Ah, Jasper?
Hollyn: Yes. Please don't tell me I'm being naive. I already know that. I realize what's happening with Jasper is not an actual relationship.
Mary Leigh: Isn't it, though? Maybe not a traditional relationship. But you're spending time together, sleeping together. It's some sort of a relationship.
Hollyn: You know what I mean. We're not dating. We have an agreement. He's straight up told me it couldn't turn into

anything. He's not an actual possibility. But...

Mary Leigh: You've developed feelings for him.

Hollyn: YES. I'm so stupid.

Mary Leigh: Remember what we talked about, not calling yourself names. You're not stupid. You're human. A human having human feelings.

Hollyn: A human having love feelings.

It was the first time she'd admitted the word aloud, and a flood of dread went through her. She grabbed the pillow again, pressing it to her face for a second to scream silently into it. How had she landed here? *Love*. She was out of her goddamned mind.

Mary Leigh was silent. If they were face-to-face in an office, Hollyn imagined Mary Leigh would be giving her the go-on, keep-digging-your-own-hole face.

Hollyn: I guess I can't open myself up to the thought of Cal until I deal with this. It's not fair to him. I need to break things off with Jasper. Clear my head before I can really consider anything seriously.

Mary Leigh: Is that what you want to do?

Hollyn: It's what I need to do.

Mary Leigh: That wasn't my question.

Ugh. Sometimes she loved her therapist. Sometimes she wanted to give the middle finger to Mary Leigh's avatar and toss the phone across the room.

Hollyn: I know but this is a false debate. I'm not choosing between two guys. Only one is a real possibility. So the debate is get together with Cal or stay single.

Mary Leigh: You're leaving out another possibility. You could also tell Jasper how you feel and see if maybe he's open to something more with you.

Hollyn sat up and scoffed.

Hollyn: NO WAY. We have an agreement. I promised this was only casual. No feelings. I'm not going to be that girl.

Mary Leigh: Relationships are continuously negotiated. What if his feelings have changed about you? Wouldn't you want him to be honest with you?

Hollyn: Obviously. But he hasn't given me any signs that anything has changed. I'm going to end up looking like the pathetic girl who fell for the wrong guy again. I can't bear the thought of him having to let me down. The mortification of that would be... I can't even think about it.

Mary Leigh: Jasper isn't that bully from school. He's shown no signs of wanting to hurt you. From what you've told me, he's been kind and attentive with you. He's given you a lot of indicators that he genuinely likes you and is attracted to you. If you tell him you have feelings for him, and he doesn't reciprocate, what is the worst that can happen?

For others that would be a rhetorical question, but Hollyn had learned Mary Leigh didn't do rhetorical. She always wanted actual answers. What would be the worst?

Hollyn: Feeling embarrassed. Ending our friendship. Him feeling pity for me.

Mary Leigh: Could you survive those things?

Hollyn: That last one gives me all the vomity feelings. And I'd have to leave WorkAround because I couldn't face that every day. That would be tough because I've made a friend there now. But I wouldn't die, I guess.

Mary Leigh: Not dying is good. What is the best that could happen?

Hollyn rolled her lips together, trying to imagine what that would look like. Jasper smiling. Jasper pulling her into a hug and kissing her and telling her he's so happy to hear it. It was a ridiculous fantasy that could've been pulled straight from one of the many rom-coms she'd been binge-watching the last few days.

Hollyn: He feels the same way and wants to be in a real relationship.

Mary Leigh: So, is that result, even if you feel like it's a remote one, worth the risk of the other things?

Hollyn: It's super remote. Like Siberia remote.

Mary Leigh: Okay. But somewhere in between the two extremes are a lot of other possibilities. For instance, another is that he doesn't feel the same way, doesn't embarrass you about it, and you part friends. Then you can have a clear head to decide if Cal is someone you want a romantic relationship with or not. You can get the distraction of Jasper off the path and really evaluate the decision and your feelings about Cal.

Hollyn rubbed her forehead. *Could* she tell Jasper? Like actually speak those feelings out loud? The thought sent a wash of clammy anxiety through her. But Mary Leigh was right on one thing. He was a big distraction right now. She couldn't even begin to pick apart her feelings about Cal because she had this bright, beautiful man distracting her at every turn.

Hollyn: Maybe I can talk to him. I'll think about it.

Mary Leigh: This is about fear. Fear is there to protect us, but fear is also what gets us stuck. You have been so brave this year. I'm so impressed with your progress. But with this, you're still afraid that you are the outcast little girl who no one wants to play with. You can't imagine that someone like Jasper would ever consider you a worthy partner. But that little girl is a part of your history. You can thank her for trying to protect you, but she is not you anymore. You have a lot to offer the world and a partner. If Jasper can't be in a committed relationship, that's his issue, not yours. Don't own other people's hang-ups. But also don't decide their answers for them before you ask. Maybe he's scared too and waiting for you to be the one to say something first.

Hollyn read the words quickly and then went back and read them again more slowly. Tears burned the corners of her eyes at the thought of that little-girl version of herself trying to protect her, putting her hands up and stopping anyone from getting too close, from looking too hard. She didn't want to stand behind that little girl anymore. She had been taking steps out into the sunlight for the last year, baby step by baby step.

She wasn't all the way there, but she'd come so far. She was a grown woman, living in the city, working hard at her job. She was tackling her worst fears to get a promotion. She was a woman who had asked Jasper for what she wanted and had boldly started a relationship with him. When he looked at her, she didn't know if he had feelings, but she knew that he liked her. She knew he was attracted to her. She wasn't a pity project for him. She needed to stop thinking of herself as a charity case. She lifted her phone again.

Hollyn: I'm going to talk to him.

The words appeared on the screen, and a jolt of fear went through her, but she swallowed it down. She had to trust herself, that she could handle whatever the outcome was.

Mary Leigh: Good. I'm here if you need me.
Hollyn: Any last-minute advice?
Mary Leigh: Be honest. Don't play games. And maybe have a shot of something strong before you have the convo.
Hollyn: LOL. Mary Leigh!
Mary Leigh: :) Kidding on the last part. I know you can do this stone-cold sober. You've faced a lot worse. At the end of the day, he's just a man. A person. Just like you. He may let you down. He also may surprise you. But you won't know unless you give him a chance to hear how you feel.

Hollyn ended the session and tossed her phone onto the coffee table. So this was happening. She was going to break her word, put herself out there, and tell Jasper how she felt about him.

Tomorrow. Definitely tomorrow.

She reached for her phone again and scrolled. After an inner pep talk, she let her thumbs fly over the keyboard.

Hollyn: So how exactly do girls' nights work?

It took only a minute for the response.

Andi: OMG ARE WE HAVING A GIRLS' NIGHT???

Hollyn laughed.

Hollyn: I have boy angst and I don't want to think about it tonight. I'm assuming this is the proper solution.

Andi: *GIF of Rachel from *Friends* jumping up and down in excitement* YASSSS. Here for it. I have about half an hour worth of editing left on this podcast and then it's on. Are we having girls' night in or girls' night out?

Hollyn: I haven't left the house in 2 days.

Andi: GURL. Queso and margaritas it is. Text me ur address. Pick u up by seven.

Hollyn forwarded her address and smiled. She may completely blow things with Jasper. She may embarrass the hell out of herself. But at least she'd made *some* progress. If everything melted down, she'd at least have someone to call for chips and queso.

That was something.

A big something.

She bit her lip and scrolled to a different number.

Hollyn: Hey, have any Saturday plans?

Her phone went dark after no response came, but as soon as she shifted to put it down, the screen lit.

Jasper: I was just about to call u and ask the same thing. U done with Cal?

Jasper had no idea how big a question that was.

Hollyn: He's headed back to Baton Rouge. I'm free.

Jasper: Cool. I wanted to talk 2U about something. Picnic lunch in City Park?

Hollyn: Perfect. See you soon. Miss you.

She had a mild panic reaction when she hit Send, but there was no taking it back. *Miss you. Miss you.*

When the dots appeared and then disappeared and Jasper didn't immediately respond, she almost moved from mild panic to freak-out, but then his message finally popped up.

Jasper: Same.

The word was a simple one but seemed to blink on the screen like a neon sign. *Same.* If that were true, maybe there was hope for her yet.

Maybe.

chapter **twenty-six**

JASPER SMOOTHED OUT THE BLANKET ON THE GRASS UNDER one of the ancient live-oak trees in the park and put the cooler of food he'd brought on one corner to keep the blanket from flying away. The gnarled branches of the oak touched the ground on one side, offering the picnic spot some semblance of privacy, but the other side was open to a wide green space where kids were playing and couples were lounging.

Jasper should've been in a great mood. He didn't have to work today. The sky was bright blue, and the temperatures weren't death-by-humidity hot. He had investors interested in his theater. He should've been running around in joy like those kids. But instead, he couldn't shake the ominous sense of dread that had been hovering over him since his talk with Fitz.

He hadn't seen Hollyn in days, and part of him was desperate to see her smiling face. But the other part of him just felt like a fraud. So when he saw the sunlight catch a mane of gold curls in the distance, he had equal parts excitement and trepidation crashing together inside him.

He lifted a hand in greeting as Hollyn got closer, and she caught sight of him, a smile lighting her face as she waved back. He couldn't take his eyes off her as she walked his way. She was wearing a red sundress that fluttered around her legs in the breeze, and her hair was blowing wild. A sharp stab of longing hit him in the chest. The woman was beautiful. And interesting. And funny. And for a minute, she'd been his. He'd written his name on her skin.

But that marker had washed off by now, as had the shine on this arrangement.

After today, he'd never get to touch her that way again.

Hollyn ducked under a tree branch and met him at the edge of the blanket, smiling. "Hey, you."

"Hey." Jasper didn't know what to do. He wanted to kiss her. Wanted to pick her up off her feet, wrap her legs around him, and kiss her until they were both dizzy from lack of breath. He leaned in for a hug instead.

She wrapped her arms around him, smelling like sunshine and Hollyn, and gave him a tight squeeze. "Long time no see."

He released her and stepped back so he wouldn't be tempted to go in for the kiss. "Yeah, it's been crazy. Did you have a good time with Cal?"

Her cheek and nose twitched, and a flash of something flickered in her eyes. "Yeah, it was good seeing him."

His stomach sank. He didn't know how he knew, but he could feel the shift in her, the shields. Cal had told her about his feelings. Cal had told her he loved her, and she wasn't telling Jasper about it. He should've been happy. That would make breaking this off easier. But he felt like punching something instead. "Great."

Hollyn bit her lip and rocked back on her heels, the weird quiet between them growing. "Um, so a picnic, huh?"

Jasper snapped out of his frozen state and motioned at the cooler. "Yeah, I picked up a muffuletta and a few other things. I thought it'd be nice to get outside."

And not have a private conversation in the confines of a restaurant.

"Cool." She looked to the cooler and then back to him, her fingers tapping a pattern against her thigh. "Why does this feel so awkward?"

The words popped a pin in him, his breath sagging out. He raked a hand through his hair. "Sorry. That's my fault. I have a lot on my mind."

She frowned and then lowered herself to the ground and patted a spot on the blanket. "Wanna share?"

He nodded and sat down across from her, trying to find the right words. He needed to pitch her on his idea of being the show's guest, make it sound completely doable and beneficial for them both. He needed to convince her this was the best way to go for both of their careers. He needed to tell her that it was best that they end the physical part of their arrangement. "Hollyn..."

"Yeah?" Hollyn shifted into a cross-legged position, gathering her dress between her thighs. The faded flourish from his signature peeked out and he couldn't take his eyes off it. Flashbacks of the morning in her bedroom came to him in a rush, the way she'd felt beneath him, the way she'd looked back at him, the things he'd felt deep in his chest.

Things that didn't feel false at all. Things that suddenly felt very, very real and not faded in the least. *Shit.*

He closed his eyes. The show. He needed to ask her about the show.

"I know Cal's in love with you," he blurted out instead. He opened his eyes, surprised at the words that had come out of his mouth.

Hollyn's lips were parted, her expression blank. "What?"

Jasper wet his lips. "He told me that night after you went to bed. He was drunk, but he told me. And so I know... I know that you're probably here to tell me that we need to end this thing between us because you're going to date Cal and you love him, and I just need you to know that…I get it. Obviously. I mean. I understand."

She frowned, lines bracketing her mouth. "You understand what exactly?"

"That this thing with us was just temporary and for a particular purpose and that of course you want to be with Cal. You guys have been friends forever. He's obviously good to you. I don't want you to feel like you owe me explanations or whatever. We were just helping each other out."

Her eyes narrowed, and her tone was careful when she spoke again. "Helping each other out."

"Right. And I just wanted you to know that I wish you both well." The words stabbed at him like a rusty knife. "I didn't want you to feel like you needed to lie to me about it. I want you to be happy. If what we were doing helped you find the guy you were meant to be with, then… I guess the relationship practice was a success, right?"

Her throat worked as she swallowed. "Right."

He nodded, trying to convince himself this was a good thing. The right thing. "Great!"

Her hand, which was resting on her thigh, started a fast rotation of tapping with each finger. Her gaze was focused on the blanket. He didn't think she was going to say anything else, but then she looked up with a determined expression. "No. Not great."

The change in her tone jarred him out of his thoughts. "What?"

"Everything's *not great*. I'm lying to you." She looked off to his left, like she was studying the trunk of the oak tree. "Cal did tell me he loved me, but he went home a few hours after you left my house."

Jasper shook his head, confused. "What do you mean?"

She quickly peeked over at him, her nose scrunching. "He told me he wanted to be with me. He told me he's moving here. He kissed me."

An involuntary sound of annoyance escaped Jasper's throat.

"Then he left because I told him I needed time to think," she finished.

"Oh." Jasper didn't know where she was going with this, but he was fixated on the idea of Cal kissing her right after Jasper had walked out the door. The dude didn't waste any time.

"Yeah. So I've spent the last two days trying to figure out how I feel." She grabbed a leaf that had fallen onto the blanket and started breaking off little bits of it. "And I know what you're trying to tell me. I hear you. This has run its course for you, and you wish me well. Got it." She looked up, a wary expression on her face. "But if we're ending this, I want to do it the way we came into it—with absolute honesty."

He tried to catch her eye, to search her expression, but she wouldn't look directly at him. "Okay."

Little pieces of leaf fell from her fingertips, and she glanced up at him from under her lashes. "I can't figure out how I feel about Cal because...all I can think about is how I feel about you."

Jasper's breathing stilled.

"I know I'm completely breaking the promise I made coming into this," she went on. "And I'm sure I sound pathetic. But the last month with you has been...the best of my adult life. Fun and filled with laughter. Intense. Exciting." She wet her lips. "Hot. And...every time I try to picture a future with Cal—Cal whom I adore and who is absolutely great—I keep picturing one with you in it instead. And it's unfair for me to lay that on you because I'm putting you in a shitty position to let me down, but I'm telling you this because I'm freeing you from that duty.

"I can't keep my promise about not developing feelings for you, but I can keep my promise of not expecting anything from you. You told me what this could and couldn't be, and I haven't forgotten that. But, I'm also tired of being too scared to speak. I've spent my life keeping my mouth shut, swallowing my opinions and feelings. I need to get this out in the open, so I can let you go and move on." She took a breath. "So there it is. I hope that I haven't made it too weird and that we can still be friends."

Jasper's ears were buzzing and his heart was beating painfully fast. The wind blew, shaking the leaves above them, like the tree was applauding Hollyn's speech. More leaves fell around them, one catching in her hair.

"Friends," Jasper repeated, reaching out to untangle the leaf from her hair.

"Yeah." She nodded, her teeth pressing into her bottom lip. He could see her hands were trembling, the leaf stem she was holding quivering like a tuning fork. This had taken everything out of her to say.

That simple sight broke him open. Everything he'd been trying to talk himself out of came rushing in like a stampede of goddamned bison. This woman who hadn't been able to even look him in the eye when they'd first met had just declared her feelings for him, convinced that they weren't going to be reciprocated, putting herself out there and expecting rejection. Doing it anyway.

She was the bravest fucking person he knew. She was...

"You should date Cal," he said abruptly.

Her gaze snapped upward, a flash of pain there.

He took her hands in his, trying to steady hers, all his resolve rushing out of him. "But fucking hell, Hollyn, I really, really don't want you to."

She blinked. "I don't understand."

He ran his thumbs over her knuckles, no longer able to tell if she was the one shaking or if he was. "I am the wrong choice by far. I don't have money or my own place. I'm still pouring coffee at twenty-five. I can be flighty as shit. I've been epically bad at relationships and will probably figure out a way to screw things up. You deserve so much better than me. I came here to tell you that. I had a whole plan. But I'm also a selfish fuck. And right now, I selfishly need to tell you that…I'm into you. Like really into you. Not as friends. Not as an arrangement. But…" He swallowed hard. "But if I'm not careful, I'm at high risk for falling in love with you."

Her lips parted and her nose ticced. "*What?*"

"And I know Cal probably gave you some romantic speech. I know he's got the better résumé and stability and history with you, but goddammit, I can't do this. I can't sit here and pretend I want you to be with him. I don't want you to be with anyone else but me."

....

Hollyn was hot all over and literally shaking. Was this actually happening? Jasper was looking at her like he was pained, like he hadn't wanted to say these things but couldn't help himself. Her eyes burned. "You want to be with me?"

"Like a whole lot," he said like it was an apology. "Like I'm kind of obsessed with you. I've tried to talk myself out of it. Clearly, I've failed."

She pressed her lips together, not sure whether she was going to cry or laugh. "Jasper Deares, I think you just beat Cal on the romantic speech."

He smiled, as unsure of himself as she'd ever seen him. "Yeah?"

"Yes. God. Stop looking like your puppy died. I want to be with you. You want to be with me. That's…pretty fucking wonderful."

His mouth hitched at one corner, some light coming into his eyes. "Yeah, it is, isn't it?"

"It's the literal best." She shifted, tucking her legs under her, and put her hands on his shoulders. "You know what we need to do?"

He lifted his brows, some of that Jasper playfulness coming back in his expression. "Kiss to seal the deal? Make sweet, dirty love on the picnic blanket?"

She laughed. "Yes to the first. Only if we move the blanket indoors on the second. But what I was going to say is we need to stop thinking of ourselves as bad choices. You know what I see when I look at you?"

He wrapped his arms around her waist and guided her to straddle his lap, her dress fanning out around them. "A hot piece of ass?"

She grinned. "Obviously. But I also see a smart, talented guy who's working his butt off for his dream. I see a guy who is kind to his friends and honest with me. I see a guy who wanted to help a stranger at work when he saw she was struggling. I'm not looking for someone to beef up my bank account. Or someone who has it completely together. Lord knows I don't have it completely together. I'm looking for someone who I can have fun with on the journey to figure all that stuff out. A travel companion. Not a tour guide who already knows all the answers. How boring would that be? I want the man, not the résumé."

His expression softened. "See? This is what I'm talking about."

"What?"

He pushed her hair behind her ears. "How am I supposed to not fall for you when you say stuff like that? I've got no shot."

A warm, sweet feeling filled her chest. She tipped up her chin. "I apologize for being completely irresistible."

He smiled. "Narcissist"

She touched her nose to his. "I learned from the best."

His hand slid to the back of her neck, gripping her there. "Ready to do this? For real this time?"

She lowered her head to his, her lips hovering over his. "Once more, with feeling."

"Hollyn and Jasper, sittin' beneath a tree, K-I-S-S-I—"

She kissed him before he could finish, sweet and soft at first and then deepening it when he threaded his hands in her hair. The whisper of the leaves, the children laughing in the background, the birds singing—all of it faded into the background—as they lost themselves to the kiss, no rules between them this time.

Just feelings.

And hope.

A new beginning.

chapter **twenty-seven**

HOURS LATER, HOLLYN WAS SATED AND SLEEPY IN HER BED with Jasper sprawled next to her after they'd exhausted themselves with two rounds of lovemaking. The first time, they hadn't even made it to the bedroom. It was as if the few days apart had been months. The minute they'd walked into the door after the picnic, Jasper had grabbed her and pushed her against the wall, kissing and touching her everywhere. They'd ended up on the couch, still half-dressed, and Jasper rucking up her dress and thanking the sex gods that he still had a condom in his wallet.

The second time, they'd slowed it down and actually made it to the bedroom. Jasper had driven her out of her mind with his hands and then his mouth before he'd dragged her on top of him and buried deep inside her. Her body had never felt so satisfied and sapped at the same time. But her body had nothing on her brain. She was riding some high that made it impossible to wipe the smile off her face. She'd put herself out there, had done the thing she was so afraid to do, expecting the worst to happen, and Jasper had said more than she could've ever hoped to hear.

Her best-case-scenario conjecturing with Mary Leigh had nothing on what the reality had turned out to be. Mary Leigh was going to feel so smug when she found out how right she'd been.

Hollyn laughed.

Jasper turned his head on the pillow. "What are you giggling about over there?"

She gave him a stern look. "First, I don't giggle. That was clearly a very mature, sultry laugh."

"Of course," he said. "Lauren Bacall incarnate."

"Thank you. And I was just thinking that my therapist is going to be buying feathers for her proverbial cap. She was the one who told me to get over myself and just tell you how I felt."

"Your therapist is a genius."

"Yep."

He grabbed her hand, lacing her fingers with his as they lay on their backs next to each other, naked beneath the covers. "This is so not how I expected my day to turn out."

She stared at their linked hands, loving the way his was so much bigger than hers, two of his knuckles dotted with burns from the coffee contraptions at WorkAround. "You and me both. Why did you ask me on the picnic anyway? Just to tell me to go be with Cal? That's like a super unromantic picnic."

He let out a breath. "Actually, that was not what I planned to talk to you about at all. I was bringing you out there to convince you to do me a huge favor."

"Oh?" She turned her body to face him. "What kind of favor?"

He shook his head against the pillow. "It's not important. I've changed my mind. I'm going to figure something else out."

She frowned, not liking that closed off look on his face. "No, don't do that. Tell me. We are rocking the honesty today. Let's not end our streak. What's going on?"

He looked at her, his brows knit. "I've got three big investors interested in my theater."

Hollyn gasped. "Jasper, that's great!"

He smiled a little. "It is. It's unbelievable, honestly. But the catch is that they need to see a live show, and I need to make it seem like a spectacle. A packed house, a lot of buzz. I need to seal the deal with social proof."

Hollyn propped her head on her hand. "Oh. Do you need me to write up my review? I had already started one after seeing your show with Cal. I could finish it up and get it to run in the next day or two."

He gave the hand she still had linked with his a squeeze. "Thank you, but I need more than that. Fitz thinks that if we promote the event with Miz Poppy as our special guest star, we'll get all the people we need. He wants the event to also be your identity reveal."

She blinked and her nose scrunched. "Guest star? You mean like me, *live onstage? To a packed house?*" The horror of that rushed through her like a roller-coaster plunge. "Jasper..."

"Yeah, I know. It's too much. Which is why I'm going to come up with something else. I'm not asking you to do that for me." He brought her hand up to his mouth and kissed her knuckles. "I'm going to brainstorm some options tomorrow. There's got to be something that will get a lot of people there."

She watched him, her heart beating hard in her chest. She knew how much these investors meant to Jasper. This could be the difference between another year pouring coffee or his dream coming true, but he wasn't going to push her to do it. God. *This guy.*

She had a potential key to the kingdom for him, but he was going to let her keep it in her pocket—without a guilt trip, without manipulation, without shaming her for her anxiety. If she promoted on her NOLA Vibe page that she was going to be a guest star at the show and reveal her identity, she had no doubt people would show up. Her numbers didn't lie. But the thought of being up there onstage, no avatar, no opportunity to edit out mistakes, everything improvised, her tics showing up under all those bright lights...it made her feel faint.

"I would screw it up," she said, talking to herself more than him.

He glanced over at her. "You wouldn't. First, there is no screwing it up. It's improv. But you don't see yourself. You're really quick on your feet. When you don't overthink it, you're really funny and smart on camera. I don't think you realize it, but your Miz Poppy comes out. I can hear the voice from your articles coming through—the real you." He rolled on his side to face her. "I'm not saying this to try to convince you, but I hope that other people besides me get to see that part of you one day. Whatever that timeline looks like for you."

Hollyn swallowed past the knot in her throat. "I don't think I can do it without panicking. My tics would be out of control."

He kissed her twitching nose. "You don't have to do it. I'm not asking you to."

She flipped onto her back with a frustrated sound and stared at the ceiling. "If I revealed my identity that way, the NOLA Vibe couldn't take it."

Jasper shifted. "Hmm?"

She watched the ceiling fan turn slowly, her thoughts going in circles along with it. "I've been thinking about the practice videos we've been doing. I watched a few over the last few days. I can see that I've improved, but I'm still...me. I have this fear that when I submit them to my boss, he's going to see my tics and my awkwardness or whatever and just decide to let me go. He can take the Miz Poppy name and hire someone else to use it."

"Which is bullshit," Jasper said, tone edged with disgust.

"Right." She turned to look at him. "But what if I steal that opportunity away?"

"Meaning?"

"If I do a live reveal at your show, I *am* Miz Poppy. I claim the name publicly. People will see my face—in all its ticcing glory probably. But then if the site replaces me, people will know it's a replacement. It will make the staff look like jerks. Because people will know I've been let go because of the Tourette's."

Jasper's mouth curved into a wicked smile. "And at worst, you'd be able to keep the moniker you made popular."

"Yep. At best, I keep my job."

"Diabolical." He leaned over and kissed her. "But you realize this means you'd actually have to be live onstage—which you just said there was no way you were doing."

A ripple of nervous energy went through her and she sat up, pulling the covers with her and leaning against the headboard. Jasper followed her. She looked over at him. "Would you be with me onstage?"

Jasper searched her face. "If you needed me to be. I could also give you roles in the improv games that were easy parts. There are some games where one person can read off of note cards and the rest of the actors improv around you. There's one where the guest just makes sound effects for the actors. There's another where you tell facts about yourself and someone makes up a song or a skit based on them. You would just be a catalyst."

Her mouth was dry and her hands clammy. She was probably insane for considering this. "What if I panic and ruin your show for the investors?"

"If I couldn't deal with someone freezing up onstage, I'd never have made it in improv. If you freeze, I'll make up a story about why. If you run offstage, I'll make a joke about why you bolted from me. I'd have your back. The whole group would."

Of that, she had no doubt. Jasper wouldn't let her drown onstage. He would take care of her. She'd seen him do it with his fellow actors in the show. They all supported each other. The *Yes, and* thing was real.

"Okay," she said, fear and determination braiding together

within her. "If you swear that you'll be right by my side and ready to bail me out if I mess up, I'll do it."

Jasper turned fully to her, the blankets falling to his waist, and his eyes wide. "Are you serious?"

She rolled her lips together and nodded. "Knowing you'll have my back makes me feel like maybe I can actually pull it off. I'll post the news on the site in the morning."

Jasper cupped her face and pressed his lips to hers. "You have no idea how much this means to me. I can't even... Thank you."

She gave him a shaky smile. "Don't thank me yet. I may scare off those investors."

"Not a chance." He grabbed her around the waist and rolled her on top of him. "They're going to love you."

"Yeah?"

"Believe me. It's an easy thing to do." He pulled her down to him and kissed her again.

Back at you, Jasper Deares. Back at you.

She couldn't say the words to him yet. But she felt them down to her bones.

She loved this man.

She hoped she didn't let him down.

chapter **twenty-eight**

THE HAIL YES GROUP WAS ON THEIR FINAL HOUR OF rehearsal at WorkAround, and Jasper was damp with sweat and beaming with pride. Hollyn had come to rehearsal for three nights in a row, preparing for the big Miz Poppy reveal show and working her ass off.

She'd been completely freaked out the first rehearsal, the energy of his group members a lot to handle all at once. But they were also amazing people, so they'd worked hard to make her feel comfortable with them and loosen up. After a few games and Jasper making a fool of himself to show her that he could always take the spotlight off her if anything went wrong, she'd shaken off the panic. Now she looked like she was actually starting to have fun.

Antonio, Leah, and Barry were running the sound-effects game with her. Leah and Antonio were pretending to be a couple lost in the jungle on their honeymoon. Barry and Hollyn were off to the side and responsible for making the sound effects for whatever happened in Leah and Antonio's scene.

"I can't believe you brought me out here. I wanted to go on a cruise, and now I'm in the devil's armpit... Oh my God," Leah said, clinging to Antonio with one hand and pointing with the other. "What the hell is that?"

Barry made a hissing sound and then accidentally coughed when he hissed too hard.

Antonio looked in the direction Leah had pointed. "Oh my God, it's an asthmatic anaconda. Here, throw this grenade!"

Leah pretended to pull the pin, and Hollyn made a funny sound for that, and then Leah tossed the pretend grenade. Hollyn made an exploding sound while Barry made pained hissing sounds mixed with gasping coughs.

"Duck!" Antonio yelled.

Hollyn said, "Splat!"

Jasper laughed as Leah and Antonio acted like they were being rained on with snake guts. Perfect. Hollyn was going to do great.

Jasper left them to it and walked out into the hallway to grab a bottle of water from the cooler Monique had left there. He was crouched, digging around for a drink for himself and one for Hollyn when he felt the air shift behind him. But before he could stand and turn around to see who it was, the person spoke.

"Hey, Jas."

Jasper stilled, the familiar female voice pinging through him like an ice cube in an empty glass. He dropped the water bottle back into the cooler and turned his head.

He'd hoped his ears had been playing tricks on him or that one of his group members had gotten really good at voice impressions, but the sight before him confirmed he hadn't forgotten his ex's voice. Kenzie was standing there in a fit-to-the-skin tailored white pantsuit, looking down at him with that little apologetic Mona Lisa smile she had. Her hair was a darker brown than it was naturally, and her skin looked like porcelain. Flawless. Cool. This was Hollywood Kenzie.

And she was standing here in WorkAround. He couldn't make the incongruent images make sense. Jasper stood. "Kenzie."

Without asking if it would be okay or not, she came close

and hugged him, smelling faintly of wine and that flower-scented lotion she liked. "God, it's so good to see you."

Robotically, he hugged her back. What. The. Hell. Was. Happening?

When she released him, he stepped back as if he was afraid she'd bite. She put her hands on her hips and gave him a once-over. "You look great."

He was sweaty and in a T-shirt and jeans. Sure, he looked like a million bucks. Whatever. "What the hell are you doing here?"

She smiled as though his sharp tone hadn't bothered her, but her throat bobbed, giving herself away. She was nervous. "I came to talk to you."

"Talk to me?" He glanced at the doorway to the stairs. "How did you even find me?"

"I called your parents' house. Your mother told me where you were working. A guy downstairs told me where I could find you." She tugged at the hem of her jacket, straightening it. "I needed to see you. Do you have time to get a drink?"

"A drink?" He scowled. "Kenzie, I'm rehearsing. And I haven't spoken to you in months. What the hell could we possibly have to talk about? Last I heard, I was holding you back. You might not want to risk being seen with me in public. I still pour coffee. I might hurt your image."

Her lips parted like she was ready to fire back, but then she frowned and seemed to gather herself. "Look, I deserve that. I know things ended badly, and that was a lot my fault. I'm not here to rehash that. But I have something important to talk to you about, something I think will interest you. Career stuff."

"Hey, Jasper Deares," Hollyn's voice called from inside the rehearsal room. "We need you." Before he could answer, Hollyn's head poked into the hallway. "Jas... Oh. Sorry."

Kenzie had turned to look Hollyn's way. Hollyn glanced from Kenzie back to Jasper, a wrinkle appearing between her brows.

He cleared his throat. "I'll be there in a minute. Hollyn, this is...Kenzie. Kenzie, Hollyn."

Hollyn's nose wrinkled, and her face ticced into a full grimace, but she stepped into the hallway and took Kenzie's outstretched hand. "Nice to meet you."

Kenzie smiled her kindergarten-teacher smile. "Likewise. Are you a new member of the group?"

"She's our special guest this week," Jasper said. "She's a local writer."

Hollyn's gaze cut his way, and she grimaced again, her tics flaring.

"Oh, fun," Kenzie said, her tone a little too bright, a whole lot condescending. "Well, I don't mean to interrupt y'all. I just need to borrow Jasper for a few minutes. You don't mind, do you?"

Jasper's fist curled. "Kenzie, I'm rehearsing—"

"It's fine," Hollyn said quickly. "We're wrapping up in here. I'll tell them to run the last game without you, Jasper."

"Hollyn—" he started. But she was already turning to head back in.

Only when she disappeared did he realize his mistake. He'd introduced her. As Hollyn. As the special guest. As a writer. What he had not introduced her as was his girlfriend.

Fuck.

Kenzie turned back to him. Her face shifting into one of concern. "Wow. What's wrong with her?"

The question snapped in Jasper's face like a firecracker, jarring him. "What?"

Kenzie pointed at her face, making a circle around it. "Is she okay? She looked like she was having a seizure."

His jaw clenched. "It was a tic."

"Oof," she said with a wince. "Bless her heart. That's going to be hard to hide onstage. How are y'all going to work around that? Is the show for charity or something?"

Jasper could feel his anger about to boil over. Kenzie could be self-involved but he'd never known her to be cruel. "Why are you here?"

She smoothed her lipstick and glanced back over her shoulder to make sure they were alone. "Right. So I got a deal with Netflix for the Aurora Boring character."

"I heard. Congratulations," he said with zero enthusiasm.

"Thanks. It's an amazing opportunity," she said in that voice she probably used in media interviews. *Amazing opportunity* was such a fucking cliché. "But we've been auditioning actors for months, trying to fill the Eddie Ecstatic role, and no one has been the right fit. We had one guy we thought would work but then it fell apart. People either play it too over the top or too goofy. And the chemistry between the character and mine gets thrown off."

Eddie Ecstatic had been his role in their sketch. Her character couldn't show excitement about anything. His would find a thrill in anything. "Okay."

"I know the original audition didn't go how you wanted it to, but I showed the director and producer some of your videos you've been putting online. And I've convinced them that you're the guy for the role. That you'd just been having a bad day the day of the audition." She bit her lip, smiling behind it.

Jasper stared at her, the words not computing. "What?"

"Jasper!" she said, a little shriek in her voice. "They want to give you the part! It'd be a costarring role."

"They want to give me the part," he repeated, voice flat. "On a Netflix show."

"Yes!" She clasped her hands together and beamed a smile at him. "And it's the right choice. I realized we messed everything up when we tried to date. We sucked at being in a relationship, but we're *golden* as comedy partners. I play the role better when I'm playing off of you. And probably vice versa. The mistake we made in that audition is that we didn't audition together."

Jasper's knees decided they didn't want to hold him up anymore. He sat down hard on top of the cooler. "Holy shit."

"I know, right?" she said, bouncing a little on the toes of her expensive stilettos. "It's pretty much a done deal. They just want you to fly out to LA so you can do a scene with me for the director and producer. They want to lay eyes on you. I know you'll nail it. And"—she looked him up and down—"you still look fantastic, Jas. You'll be perfect on camera. And they'll do all this to you." She swirled her hand around her head. "You know, the designer haircut, the wardrobe, the polish."

His head was spinning. The room was actually tilting in his vision. They wanted to offer him a role in a TV show. One that he would possibly have a part in writing since it had characters he and Kenzie had created. It was...the dream.

"So, you in?" she asked, a hopeful note in her voice.

He pinched the bridge of his nose, trying to get his vision to clear. "How am I supposed to say no to that?"

"Yay," she said and pulled her phone from her purse. "How quickly can you be ready? The audition is Friday, but it would help to get you in town a few days earlier so I can introduce you to some people. And maybe go shopping so we get the right outfit for the audition." She scrolled through. "We can get a flight out tomorrow that goes through Dallas."

Jasper's brain snapped back online. "Wait. You need me to go that soon?"

She frowned. "I know it's last minute, but Hollywood waits for no one. That's the day they want you there. We're already behind schedule because of the casting problems."

He stood and dragged a hand through his hair. "I have a big show here Saturday night. I can't miss it."

Kenzie pursed her lips. "Jas, I'm sure they could do without you at the bar for one show."

"No." He shook his head. "You don't understand. That's the show we're rehearsing for. I have investors coming to see the show."

She tilted her head. "Investors?"

"I'm trying to buy a theater here. Move the show to my own place. I need to be there on Saturday."

She gave him a patient look. "Come on, Jas. I mean, that sounds like a fun project and all. But local theater? That's your endgame?"

"Kenzie."

"This is a chance to be on a television show that will be worldwide. This is it, the big break. Netflix. Starring role credit. Fame. Money. All that stuff we've both spent our whole lives working toward." She gave him an exasperated look. "Get your head together, Jas. Local theater is where actors who can't make it go to fade into obscurity. No one would walk away from this."

He had sworn to his group that he wouldn't bail on them again. He'd promised Hollyn he'd be beside her onstage. But... Kenzie was right. How the hell could he walk away from this chance? If any one of his group got this opportunity, he'd never hold it against them. This was the dream. "I have to be back by Saturday night. I need to be here for the show."

Kenzie rolled her eyes. "Then be back by Saturday night. Audition is Friday. Get an early flight out on Saturday morning."

He let out a breath and squeezed the back of his neck. That could work. He could do both. "All right. I can do that."

Kenzie rushed to him and gave him another hug. "Awesome. What's your new phone number?"

He rattled off the digits, his mind numb.

"I'll look up some flights and text you later. I can't wait for them to see you, Jas. This is going to be great." Kenzie kissed him on the cheek and then stepped back and wiggled her fingers at him in a little wave. "Later, loser."

It was a little joke they used to say when they left each other. He didn't like the way it made him feel, though. He was down for the audition. He was not down with starting anything back up with Kenzie.

The audition.

Fuck. How the hell was he going to tell the group?

More than that, how was he going to tell Hollyn?

chapter **twenty-nine**

HOLLYN ESCAPED INTO THE WORKAROUND BATHROOM AND leaned against the bathroom sink, trying to wrangle her emotions and not lose her shit. She'd already been rocked by seeing Jasper with his ex. His *stunning* ex. That woman wasn't just pretty. She was the kind of gorgeous that would make anyone of any gender or orientation turn their head. Polished and poised and tailored.

Hollyn had felt every bit of her own awkwardness facing the woman. And then Jasper had introduced Hollyn as the guest, the writer, basically "just some chick you don't have to worry about."

She might've been able to deal with all that if she hadn't heard what Kenzie had said when Hollyn had stepped back into the rehearsal room. She hadn't heard Jasper's response, but she'd heard Kenzie's question. *"What's wrong with her?"*

Mortification worked its way through Hollyn all over again, making her eyes fill with tears. *Dammit.* It shouldn't matter what some random woman thought of her. So what if that woman was Jasper's ex? So what if she was going to be some famous actress one day? But after days of trying to talk herself up about the upcoming show, Hollyn didn't need to hear the knee-jerk reaction of a stranger seeing her tics. Was that what everyone was going to think when she got onstage Saturday night?

What's wrong with her?

She stared at her reflection in the mirror, her eye makeup starting to smear and her cheek tic jumping. *What's wrong with her?* She hated that she couldn't make her muscles cooperate. That she couldn't smile serenely and pretend like everything was okay. Everyone else got to wear a mask out in the world. Hers constantly slipped and told her secrets. *Looks who's nervous. Look who's insecure. Look who's got something wrong with her.*

Tears slipped down her cheek and she gripped the edge of the sink, trying to will herself to calm down.

The doorway to the bathroom swung open, and Hollyn straightened, quickly swiping at her face. Monique caught sight of her, though, and frowned. "Hey, honey. You okay?"

Hollyn nodded a little too vehemently. "I'm fine."

Monique cocked her head. "Sure you are." She walked over and put an arm around Hollyn's shoulders to give her a squeeze. "What's going on? Have we thrown too much at you tonight?"

Hollyn choked, a little sob escaping. She'd noticed the whole Hail Yes group was very easy with physical affection with each other. The side hug made her feel even worse because it was like Monique was signaling to her that she was part of their little comedy family now. And she was going to have to disappoint them. "I'm sorry. I don't think I can do this."

Monique didn't let her go, and her tone was soothing when she spoke again. "Did something happen? You were doing great out there. You seemed like you were having fun."

"I was," she said, "but I don't think I can handle strangers looking at me, wondering what's wrong with me."

"What's wrong with you?" Monique said, frowning at her in the mirror. "Hollyn honey, nothing is wrong with you. We are all God's children. Beautiful and wonderful in our own individual ways. And if anyone judges us for the things about ourselves we can't control, then fuck them and the horse they rode in on."

Hollyn choke-laughed. "That's quite a colorful sermon."

Monique grinned as she pulled a paper towel from the dispenser and handed it to her. "Now you know why my church doesn't invite me to speak."

Hollyn took the paper towel and dabbed at her eyes. "I don't know. I feel like the minute I get some confidence, the world reminds me to take a seat."

Monique released her from the side hug and turned toward her with an empathetic expression. "Honey, that's okay. The first few months I did improv, I literally felt so sick with nerves that I threw up before every show."

Hollyn's lips parted. She could never imagine the bold Monique the Mouth being scared of anything.

"You're not a freak for being anxious about getting onstage. It's a one hundred percent normal reaction to being vulnerable to others. That's why, in those improv classes we've been teaching, so many people either don't come at all or they sit in the back." She smiled. "But the thrill comes from walking with that fear and doing it despite all those emotions. When you do that, you walk off feeling like you can conquer the goddamned world because you realize, especially in comedy, that you've taken away the power of others to shame or embarrass you. You're already making fun of yourself. What have you left them with? You've taken all their ammunition away and tucked it in your own pocket." She spread her hands out to her sides. "People want to make fun of my size. I've already beat them to it. They want to call me a loud mouth. I've already claimed that nickname as my own. They've got nothing. They don't get a vote on how I feel about myself."

Hollyn smiled, the woman's warmth like a balm to the sharp edges inside her. "I want to be like you when I grow up."

Monique put her hands on Hollyn's shoulders. "Then start by doing this show. You're going to do great. And we'll all be backing you up. Not to mention, Jasper will be right there. And that boy is goo-goo eyes over you, girl, so he'll do anything you need onstage. He'd probably strip naked and do jumping jacks just to take attention off of you if he felt you were panicking."

Hollyn laughed. "I have a feeling Jasper just likes to strip onstage."

Monique snorted and lowered her arms to her side. "Ain't that the truth."

Hollyn tipped her head back and pressed her fingertips to the corners of her eyes, trying to center herself. "Okay."

"Yeah?" Monique asked, her excitement clear in her voice. "My pep talk worked?"

Hollyn gave her an exaggerated thumbs-up. "You are excellent at pep talking."

"Damn straight." Monique winked. "And now I better pee before we get a comedy show no one signed up for."

Monique hurried off to a stall, and Hollyn got herself cleaned up so she could go back out to the group. To find Jasper. And to figure out why the hell Kenzie was back in town. But when she went in search of him, Barry let her know that he'd already left and had said to tell her he'd stop by her place later.

Jasper's gorgeous ex had shown up. And he'd disappeared without even telling Hollyn goodbye.

Fantastic.

This night was getting better and better.

....

The clock had moved past eleven when Jasper finally showed up on Hollyn's doorstep. He was in his same clothes from earlier, but his hair was a mess, and his face had that grim look of a cop stopping by to tell a family that there's been an accident.

Hollyn's stomach dropped to her toes. "You slept with her."

Jasper looked startled. "What?"

A sick feeling welled in her, the suspicions she'd been circling around for hours bubbling out of her like poison. "Look at you. I'm not a mathematician, but my new boyfriend's stunning ex-girlfriend shows up, he disappears for hours, and then shows up with bedhead and a bad-news look on his face. I can figure out the answer to that equation."

"Shit, Hollyn. No," he said, frowning and stepping inside. "Of course I didn't sleep with Kenzie. What the hell?"

She looked down at the floor as he shut the door, anger and heartbreak mixing into a brew inside her. "Don't say it like it's a ludicrous suggestion. You left, Jasper. You didn't even bother to tell me goodbye. After blatantly not telling your ex that you're dating me. What am I supposed to think?"

Jasper let out a rough sigh, looking ten shades of beleaguered. "I'm sorry. You're right. That was a dick move." He reached out and took her hand. "But I promise, that's not what this is about. I was just so shocked to have Kenzie there at all that I messed up not introducing you. That wasn't intentional. I swear."

She didn't respond, and he tugged her hand, leading her into the living room. She let him guide her to sit next to him on the couch.

"And I didn't go anywhere with her," he said, dipping his head to try to catch her gaze. "She's not here for us to get back together. Even if she were, I'm not interested."

"She's gorgeous, Jasper," Hollyn said quietly. "Like whoa pretty."

Jasper squeezed her hand. "And you're beautiful. Like whoa hot. I have excellent taste."

Hollyn looked up, finding him with a little smile.

"Look, I get it," he said. "I spent the whole night we went out with Cal sizing him up. Knowing he was your ex, that you had this deep friendship connection still, and seeing that he wanted you? It was driving me fucking crazy."

"Jasper—"

"Kenzie has nothing on you," he said softly. "I loved her once. But seeing her again just confirmed that those feelings are dead and buried. We weren't right for each other then or now. End of story."

Hollyn believed him, but her thoughts were still a tangle. "Then why was she here? And why were you looking so grim when you walked in?"

The tense expression he'd been wearing at the door reappeared, and he raked a hand through his hair, revealing how it had gotten so messed up. He leaned back on the couch. "She wasn't here to get back together, but she was here about an acting gig."

"An acting gig? I thought she already had one. That Netflix thing."

"She does," he said, cutting his gaze toward her. "She was here to offer *me* one."

Hollyn turned, pulling a leg up on the couch to fully face him. "What do you mean?"

He looked down at his hands, which were rubbing tracks on the thighs of his jeans. "The show she's doing for Netflix is based on a sketch she and I used to do. They apparently can't find the right actor to play the part I used to play. She convinced them that I'm the guy who needs to be in that role." He looked up. "The costarring role."

The words were like syrup in her brain, slow and sticky sliding through her consciousness, taking a while to make sense. "A role on a Netflix show. With Kenzie."

His shoulders rose and fell with a breath. "They won't offer it to me until I do an audition for the director and producer, but from what's she's telling me, it's mine if I want it."

The reality of that sank in. A TV show. Netflix. Starring. "Holy shit, Jasper."

He laid his head back and scrubbed a hand over his face. "I know. It doesn't even sound real when I say it out loud."

Hollyn's heart was beating fast as if her body already knew the answers to the questions she needed to ask. "What does this mean?"

He lifted his head and met her gaze, a somberness there. "It means I'm supposed to get on a plane for LA tomorrow with Kenzie. The audition is Friday."

"Friday? But the show…"

"I'll fly back Saturday morning. I can still do the show," he said, voice dull and flat. "I promised I'd back you up onstage and I will."

He could still do the show, but she could hear what he wasn't saying. She forced herself to ask the question. "But if you get the part, what about the theater project?"

And New Orleans. And their relationship.

He had heartbreak in his expression. "I know. It's killing me. The last thing I want to do is let down the group again. Or leave"—he looked at her as if searching for the right word—"everything."

She closed her eyes, breathed in, breathed out.

Reality was a funny thing. Something that should've made her feel hysterical or angry or dramatic instead made her feel very, very still. Resigned. Some sense of inevitability settled into her, like she had already known this was how things would have to be. *Too good to be true* had always proved to be an accurate aphorism in her life. Jasper was going to do this. He was going to audition and he was going to get the part and he was going to leave. For good.

"Right. Everything. Meaning, me. Us."

"Hollyn—"

She opened her eyes and forced a smile, though her heart was fracturing at the thought. "No, I get it. Please don't give me some speech. I mean, of course you're going to do this. It's all you've ever wanted. I can't compete with that. I don't want to."

"Fuck," he whispered, pain on his face. "The last thing I want to do is hurt you. But…I can't turn down this part if they offer it to me."

Her gaze went watery and she looked down at her hands, trying to gather herself together. "It's okay, Jas. This thing between us...it's new. You don't owe me anything."

He made a frustrated sound. "Don't let me off that easy. Yes, it's new, but you're my girlfriend. Of course I owe you something."

The word *girlfriend* hit her ears like a record scratch. As much weight as she'd pinned on that title, she realized now how paper-thin it was. The designation could disintegrate with one little shift in the universe. She met his gaze, tears slipping down her cheeks.

"You could come with me," he said, a hopeful note in his voice. "If I get the part, you could move there, too. You can write from anywhere."

The offer warmed her, but she shook her head, sad inevitability moving through her. "Do you realize how much your life will change when you get this part? You'll become a public figure. Press and cameras and people digging into your private life. I... That's not for me. I'd drown in that kind of fishbowl. Plus, I can write from anywhere, but my job is here. No one knows Miz Poppy anywhere else. I'd have to start over."

His head dipped like he'd just realized there was no answer that solved this equation for them. He couldn't have both. "I hate that I have to choose between an amazing break in my career and an amazing woman."

Hollyn let out a breath. "It's not really a choice, is it? I mean, part of me wishes it was. I've fallen in love with you."

He closed his eyes like her words pained him, but it wasn't lost on her that he didn't say *I love you, too.*

"The idealistic side of me wants to believe that love conquers all. I'm that girl who watches all the romantic movies with the love at first sight and the fates aligning and the grand gestures where the characters declare that their love for each other is the be-all and end-all." She swallowed past the tightness in her throat. "But

I know that's not real life. I know I'm not that girl in the movie. I maybe let myself forget that for a little while with you these last few weeks, but of course you're not going to choose staying here with me over your dream. I would never expect you to do that. You've worked too hard to get this chance."

"Hollyn." Anguish crossed his face and he reached out, swiping tears from her cheeks. "You deserve to be that girl in the movie. You deserve to find someone who would sacrifice it all to be with you." He shook his head. "*Fuck.*"

"What?" she whispered.

"That person is Cal," Jasper said, his face all grim lines. "He told me he'd walk away from anything and everything if it meant he could be with you. I believe him."

The fact that he was suggesting Cal should be her guy cut deeper than anything else. It meant Jasper didn't love her. Not like she loved him. She could never see herself telling him to be with someone else. A snap of anger went through her. "You want me to be *with Cal*?"

He closed his eyes and squeezed the bridge of his nose. "No. Even saying it makes me want to punch things, but maybe he's the better choice. I want you to be happy. He could give you what I can't."

"Don't do that," she whispered.

He lowered his hand and gave her a wary look. "Do what?"

"Play the martyr. Pretend like he's better than you," she said, frustration in her voice. "You're capable of love. You're capable of making someone happy. If you need to put your career first, then do that. But don't act like you're doing me some favor by sparing me a relationship with you. I didn't fall in love with some flake. I fell in love with *you*, and I'm a pretty good judge of fucking character, so don't insult me."

He stared at her a moment, clearly taken aback, and then he let out a breath. "Okay. I'm sorry."

"Thank you." She poked him in the shoulder—hard. "You're great and this hurts. So you let me have my broken heart, goddammit. I have earned the right to feel this way."

His shoulders sagged and a look of utter sadness crossed his face. "I don't want to break your heart, Hollyn. It's killing me to see you upset. I care about you so much."

The catch in his voice made her chest ache. This wasn't a brush-off. Jasper really was hurting over this decision. She reached out and took his hand. "I believe you. I know you're not trying to hurt me. You just already have the love of your life—your career. I never had a shot in that competition. If you don't take this opportunity, you'll just resent me, and it'll doom us anyway. Either way, we've reached the end of our story."

"God, this sucks," he said, exhaustion in his voice.

"Yep. A whole lot." Tears started up again despite her attempts to hold them in.

"Come 'ere," he said finally, pulling her against him. She went willingly, leaning against his chest, his arm around her shoulders. So this was it. She closed her eyes and listened to the rapid beat of his heart, inhaled his scent, tried to imprint it all on her memory. *Once upon a time, I was in love...*

"Maybe I won't get the part," he said softly.

She sniffed. "Shut up. You're going to nail that audition. Kenzie wouldn't have come all the way out here if she didn't think she was bringing them a sure thing. You think she wants to come to her ex for anything? She needs you for this. That's the only explanation."

Jasper pressed his nose to her hair, a deep exhale making her hair flutter. "I hate this. Why would the universe bring us together just to bait and switch us when we're getting started?"

She draped her arm over his waist, wishing she didn't have to let him go. "Maybe because the universe knew *I* needed *you.*

Without you, I'd still be hiding in that office of mine, probably without my job. Even if it was only a couple of months of knowing each other, the time we had together has set my life on a different course—a better one. I don't regret it, even though this is going to hurt like a sonofabitch when you leave."

Jasper tightened his hold on her, pressing her against his chest. "You've helped me, too. This time with you has been..."

She wiggled, loosening his hold, and sat up to press her hand over his lips. "No speeches. Please. That will make it hurt worse."

Jasper's expression was drawn, but he nodded, and she lowered her hand. "Okay. No speeches."

She searched his face, another thought popping into her head. Hers weren't the only hopes that were about to be dashed. "Does the group know yet?"

He grimaced. "No. I don't want them to know until it's one hundred percent a done deal. Please don't say anything."

"But—"

"They're going to hate me and that will distract them. I want them giving their all on Saturday night, and they're only going to do that if they believe the stakes are real. They're all talented. And really, they don't need me to get the theater. If the investors see the show and want in, I'll ask Monique to take over the role I was going to play in running the business if she wants it. They can have the theater without me."

Hollyn frowned. "You're an integral part of the show, Jas."

"They can carry the show without me," he said firmly. "I won't deny them another opportunity. I will be there Saturday with you, supporting you and the group onstage, giving it everything I have, and we're going to make it happen for them. I want my dream, but I'm not going to sabotage theirs in the process."

Hollyn met his gaze, not feeling great about keeping that secret from the group. "Okay. But you promise you're going to be there? I don't want to have to explain why you're not."

He reached up as if he were going to touch her face but then he lowered his hand. "I swear. I'll be there."

She nodded and swallowed past the knot in her throat. "So I guess it's time for our final practice session in our fake relationship, huh?"

"What do you mean?"

"The breakup."

"Hollyn," he said, pain in his voice.

"Am I supposed to throw things?" she asked, trying to smile. "Or call you names? Maybe slam some doors or slap your face?"

The corner of his mouth lifted in a sad smirk. "Would that make you feel better?"

She lifted her hand and gently swatted his face. "Didn't work."

"Maybe try something else."

She stared at him, memorizing every little feature of his face. "Maybe I need the opposite."

"What's that?" His voice was soft, knowing, like he could read every thought in her head.

"A proper goodbye." She climbed off the couch and put out her hand. "Come to bed, Jasper Deares. It's late."

His eyes searched hers, longing there. "Hollyn, are you sure..."

"I'm sure. Let's end this with a good memory."

Jasper took her hand, kissed her knuckles, and let her lead him to the bedroom.

They couldn't have this forever. But they could have one more night.

It would have to be enough to last her a lifetime.

Because she knew one thing for sure. No matter which men came into her life in the future, she'd never meet another one quite like Jasper Deares.

chapter **thirty**

KENZIE HAD TRANSFORMED HERSELF. SHE STOOD ACROSS from Jasper in the audition room with her hair parted down the middle and rolled into a tight bun at the back of her neck, her dress a drab shade of gray, and her makeup so understated it made it look like she wasn't wearing any. Aurora Boring come to life.

She'd insisted Jasper shave his face smooth for the audition—Eddie Ecstatic wouldn't have stubble—and he was wearing a bright-pink polo and chinos. They'd been practicing this office scene for hours every day since they'd arrived in LA. But this time, the director and one of the producers were sitting in the room, ready to see them perform and determine Jasper's fate.

The four of them had met beforehand to discuss the concept for the show, and Jasper had gotten every impression that this part was ninety-nine percent his. He just had to not screw up during this audition, and it would be done. This was it. The moment he'd been waiting for as long as he could remember. He took a deep breath and nodded at Kenzie. She winked, all confidence.

"Ready, guys?" Angie, the director, asked as she leaned back in her chair and set her reading glasses on top of her sharp-edged black bob.

"Yep," Kenzie said. "Ready, Jas?"

"Ready." He rolled his shoulders, getting into character. This was just another stage. He didn't need to freak out about it.

"Start at the beginning of the office scene," Angie said.

Kenzie started the scene, delivering everything with a flat tone and life-is-exhausting expression. Aurora Boring in every mannerism, every word. The sight eased some of Jasper's nerves. He and Kenzie had done these two characters so many times when they were performing sketch along with the improv that it felt like visiting old friends. He waited for his cue and then walked into the scene, saying his lines and slipping into the overenthusiastic role.

The two of them went on for a few minutes, and he and Kenzie fell into a well-worn rhythm. He could anticipate her choices, play off them. Kenzie had been right. They were bad in a relationship, but onstage, they had the dance down. Symbiotic in the way that only came from years of improv together.

"Stop," Angie said, the word clipped.

Jasper startled, having forgotten there were two other people watching. He turned to the director. Angie had her hand lifted and her eyes on the pages in front of her, the reading glasses back on her nose. She glanced up and met his gaze. "Jasper, can you stay on script?"

He blinked and cleared his throat. "Uh, sure. I thought I had. I'm sorry."

The director frowned. "Your lines were on script, but you're improvising a lot of the stage directions. I know you both have improv backgrounds, but we really want to keep this pretty tight to script."

He stiffened. No improvising. That was like telling him not to breathe. But he understood. If they were on a tight production schedule, he couldn't do a scene ten different ways and expect them to take the time to cut all of that together in a cohesive way. "Right. Sorry. Got it."

Kenzie gave him a look. He recognized that one from their time dating. It was the don't-fuck-this-up look. He nodded at her. *I've got this.*

"Start again from the top," Angie said.

Kenzie began the scene again, and Jasper gave it everything he had, sticking to the script like glue. By the time they'd made their way through the scene, his blood was pumping and he almost felt high. Kenzie delivered the last line and then grinned wide at him.

They both looked over at the people in charge.

"Thank you. Give us a few minutes," Phil, the producer, said, and then leaned toward Angie to confer.

Jasper followed Kenzie out into the hallway. As soon as the door shut behind them, Kenzie rushed to Jasper, threw her arms around him, and gave him a smacking kiss. He was too stunned at the contact to respond. She pressed her hands to his face, squeezing. "Oh my God. You nailed it! We just *nailed* it. This is going to happen!"

She leaned in to kiss him again, but he grasped her shoulders and eased her back. "Don't."

She blinked. "What's wrong?"

"We can't do that. The kissing thing," he said, lowering his arms to his sides. "We're acting partners. That's it."

She frowned. "Jas, we're going to be kissing all the time on the show. Aurora and Eddie have a romance story line the first season."

His stomach turned at the thought. "That's for the part. We aren't Aurora and Eddie. I'm not here to start things up between us again. We weren't good for each other."

She gave him a smug look. "That's fine. But you're naive if you think we're going to be working this closely and things aren't going to happen. Our relationship has never been one hundred percent professional. We're not very good at boundaries."

"Kenz—"

"You can come back in," the producer said.

Jasper swallowed hard and followed Kenzie back into the room. Phil invited him and Kenzie to sit down at the table with the two of them. Angie was tapping a pen against the script, a pensive look on her face. Jasper thought he might throw up. He remembered the last time he'd been told no at an audition, how that had felt puncturing through all that hope. But then Angie smiled.

"Well, Kenzie, you were right," she said, turning to Jasper. "Jasper, we think you're perfect for the part. We like your whole vibe, and once you stuck to the script, the entire scene came to life. The two of you have fantastic chemistry. I know you're going to be using Kenzie's agent, and we have to go through the fine print of all that, but I'm not going to make you wait for our thoughts. We'd love to offer you the part."

Jasper sagged back in his chair, his ears buzzing and his heart pounding. Kenzie squeezed his knee under the table, her excitement palpable. They were offering him the part. He'd just landed a costarring role on a Netflix show, playing a character he'd help create.

Jasper Deares, you've just been handed your dream.

"So what do you think?" Angie asked, her brows disappearing beneath her black bangs.

Jasper shook his head. "I think I'm speechless. Thank you."

He couldn't access his words beyond that or even his emotions. There was just a lot of undefined internal screaming. All his feelings seemed locked in some vault he didn't have the key to.

All he could think was *I did it. I finally did it.*

And everyone would know it. His birth parents who'd abandoned him. The foster parents who'd told him he'd never make anything of himself if he didn't get some self-control. The teachers who'd gotten frustrated with him. And the Deares family who had loved him through and through and who he wanted to make proud more than anything. Everyone would know that he'd finally done it.

But as he shook hands and thanked the director and producer, as he accepted another hug from Kenzie, as he went out to dinner with all of them to celebrate with a fancy meal, he couldn't help thinking, *I thought it would feel better than this.*

Was this what happy felt like?

Maybe he'd experienced so little of it that he didn't recognize what it was when it showed up.

But in that moment, what was supposed to be euphoria felt a lot like numb.

So when Angie ordered expensive champagne to celebrate and the drinks kept flowing afterward, Jasper accepted every glass handed to him. He drank until the numbness faded and fizzy giddiness filled him. He drank until the sharp edges of his thoughts blurred into soft ones. And when Kenzie brought him to her place instead of back to his hotel room, he didn't remember to protest.

....

Hollyn gave up trying to get in touch with Jasper Friday night. She'd sent him a few texts to see how his audition had gone, but since his message from early that morning, asking her to wish him luck, he'd been radio silent. And the one time she'd tried to call yesterday evening, it'd gone straight to voicemail. Without a doubt, she'd known that meant he'd gotten the part. If he hadn't, he would've called, told her he was coming home and they could still be together. The only reason not to call was to save her the news for another day.

She would lose him officially now. She tried not to think about the fact that he was in LA with his ex. She tried not to think about how the night before he'd left for the trip, they'd spent all night with each other in bed, pouring everything they had into what would probably be their last time together. She had no claims on him now. She was back on her own—again.

She got ready for bed and plugged her phone into the charger before setting it on her side table. She'd just climbed under the covers and turned off the lamp when her phone buzzed with a text. She reached for it so fast, she almost knocked it off the table. But when the screen lit, she didn't see Jasper's name. It was Cal.

Cal: Just checking in.

She rolled her lips together, staring at the screen. She'd told Cal she needed time. He knew she was still with Jasper and he was trying to respect that, but in the lingering awkwardness, she hadn't been calling him. They'd exchanged a few texts, but she'd let what he'd said affect their friendship, which wasn't fair. Regardless of her confused romantic feelings, she didn't want to lose Cal as a friend. He was too important to her.

She scooted up along her pillows and considered her screen. Without thinking too hard on it, she hit the button to call him back. He answered on the first ring. "Hey, stranger."

She smirked in the dark. "Is that your passive-aggressive way of telling me I've bailed on you?"

"*Panic station*. Yes. Not that passive really," he said with a smile in his voice. "I'm saying it. You definitely bailed. But it's cool. I get it. *Kill the lights*. You need time. Space. All that fun stuff. I know I blindsided you."

Hollyn leaned her head back, the sound of his familiar voice a balm to her frazzled nerves of the last few days. "I'm sorry. Blindside or not, I don't want to stop talking to you."

"Glad to hear it," he said, the squeak of his couch sounding in the background.

"You're not in bed yet?"

"Nah. We did a *rolling stone* show tonight. Just getting in." She could hear the weariness in his voice.

"Living the rock-and-roll life. How'd it go?"

"Great." He yawned. "No panty-throwers, though."

She laughed under her breath. "Bummer."

"Right? We must've done something wrong." He was silent for a few seconds. "You okay, Tate? You seem...quiet."

She closed her eyes. Cal knew her too damn well. "I'm always quiet."

"Not with *panic station* me." He cleared his throat. "Everything all right? How's the job training going?"

She heard the unspoken question in that. He wasn't just asking about her job. He was asking about Jasper. "I'm supposed to go onstage for a live appearance tomorrow night at the improv show. I'm going to reveal Miz Poppy."

"Holy shit," he said on an exhale. "That's...wow."

"I know. I'm completely freaked out about it," she admitted. "But I've been rehearsing all week. I need to do this. It will let me keep the Miz Poppy name even if NOLA Vibe lets me go."

"It'll also help the *kill the lights* boyfriend, I imagine," he said, a bitter note entering his voice.

"Don't," she said, too tired to get irritated. "Please. Jasper doesn't need my help. I think he just landed a starring role in a TV show. He's going to be moving to LA."

The couch squeaked again. "Wait, *what*?"

She closed her eyes. "It's an amazing break for him. It's what he's been waiting for his whole life."

"Motherfucker," Cal breathed. "I knew it. I knew that guy would let you down. Hollyn, I'm so sorry."

"He didn't let me down," she said, her tears quietly slipping out. "I told him to go for it. How could I not? Who am I but some random woman he met a few months ago? He can't stay for me. I would never ask him to give up his big break."

Cal groaned. "See, that's where you're *hella good* wrong, Tate. You're worth giving up everything for. You're worth loving that hard. You *are* the big break. You need to start seeing that. *Panic station.*"

Her heart fissured in her chest. Why couldn't it be Cal? She loved Cal so much, but after that last night with Jasper, she knew in her gut that she could never feel with Cal what she felt with him. So even though Jasper was leaving, she wasn't going to default to Cal. He deserved better than that.

Being around Cal made her comfortable to be herself. But being around Jasper made her want to fight to be the best version of herself she could become. She liked who she was when she was with Jasper. He pushed her. So even if she couldn't have him, she knew that she needed to wait until she felt that magic again with someone. Love wasn't enough. She could love a lot of people. But only one had set her heart on fire. She needed to find that again or be okay being alone. She wouldn't settle for less.

"I love you, Cal," she said, her voice scratchy with tears.

He sighed. "I love you, too, Tate. And it's okay. *Kill the lights.*"

She sniffled. "What is?"

"That even with Jasper leaving, you're still going to tell me no," he said, his tics quiet. "I knew the minute you let me leave New Orleans that it wasn't going to happen."

"Cal..."

"I deserve someone who wouldn't let me walk out," he said, no ire in his voice.

She pressed her lips together and nodded even though he couldn't see her. "You absolutely do. You deserve the world. I'm sorry I can't be that person."

She could hear him shifting on the other side of the phone. "It's okay. *Kill the lights.* I've thought about it a lot since we talked. You're my comfort zone, too. Maybe I've held on a little too long because I know you'll always *hella good* accept me how I am. Girls like that I play guitar. Some like how I look. If I want to do the hookup thing, it's usually not a *hella good* problem. But when it comes to longer-term stuff, the tics are a lot for most people. Maybe I'm just as scared as you that I'll end up alone."

Her chest compressed, her heart squeezing for him. "No, you won't."

"No?" he asked, sounding exhausted by it all.

"No matter what happens," she said, pulling the covers higher, "I won't let you be alone. We've always got each other. Maybe not for the kissing stuff. But for the friendship stuff. I will always be here for you."

He let out a long breath. "Back at you, Tate. You can always be the Dorothy to my Blanche."

She grinned through her tears. "Why do you get to be Blanche?"

"Because I'm the unashamed slut. *Hella good.* Obviously."

She sagged back against her pillow. "I missed you."

"Me too." He made a sound in the back of his throat. "I'm sorry things didn't work out with Jasper."

She rolled her eyes. "No, you're not."

"Okay, fine. I didn't like the guy. But I liked knowing you were happy."

She put her hand to her chest, pressing there, wishing she could fix the hurt those simple words stirred. You *were* happy. Past tense.

Cal shifted on his couch again, and she wondered if he was having problems with his tics. Sometimes when he got tired, the motor ones got more pronounced. "So, what time is this event of yours tomorrow night?" he asked. "I think I have an itch for a comedy show."

"Oh, seriously, you don't have to come," she said. "It'll probably be a disaster."

"It won't and Blanche would never miss Dorothy's improv debut. Give me the time. I'm going."

Something unlocked in her muscles. Despite everything, knowing a friendly face would be in the audience sounded like a godsend. "Seven thirty."

"I'll be there."

"Thanks, Cal."

"Anytime, Tate."

She cradled the phone closer to her ear. "I love you."

"I know."

She laughed. "Overused line."

"Don't care. A classic is a classic."

She told him goodbye, feeling a little better that they had set things right between them again. Even with her heart broken, she didn't have to be alone. Love came in many forms. Maybe she needed to be satisfied with the friendship kind.

For now, it would have to be enough.

chapter **thirty-one**

JASPER WOKE UP WITH A HEAD FULL OF STAMPEDING elephants and a mouth full of ash as sunlight pierced his eyelids. He groaned and rolled to his side, trying to hide from the light, and pressed his cheek to the cool silk of the pillow. His thoughts stumbled. *Silk?*

The unexpected sensation had him squinting his eyes open. Gauzy white curtains and bright sunlight filled his gaze. He didn't recognize the room at all. Where the hell was he?

He tried to blink and clear his thoughts, but before he could, the bed shifted next to him. His breath stalled in his chest. Then a decidedly feminine sigh filled his ears. A familiar one.

Oh no. *Oh fuck.*

The scent of the silky sheets filled his nose then. A familiar perfume. *Kenzie.* He was in Kenzie's bed, and he had no memory of how he'd gotten there. Based on the pounding in his head, though, he'd guess he'd gotten there via a river of booze. *Christ.*

Kenzie groaned. "God, I need to get blackout shades. This California sun is no joke."

Jasper didn't want to turn over. He didn't want to face this. But what else was there to do? Reckless Jasper had done something stupid. Again. He closed his eyes, counted to five, and then eased onto his back. He hadn't been imagining the sounds and scents. Kenzie was there as real as ever. She propped her head up on her fist and looked down at him. "Welcome back to the world of the living, loser."

Jasper flinched, her voice piercing his pounding head. "Kenzie."

"Well, at least you still remember my name. I'm not sure you remembered your own last night." She gave him the hairy eyeball. "You're lucky I got you out of there before you made an ass out of yourself in front of Angie and Phil."

Jasper rubbed his head. "I don't remember leaving the restaurant."

"Yeah, sweetheart," she said, all sarcasm. "You celebrated like a rock star. I half carried your ass up here."

He glanced down at the flimsy tank top she'd slept in. "Did we...?"

Her nose wrinkled. "Jesus, no. Give me some credit. I'm not a date rapist. You were out of it, Jas. I didn't think it was safe to leave you in some hotel room. So I brought you here, dumped you in bed, and you passed out."

A tidal wave of relief flooded through him. "Oh, thank God."

She gave him an affronted look. "Gee, thanks. I'm glad the thought of sleeping with me is so repellent."

"No, it's not—" He winced at the stabbing pain in his head. "It's just, I have a girlfriend."

Have not *had*. He didn't know why the words had come out that way. He and Hollyn had broken up. But he didn't correct the statement. He didn't want to.

Kenzie's eyebrows went up. "You have a what now?"

He pushed himself up on his elbows, his stomach pitching a little. "The woman you met at rehearsal the other day. Hollyn. We're dating."

Her eyes widened. "Wait. The chick with the tics?"

Jasper pinned her with a hard look. "Don't fucking call her that."

Kenzie sat up and lifted her palms in surrender. "Sorry. I just... That's unexpected. She's..."

"Smart and beautiful and talented," he said, fully annoyed now.

"Hey, I wasn't going to criticize. If you like her, that's cool. But..." She lifted her shoulder in a shrug.

"But what?"

She pressed her lips together as if choosing her words. "Look, I'm not trying to be the storm on your parade or whatever, but you just landed a starring role on a TV show. Some new hometown relationship doesn't exactly have the best outlook. Is she going to move out here with you?"

Jasper rubbed the spot between his eyebrows, trying to get the ice pick of pain to stop stabbing him. "No. She can't."

"I'm sorry." Kenzie reached out and gave his leg a pat. "But honestly, it's probably for the best. Everything in your life is going to change when you get here, Jas. Think of all the people you're going to meet, all the opportunities you're going to get. The most beautiful and talented people live here. You don't want to be tied down to some part of your old life. That's like walking around the clouds with an anchor tied to your foot. You need to leave that stuff behind."

The words rang like a bell in his head, the familiarity reverberating through him. He looked up and met her no-nonsense gaze. "That's what you did with me, wasn't it?"

Her brow creased. "Huh?"

A sick feeling that had nothing to do with the hangover filled his gut. "You broke it off with me because I was the hometown boyfriend. *I* was the anchor. You wanted to be freed up to find a richer, more well-connected boyfriend. I wasn't him. Until now, when I may have a chance to be that for you. Now I'm interesting to you again."

She tilted her head and gave him a patient look. "Don't do that. Don't make me out to be the bitch and you some maligned party. You know what happens to relationships out here when one is a star and the other is a civilian? The regular person gets crushed under the weight of it. The media eats them alive. Or they get to sit home and watch the person they love hang out with the most beautiful, talented, famous people in the world, always on the outside looking in. They get to sit home and watch the kids while the other person is on location for months doing love scenes with someone on *People*'s Most Beautiful list. I didn't want that life for either of us. So when you sabotaged that last audition before you left LA and I landed a role, I saw the writing on the wall."

His jaw clenched. "I didn't sabotage that audition."

"They told you not to improvise, and you improvised your ass off. You wanted to prove that you knew better, that your way was the better way instead of listening to what they wanted you to do." She pulled her hair to the top of her head and secured it into a bun with the hair band around her wrist. "I thought you were going to do it again yesterday, but you finally got your shit together and showed them you could take direction. Thank God. You need to let the improv go. It was good training, but you've got a real acting job now. Let the writers do their job and write for you. Memorize the script, follow the stage directions. Be a professional."

Let improv go. Memorize scripts. Be a professional.

He tried to imagine never being onstage again without a script, never getting the rush of that living-on-the-edge state in improv.

Onstage. Improvising.

Panic hit him like a baseball bat to the gut. "*Oh, fuck.*" He scrambled out of bed, his head protesting at the sudden movement, and scanned the room for his phone. "What time is it?"

"What's wrong?" Kenzie asked, the covers falling from her and revealing she'd slept in only a tank top and underwear.

"The time, Kenzie."

She reached behind her for her phone, which was sitting on the side table. "A little past ten. Why?"

Dread and panic filled him. "Fuck! Where's my stuff? I need to go."

"What the hell, Jas?"

"I missed my flight." His heart was racing as he found his jeans draped over a chair and tugged them on. "I need to get to my room, grab my stuff, and go to the airport. I need to get back to New Orleans to do the show tonight."

Kenzie frowned. "Jas, that's sweet of you to want to help out the group and all, but what's the point? You got the part."

He found his phone in the pocket of his jeans and started typing, trying to get to the airline's website. "The point is I promised I would be there."

I promised I wouldn't let Hollyn be onstage alone. I promised my group I'd help land these investors.

Legitimate panic was making his fingers tremble as he tried to search for a new flight. *Full. Full.* "Dammit!"

"I think you're going to be too late anyway. New Orleans is two hours ahead of us. And the traffic to get to the airport..."

"Screw my stuff. You can send it to me. Get me to the airport. There's got to be something. Standby or something."

"Jasper."

"Fine. I'll call a fucking Uber."

She threw the covers off. "Don't do that. I'll bring you. Damn. I just think you're being ridiculous. What's the worst that could happen? The girlfriend you have to leave behind anyway is going to get mad and break up with you?"

Jasper couldn't answer. That was by far not the worst thing that could happen. Hollyn was going to have to go onstage with or without him because of all the Miz Poppy promotion she'd done. He'd sworn to her that he'd be there to back her up and support the group, that he wouldn't leave her up there on her own. He'd already let her down by going out to California. He couldn't do this to her, too.

But as they pulled into LA traffic a half an hour later, home had never felt so far out of reach.

chapter **thirty-two**

HOLLYN STARED DOWN AT HER PHONE AGAIN, THE WORDS on the screen sending a chill straight down to her bone marrow.

Jasper: Missed my flight. Phone running out of charge and no charger. I don't know if I'm going to make it there in time. Trying everything I can. I'm

Hollyn had gotten the incomplete message a couple of hours ago. She'd read it again and again, hoping she'd read the words wrong, but they were the same on the second and third and hundredth time. *Missed my flight?* How the hell had he let that happen? He knew she was counting on him, knew his group needed him there. But maybe after his big audition, that didn't seem so important anymore. *Oops. Sorry. Can't make it.* Irritation had flooded her. She'd tried to text Jasper back and call him, but his phone had apparently died mid-message.

He might not make it on time. I might have to go onstage without him. Those realities were flying around her head like belfry bats, setting off all her deepest anxieties.

Hollyn sat on a box in the storage room of the Shifty Lizard, trying not to have a meltdown. The show was supposed to start in thirty minutes. The bar was already packed, the sound of the crowd rumbling through the walls. The rest of the Hail Yes group had already come into the storage room to change and were outside getting some air before the show. Everyone seemed excited. But no one had realized yet that Jasper being late wasn't "normal last-minute Jasper" and was possibly a "Jasper's not coming" disaster. The rest of the group was under the impression that he hadn't been able to be at rehearsal for the last few days because he had to take care of something for his family.

Hollyn breathed in through her nose and out through her mouth, trying to calm herself. Fitz poked his head into the room. He smiled when he saw her. "Hey, there. Ready for your big debut, Miz Poppy?"

"If feeling like I'm going to throw up and pass out is ready, then yes?"

He chuckled and stepped inside, letting the door shut behind him "We've got a packed house and all three investors are here, looking impressed with the crowd so far. You need anything?"

"Jasper would be nice," she blurted out, immediately regretting the slip.

Fitz frowned. "He's not here yet? That dude needs to learn the concept of cushion time."

She looked up, pulling her knees up onto the box with her and hugging them. Her nose scrunched a few times. "No, he's not here. Like in the state."

"What?" Fitz looked back toward the door as if he was expecting Jasper to appear. "He was supposed to have an early flight in."

Jasper had confided what was happening to Fitz, though not how likely it was that he was going to get the part. Fitz had just spun it as another opportunity. If Jasper got the part, he could use his fame from the new show to promote the theater they'd all invest in. Fitz wasn't successful for no reason. The guy always had an angle.

"He sent me a text earlier that he missed his original flight," she said, sharing the confession with someone else making her feel a little less alone. "He wasn't sure if he was going to make it. I haven't heard from his since."

"Shit, Jasper." Fitz ran a hand over his head and then squatted down to her level. "Hey, you know you've got this either way, right?"

She shook her head, her cheek tic going crazy. "I don't know. I've never been onstage live. I've had nightmares that start like this. I'm about three seconds from bolting out the back door if you really want to know."

"Don't do that. Not to put more pressure on you, but you being here is what's brought this crowd. This is going to help your career, but it's also going to help the group and Jasper. You're part of this team."

She inhaled a shaky breath. "I'm going to blow it for everybody—including myself. I can feel the panic attack coming. I can't do this. Jasper was supposed to back me up if I froze. That was the only reason I agreed to this."

Fitz gave her a football coach look. The I-don't-want-your-excuses look. "Hey, I want Jasper here, too. Believe me. That's who the investors want to see most, but this entire group is talented as hell. They'll back you up. And they all want this theater thing to happen so they're going to be on top of their game. Y'all are on a team together, and you're *the* Miz Poppy. People just want to meet you." He put his hand on her shoulder and squeezed, grounding her.

"There's no need to panic. You're not here to impress the crowd with your improv skills. You've already impressed them with your writing. You don't need Jasper to carry you through this. He has nothing to do with Miz Poppy. *You've* created that business. Now you get to own it. Grab on to that shit and be proud of it. Don't let the nerves steal that from you."

Own it. Be proud of it. The words wound through her like a shot of adrenaline. She didn't want this taken from her. Her anxiety had already stolen so much from her in her life. The Miz Poppy business *was* hers. If she walked out, she risked giving up what she'd worked so hard to create for herself. She wasn't going to let the NOLA Vibe steal her name, this thing she'd made. Miz Poppy wasn't a separate person. She wasn't her cooler, more interesting twin. *Hollyn* was that person. No one else could step in and do it better. Her shyness was just a layer that made it harder to see the real parts of her. It didn't make them any less real. She needed to go out there, be the person she was, tics and awkwardness and all and own it. "I am Miz Poppy."

Fitz patted her shoulder and rocked back on his heels. "Damn straight you are. Say it again."

"I am *Miz. Fucking. Poppy.*"

He laughed and got up from his crouch. "There you go. You got this."

She stood and gave him a hug. Her body was still trembling with nerves, but the determination stirring deep within her was starting to take over. "Thanks. I think I'm tired of needing pep talks. I'm designating you the last one I'm going to need."

"I'm honored." He stepped back and held up his fist for a fist bump. "I'll see you out there. Make me some money."

She laughed and bumped his fist. "Eye always on the bottom line, huh?"

"Always." He gave her one last grin and then headed out.

When she was alone again, she vowed to stop looking at her phone and hoping to see Jasper's name. He had made a promise to her that he'd be here, and he'd broken it. He'd been right. She deserved better than that. She turned off the phone and dropped it into her bag. She was going to have to do this without him. It would be good practice.

She was going to have to get used to that. Even if Jasper got back in time, he was only coming back to pack his stuff and tell her goodbye.

She tossed her bag on the floor and went out to join the group. It was almost showtime.

....

Twenty minutes later, Monique was standing in the storage room with Hollyn. When Hollyn had broken it to the group that Jasper couldn't make it, the group hadn't looked surprised. Barry had just nodded, a grim set to his jaw, like he'd been expecting the day to come. "All right. Stick to the plan. We know how to do this without him."

The others nodded in agreement.

The solemn acceptance made Hollyn's chest hurt. But there was nothing to be done about it at this point. The crowd was waiting. Because of Jasper's absence, they'd had to shift around how Hollyn was going to be introduced. Antonio was going to do her intro. Monique was going to give her the cue to walk out.

Monique leaned against the doorframe, the door open, and looked her way. "Almost time, lady. You ready?"

For the first time all night, Hollyn could confidently nod. "I'm ready."

Monique gave her a proud smile. "Good. Let's kill it."

The lights of the bar went dark. A roll of anxiety went through Hollyn. "What's going on?"

"They're making your reveal dramatic," Monique whispered and took Hollyn's hand. "Come on."

Monique led her out to the area behind the stage. The NOLA Vibe had gotten on board to sponsor the show tonight and had set up a large, black backdrop for the stage with their logo on it. The bonus was that it provided a place to act as a backstage area.

Monique gave her hand a squeeze. "Here we go."

A spotlight flipped on, a circle appearing on the backdrop, and Antonio's voice came through the microphone. "Welcome to the Hail Yes Improv show and Miz Poppy reveal party!"

The crowd cheered, and the sound of so many people made Hollyn's stomach flip over, but she breathed through it. She wasn't going to run now. For better or worse, she was getting on that stage.

"We have a great show planned for you tonight," Antonio went on. "Start getting drunk now. We're better looking and more talented through beer goggles."

The crowd laughed.

"But you'll need no inebriation for tonight's special guest. Stone-cold sober you'll be able to see how wonderfully talented and fun she is. You've known her as her cartoon avatar. You've met her through her well-written posts and have gotten to see her snarky side in her words. She's the lady who tells us where New Orleans's best-kept secrets are. She's that best friend who makes sure you know the cool stuff first."

Hollyn could feel her face burning, but she couldn't help the smile that touched her lips. Monique playfully bumped her shoulder into Hollyn's. "This woman sounds pretty awesome."

Hollyn gave her a grateful look.

"It's my honor," Antonio went on, "to give you lucky people the privilege of being the first to meet the real Miz Poppy. Please welcome to the stage Hollyn Tate."

The crowd erupted with applause and Monique nodded at her. "It's your time, honey. Enjoy it."

Hollyn took one last deep breath and then stepped from behind the curtain. The lights and the number of people froze her in place for half a second, but then her brain kicked in and made her feet move forward. She had a smile pasted on her face, and she could feel her nose scrunching in a constant twitch. No way was she going to be able to squelch the tics for these minutes onstage. But people were clapping and everyone was looking at her and she had to keep moving. She got a flash of blue hair in the audience and her gut twisted. Billy Blue. Her competitor. Of course he'd be here. But she forced his presence out of her mind.

When Antonio took her hand and guided her toward the mic, she caught sight of a few familiar faces in the front row. Cal, clapping hard, and Andi with her hands cupped around her mouth, shouting "Woo!"

They both looked so enthused that Hollyn couldn't help but laugh. Knowing not everyone out there was a stranger helped. She stepped up to the microphone and tried to get her heart to stop racing. She was onstage. As Miz Poppy. Holy shit.

The crowd quieted after a few seconds, and she cleared her throat. The sound was loud in the mic and she cringed. Her tics followed the cringe, adding a few more seconds to it. Panic started to well. She gripped the mic. "Um, so hi. I'm Miz Poppy."

The crowd responded with more claps and sounds of encouragement. People were taking photos with their phones. Some dude in the back yelled, "I love you, Miz Poppy!"

That made her laugh and forget the nerves for a second. "Thanks. You seem nice, too."

The crowd murmured with quiet laughter.

She wet her lips and forced herself to not look down at her feet. "First, I want to thank the Hail Yes group for inviting me as a special guest tonight. Y'all are in for an amazing evening." She swallowed past the dryness in her throat, trying to focus on what she wanted to say instead of what people were thinking about her tics going crazy. "I've been doing these reviews for a while now, and I'm often amazed at the level of talent our city has. But it's a special experience when I feel like I've stumbled upon some hidden gem, people on the cusp of greatness. That's what you're going to see tonight. Talented actors who will leave you laughing and feeling better about the world when you walk out the door. Because what greater gift can anyone give us than the ability to take a break for a while, to laugh—at them, at ourselves, at the world?"

She looked over to the side of the stage where the group awaited.

"In fact, I wouldn't be standing up here if not for these people. I make my living as a writer because I want to be heard without being seen. As I'm sure you can tell"—she pointed at her twitching nose—"I have Tourette's, which makes my face do this when I'm nervous." She leaned closer to the mic. "Don't tell. But y'all make me a little nervous."

She caught Cal's gaze in the front row, the lights revealing the shine in his teary eyes.

"But someone in this group taught me that we're all human and that we shouldn't have to hide that. It's okay to be seen. It's important. Improv is about working with the happy accidents, the unplanned mistakes, and the drunk heckler in your life."

"I love you, Miz Poppy!" the guy yelled again, perfectly on cue.

The audience laughed.

She smiled and pointed his way. "Give that guy a free beer for helping with my metaphor."

He gave her a devil horn's rock-and-roll hand signal.

"So," she said, "if you're sitting here right now, afraid to do something in your life, know that I'm calling you out to change that. Because if this chick with the tics can get up here and make a fool of herself with the improv pros, then I bet you can do just about anything." She tipped a pretend hat. "And thus concludes my motivational speech for the night and also my disclaimer that if I suck, it's not on these guys."

The audience's clapping filled her ears, and she pressed her lips together, taking it in. She'd done it. She'd gotten onstage as Miz

Poppy and hadn't lost it. Regardless of what happened the rest of the night, she'd won.

Monique joined her onstage and gave Hollyn a side hug. When the crowd settled down, Monique addressed everyone without the need for the mic. She gave them the speech about how their improv worked and then they were off and running.

The group handled the first game where they got an audience suggestion without her. They'd planned that so she could have a moment to recover in case she'd had a rough time during her intro. But by the time the first scene ended, they were already calling her back onstage.

Leah had the mic, and Barry led Hollyn over to one of four chairs they'd dragged onto the stage. Hollyn sat, and Antonio, Church, and Barry took the other three chairs.

"For this game," Leah started. "We're going to make Miz Poppy go on the Hail Yes dating show."

Hollyn groaned, and Andi grinned at her from the audience.

"You guys," Leah went on, "are going to be able to read what role each potential suitor has been assigned. But dear Miz Poppy won't be able to see what's happening because..."

Danica and Monique lifted up a sheet, separating Hollyn from the three guys.

"She's behind the magic dating wall," Leah said. "Her job will be to ask them questions and then try to guess who or what they are."

Hollyn scanned the audience, searching for the investors, but she couldn't pick them out. Everyone was focused on Leah, most were smiling, and the whole place seemed fully engaged. Jasper would've loved to have seen this. Hollyn shook off the wistful thought. *Stop thinking about Jasper.* If he had wanted to be here, he would've made it happen. She was mourning the loss of the person she thought Jasper was, not the real one who'd bailed on her and his friends tonight.

Leah walked over and handed Hollyn her index cards, which held the prepared questions. They'd practiced this game in rehearsal, but the guys would be different characters this time and she didn't know what the questions were. However, she had the easy part. Jasper had made sure her parts in the games were as straightforward as possible.

The game began, the spotlight hit her, and she picked the first card. "Bachelor Number One, if you were to take me out on a date where cost wasn't an issue, what would we do?"

"Well," Barry said in a deep, serious voice. "First, I would take you to my laboratory and show you my big...beakers. And then we'd do experiments on each other all night long."

Hollyn lifted her eyebrows. "That sounds...interesting."

"It would be, my little Bunsen burner. Then we would—" He started to scream. "No! You can't be alive. What are you doing? Put that down. No, no—" He made a choking sound.

"Bachelor Number One, are you okay?" she asked.

A deep grunting sound was the response. He repeated it a few times. The audience was laughing so she suspected Barry was doing crazy movements on the other side of the sheet.

Hollyn feigned a worried face and flipped to the next index card. "Okay, then, so since Bachelor Number One is Dr. Frankenstein who just got killed by his monster, why don't we move on to the next."

The audience clapped at her apparently correct answer.

"So, um, Bachelor Number Two..."

She went through the routine with Church, who seemed to be a Broadway singer who was unable to speak in anything but song. Church had some of the front row in tears with laughter by the end of his performance.

"Okay, Bachelor Number Two, I'm not sure I could date a guy who has to say everything in song." Finally, she moved on to Antonio. "Bachelor Number Three, tell me why I should pick you over the other two bachelors."

"Because I'm already in love with you," he answered in a deep, affected voice that was without his normal accent.

She tilted her head. "But you don't know me."

"Don't I? I know that you like sappy romantic comedies and watch them late into the night. I know that you dot your *i*'s with little circles. I know that you always smell like berry-burst body wash."

Hollyn frowned, the observations true. "Uh, Bachelor Number Three, are you my stalker?"

The crowed laughed, and she noticed most were looking at her now, not at the other side of the curtain. Andi's head was on a swivel, looking back and forth between both sides. Cal was staring hard toward Antonio. She shifted in her chair.

"I know you like spicy food and you have a wicked sense of humor," Bachelor Three went on. "I know you're a badass and a talented writer and superhot."

Hollyn swallowed hard, the voice shifting in her ears and making the hair on her arms prickle. "You seem kind of sure of yourself, Bachelor Three."

"True." The voice was closer, just on the other side of the sheet. "Some have called me a narcissist. And selfish. And really, really stupid for walking away from the best thing that's come into my life in a long damn time."

Her hands trembled at the familiar voice. She closed her eyes. Breathed. "How do I take my coffee, Bachelor Number Three?"

"Decaf. Handsome."

Monique and Leah dropped the curtain. Hollyn had known who'd be standing there. No one else could've known those things about her, but the sight of Jasper still stole her breath. He was standing there with a weary smile, tousled like he'd been wearing the same clothes for days, and was holding a sign that labeled his character for the audience, but it was flipped downward.

"Hey," he said softly.

It took a second for Hollyn to find her voice. "Hi."

"Sorry I'm late."

She stood, forgetting anyone else was there. "What are you doing here?"

"Show her your sign, bro!" the heckler shouted.

Jasper smirked and turned to the audience. "Thanks, man. I'll take it from here."

Hollyn glanced down at his white-knuckled grip on the sign. "Should I take a guess?"

"Yes!" a female voice shouted, one that sounded suspiciously like Andi.

Jasper didn't lift his sign. "You can try."

Hollyn swallowed hard. "Guy who got the part?"

He nodded. "I am, but that's not what's on the sign."

He got the part. The knowledge sent a sharp kick of grief through her. "Guy who's going to be a great, big TV star?"

He shook his head and lifted the sign. The words were scrawled in Jasper's handwriting.

THE GUY WHO MESSED UP AND IS HERE TO SAY HE'S SORRY

She sucked in a breath.

He dropped the sign to the floor. There was another behind it.

THE GUY WHO'S GOING TO TURN DOWN THE PART

Her hand flew to her mouth.

He dropped another page.

THE GUY WHO BELONGS IN THIS CITY, ON THIS STAGE, WITH THESE PEOPLE, AND WHO...

Another page dropped.

HAS TOTALLY FALLEN IN LOVE WITH YOU

THE GIRL WHO MOST DEFINITELY, WITHOUT A DOUBT DESERVES ALL THE BIG ROMANTIC GESTURES

Tears brimmed in her eyes as the audience caught sight of the words and started cheering. The heckler called out, "He loves you, Miz Poppy!"

Hollyn choke-laughed on her tears and lowered her hand.

Jasper stepped forward, took her hands in his, and put his mouth next to her ear. "I love you, Miz Poppy. And Hollyn Darling. And every other version of yourself you might want to be in the future."

The future. "Jasper."

"Kiss him!" Andi shouted.

The crowd chimed in, cheering them on.

Jasper looked down at her, questions in his eyes, vulnerability there.

"Are you sure about this?" she asked, still reeling from all the things he'd said. He'd gotten the part. He was turning it down. He was staying. He *loved* her.

"Never been surer of anything," he said. "Sometimes when you get the dream, you realize it wasn't what you were looking for at all. That you already had what you most wanted right where you were standing. You just weren't looking hard enough."

All the tension she'd built up being onstage relaxed, and a big smile took up residence without her permission. "This is the least funny improv scene ever."

He grinned. "Let's give them a show, Hollyn Darling."

"Let's." She wrapped her arms around his neck and he dipped her back low, putting his lips to hers and kissing her with dramatic flair. It could've been the intro sequence to the Jasper Dearest and Hollyn Darling show they'd joked about that first night together.

The crowd exploded with cheers, and Jasper eased her back up, cupping her face and kissing her for real this time. The sound of the other people in the room faded into the background, and Hollyn forgot to be self-conscious or nervous or worried about what anyone else in that room thought. She no longer cared.

All that mattered was how she felt inside. That this was right. That this was real. That this was meant to be.

For the first time in her life, Hollyn didn't have to pretend she was in a movie to escape. She didn't have to imagine she was anyone else or anywhere else but right there in her own shoes. Happy. In Love. Brave.

She was finally the star in her own story.

chapter **thirty-three**

JASPER HAD NO IDEA HOW HE AND HOLLYN MADE IT through the rest of the improv show. He'd wanted to sweep Hollyn out of there the minute they'd kissed, but they'd stayed onstage and had given it everything they had. The whole group had walked off to a standing ovation.

The applause was still ringing in his ears as he grasped Hollyn's hand and tugged her toward the back of the bar. But before they could make it to the storeroom and get some actual alone time, Fitz intercepted them. He threw his arms around Jasper and picked him up off his feet. "Holy shit, Jasper!"

Fitz squeezed the breath out of him. Only Fitz could make Jasper feel like his six-foot-two frame was small. "Dude, calm down. I didn't announce onstage that I loved *you*."

Hollyn was laughing at them, her eyes sparkling. "Should I be jealous?"

"Maybe," Fitz said, releasing Jasper and thumping him on the back "Because I love this guy. That show was...wow. The signs, man."

Jasper straightened his collar. "Aww, Fitzwilliam, I didn't take you for a romantic."

"It's Fitzgerald, asshole. Do I look like a Mr. Darcy?" Fitz grimaced like the idea of being considered broody offended him on a personal level. "And though I'm happy for the both of you, this isn't about the romance. This is about setting yourself up to go viral. That shit y'all pulled up there?" He shook his head with a smirk. "Golden. You should see the hashtags popping up already. Hashtag LoveAtImprov, hashtag GrandGesture, hashtag ImTheGuy." He glanced at Hollyn. "Hashtag MizPoppyInLove."

Hollyn grinned.

Jasper shrugged. "I didn't do it for the hashtags."

"And I don't give a damn about your intentions," Fitz fired back. "Because all that matters right now is the fact that at least two of the investors are in. The third is a strong maybe. Either way, you're going to have enough. You and Hail Yes are going to get your theater, Jas."

Jasper rocked back on his heels, the news hitting him like crashing surf. "Are you serious?"

"They want you to be part of it, too, Hollyn. A regular special guest," Fitz said, looking to her. "People are going to connect to your story and the story of the two of you together."

Hollyn's eyes widened. "I'm not an actor."

"That doesn't matter. You did great tonight, and you're likable onstage. They can work you into games without you needing to be a full member of the team," Fitz said. "Bringing in guests will keep it fresh."

Jasper laced his hands behind his head. "I can't believe this."

Fitz gripped Jasper's shoulder and gave him a little shake. "I told you not to doubt me."

Jasper laughed. "My mistake, man."

"Damn straight," Fitz said. "Now, I'll go bring the good news to your group. You take your girl and run."

"I plan on it." Jasper looked over to Hollyn, his chest filling up with so much he couldn't sort it all out at once. "You ready to go, Hollyn Darling?"

She stepped into his space and pressed a kiss to his lips. "Give me five minutes to say goodbye to Cal and Andi and then I'm all yours."

He lifted a brow. "Is Cal going to challenge me to a duel out back?"

She laughed and patted his chest. "It's okay. We've worked it out. I let him know my heart was elsewhere."

That gave Jasper pause, and he grabbed her around the waist before she could escape. "Wait, you told Cal your heart belonged to someone else even though you knew I was leaving?"

She gave him an exasperated look. "Jasper, don't you get it? I love *you*. I chose *you*. Whether you were leaving or not, that didn't change what is."

I chose you. The words were everything he hadn't known he needed to hear. This meant something more to her like it did to him. He'd loved a woman before. He'd thought he'd loved Kenzie. But from the very start with Hollyn, he'd sensed the shift. She was different. He'd tried to dismiss that feeling because he'd figured it was just his impulsiveness jumping the gun again, but his gut hadn't lied. The feeling he had for her was singular.

He knew they were still new to each other in a lot of ways, but something deep in his DNA just knew—*her, this one*. It was why when he'd finally gotten on the plane today, he hadn't had to wrestle with the decision about turning down the part. Sitting in that plane, heading back to New Orleans, to Hollyn...all of it had felt as if things were going exactly as they should be. Like all points in his life had been converging to get him to this moment.

Everything in LA had felt wrong, off. He didn't want to give up improvising. He didn't want to stick to script. He didn't want to go hang out with the "beautiful" people. He didn't want to spend all his days working with Kenzie. He didn't want to be away from Hail Yes or his family. He loved this city. He loved improv. He loved his friends.

This theater. This life. Would give him what he'd always wanted. A place on the stage and a job he could feel proud of. His family and friends nearby. And most of all, this life would give him Hollyn.

Hollyn came back to him after saying goodbye to her friends. "You ready to go home?"

He dipped down and kissed her one more time. "I'm already there."

He took her hand and they ran to the back door before anyone else could stop them.

....

Hollyn had so many questions running through her head as they made their way back to her place, Jasper's hand firmly around hers as he drove. But she couldn't seem to get any of them out. She was almost afraid to ask.

"You're quiet," Jasper said finally. "You okay?"

"I'm possibly in shock," she said with a smile. "What happened since I saw you last?"

He glanced over at her as he stopped at a red light. "The short version is I went to LA, got offered the part, went out to dinner with the director and producer to celebrate, and ended up passed out in my ex-girlfriend's bed."

She stiffened.

"Nothing happened," he said quickly. "Except that I woke up feeling like I'd been run over by a truck and had missed the flight. Which, God, I am so sorry about." He started driving again. "But while all of this was happening, it hit me why I drank so much last night. I wasn't celebrating with them. I was mourning."

She frowned.

He glanced over. "I've been so focused on what could be in the distance that I missed how happy I already was here. Even if the theater didn't come through and I had to keep slinging coffee for a while longer, I've never felt so...peaceful. I have my family here. I've reconnected with my group and with Fitz. I've always loved improv, but I never realized how much I'd enjoy teaching it. I've even thought about doing classes for teens once the theater opens because improv saved me, so maybe it could help some other ADHD kid who can't find his place."

Hollyn squeezed his hand.

He pulled into her driveway and brought her hand to his mouth, kissing her knuckles. "And I couldn't stop thinking about you. From the outside looking in, it sounded crazy to turn down a TV role to stay for a new relationship no matter how much I liked the woman. That's what I was telling myself on the way there. That's what *you* told me, too. We were being smart. Rational."

"Right."

He shut off the car and turned toward her. "But then I started thinking—we're not giving up a new relationship, we're giving up the possibility that the other person could be the one. We're throwing out the lottery ticket when only a few numbers have been pulled. And if this turns out to be it, if we turn out to be the loves of each other's lives, giving that up for a part in some TV show is ludicrous. It's a really bad bet."

Tears burned her eyes. "But we don't know that answer. We don't know if this is forever."

"No, but the only way to guarantee it isn't to give up now when things are just getting good." He reached out and tucked her hair behind her ear. "Love isn't rational. It's a risk. It's always a risk. So there's only one thing we can do."

"What's that?"

He grinned. "We're going to have to improvise this sonofa-bitch."

She laughed, the sound getting caught in her throat. "Love improv."

"Exactly. Life is one big improv stage anyway. You're only as good as the people standing there with you. And you, Hollyn Darling, are the very best."

He touched his forehead to hers, and she let her fingers slide into his hair. "You could be a famous TV star."

"I'd rather be happy and surrounded by people who love me. And let's face it, everyone here *adores* me." He smirked.

"Narcissist," she teased.

"You know it." He closed his eyes. "So will you have me? Even if I'm not a famous TV star?"

"Will I have the sexy theater owner slash improv professor slash kick-ass maker of coffee?" she asked and pressed her lips to his. "Every damn day I can."

He inhaled deeply and cupped her chin. "How about right now?"

"Especially right now." She reached out and took the keys. "Inside. This introvert has had enough public displays of affection for one night. I'm ready to get very, very private."

Jasper didn't have to be told twice. He came around and opened her door for her. He was already kissing her by the time they reached the door. She had to grapple for the lock blindly behind her. He finally grabbed the key and the door swung open, dumping them into the foyer.

The door slammed shut and her shirt was up and over her head before her next breath. Jasper tossed her shirt to the floor and kissed down the curve of her neck. "God, I missed you."

"It's only been a few days."

"Yeah, but the last time I thought I was saying goodbye." He slid his hand up her side. "Knowing it was the last time, I was missing you before we were even done that night. But now…" He got a hungry look in his eye as he cupped her through her bra. "Now we've got all the time in the world."

She arched as he thumbed her nipple through the thin fabric, and a bolt of want went through her. "God, I missed you, too."

He looked down at her, those hazel eyes of his going solid green in the low light. Part of her couldn't believe that he was hers. This gorgeous, talented, kind man was hers.

Or maybe she could. She was pretty damn fantastic herself. Lucky him.

"What are you smiling about?" he asked, hooking her leg around his hip and leaning in, letting her feel just how much he'd missed her.

"I was thinking how lucky you are to have me. Didn't you hear? I'm Miz Fucking Poppy."

He laughed. "Hell yes, you are. And tonight, you were spectacular. I watched your whole intro from the back corner. I was so fucking proud of you."

"Thank you. I had a good teacher," she said, looping her arms around his neck. "He taught me a few other things, too."

"Yeah?" he asked, a sinful smirk touching his lips. "Like what kinds of things?"

"Bring me to the bedroom and I'll show you."

He reached down and lifted her, hooking her legs around him, and carried her to her room. When he tossed her on top of the bed and she landed with a bounce, they both laughed. He stripped her down and discarded his clothes like they'd offended him. Soon, they were tangled up on the bed together, skin to skin, every part of her alive with want.

He pressed her hands to the bed above her. "My turn to explore. Keep these here."

She bit her lip, her blood rushing, as he shifted along her body, his cock brushing her thigh and making her ache. But he wasn't in a hurry to get to the main event. He kissed down her neck, along her collarbone, down her sternum. His tongue found the sensitive underside of her breast, licking a path up toward her nipple and making her hips arch off the bed. When he closed his mouth around the tip of her breast, she cried out.

He sucked her there, his tongue driving her crazy, and he pinned her legs beneath him, keeping her from shifting around. He lifted his head a bit, his warm breath coasting over her damp skin. "That first night, when you came from this, I don't know how I made it through the rest of the night." He glanced up at her, his gaze burning into her. "You were so fucking hot, Hollyn. And you had no clue how sexy you were."

"I was so embarrassed," she confessed. "It made me look so hard up."

"Hard up? Fuck, no. It made you a fantasy. A woman who was so sensitive, I could make her come in all kinds of inventive ways." His tongue brushed along the hard peak, making her gasp again. "As soon as you left that night, I went to bed, wrapped my hand around myself, and pictured you just like this, spread out naked beneath me, coming from my hands, my mouth, my cock. It wasn't the last time I'd picture you like that. You're a dream, Hollyn."

A hot shiver went through her as she let the words sink in. She'd never let herself imagine being in that role. The one a guy fantasized about or ached for. But he made her feel that way. Sexy. Free. In her own skin. "Want to see if we can do it again?"

His lips curved, and his eyes sparked with desire. "Challenge accepted."

Hollyn let her head sink back into the pillow and kept her hands above her as Jasper moved to her other breast and sucked, the fingers of his other hand massaging the place he'd left. Sensation wound through her like a drug, the tight bundle of nerves between her legs throbbing like Jasper was kissing her there. Every part of her felt alive, connected. She didn't have skin hunger anymore, she had Jasper hunger. Her body craved this man. His hands. His mouth. His body inside her.

Jasper took his time, winding her up and teasing her, making her breath catch and her fists clench. Her body had never felt so good and so restless at the same time. She wondered if he was going to tease her to the edge all night, but then his teeth grazed her breast and light exploded behind her eyes, sharp and sudden. Her hips tried to lift off the bed but he had her pinned. The orgasm rolled through her, making her cry out and heat surge between her legs. He hadn't even touched her there yet, but her body was aflame. Slick and needy for him. "*Jasper.*"

"Fuck, baby." Jasper groaned, need in his voice, and lowered himself down her body, holding her hips to the bed. "Need to taste you." Then his mouth was on her center, licking her as she bucked her way through the tail end of the orgasm, only to be shot up the mountain again when his tongue circled her clit.

She couldn't keep her hands where they were anymore. She gripped his hair hard and made sounds in the back of her throat that she could no longer control. She was going to break apart. Just be a pile of bones and bliss left behind, a little curl of smoke above it. *Here lies Hollyn. She spontaneously combusted.*

She started to laugh. She was still coming and the sounds came out hysterical, but she couldn't stop. Jasper lifted his head and she could feel him shift up her body. When she managed to open her eyes, still laughing, tears streaming down her face, she found him with an amused smile. "I'm not sure if this is good or I totally fucked something up."

That just made her laugh harder, and she pulled him down to kiss him.

He smiled against her mouth and when they broke apart again, he said, "Good then. Got it."

"So good," she managed, her laughs calming. "You make me delirious."

"We're even then. Because you make me deliriously happy." He slid his hand down her thigh. "You need a break?"

"Never from you," she said, reaching up to rub her thumb over his mouth.

"I love you, Hollyn Darling."

"I love you, Jasper Deares."

"Ready to start our *Darling and Dearest* TV show?"

"Looks like it's going to be a dirty one."

He smiled and entered her, joining their bodies and keeping his gaze on her. "And a long-running one."

"One of those sappy happily-ever-after ones."

"God. Those are *the worst*." He grinned and leaned in to kiss her, their bodies moving together. "I can't wait to see what happens in the next episode."

And the next.

And the next.

And the next.

Epilogue

One year later

HOLLYN PUT HER LIPS NEAR THE MIC FILTER, WAITED FOR the signal from Andi, and then repeated the line she'd messed up. "And don't forget, y'all, the grand opening of the Hail Yes theater is this weekend. I'll be the guest player for the Saturday night show with the fabulously talented Hail Yes group, and I'll be doing a live interview with the actors afterward for the podcast. Come hang out with us and bring your best questions."

Andi gave her a thumbs-up.

"Until next time, thanks for listening and I'll see you out in the city," Hollyn said, wrapping up the show.

She flipped the switch on the mic. "Done."

Andi smiled. "Yay! We kicked butt."

"Thanks for letting me interview you," Hollyn said. "That was fun. I should have more local authors on. That's part of the entertainment scene, too."

"None will be as fantastically entertaining and effervescent as me, though," Andi said, standing up and stretching.

"Obviously," Hollyn agreed. "And you run circles around me

with the podcasting skills. I still feel like I'm getting my sea legs with the technical stuff."

"You'll get the hang of it," Andi said with a flip of her hand. "You sound great and are entertaining. That's what matters. Spending money on a producer is worth it. Let them handle all that technical stuff."

Hollyn had lasted another few months at the NOLA Vibe after the Miz Poppy reveal, but doing the video reviews had been a drain. Being capable of doing something and actually enjoying it turned out to be two different things. Being on video meant trying to suppress her tics. She could do it, but it was exhausting and it made the rest of her performance flat. When she'd brought it up to her boss at the NOLA Vibe, he'd insisted they needed to stick with video.

So, she'd left. And had taken her Miz Poppy name with her.

Andi had convinced her to give podcasting a shot—doing local entertainment reviews and chatting about movies, but adding interviews with local performers and artists to the docket. Hollyn had been reluctant at first, but when she'd finally given it a chance, she'd realized podcasting was the perfect medium for her. Her snark could still come through on audio, and she didn't have to worry about her tics. She could relax and enjoy herself. Even when she was interviewing someone face-to-face.

The move had been the perfect one for her. She'd spent a lifetime trying to be something she wasn't, to fit into some mold she thought she needed to be in. But she didn't want to change her personality. She'd worked on her social anxiety, but she was never going to be a bubbly, on-screen talking head. She didn't *want* to be. She had strengths that were better utilized in other ways. She was over someone trying to force her into something that didn't come naturally. Not everybody had to be a damn extrovert.

Jasper poked his head into the podcasting room. "Hey, how'd it go?"

Speaking of extroverts. Hollyn smiled. "Aren't you supposed to be at the theater making final preparations?"

"They kicked me out," he said with a derisive sniff. "Said I was being too...intense."

"You? Intense?" Andi teased. "No."

She ducked beneath the arm Jasper had stretched out to grip the doorjamb and slipped out of the podcasting room.

"You wound me, Andi," he said.

"My deepest apologies. See you guys this weekend," Andi said with a little wave. "Break a leg, you two."

They told her goodbye and then Jasper slipped into the room, locking the door behind him. He grinned. "So. Hey."

Hollyn laughed and lifted a finger. "Don't give me that look, mister. We've already defiled the video room. The podcasting room is sacred."

He stepped up to her and wrapped his arms around her waist, pulling her to him. "Guess what?"

"Hmm?" she asked, loving the feel of him against her.

"Opening weekend sold out."

She gasped. "Really? That's amazing!"

"Yeah, rumor has it the owner is planning some big stunt," Jasper said cryptically.

"Oh is he? Are you going to get naked onstage again?" she teased.

"No." He dipped his head close and whispered, "Word on the street is that he's going to propose to his girlfriend."

Her eyes widened and then she snorted. "Oh my God. Who started that one? I bet you it was Fitz. He has no shame."

Jasper shook his head. "It wasn't Fitz."

"Then who? Monique?"

"Nope." Jasper stepped back, and before she realized what was happening, he lowered himself to one knee. "It might possibly have been me."

Hollyn's mouth gaped open as Jasper pulled something from his back pocket and then opened a ring box in front of her. The diamond inside glinted in the overhead light in the room. "Oh my God."

"Hollyn, I would never do this onstage. This is just for us. But the last year of my life has been my absolute favorite. I searched all my life, trying to find where I belong. And over this past year, I know without a doubt where that is. I belong with you. You have lit my world on fire in the best possible way. I love you."

Hollyn's hand pressed over her mouth and tears flooded her eyes.

"Hollyn Darling Tate," he said, his voice choking up, "want to be a Dearest?"

Hollyn sank to her knees in front of him, her nose twitching like mad and tears leaking out. "You're proposing to me in the podcasting room?"

He smiled, chagrined. "This wasn't how I planned it. I had a whole script. A romantic night mapped out. But then I saw you standing there and you looked so pretty and I couldn't wait and..."

"You improvised," she said, her heart feeling too big for her chest. She reached out and cupped his jaw in her hands. She knew Jasper had been told all his life that he was impulsive, that he didn't think things through, that he didn't stick to the plan. But those people had gotten it all wrong. Jasper wasn't broken. He didn't need to be fixed. Jasper just knew how to follow his heart. She wouldn't want the man she loved to be any other way. "It's perfect. You're perfect." She kissed him. "Yes."

Jasper let out a breath like he'd been legitimately worried. "Yes?"

"Yes, yes, yes. A whole lot of yes," she said kissing him between each yes. "I love you so much I could die."

"Thank God. But don't die." He snapped the ring box closed and tossed it to the side.

She turned, reaching for the flying box but missing it. "Jasper!"

But he was already toppling her over and putting her onto her back. She gasped. He grinned down at her and waggled his eyebrows. "The door's locked."

"We *are not* getting naked in the podcasting room."

He smirked. "We just got engaged. I'm like epically in love with you. Of course we're getting naked in the podcasting room."

She laughed and he kissed her and she forgot to care what anyone else would think.

The *Occupied* sign stayed on for a long, long time.

Neither was in hurry to get anywhere anymore. Both were exactly where they wanted to be.

Acknowledgments

First, dear reader, thank you for reading this book. The fact that I'm still able to do this dream job after a decade is because of you. I appreciate that you keep showing up for the party.

To Donnie and Marsh, a writer under deadline is not always the most pleasant creature to be around, so thank you for loving and supporting me even when I've worn the same yoga pants for a week, can't remember anything you've asked me to do or buy, and have served spaghetti for dinner—again.

To my parents, your positivity and unwavering support have always been the wind in my sails. Thank you for pushing me but always letting me choose my own direction.

To Dawn, I am truly blessed to have a friend like you. Thanks for all the help with my books, my classes, and the queso consumption.

To my editor, Mary Altman, for helping me make this book the best it can be, and to the whole team at Sourcebooks for always being so enthusiastic and supportive.

To my agent, Sara Megibow, who is not only a badass agent but also one of the warmest people you could ever meet. Thank you for continuing on this journey with me.

And finally, thanks to my former editor, Cat Clyne, who was the first to love the idea for this book and who gave me the opportunity to write it.

About the Author

Roni Loren wrote her first romance novel at age fifteen when she discovered writing about boys was way easier than actually talking to them. Since then, her flirting skills haven't improved, but she likes to think her storytelling ability has. She holds a master's degree in social work and spent years as a mental health counselor, but now she writes full time from her cozy office in Dallas, Texas, where she puts her characters on the therapy couch instead. She is a two-time RITA Award winner and a *New York Times* and *USA Today* bestselling author. Visit her online at roniloren.com.